Sister Vision
Black Women and Women of Colour Press

PLURAL DESIRES: *Writing Bisexual Women's Realities*

EDITED BY

The Bisexual Anthology Collective:

Leela Acharya, Nancy Chater,

Dionne Falconer, Sharon Lewis,

Leanna McLennan & Susan Nosov

ISBN 0-920813-19-4

Grateful acknowledgement is made to the following for permission to reprint
copyrighted material: *Link* journal, Fall 1994, for "Queergirl" by Michele
Spring-Moore; *Broadside*, 1983, for "Lesbians Who Sleep with Men" by Lilith Finkler;
Asian/Pacific American Journal, Spring/Summer 1993, for "Cinderella" by Indigo Chih-
Lien Som; Sister Vision Press for "The Queer Kitchen" by Indigo Chih-Lien Som in
Piece of my Heart: A Lesbian of Colour Anthology, 1991; Queer Press for "The Fuckin'
Faggot" and "Say What?..." by Leanne Franson in *A Queer Sense of Humour*, 1993;
Deneuve magazine, February 1994, for "Naming Her Destiny — June Jordan Speaks
on Bisexuality" by Zélie Pollon; *Fireweed: A Feminist Quarterly of Writing, Politics,
Art & Culture*, Winter 1993, for "Marks" by Margaret Christakos; and
Women's Press for "Mama Nature" by Victoria Freeman in *Imagining Women*, 1988.

Canadian Cataloguing in Publication Data

Main entry under title:
Plural desires : writing bisexual women's realities
ISBN 0-920813-19-4
1. Canadian literature (English) – Women authors.*
2. Bisexual women – Literary collections.
3. Bisexuality – Literary collections.
4. Canadian literature (English) – 20th century.*
I. Bisexual Anthology Collective.
PS8235.W7P58 1995   C810.8'0353   C95-930677-3   PR91994.5.W6P58 1995

Sister Vision Press acknowledges the financial support of The Canada Council
and the Ontario Arts Council toward its publishing program.

Cover Art: Maureen Paxton ©1995 / painting based on photograph by David Hlynski
Cover and Book Design: Stephanie Martin
Typesetting/layout: Jacqueline Rabazo Lopez
Editor for the Press: Makeda Silvera
Copy Editor: Margaret Christakos
Pre-Production: Leela Acharya

Published by:
Sister Vision: Black Women and Women of Colour Press
P.O. Box 217, Station E, Toronto, Ontario, Canada M6H 4E2

Table of Contents

Introduction: More Than Two Sides to Our Stories

Introduction: More Than Two Sides to Our Stories

We began *Plural Desires: Writing Bisexual Women's Realities* four years ago with a dream and a sense of something missing. What was missing were the voices and images of bisexual women, particularly in a Canadian context, reflecting on the pleasures, pains, challenges and strengths of being bisexual. Whether we look to the homophobic and heterosexist dominant society that views bisexual women as kinky, exotic, hypersexual, something to entertain men, perverted non-heterosexuals or lesbians; or whether we look to often biphobic lesbian cultures where bisexual women tend to be seen as confused, fence-sitting, male-identified dabblers with heterosexual privilege who make unreliable sexual, political or life partners, images by and about bisexual women that affirm our existence, our validity and our complexity are in short supply. And in both the heterosexual and lesbian/gay worlds, an "either/or" view of sexuality prevails which renders identifying as bisexual apparently impossible.

Our dream was of a forum in which bisexual women could be ourselves without defending ourselves, of a vehicle for self-expression and self-affirmation, of a space in which to listen to ourselves and each other. The format of an anthology is well-suited to this dream because of the way it brings many voices together — voices that tended to be previously isolated or raised only in private — and creates an atmosphere of dialogue, exchange and collectivity for its contributors and its readers. This is important for bisexual women generally; it is particularly so in Canada where the open forging of community, or at least of a sense of collective support and alliance, be it social or political, is still new.

This book was also inspired by the growing wave of bisexual visibility, self-confidence and activism in the early 1990s — a wave that results from well over a decade of political organizing and networking by bisexual women and men in the U.S.[1] and, more recently, in Canada. During the compilation of *Plural Desires* it became ever more clear that the moment to speak and inscribe our realities as bisexual women was upon us. In the arenas of publishing, feminist and lesbian/gay/queer activism, popular culture and academia, an upsurge of the B-word through the increasingly open presence of bisexuals and debates around bisexuality was evident. Too numerous to detail here, we offer a small, random sampling from what adds up to a sea change in the informed inclusion of bisexuality in feminist and lesbian/gay circles — and beyond — arising from bisexual activity taking place autonomously and in coalition with lesbians and gay men.

When we came together as an editorial collective in 1991, the important anthology *Bi Any Other Name: Bisexual People Speak Out* had just been released. *Closer to Home: Bisexuality & Feminism* followed in 1992. Articles appeared in magazines and newspapers, both mainstream and progressive. Talk shows did surprisingly sensitive shows on bisexuality, featuring some of the writers and editors of the two books just cited on panels made up of bisexuals rather than psychology "experts." Some Canadian gay and lesbian weeklies added the name "bisexual" to their mastheads and mission statements with inspiring editorials explaining the change, for example, *Go Info: A Voice for Lesbians, Gays and Bisexuals* in Ottawa in 1991 and *Angles: The Magazine of Vancouver's Lesbian, Gay and Bisexual Communities* in 1992. Several university and college lesbian and gay organizations, as well as grassroots groups in Canada moved to include bisexuals in their names and thus to recognize bisexual participation in their activities. The historic National March on Washington, D.C., in April of 1993 demanded "Equal Rights for Lesbians, Gays and Bisexuals." All of this exciting activity propelled our conviction that as bisexuals we have to raise our voices if we want to make ourselves known to the world and to each other. At the same time, we view with some caution an approach to coalition politics that simply adds on the name "bisexual" to "gay and lesbian" if it is not accompanied by a recognition that we are linked by our struggles against homophobia, heterosexism and biphobia.

The crossroads of time, place and individuals from whom this book emerged shapes its contours. Toronto, Canada, was the place and the summer of 1991 was the moment we came together. Initially, a series of potluck dinner-meetings were organized through word of mouth, with the primary goal of finding other bisexual women to begin work on an anthology and the secondary goal of forging some bisexual feminist community in Toronto. Through these gatherings, the six editors of this anthology met and coalesced.

Members of the Bisexual Anthology Collective are Black, Black-Asian, South Asian, Ashkenazy Jew and white Anglo Saxon. We are middle class and working class; we are university educated; we are not currently living with disabilities; we are in our twenties and thirties. We are writers, actors, directors, community AIDS workers and workers in feminist publishing, restaurants and film production. Some of us are new to publishing, others have experience. We are daughters, sisters, lovers, friends and allies. And we are feminists, which we take to mean that we are part of a collective struggle against intersecting forms of oppression and domination, and for a just, humane, welcoming world.

As a collective of six diverse women we came together at the intersection of "bisexuality," "feminism," "anti-racism" and "desire." Aware that diversity of every kind is found among bisexual women, and that representation by and about bisexual women was still in its infancy in Canada, we were determined to take the early and groundbreaking step of producing this anthology in a way that would disrupt from the outset any notion of homogeneity among us.

One of our commitments and the (wo)mandate of *Sister Vision Press* was that at least half of the book be written and edited by women of colour. This took time. There are particular issues faced by women of colour who take the risk and have the confidence, time and mental/creative space in our lives to come out as sexual,[2] let alone as bisexual, in the form of writing or visual art. The impact of sexist racism in the area of sexuality, with its stereotypes of hyper- or asexuality for women of colour, works in tandem with male dominance in many cultures to silence, or to increase the risk of speaking out. The politics of cultural production — who gets access to speak and about what and in what forms and forums — combined with often harsh economic realities of racism make writing or being creative a difficult enterprise. As well, both the convention of binary thinking about sexual identity that prescribes that one is "either straight or lesbian" and the fact that bisexuality is still just developing an aura of legitimacy have an impact on all women, sometimes making us hesitate to name ourselves bisexual. We celebrate all of the women in this anthology for their perseverance and vision.

We chose to work as a collective. This brought the strength of six different perspectives to our process of seeking and deciding upon work. It also brought the challenge of coordinating six busy schedules and reaching consensus on the more than one hundred submissions that we read.

Collective members moved to different cities, became unemployed and changed jobs, apartments and relationships. While we meet at an intersection of politics and identification as bisexual, we differ in many ways, including in the texture of our lives as bisexual women. Some of us are single, some of us are in short, medium or long-term relationships with one or more women or men. Amazingly, we got through this with no major conflicts. We still like each other! Flexibility and commitment to the project were the keys to this success.

The combination of a collective process, the groundbreaking nature of the project itself and the large size of the complete manuscript add up to a book that required four years to come into being. We were heartened to learn that this is not uncommon for collections anthologizing previously un- or little-heard voices and issues. Our many mail-outs seeking submissions (with their ever-extended life/deadlines) went to groups in most regions of Canada, in rural as well as urban areas, to the United States and to international organizations. We sought work through word of mouth and generated pieces ourselves through interviews and transcribed discussions. We extend our thanks to all of the women who generously shared their stories with us; it was a privilege to read the many thoughtful and honest submissions that we received.

This collection of writing and artwork by bisexual women moves through and makes waves in the fluid map of desire, sexuality, identity and politics. Indeed, the fluidity that characterizes this terrain in each contributor's life — the changes often surprising, the risks often unacknowledged, the moorings unsettling and resettling over time — is a key element of bisexuality witnessed and recorded in *Plural Desires*. What unites all of the contributors is a willingness to explore bisexual identification and how it intersects with other multiple facets of identity. More than one writer speaks of connections between bisexuality and other mixed, split or doubled elements in her history and herself, such as being biracial and bicultural. As editors, our working definition of bisexuality was simply *self-identification as bisexual*. This allowed the inclusion of a questioning stance, reflections on self-definition and a range of relationships with the name "bisexual."

The proliferation of forms of work in *Plural Desires* attests to the creativity and variability of bisexual women. Poetry, cartoons, fiction, experimental and more traditional non-fiction, photographs, paintings, slogans, interviews, conversations and collective discussions are all included, adding to the multivoiced quality of the anthology. In some cases, the oral-into-written form of transcribed interviews, conversations and collective discussions was a way to facilitate the inclusion of women for whom writing poses a barrier because of time shortages or under-confidence in the value of their thoughts and skills. These forms also provide an "on-the-ground" documentation of political analysis and insight that would not otherwise be preserved in writing or find its way into an essay. As such they are an important part of historicizing bisexual activism and thinking. Their conversational, polyvocal qualities aptly characterize the sense of travelling-community-in-paper-form provided by an anthology.

Within the feminist bisexual framework of *Plural Desires* the relationship between bisexual women and lesbians is especially important and highly charged. The dynamics, frustrations and rewards for bisexual women of what is experienced on one hand as a "les/bi divide" and on the other as a natural social and political alliance between women-loving women as sexual outlaws is an issue that concerns many contributors. In terms of the les/bi divide, which can emerge when lesbians judge and dismiss bisexual women as traitors with divided loyalties and allegiances, it is the thorny question of bisexual women's relationships with men upon which the judgements pivot. What several contributors illuminate is that such judgements are oversimplifications of how bisexual feminists contribute to struggles against homophobia and heterosexism and how we can exercise agency in relation to men in our lives. Recognition of the reality overlapped by the lives, interests and goals of bisexual women and lesbians holds the potential to move forward the debate around this divide, so that we all gain from our alliances.

Plural Desires opens up dialogue between bisexual women and lesbians, among bisexual women, and with anyone who cares to drop in and listen to a sampling of bisexual women's realities. For the more than forty contributors to this volume, desires are plural, encompassing the wish for community, for honesty, for self and social acceptance, for change and for a different world, along with sexual desire felt toward and potentially acted upon with either men or women.

The anthology is divided into five sections. LEAKY CATEGORIES: CROSSING LINES & REDEFINING borrows its name from Trinh T. Minh-ha's apt assertion that "categories always leak."[3] By our very existences and through our reflections on them, bisexual women cross the heterosexual/homosexual line laid down and policed by dominant sexual discourses. We also challenge the extent to which lesbian and gay discussions of sexuality and identity have similarly adopted an "either/or" model. We are redefining ways of being sexual in a homophobic, heterosexist culture. For those who advocate watertight categories of identity, bisexuality threatens and disturbs. The pieces in this section flow over the confining edges of labels and prescribed behaviour.

HOW WE ARE SEEN & SEEING OURSELVES explores one of the issues crucial to bisexuals as a group that is devalued and marginalized — seeing ourselves through our own eyes and experience while naming and refuting the stereotypical and distorted ways in which we are often seen.

The personal histories of bisexual women include many surprising twists and turns through lesbian, heterosexual and bisexual social and political worlds. They also include growth and recovery from trauma and alienation. JOURNEYS OF TRANSFORMATION charts a number of these courageous histories.

The notion of making sexual life choices, the assertion of agency (as in an "active exertion of power that produces an effect"[4]) and an awareness of the startling range of life possibilities are three themes that emerged in contributors' works, gathered in AGENCY, CHOICES, POSSIBILITIES.

Some of the overlap as well as the discontinuity and contradiction among community, politics and organizing is addressed with fresh insight in the final section, COMMUNITY, POLITICS, ORGANIZING.

This anthology is just the crest of that wave we spoke of earlier. As the first book about bisexuality produced in Canada, it propels us forward and eagerly anticipates the waves to follow. The voices and perspectives you will hear in *Plural Desires: Writing Bisexual Women's Realities* are passionate, engaged, witty, erotic, challenging and full of insight, love and vitality. They amply testify that there are many more than two sides to our stories as bisexual women. Enjoy!

Leela Acharya, Nancy Chater, Leanna McLennan & Susan Nosov
for THE BISEXUAL ANTHOLOGY COLLECTIVE, February 1995

NOTES

1 See *Closer to Home: Bisexuality and Feminism*, ed. Elizabeth R. Weise (Seattle: Seal Press, 1992) and *Bi Any Other Name: Bisexual People Speak Out*, ed. Loraine Hutchins and Lani Kaahumanu (Boston: Alyson Publications, 1991) for full details.

2 This point was made by Ritz Chow in a dialogue between lesbians and bisexual women on CKLN 88.1 FM's "Queer Radio" in Toronto 1992. See "Bi & Out: Discussing the Les/Bi Divide on Queer Radio in 1992" in *Fireweed: A Feminist Quarterly of Writing, Politics, Art & Culture*, No. 36 (Summer 1992): 63.

3 Trinh T. Minh-ha, *Woman, Native, Other: Writing, Postcoloniality and Feminism* (Bloomington: Indiana University Press, 1989).

4 Oxford Concise, 1982.

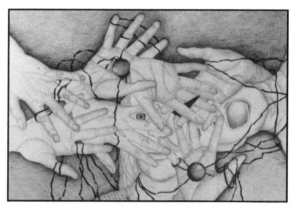

Tracy Charette Fehr   Hands © 1992
pencil, pencil crayon, ink on paper

LEAKY CATEGORIES: CROSSING LINES & REDEFINING

Ann Decter

From A. to Z. — with love & monsters

> ...imagines a logosphere in which the ideologically charged
> pair, *homosexual/heterosexual*, will be no more significant or
> worthy of attention than, say *horizontal/vertical*.[1]

And nothing in between. No between, no barriers, common identity, somehow, without barriers. No closets, no need for places to hide. For hiding.

Straight, bi, lesbian.
And Adrienne's continuum.[2]
"Bi now, gay later."
I don't think so.
The static imposition of approved identities is not liberating.

Let's talk about ourselves. Let's exchange stories, of our needs, our
feelings, our desires. Desires for life as we would choose to live it, a society
we would choose to live in. Without, of course, controlling everything.
There must be surprises. Surprises like sexuality that changes and evolves.
Surprises like acceptance and rejection, experiencing and experiencing until
you finally realize the choice is yours — who and what to accept. Choice of
who you are in the world, of how you move through it, how you love and
treasure it, fight it and betray it. How it fights you.

Straight, bent, curved.
How you fight not to betray yourself.
To be exactly who you are and make the definitions fit you, not vice-versa.

A. is thirty years old. She has a lover, a man. She has a friend who
tells her, "you are the most male-identified woman I know." Not that it's
much of a contest, and this friend is prone to passionate exaggeration. Still,
A. is ensconced in female-male, sexually at least. All her lovers have been
men. And even though she was late to take an interest in sexual pursuits —
the requisite coyness of adolescence had never been comfortable — she has

been steady in this course. She has turned down the women who have approached her, surprised at their interest. If she was somehow responding, somehow there, where the world starts to curve, she was not aware of it. Not conscious of it, at all.

A. is a thirty-year-old heterosexual.
Straight. Living in that world where attraction is assumed to be in opposition.

For me: the manifestation of desire and the *birth* of homosexuality.

And an assertion; that there is a "birth of homosexuality" as opposed to the helpless conventionality, "I was born that way."

How the world changes in a moment, stretching, easing around corners, how figures change, the gaze shifts, the corners disappear. Peering around them will get you anywhere.

A. was born headfirst and happy. Her mother's doing. Headfirst and happy. Own your own emotions, your thoughts, your desires. Honour them. A.'s mother and father were heavy believers in honour. Respect. Yourself and others. The world turns on it, the round world.

Let's exchange stories.

A. is thirty-one, and sees around a corner. Desire begins to bend, the shape of desire softens and broadens. Hands are smaller, skin is smoother, closer. A. is sure and unsure. Taken by surprise, shifted over the rainbow, to somewhere she's never been before. But that is...that is...that is life. If you're lucky. A. thinks this must have been in her somewhere, must have been something she had always been feeling, but how could she not have noticed?

A. thinks this is a beautiful bend, this bend in the world. Gradually, A. realizes it is more and less beautiful than she first thought. Women are not uniquely loving, clear and non-manipulative. Desire plays into a prism, her vision roams red orange yellow green blue indigo and violet. She perceives. How humanity is created and denied in each individual woman, how there are monsters everywhere, but how between women, maybe, just maybe, there is one many-headed monster missing.

Between women, love can be more of a fair fight. Because it's only between two individuals and their personal monsters. Because you can trade facing the great multifaced ghoul of patriarchy every time you disagree with your lover for tripping over a range of goblins and ghosts, the legacy of fear each woman carries, depending on her personal history. Depending on what the multifaced ghoul has meted out to a creature of her form and circumstance — her race, class, culture, history and geography. And so you love her. Not for all that, but in between it. For where she is when she's not fighting. For where she comes to rest in your arms. A.'s arms, curved around that bend in the world.

> It does not have *a* cause. Perhaps it is more appropriate to refer to each person's sexual etymology, rooted in events, persons, a geo-political milieu.

Who is A. — straight, bent and curved?

Where can we situate her in a world that perceives same-sex sexuality as obscene by definition, as a birth abnormality justified only as an autonomic response? Socially permissible only if she can be sexual, no other way; permissible only if A. is otherwise consigned to a life that is celibate and lonely, only if she will live in a twilight zone, repeating, like a mantra, "I can't help it. I don't really like it. It happened to me and I wish it hadn't, but it's this or nothing at all so please, just let me be a lesbian and I won't ask for anything else. I'm sorry."

But A. is not sorry. Not about who she is or what she does. She's fine, just fine. She doesn't hate herself. In spite of the surrounding poison of homophobia breathed daily, A. is still intent on being headfirst and happy. Mmmm-hmmm. She sees who she is, in the curve of her lover's chin resting quiet in the palm of her hand, in the struggle of friends, lesbians, to have children and full parental rights for their children. She understands who she is in her desires and in the structures that oppose them. Mmmm-hmmm.

Who is she?

A. is a dyke. She remembers that birth. A lesbian. A woman loving woman loving woman.

Isn't she?

A. lives with her lover. Z. of the small, round chin. Z. is a woman, small hands, forest-lost voice when she's tired. Anger that rises and jumps when the monsters are looming red green yellow and blue. Lands where it will. Z. has lived as a lesbian for years and years. For more than a decade. As she met Z.'s friends, A. was amazed so many were lesbians.

"How do you know so many lesbians?" A. asked.

"Time, I guess," Z. answered.

Often, Z. and her friends shared stories of old times. Who slept with whom, ten, eleven, twelve years ago.

"Anyone who has been lovers with the luscious P., raise your hand!" someone shouts at dinner one night.

Everyone at the table does, except A.

Stories of their young days, wild days, discovery days. Bar scenes A. never participated in, parties she didn't go to, benefits she hadn't heard about. Women who had been friends, connected by time, place, politics and sexuality. A. listens, learns and, after a while, begins to think about more than how she wasn't there at all these events. As F. and Z. swap memories of shooting pool in a dyke bar that closed in 1983, A. begins to think about 1983, instead of trying to imagine a dyke bar she never visited, F. and Z., so many years younger, sliding pool cues above rich green felt.

In 1983, A. was on the Atlantic coast, then back in Toronto, re-settling in Toronto with B.

B. was not, is not, a woman. Now that A. does not only remember how much too long it went on and how it ended with embarrassing melodrama, she can remember liking his hands. How even though they didn't really get along she liked his round fingers, and the way he situated himself a long way back from turmoil, how he often just let it go on around him and went on sardonically about his way, dabbling in life. She hadn't thought kindly about B. in eight years. A. is pleased to find some fondness beneath all the bitterness. It's a relief.

A. listens again. F. and Z. are still talking about nights long past. A. wonders if Z. misses those freewheeling days, if she really feels comfortable in their monogamous, live-together situation. A. recalls months of Z.

repeating that she wanted a one-to-one sexual life, each time A. said, "I keep waiting for you to just turn to me out of the blue and say 'I'm going back home.'" Home where Z. lived with the love of her wild years.

"I told you," Z. would answer, "we haven't been lovers for two years. And besides, I'm not like that."

A. puzzling and puzzling over how a woman lives with someone who is no longer her lover, shares her bed and her home, and both date other women. So far from A.'s experience. She listens, she watches. Okay, she thinks, this is a different world, don't impose the values of heterosexuality.

But deep down, she suspects she may arrive at the same conclusion here that she did in the straight world. That non-monogamy is not the simple freedom it's cracked up to be. That there is always power at its root. There is always, in practice, an imbalance between the two lovers, an imbalance in their desires for other lovers. And the one who *wants* the most gets the power in the relationship. *In principle*, A. had no problem with non-monogamy in a long-term, live-in relationship. *In practice*, it appeared to move inevitably toward manipulation and inequality, at least in the hetero-sexual world.

But, A. was not going to impose any knowledge gleaned from a sphere in which power was held so differently. She suspended judgement, watched and listened.

Now A. is thirty-four, now she lives with Z. She has spent three years ignoring her sexual history, her sexual knowledge of the world learned in pre-dyke history. Years of listening and imagining events she never attended. Before she begins, instead, to let herself remember what she knew.

Why?

Because this is a different world, out here, where sexuality bends and curves. Where we make our own rules. Our own patterns. Where we are not quick to judge, because of all the judgements that have been lain upon us. Dyke, queer, pervert.

Rapists and murderers are perverts, A. thinks. I'm a lesbian.

A lesbian in a lesbian world where she has seen love, sex, power, jealousy, manipulation, caring, generosity, kindness, where she has talked about barriers and identity, closeting and being out, pride and privilege. As a lesbian, A. does not understand non-monogamy as a non-manipulative phenomenon. But now she feels some credibility in her viewpoint.

Why did A. suspend her knowledge?

Because she respected the experience of others, she invalidated her own history and, with it, her experience.

A. is thirty-five. Everyone she has met in the past four years thinks of her as a lesbian.

For always.

In the course of their dreaming, Utopians invented andro-gyny, *égalité*, "the death of the family," critiques of roman-tic love, promiscuity and aspects of sadomaso-chism. All these were but experiments, occasionally nightmarish, toward a utopian goal: a world in which no one thought of himself as a "homosexual" or a "hetero-sexual"; that is tran-scendence of binary opposition in the discourse of sexuality.

And *herself*? What utopia does she imagine in the course of her dreaming?

A world without closets, a manner of celebrating identity without walling out non-members. A community of communities wherein the complexity of identity is unfolding and unfolding. Interweaving.

And what of the unimagined world? The one that stares back at us, surrounds us, closes us in and off, makes us invisible, alone, weak and warring. She is not what I am, we are not what she is, they are not a part of, a part of, *this* community. This is a closed circle and that is a separate and other circle, and they are not contiguous. The unimagining world makes this true. You are you and I am I and we are either the same or different.

Automatons or degenerates.

A world without closets.

Headfirst and happy, honour yourself and others.

Each individual defines her or his own sexuality according to how she or he experiences the world.

No more lesbians closeting straight affairs, no more bisexuals living publicly as heterosexuals, closeting lesbian affairs, dropping the woman when the man becomes angry, threatening or abusive.

It is about respect in a dangerous world. Living publicly as a heterosexual is as safe as it gets for a woman.

Respect yourself, and others.

Each individual has a sexual etymology.

Each individual hides part of that sexual etymology to save herself from pain.

It is an unimagining world.

But we can imagine it differently.

We can imagine concentric, overlapping circles.

A. lives as a lesbian. Year by year, she is more confident about her life and she lives it, even though it came as a surprise. An unexpected gift. Mmmm-hmmm. She honours her deceased parents by seeking, deep in herself, to live from a position of respect for herself and those around her. She loves Z. She uses all the skills of her many years to keep them together, even when their home is a rampage of Hallowe'en monsters. She watches frightened memories hurl and slash across the living room ceiling, and tries to stay calm. To keep her own vile pets of fear and rage out of the fray. There is no point in being afraid of anything, A. thinks, as Z. rails, drinks and smokes.

Hollers. A. will holler back, or not. It depends on the monsters, whether they scare her into believing she is responsible for them. It just depends. But the longer she thinks there is no point in being afraid of anything, the less she feels afraid. Soon A. will not be afraid of anything. Not of flying, or the sun exploding in the middle of the afternoon, or Z.'s monsters or her own monsters, or of leaving Z. or of Z. leaving her, or of loving Z., or even of being alone for the rest of her days and nights on this tumultuous planet.

A. lives as a lesbian.

She believes that women and men must honour their whole selves, as they are in this world.

She believes that there is strength in coalescing around identity, she has seen this strength manifest many times. A power alternative to the unimagining world, the commodifying world. The strength of community, un-commodified. For that is our strength as a community, that if we retain community and sharing within it, we can refuse to be commodified, we can not be reduced to consumable and consuming, a unit of labour that purchases goods.

A. sees the world, in her monster-free moments, as a community of communities that are not distinct. Sees that as we explore and develop ourselves, as we gather in new communities, we need to remember that our purpose and strength lie in sharing our commonality, not in creating exclusions. Exclusions may be necessary to create safe spaces, but they are not purposeful, they are only functional.

A. once lived as a heterosexual.
Now she lives as a lesbian.

She draws a map of her sexual etymology. Shares a story, and asks for another in exchange. She takes a long historical gaze back around a lovely curve, gives her love to a woman she knows as Z., and says, yes, I too am a bisexual woman. This is my map and this is how I draw it:
Here, there is a circle of lesbians, I stand within it.
Here, there is a circle of bisexual women, I stand within it.
Here, where these circles overlap, I stand.
In this sweet, fresh space I am history, I am present and I am future.
There is no point in being afraid of anything.
Especially yourself.

NOTES
1 All quotations are taken from Stan Persky, *Buddy's: Meditations on Desire* (Vancouver: New Star Books, 1989, 1991).
2 "Adrienne's continuum" refers to the concept of the "lesbian continuum" articulated by Adrienne Rich: "I mean the term lesbian continuum to include a range — through each woman's life and throughout history — of woman-identified experience, not simply the fact that a woman has had or consciously desired genital sexual experience with another woman." From "Compulsory Heterosexuality and Lesbian Existence," reprinted in *Blood, Bread and Poetry: Selected Prose 1979-85* (New York: Norton, 1986).

Leanna McLennan

The Bisexual Problem

I am 1/2 Queer
I have been told.

7/8ths Queer
9/10ths Queer
Depending on who is looking,
4/5ths Queer

Last year:
45% Queer
At the end of this quarter:
98% Queer

Predictions for the coming decade:
(23% of the square root of 48.3% queer) x 1

A problem:
If 2 queers travel three light years
and one of them is 98% Queer
while the other is 23% queer:

a) who arrives first?
b) where?
c) and with whom?

Sharon Lewis

The Good-Bi Girl

i was raised to be everything nice like sugar'n'spice — to be a
GOOD GIRL.

when i started to "actively" explore my attraction and love for
women i went looking for a way to be "good" — to be accepted,
affirmed, reflected and approved.

but i got stuck.

looking for boxes was part of my psyche, part of being a GOOD
GIRL. being named or fitting into pre-scribed boxes gave me a
checklist of what i needed to do in order to be GOOD. the
checklist i had was shaped by the values, philosophy and power
of primarily white, straight men.

i needed a label that would help me challenge a sexist and racist
world view. but i also wanted the label to tell me who is an
acceptable partner, the definitive answers to political debates, a
way to analyze the news, a way to deconstruct professors, friends
and family into boxes apart of or outside of my own. a label or
checklist that i could measure myself against and be GOOD.

while working at the women's centre, i was the GOOD straight
asexual GIRL. i wasn't ready to come out as anything, so i
submerged my sexuality and became the straight asexual
coordinator. i didn't know enough about my sexuality to fit into
any of the labels i saw, so i used a political label as the only way of
identifying myself. i came out as a black feminist which provided
me with a structure against which to challenge my pre-existing
views and find a new checklist that more clearly reflected and
affirmed me.

i'm sure i would've been content to live a happy sugar'n'spice good girl asexual life.

but i got stuck.

my old hormones started to act up and without any regard led me into unlabelled territory. i developed quick crushes on several women, and a serious attraction to a MAN! shiit! what now?

there i was in unlabelled territory. BAD.

i quickly realized (as did my male partner at the time) that the label lesbian or straight asexual wasn't quite reflecting where i was at.

exploring my bisexual feelings challenged my GOOD GIRL pattern.

allowing myself to embrace the label bisexual opened up the possibility of not seeing myself in either/or terms. i began to examine my mixed identity as a black–south asian woman. i changed jobs and began to explore my potential as an activist and an artist.

but old patterns die hard. i got stuck.

where was the approval? where was the community-home that i could fit into? girls are nice like sugar'n'spice...

i set out to find a way to be a GOOD BI-GIRL. i tried using the label lesbian-identified feminist bisexual in order to differentiate myself from "those" other bisexuals whose politics i don't share. this would offer me a more specific checklist for approval.

but a process had taken place in exploring my sexuality, and the way i began to use labels to define myself was less didactic and more fluid. as a blacksouthasianfeministmiddleclassablebodied-actoractivistcaribbeanposttherapybisexual, i am never going to find a box that can reflect that back to me exactly.

two alternatives — suppress certain aspects of myself in order to be GOOD. (did it, hated it, can't.) or challenge the sociopolitical and psychological pressure to be GOOD.

challenging the need to be GOOD has allowed me to explore my sexuality, my race, my work outside of labels — pure ME-ness. that ME-ness gets suppressed whenever anyone assumes i'm straight, confused, male-identified or stupid because i'm a girl. that ME-ness gets oppressed whenever someone with institutionalized power tries to silence me.

my ME-ness stays suppressed and oppressed whenever i feel that i can't challenge or be a BAD BI-GIRL. most times it feels GOOD to say exactly what i think we little girls are made of.

Nancy Chater & Lilith Finkler

"Traversing Wide Territories":
A Journey from Lesbianism to Bisexuality

INTRODUCTION

THIS TWO-PART ARTICLE IS ABOUT ONE WOMAN'S journey from lesbianism to bisexuality. The first section is a reprint of Lilith Finkler's article called "Lesbians Who Sleep With Men," originally published in 1983 in the now-defunct Canadian feminist newspaper *Broadside*. In this risky and groundbreaking article, Lilith Finkler discusses the complicated political and personal questions that arose for her when, after many years as an out, politically active lesbian, she had a relationship with a man. During and after this relationship, Lilith Finkler identified as a lesbian and was deeply involved in lesbian community and political struggles in Toronto. Identifying herself as a working-class, white, Jewish anarchist-feminist, Lilith Finkler continues to organize, mobilize and make links between various political movements — anti-poverty, psychiatric survivor, disability rights, and with Jews in solidarity with Palestinians.

Ten years after the *Broadside* article, and seventeen years after coming out as a lesbian, Lilith Finkler decided that, despite some limitations to the term, "bisexual" most accurately described her changing sexual identity. I first met Lilith at a bisexual women's potluck gathering in Toronto, where she sought support for her journey. Reflecting on the important issues Lilith had raised in her 1983 article concerning identity, community and politics, I interviewed Lilith about the shifts and continuities in her current perspectives. This interview comprises the second section. With a seasoned critical consciousness informed by her particular social location, Lilith Finkler offers insights into the pleasures, pains and potentials of bisexuality in a heterosexist world.

PART 1:
Lesbians Who Sleep With Men
By Lilith Finkler. Originally published in Broadside, *1983.*

EVEN AS I WRITE THIS ARTICLE, I AM BECOMING more aware of the potential to distort the information it presents. This essay could be construed as a denial of real lesbianism, or as a suggestion that lesbianism is merely a "stage," or even perhaps that if one finds the right man, a dyke could be "cured."

This is not the point of my article. I am trying to describe a very complex situation. What happens when a lesbian-feminist (and a political activist at that) decides to sleep with a man? What does she experience? What kinds of questions does it raise for her and the community to which she belongs?

My ideological reference points are a combination of lesbian-feminism and anarchism. For me, lesbianism is not just a sexual orientation. It is a political statement, a rejection of male supremacy at work, at home, and in bed. I allowed myself to become intimate with a man because I felt it was part of a personal process. I had to reclaim a part of my traumatic past that included many violent rapes. Heterosexual sex triggered many painful memories; it broke through the blocks and forced me to actually deal. Of course, I trusted the individual male in question, and was attracted to him, or I would never have let him so close.

Nevertheless, it proved very difficult to reconcile my emotional situation to the current political reality. While allowances are made for "women-identified" women, lesbian feminists often think of themselves as superior to their heterosexual counterparts. After all, as Ti-Grace once said: "Feminism is the theory, lesbianism is the practice."[1]

I myself adhered to such a belief system, although I would not have necessarily admitted it in public. While I was sleeping with a man, I convinced myself that since feminists had always fought for "the right to determine our own sexuality," I did not have to worry about my own political credibility. I could not forget, however, participating in one group a few years ago where being heterosexual (celibate or otherwise) was a political liability. Nor could I forget "A Fine Kettle of Fish"[2] which deteriorated rapidly into a session of angry declarations and anti-*man*-ifestoes.

More importantly perhaps, I realized that the woman I had quietly mocked before was the very woman I now faced every morning in the mirror.

I, Lilith, am a working-class, white, Jewish, anarcha-feminist lesbian. (Talk about labels!) Yes, a lesbian, although I ended a ten-month relationship with a man in April of this year. I do not intend to have another relationship with a man. I identified as a lesbian throughout my sexual involvement, making it quite clear that my emotional and political priority was other women. This attitude was undoubtably the source of many tensions in our time together as a "couple."

During the time that I saw Robert, I operated in a no-woman's land of social semantics. For the past six years, I had identified myself as a dyke, but now for the first time, I was seeing a "MAN"! (So I'm bisexual, but I'm not sleeping with a woman so maybe I'm heterosexual with past lesbian experience? But lesbianism is not just who you sleep with, it's a whole politic, a way of life...)

I felt confused, unsure and afraid to approach other lesbians with my own personal truths. After all, I as a lesbian had not wanted to hear about other women's straight experiences. And a dyke gone "het" is just ten times worse. I was a traitor to my cause.

I found out during the course of my "phase" that there were many lesbians like me who for a variety of reasons explored sexual relationships with men.

Some were actually questioning their sexuality, others had ended painful relationships with women and yet others had moved to smaller communities where there were no "out" lesbians.

Once I had spoken to these other women (they called themselves "lesbians" in spite of their temporary liaisons with men), I began to feel validated; there were others like me. I was not alone in the pursuit of my own unique label.

Some, having read the above, may feel that I have not analyzed correctly. One could posit that women turn to men not for personal exploration, but for political gain, i.e., Social Acceptability. To deny that particular element in social dynamics would be pure folly. Of course, being Normal is tempting.

Nevertheless, all the lesbians I have spoken to, without exception, are strongly woman-identified, and carry in their hearts some vision of a matriarchal world. One cannot so easily discredit their personal struggles.

Many of these women mentioned being afraid to be affectionate in public, lest they be spotted by past acquaintances. I, too, was fearful of others discovering my political inconsistencies and personal confusions. How ironic that I, who insisted on kissing my woman lovers everywhere and anywhere, would a few years later be terrified to hold the hand of a man.

For a while, I avoided attending "women's" events and local demonstrations where I was likely to meet old friends and acquaintances. Then I realized that, in spite of my circumstances, the lesbian community was and would continue to be my community. My essential values had not changed. But how was I to reconcile what was in my heart to what was in my head to what was in my cunt?

It was no mean feat "coming out" once again to my "family," my circle of lesbian friends. I was afraid of being rejected and of being judged "politically incorrect." I am glad to say that without exception the members of my immediate "family" accepted me as I was. Other women were not so lucky. One woman's friend refused to discuss the male lover. Another actually spit on the floor and walked out in the middle of a conversation. I feel tremendously lucky to know that at least for me, sisterhood is powerful.

During the time that I spent with Robert (no, that's not his real name), I discovered heterosexual privilege. I was finally "normal" to the outside world. I could talk about my boyfriend to virtual strangers and they would nod sympathetically, acknowledging the primacy of our relationship. This was so different from talking about my "friend" or "roommate" in the hope of disguising the level of our intimacy.

I didn't have to inquire whether events were actually "gay" or not because I was "straight" and everything in this world is heterosexual unless designated otherwise. I'll never forget going to a restaurant I had frequented with my woman friends. I had always been allocated a small table beside the door, even when booths were available. When I went with Robert, the hostess smiled and, judging us to be a couple, gave us a private booth at the back. I couldn't believe the difference. So this is heterosexual privilege.

Sleeping with Robert brought up a lot of political questions too. What is a lesbian? Is she simply a woman who sleeps with other women? Is she a woman who commits her life to women emotionally and politically? Or, is she all of the above?

Was it "politically correct" (forgive the cliché) for me to call myself a dyke while I slept with a man? Was that dishonest or misleading? Or, on the other hand, would it have been a cop-out for me to peel off the label "lesbian" and apply "bisexual" instead?

While I would not presume to judge the lifestyle, I personally do not like the term "bisexual." It implies a political equality that does not exist. Sleeping with a woman is not the same as sleeping with a man. A woman must consciously decide to be lesbian. She need not question herself at all to be actively heterosexual. The prefix "bi," or the implication of two equal sides, is therefore an inaccurate representation of present-day sexual relationships.

One major concern of lesbians who sleep with men is their actual position as members of the lesbian community. I often asked myself whether an oppressed group should be expected to retain individuals who no longer fit the official criteria. As a member of at least three minority groups, I recognize the need for some mechanism that will help me to identify those who share my own oppression. Standardizing the approach, however, also standardizes the procedure and resultant interaction. I am not willing to give up on spontaneity.

We, as lesbians, do need constant validation for our lifestyle. The male-stream media is certainly not renowned for its accurate portrayal of our experience. Having women who are "uncommitted" or "confused" enter the movement dilutes the strength and character of the lesbian milieu — but does it?

There are many women who do not identify as lesbian: not all are heterosexual or have lovers of both sexes. Some are closeted lesbians who may risk their homes, their jobs, their kids or all three. Some of us can be more sure of ourselves or more public than others. I believe that diversity, in all its manifestations, is our strength.

I would suggest that we continue to be open to hearing about the myriad of lesbian experiences and refrain from passing judgement. Let us integrate the whole spectrum of lesbian sexualities in our discussions, newsletters, conferences, etc. We should redefine the word "lesbian" to include those of us who have questioned ourselves in the past or who may do so in the future. Our ranks may well be thinned by the inevitable percentage who will attach themselves permanently to men. However, we will be much stronger by having allowed those amongst us to be open and honest about who they are.

A great many women I know have questioned themselves, experimented, had one-night stands. It is a lot more common than any one of us would like to think. Yet coverage of this issue merits precious little space in the feminist press: one column in *Our Right to Love* (ed. Ginny Vida) and one short article in *Off Our Backs* (October 1982). Is this really all there is to say?

Unfortunately, the unspoken lesbian feminist politic has often led to a narrow chauvinism that does not allow dykes to indulge in personal insecurities or to discuss them with one another. Silencing is not an effective tool for consciousness raising. Criteria of any sort spell the creation of a hierarchical setting. Thus, it is for each woman to declare herself lesbian or not. If we develop standards and seek to impose them, are we not the very people we choose to battle?

PART 2:
"Traversing Wide Territories": An Interview
with Lilith Finkler by Nancy Chater, October 1993

N: What was the reaction to the *Broadside* article when it was published?

L: Well, a couple of days after the article came out there was a lesbian dance. I went to the dance, and I was surprised because I was approached by at least three lesbians who came to me with their own stories. I had expected to spend the night kind of flirting around and I ended up spending it in corners hearing (*laughter*) from these other dykes that had also been with men. The big problem was, how do you get birth control when all the feminists work at the birth control clinics?! (*laughter*). And you didn't want them to know what you were doing! So the reaction was actually really positive, much more positive than I ever would have anticipated when I was writing it.

N: You've identified as a dyke for seventeen years and now identify as bisexual,...

L: Yep.

N: ...increasingly publically so; why is that?

L: Why do I identify as bisexual?

N: Yes, and how did that come about?

L: Because I feel like it's more honest to say that I'm bisexual. When I wrote the article I didn't think I'd ever sleep with a man again. But now I'm pretty clear that when I think about potential partners — and up until two weeks ago I was with a man too, so I think that there's the immediacy of that relationship — I can see myself being with a man, and I can see myself being with a woman. I felt like I had to be honest about saying that, and so I use the term bisexual. Even though I have tremendous problems with it, I don't know what other word there is to use.

N: Can you say more about that? You also mentioned in your 1983 article having some problems with the term.

L: For me, "bi" means a duality. Implicit in the duality is the concept of equality, that both of those sides are equal. In this society sleeping with a woman is not equal to sleeping with a man. One gets tremendous benefits from heterosexual privilege and from associating oneself with a man. One gets no privileges and tremendous harassment and oppression from being with a woman. So there's a lot more social pressure to be with a man than there is to be with a woman. So the nature of "bi" and its implied equality is inaccurate.

N: And I know a lot of bisexual women say that being bisexual does not necessarily mean they're equally attracted to men and women, or that they have had equal numbers of male and female partners in their lives. In your history it's not fifty-fifty...

L: Right. My history has been almost exclusively with women for many, many years. Well, I say "exclusively" — I have had two substantial, one-year relationships with men, the one in '82 and then this one recently. When I was thinking of the duality, I was thinking of it in regard to the social and political context rather than my own personal context. I also feel — and this is something that is coming out more in discussions of the construction of gender — that "bi" presumes that there's only two...

N: Uh huh!

L: Right? And there's lots of sexualities. It's just that the way this world is structured you have a concept of sleeping with a man or sleeping with a woman, and no real analysis of butch or femme, or top or bottom, or any of the other myriad sexualities that are present both within the lesbian communities and within the heterosexual and bisexual, or whatever, communities. So those terms are really limiting in the way that we can describe ourselves with them.

N: Yes, I would agree with you. And "bisexual" seems to be the closest thing at hand, even though I don't feel it's a perfect term either.

L: If I think of something I'll let you know.

Identity & Multiplicity

N: Do you still name yourself, as you did ten years ago, "a working-class, white, Jewish anarcha-feminist?" I'm wondering if other elements of how you identify have also gone through changes over the years?

L: It's really interesting that you bring that up. Because it seems like a lot of me has sort of split — or maybe I've opened myself up to my own multiplicities, so to speak. For example, I am white, in that I have white skin and I get white-skin privilege, but I also come from a mixed racial background. My father is European, he's from Poland, and my mother is from Libya, in North Africa. That was a tremendous struggle for me in my life. I now identify as biracial because to me it is more accurate a term. Though, again, the whole thing about "bi" is misleading, and the idea of racial purity has to be questioned, because of course in this society none of us is actually racially completely one way or the other. We are mixed from lots of cultures — and then of course there's the whole question of the actual scientific nature of "race," right?

N: That race is a social construct to begin with.

L: Yes, exactly. Because I want to let people know that part of me is European, Eastern European, and part of me is North African, I use the term biracial. And I'm still an anarchist, because to me an analysis of power is absolutely imperative when we're looking at other issues in our lives, issues of hierarchy and dominance. I want to eliminate all power relationships based on any form of privilege in this society, whether it's class or gender or race or ability or anything, so of course I'm absolutely committed to being an anarchist.

Regarding feminism, my most recent activism has been in the psychiatric survivor community, and so I found it very alienating to be in the women's movement because it tends to be so therapeutically oriented and very much into the individual model of dysfunctional families — which individualizes women's experience of oppression. So sometimes I don't even want to call myself a feminist. I think feminism is so often a bourgeois kind of term that I call myself an anarchist, and sometimes an anarchist-feminist. But I don't really situate myself politically in the women's movement. I don't feel like that's where my liberation is going to be won.

Lesbian & Bisexual Oral History: "A Fine Kettle of Fish," 1979

N: Bisexual women and lesbians working together politically is still a controversial subject and still an area that needs a lot of work, even though it has been taking place in an unrecognized way for many years. Now that more bisexual women are coming out, the issue is more on the table. Can you tell me about the 1979 public meeting called "A Fine Kettle of Fish" in Toronto (*laughter*) where lesbians and bisexuals tried to come together?

L: It was an intense meeting where a lot of members of the community got together, and they put on this play. It was called *To Tell the Truth*. Have you ever seen the game show, *To Tell the Truth*?

N: Yes, I remember that.

L: In the play the woman goes, "I'm the real feminist," then the next one goes, "I'm the real feminist," and the next one goes, "I'm the real feminist" and then, "will the real feminist please stand up?" and all three of them stand up (*laughter*). It was really funny and people had a good time during the performance part. Unfortunately once it got down to a discussion of what was actually going on in the movement, there were a lot of splits. I remember a number of women talking about being bisexual and the women who were lesbian just saying, "you're sleeping with the enemy."

N: Was that the stated purpose of the get-together, was it framed as lesbians and bisexuals coming together?

L: What happened as I understand it is that International Women's Day, I think it was in 1976, or '77, maybe it was '78, one of those years, International Women's Day had finally gotten started here in Toronto. The women from LOOT, Lesbian Organization of Toronto, and women from WAVAW, Women Against Violence Against Women, really wanted to have a women-only International Women's Day. Some of the other women who were from Organized Working Women and other women's, or left, organizations like the Revolutionary Workers League, wanted to have a mixed event. So the first year, International Women's Day had two marches. One march was mixed men and women, and then there was the march just for women. Of course, being a dyke, I was on the women-only march. And you know how they have parades and they have women who are sitting at the back waving very politely to the crowd? Well, I was the woman who sat at the back on the car, and instead of smiling sweetly and dressing very femmily, I was dressed as a butch. I think I had a hard hat and oven mitts on! (*laughter*) I was waving to people as we went by.

Subsequently what happened was a big brouhaha and a big fight and all the women from WAVAW had walked out, or was it LOOT? Mostly the lesbians, anyway, had walked out and said, "we want this to be a women-only event." They walked out in anger. I think that "A Fine Kettle of Fish" was a way for heterosexual, bisexual and lesbian women to come together and try to work out some of the politics. My experience of it was that people went away from it more convinced than ever that their particular position was right. If you talked to other women, they may have a different perspective, but that's how I saw it.

N: So there were a lot of negative views toward bisexuality?

L: Yeah! And I was part of that. That's what I feel most sad about now, that I was actually perpetuating that myself. I'll never forget there was a woman who was bisexual who I actually quite liked and because she was potentially ever going to sleep with a man, I didn't feel comfortable to be with her. That's very painful when you have to look back and admit some of your own actions.

Identity & Communities

N: You raise important questions in your article about community. About one's sense of belonging or being excluded and the role of self-defining one's relationship to a particular community. Following your relationship with the man, back in 1983, you realized that "the lesbian community was still my community. My values had not changed." Is this still the case?

L: Oh absolutely. But that is also the really hard thing for me as somebody who is actively bisexual, that my community, the people that I see in my life, the places where I go, my commitments — like last night I went to hear Joanne Loulan [a lesbian comedian] — are within a lesbian framework. What I really want is a bisexual framework.

I have to be very clear that I was actually *raised* by the lesbian community. Raised in the sense that my values, my attitudes, my life choices were very much influenced by the women around me who were lesbian. I came out when I was seventeen, and I didn't have a family. I had been rejected by my family of origin. So the lesbian community has been my family for seventeen years. You can't just — I am choosing *not to* reject those very precious times in my past when I felt part of that. And because of the nature of the relationships I have developed I still see that as very much a part of my life. I'm very conscious that if I were to choose to be with a man long-term, that I might lose some of that.

N: That would be a very big price to pay.

L: Yeah. And I must be clear that it wouldn't be because I would be rejected, that's not what would happen. Most of the events that are lesbian are women-only, so it means that I can't bring a male partner.

N: Yes, that social division.

L: Yeah.

N: That ends up being a personal division and, to some extent, a political division, too.

L: Yes. When I say that I'm in the lesbian community, I should say more specifically the Jewish lesbian community. And also community among psychiatric survivors who are gay and lesbian. I'm in very specific parts of the lesbian community. So it's also an issue that because I have so much in common with these communities, I can't just let them go.

N: And being bisexual you still have those things in common.

L: Absolutely.

N: In those lesbian communities that you just referred to, what have the reactions been like over the past year as you've been coming out more as bisexual?

L: Mostly it's been very supportive. I have to say that it's a testament to my friendships with people. There may be an implicit or unarticulated expectation that I'll go back to being exclusively with women, since that's what I did before. I don't know. That hasn't come up in discussion. In fact, a number of my friends have said that it's really been a challenge for them to think of me as bisexual, because mostly people whom they have thought of as bisexual are people whom they see as unwillng to say that they're lesbian. I, on the other hand, have spoken actively as a lesbian. In the newspaper, even, I can show you articles where even though it's not the subject matter, I make a point of saying that I'm lesbian, so people can't assume I'm heterosexual. Friends know that I am not reluctant to be out. Then they have to unearth other reasons why I would be bisexual. I think that it's offered them opportunities to look at other stereotypes.

N: You said, in 1983, "I do not intend to have another relationship with a man..." (*laughter*) I'm wondering if this was the result of a sense of pressure to disavow the act that you were at the same time self-affirming in your article?

L: Absolutely not. It had nothing to do with it. What had happened was right after I broke up with the man that I had been involved with, I had memories of child sexual abuse. The memories were quite overwhelming. Quite frankly, the thought of being with anyone was just much too much for me. In one of my other pieces of writing, I talk about an expectation of celibacy, simply because the fear of being sexual was much too much for me at the time.

I didn't have the negative reactions to my male lover that a lot of lesbians might have. I got a lot of support from my friends. In fact, it was primarily my lesbian friends who took care of me when I was having memories.

A Bisexual Politics

N: It's often been said, and this is something that you touched on yourself, that being a lesbian is not just who you sleep with, it's a whole politic, a way of life. Do you see bisexuality in that same way, as a whole politic, a way of life? If you do, how would you describe your politics of bisexuality?

L: There's a lot of things that I would say. One thing is that the lesbian politic as I knew it was very much one that affirmed woman-ness, and woman-hood. There was an emphasis on unity, it was almost the creation of an enforced homogeneity. A homogeneity that is just now

25

beginning to crack, when Black lesbians, and Jewish lesbians, and Asian lesbians and Latina lesbians and disabled lesbians are splitting off into their own particular groups of lesbians. What that change allowed for me was to say, okay, I am not part of this homogeneity either, and then to look at bisexuality.

Bisexuality is willing to explore multiplicity. A bisexual politic also allows others to explore those differences within themselves that don't often get addressed. It's easier to be just one way or the other. But that's not the truth for most of us I would say, being in one category of identity or another.

Another thing is that the lesbian politics that I've come from said "we don't have to educate the men, we're just going to focus on women and let the men go." What that means in essence is that we're no longer willing to be in a place of struggle with our oppressor. Bisexuality, on the other hand, acknowledges that there are gonna be places where we have privilege, and there are gonna be places where we are oppressed, and that we're willing to engage in both of those as part of our own process.

For me that's more true to who I am because there are places where I have privilege in the world, for example, as a supervisor in my work, and there are places where I am oppressed, for example, in a lot of my relationships. In my friendship with a friend who uses a wheelchair, I get to walk up the stairs and she has to wait outside. In a friendship with a person who is middle class and owns a house, I end up feeling like I have less physical security because I rent. With my friend who is a wheelchair user I get to be accountable to her and try not to go to places where she can't come with me. And there are places where I end up trying to get more security for myself and want my friends to share that with me.

What I would say is that being bisexual makes me willing to be, at certain times, in painful places.

Another thing about lesbian politics is that there is this assumption, or there had been previously, that lesbianism was a way of equalizing relationships between women, without recognizing that not all women were the same. For example, in my relationship with another woman who was Jewish and a lesbian, there was the whole issue of class. As a woman who owned property, she had more privilege than I did. Even though we were two women, two Jewish lesbians, there was still tremendous power politics.

I think that bisexuality addresses that, or is more willing to address power politics in relationships.

N: Do you think some of the problems that you are talking about in lesbian politics being based on a oneness, a unity, a homogeneity, are because of the extent to which that particular vision came out of a white lesbian perspective?

L: The fact that it was influenced by a white middle-class ideological orientation might have had something to do with it. Certainly people who come from non-dominant cultures are less willing to split off from their families of origin. Because those families of origin are also sources of refuge from ethnocentrism, racism or anti-Semitism. In that way, there might have been some of those white middle-class assumptions in the emphasis on unity or oneness among lesbians.

I also think that there are ways that lesbians are isolated in the world. Most of us as lesbians have lost our families of origin. Sexual outlaws, you know. The intensity of the homophobia resulted in us being rejected from our families, so we clung to one another to have some source of emotional support. Maybe part of what allows us now to splinter off into all these small groups is the sense that we have something more than we might have had before.

N: Do your politics of bisexuality stem from a feminist analysis of sexuality? For me, that's the case. I identify very much as a feminist, a bisexual feminist, in the sense that I look at issues of sexuality — things like its social control, social definition and the power issues within sexuality — from a feminist perspective. One that critiques heterosexism, and the institutionalization of heterosexism.

L: What I was trying to say before is, I don't identify as a feminist. I think it's primarily a bourgeois liberal term that keeps the patriarchy happy. Women can be feminist and still participate in screwing around other women. I prefer to call myself an anarchist because the intensity of the word has something to it. To answer you though, historically, I would say that feminism is the way in which I entered my sexuality. Or, that as a result of my lesbianism, I embraced feminism. What happened for me was really that I was looking for dykes. I wanted to be with a woman, so I went to CHAT, Community Homophile Association of Toronto — that was '76. I went looking for lesbians, because I had decided I was one. I went looking and the CHAT place wasn't open, so I went downstairs to the Hassle Free Clinic and this woman, who I'll never forget, said to me, "Oh well, if you want to meet lesbians, there's a lot of them in the women's movement, they're all feminist." And I said, "wow!" (laughter). I immediately went to The Other Woman newspaper, and then I went to a march because it said something about feminists. I thought, well here I'm going to meet lesbians. Instead what I met were a bunch of really angry women. What they were talking about though were issues that related to my life. Stuff about violence against women and stuff that I had endured, so I related to it. It was as a result of actually seeking out a sexual partner that I ended up coming to the recognition of women's oppression in society. But really what I wanted was a lover. I didn't want to be intellectually stimulated. (laughter)

N: An intellectually stimulating lover is the best kind of lover, I think... (laughter)

L: But I was seventeen, you know. (chuckle) Give me a break. Through the women's movement I came to understand about feminism. But now, looking at who I am, I would not define myself that way.

I'm looking toward an analysis of oppression that includes all disempowered peoples, and feminism doesn't have that.

N: You don't think feminism can have that? My idea of feminism is that it can, it often has not, absolutely has not had that, but to my mind it certainly can.

L: The lesbian dance that took place last night was not accessible to women who use wheelchairs, you know, so, I'm sorry. Until the so-called women's movement actually makes real practical steps to include all women and not reinforce the power structures that exist in the outside society, I am unwilling to refer to myself by that name.

Bisexuality & the "Nature or Nurture?"
Question of Orientation

N: The question that sometimes gets phrased as "is it nature or nurture" that determines one's sexuality is asked especially often in relation to "homosexuality." Is it a "choice," and therefore it enters the discourse of individual rights, individual choice; or is it something that is innate, natural, uncontrollable, just what one feels, so that's what one is. Both of those arguments have been put forward in defense of the validity of being lesbian or being bisexual. Sometimes they conflict. For instance bisexual women, it seems, often speak about *choosing* to identify as bisexual. I've heard that challenged by lesbians who say, "I don't make a choice, it's just the way I feel." How would you relate this to your earlier statement that "a woman must consciously decide to be lesbian. She need not question herself at all to be actively heterosexual."

L: What I was talking about is that because heterosexuality is the norm in this society, it is quite simple for women to be heterosexual without really having to look inside themselves and determine if that's truly who they are. However, if one is lesbian — whether one feels one was born that way or whether one comes to a political understanding and chooses to be that way — the fact is that just the very nature, the conscious understanding, of being different forces us to evaluate who we are, and whether we want to act on what it is that we think we are.

For example, I can remember being eight years old, and we had Valentine's Day and everybody was sending Valentine's Day cards. You know in class you get little cards...

N: Yes! Yes.

L: *(laughter)* My mother gave me and my sisters I think it was like twenty-five little cards each to give to all the other kids in the class. Well, everybody gave one to every other kid in the class. No, not me! I gave one to my teacher, and twenty-four to Joanna. *(laughter)*

I had a crush on Joanna at eight years of age, but *somehow I knew* that it wasn't right for me to give all these cards to another girl, so instead of putting my name, I asked my mother to spell for me "guess who?" 'cause I didn't even know. And I very painstakingly wrote "guess who?" on twenty-four different cards. Somehow it had occurred to me that it was wrong for a little girl to give them to another girl. But what was even more striking was that when I went later and Joanna, of course, had a lot more cards than everybody else in the class, and I said to her, "Oh you have a lot of cards. Where did they come from?" she said to me, "Geez, I don't know, there's a whole bunch of "guess whos?" and I can't figure out which boy gave them to me." I remember thinking, *oh my God*. Not only did I unconsciously know it was wrong from my end, but Joanna had no idea. Because she was going on in that heterosexual model. So that's what I was talking about.

When I think about it *now*, in my understanding of the world, I believe that both kinds of lesbians exist. I believe that there are women who for whatever reason, as myself, are born-and-bred lesbians. I had things like dreams about Barbie, wanting her to grow up. I remember I would — you know how they have Tabatha on television, she would rub her nose and things would get big — I spent half an hour with my Barbie doll rubbing my nose hoping she would grow into a big girl. (*laughter*) And when she didn't I got so upset I took her and threw her down the stairs! (*more laughter*) I was eight or nine! In my lesbian sensibilities, I would say I was born lesbian.

However, I also have very good friends who are lesbian who tell me clearly that they could be with men, and they could be with women. For them it's a political choice to reject male supremacy at home and in bed, by choosing to be just with women. Now, that premise is based on the idea that a relationship with two women is always equal. Therefore, you're rejecting the patriarchy by rejecting a man. As a woman who comes with many different experiences of oppression, based on ability, based on race, based on class, on religion, based on all kinds of other things, then for me if I were to reject every person who has power over me in every different part of my life, I would be very limited in who it is that I could be intimate with.

N: How do you relate that to your bisexuality? Does that seem to be more a choice, a conscious choice...

L: For me it is. In my own understanding of myself, it is a choice. I think I will probably be more with women than with men, but maybe not! I don't know. I think that I'm willing for myself to say that it's a choice. Because I think at this point I could be with either one.

Another point I want to make is that we have to be very careful about these biological arguments, because I believe that they're dangerous. People have used biology to justify oppression for many, many different groups of people. For example, women were oppressed because of our wombs. Our uterus! We're natural housewives because we have babies! Black people were put down because they supposedly had smaller brains than white people. People with developmental disabilities were segregated in institutions because of the fear of the contagion of "feeble-mindedness." Now we can see biology being used to ostensibly get gay and lesbian people off the hook. But I see it as quite possible to use the argument the other way, that gays and lesbians can't be teachers because they could "give it to their students."

N: Uh huh! And the search for the alleged gene that "causes homosexuality..."

L: Yes! And what are they gonna do when they find the gene?

N: Yes, exactly...

L: You know? Absolutely! The other thing is that "choosing" a particular experience doesn't mean that they won't oppress us. Or if it's biological that somehow it's okay and they're not going to oppress us. Besides which, what's wrong with choosing? What is fundamentally wrong with affirming a way of life that is supportive and nurturing and capable? There's so many wonderful things about being lesbian, being bisexual. What is wrong with choosing them?

N: And there's the danger of defining ourselves in response to those who would attack and undermine us, the danger of formulating a reason for being that is in defensive reaction rather than a first statement of yes, this is who I am. We shouldn't need to defend our existence! I think it's important to remember that it is inherently wrong to always be put in that position.

L: Absolutely.

"Traversing Wide Territories": The Potential
of Bisexuality in a Heterosexist World

N: Your discussion about being a lesbian who sleeps with a man or with men raises the question of how identities grounded in sexuality are defined. Answering the question "what is a bisexual?" problematizes fixed notions of sexual identity, and other elements of how people identify, perhaps even more. How would you define what bisexuality is? Do you think that's a useful thing to do?

L: Oh, geez. I think that we have to look at the question in its social context today. In California there's bisexual activism, so answering the question there is in the context of a world that is conscious of bisexuality as a lived experience. In some ways I think bisexuality in Toronto lacks that. We don't have what I consider to be a bisexual community. We don't have a bisexual community centre. We don't have a bisexual newspaper. We have one bisexual group, it's mostly men, and the women's group isn't going, so there's not a whole lot of what I would refer to as a bisexual community. Answering what is bisexual in a social vacuum is difficult.

What I can answer is what I like to think bisexuality would be and I can also tell you what I think the potential is that bisexuals offer to other communities.

N: Oh! Okay...

L: In its ideal sense I would see bisexuality as a way of exploring marginal territories. People who don't fit into either place often end up going to new places, because we need to find a home. So, for example, I'm biracial — I'm partly in the Eastern European world and partly in the North African world. And I find myself being kind of interested in Yiddish and kind of interested in Arabic, because those were the two languages of my parents. Sometimes I combine them and mix them in the way that I talk, and the way that I think, and I'll find myself speaking a little bit of one or even mixing the sounds. In the way that I explore those kinds of elements, I can also explore how being with men and being with women fits with how I am. I take some of what I get from being with men into my relationships with women, and some of what I get with women into my relationships with men.

I see bisexuals as the wanderers, because we can traverse the ground of the female world and also of the male world. Being able to do that allows us to glean from both of those gendered experiences. That's another thing, that being bisexual, or being lesbian or being heterosexual are each different gendered experiences. In our relationship to others we also have a redefinition of our own gender identity. In my experience being with women I behave differently than I have in my relationships with men. Even though I'm fundamentally the same person. So I would say that we traverse wide territories, allowing for the depth of exploration that doesn't exist when you stay in one place. That has both its stresses and its benefits. When you traverse a large ground, you get the depth of the experience, but a certain lack of security.

The potential I see for us as bisexuals is to offer to others what they themselves might not choose to do. Which is that exploration. Also I think we can offer an analysis of power inherent not only in male-female relationships but also in the dynamics that exist in other hierarchical relationships. If as bisexual women we can create models for egalitarianism, or for potential egalitarianism in relationships with men, then there's also the potential to use those models between women. If we can build alliances with men, who are our oppressors, then also it means that for those of us who are white women, or who are able-bodied women, that we can also begin to know our role as allies to women of colour, to disabled women, to psychiatrized women. You know, there's that possibility

Experience, Identity, Politics

L: Building alliances takes a lot of work. And a lot of struggle. What I have to remind lesbians is that as *they say* they choose *not* to struggle with men — and I'm talking here specifically about white, able-bodied, middle-class lesbians who say they don't want to struggle with men — then I would say to them, as a psychiatrized woman, and as a disabled woman, well then maybe I don't want to struggle with you. As a working-class woman, I'm fed up. I also understand the need to separate and take care of ourselves, but when they say that they also have to remember that it can be said to them.

N: That leads into my next question, which is that bisexual feminists are raising questions, as you have been, about the complex relationships and often the outright contradictions within individuals among experience, identity and politics. Sometimes those things don't match up. There's contradictions between one's past history and how they currently identify, and what they might be doing politically, or not, but there's an assumption that all of those things are collapsible. There's an assumption that your behaviour equals your identity equals your politics. Do you see any need to reconcile some of the contradictions within ourselves in order to formulate the grounds for an integrated or coalition politics? Or can those contradictions and tensions be there and still proceed with political work given the urgency of the work...

L: Well of course! I work with my enemies all the time! (*laughter*) That's how I struggle. Like I say, if I'm willing to struggle with men, I'm also willing to struggle with women who I experience as oppressors. My commitment is to social change. I don't change the world by being with people who are just like me.

In terms of dealing with the contradictions, I deal with them every day, every way, in all parts of my life. I work in a situation where I deal with poor people, all the time. Homeless people. All the time. The people that I see and care about will search the garbage cans for something to eat. They'll take cigarette butts off the street, and smoke them, because that's all they have. I struggle and I share with them. I'm very conscious that I have a job because those poor people exist. To me that's an inherent contradiction. As I work to end poverty, to end the psychiatric system, I participate *in it* by assisting those individuals and advocating on their behalf. If that system of oppression didn't exist, however, I wouldn't have a job.

N: Or not this job.

L: Or not this job, right. So to me the very nature of my day-to-day work is a contradiction in terms. Most of my life is like that.

Community & Politics:
Allowing "a More Complex Continuum of Sexualities"

N: Anything you'd like to add?

L: Yeah. A few thoughts. In this society, ideas come rapidly at people either on television or radio or whatever — what's referred to as "sound bites." Ideas travel a lot of ground really quickly, they come from one part of the world to another really fast. In some ways I see that expansion and proliferation of ideas also happening in the lesbian community. In the 1950s and '60s, and even in the '70s when I was coming out, we were a very insulated kind of group, because we needed to be to protect ourselves. It was a matter of self preservation. If we were out in our jobs or in our personal lives we could risk our homes, our children, our jobs, or all three, so we had to be more secretive. That also prevented the penetration of ideas within our communities.

Now that we feel more free, ideas from the outside are coming in. What it does is challenge us to be more consciously aware both of what's out there in the world and also what's happening in our own communities. As a lesbian, I was often aware that there were women who had slept with men — because of my article. I was also aware that there were women who were bisexual who were choosing not to say so because it was not safe. Now, because our community is more open, that honesty is more possible. I think that honesty will do two things. It will allow the lesbian community to be made more aware of the political, social and cultural contributions of bisexual women. I also think that it reflects a growth and maturity that we allow ourselves to be a more complex continuum of sexualities than we might otherwise have perceived ourselves to be.

The other thing that occurs to me, is that perhaps just as people are more transitory in the world, perhaps our notions of our own sexuality are also more transient. This is a thing that worries me. We explore an idea for a while, try it out for a while, decide it's cool — like I had somebody tell me the other day that it's really cool to be a lesbian now. And I got really upset, because I spent all these years being a dyke, getting people throwing rotten tomatoes at me, and now it's cool to be lesbian, and I'm bisexual! (*laughter*) I thought to myself, "Lilith, you never get it right!" (*laughter*) But to me that's one of the worrisome things about the whole nature of this society and the way in which we move, like people move from apartment to apartment, from fashion style to fashion style, and what would worry me about that transience is the way it might get applied to our sexuality.

It's something to try out for a while. Bisexuality, for that matter. Our notions of our sexuality are changing. Some people see that as a positive thing. As I've discovered for myself it's been a matter of much growth and self-searching, but I can also see what the lesbian community would be really afraid of in bisexuals. That we would be coming as transients to explore a new flavour, not really making a commitment to the underlying philosophical goals.

N: And therefore threatening the continuity...

L: Of the lesbian community. I suppose for me I would look at it more as some kind of ongoing circumstance where heterosexual women make the move toward bisexuality, or to lesbianism, and some of us as lesbians making the move to bisexuality or heterosexuality.

N: I've also known women who identified as bisexual and now identify as lesbian.

L: Right. It's an ongoing situation. I think in my own journey that because I was able to understand the whole notion of my being split, or being multiple, as I said earlier, and finally come to terms with that, also allowed me to come to terms with my split or multiple sexuality.

N: Certainly, women talk about bisexuality as, for one thing, disrupting clearcut "either/or" social categories and in that sense, as you're touching on, providing insights into all kinds of other in-between identities, mixed identities.

L: Um hum. It was allowing myself, trusting myself enough to look in one area of confusion that allowed me to trust myself to look at another. It's a process. And it doesn't mean that it's not really painful sometimes, too. I incorporate both the oppressor and the oppressed within myself.

NOTES

1 Although often quoted this way, Ti-Grace Atkinson's line was actually "feminism is a theory, lesbianism is a practice" — a subtle but crucial difference. — N.C.

2 A public meeting [held in Toronto] in 1979 for lesbian and heterosexual feminists to discuss working together in the movement.

karen/miranda augustine

what some call community...others call clicks
(in memory of Audre Lorde, Marlon Riggs & Melvin Dixon)

...THE INTRO

THE PROCESS OF COMING OUT BI, HAS, IN THE WORDS of a friend, "been the most self-loving thing I could ever do for myself." Having defined myself as lesbian for five years and being an active participant within the gay community for seven, the fear of ostracism became a constant preoccupation as I lived my life more openly. In a community where the right to love who you want is at the heart of the struggle, unfounded distrust/disgust from my lesbian sistuhs were either verbalized or acted out. In other words...girlfriend now feels she has license to be *extra...extra* rude, disrespectful and dismissive.

That bi's carry privilege is a loaded myth — homophobia is homophobia — the oppression is different. Gay women are hesitant to become involved with bi-the-way-girls because WE SPREAD AIDS or will leave them for a man (which apparently is worse than leaving them for another woman, their ex, or best friend). WE ARE CLOSETED or WE ARE BEING FASHIONABLE. Men, on the other hand, can truly be a trip. Many are sexually intrigued by you, hoping WE'LL FUCK A DYKE FOR THEM. I call it the CAN I WATCH? SYNDROME. Intimate contact with straight men, 90% of the time, means educating them on issues of sexism and homophobia.

For the dark lesbians who challenge the essentialism inherent within the mainstream of queer politics: that which suffocates Black queers, narrowly defines how we should look, how we should fuck and who. For you this is. For the dark queer women who have the courage to walk the walk and talk the talk. For you this is.

Especially for...Manisha Singh, Nicole Redman & Roberta Munroe

...The Scenario

I'm eighteen & think I'm bisexual — I go to the Lesbian and Gay Youth of Toronto support groups & am told by one of the members that BI'S ARE "ALL CONFUSED, FENCE-SITTERS...closer to straight." A year later I officially come out as a dyke & am told by another member that I DON'T "LOOK GAY" because I wear makeup...do my hair Motown...wear fishnets — I get labelled a "fruit fly" (read: fag hag).

> *...FORGET crushes on high school girl friends...gut-lust for well-endowed strippers, billboarded outside the local Zanzibar...Cherie Penthouse Players: a not-so-secret porn stash, hoarded since age eleven...At a time when femmes are far & few between...* TO MAINTAIN SUPPORT-FRIENDSHIPS-COMMUNITY, TO FIT IN, TO GET A DATE, TO BE A GOOD FEMINIST, TO BE THE GOOD LESBIAN
> ...I became someone else:

Baby/...honestly...
i want to fuck you unsafely/ feel your skin

> hard flesh
> grow
> thick in my hand/

Can you go deep enough (love deep enough)/to risk
being a Brown brother
being a Black brother/

w/me

when one time hittin'.../when one time un-jimmy'ed/

when one time

bare cock

deep brown/swollen & erect-nasty

fuck'n-up me wide/open

may chance

positivity?

jack-on/jism spray

white/

clear

drip'n-it quickly across my belly & 2 titties...

you tug gently/ sucking slow

biting once

(baby boy)

Man fills me

back

assed

doggin' it/ slamming

beneath the weight of his deepest brown

sliding woody-Crown'd

up the crack of my ass/   his sweat — canopy

soaking purple stains of heat against my hip-bone

leaving a trail of irises... red

above my thigh   Speech lost in my chest

I heave moans

deep

so rough

he thinks I'm the Man

fuck • long and slow • never tiring • her body shook twice before she came in the cradle of my sweaty palm • came twice before i pulled on her fat nips • came twice/ & so pussy — funk damn stank up the air •

she has...
legs so long she could wrap them around my neck... twice... and break it
• but
glides them instead, coyly over my shoulders • hisses obscenities while kumming
loudly • w/ 2 fingers jammed up in moist
/contracting fuck muscles • she whispers
"Sweet kunt,"
& i want to spread those legs wider...

can i play pussy •
cat games • tug on the lips let kitten give me soft, wet licks while I stroke it?

baby's hot, brown & more woman than Pam Grier
Ebony Ayes
Mary J.

doll,
let me have
you...spread-eagle...breasts heavy...
restrained w/ silver nipple clamps
restrained w/ a firm hand on your neck
uninhibited
...your back arched...your ass upward

Age 20 ~ I've finally found Black queers ~ A reception is held for South African gay activist Simon Nkoli ~ I go with members of the group...I am one of two Canadian-born Blacks ~ At my expense, a joke is made to Simon about how good my English is...Weeks later, at a new dyke bar, we jam to a reggae tune ~ The B-52's are mixed in the set ~ I exclaim! I used to love them when I was fifteen ~ A member sucks her teeth, turns to the others and says This is Karen's music:

givin' up
trying to impress
trying to enchant
trying to passively
aggress/ control/ coerce

a bad connection.
just because she's dark like me fucks like me/
just because Rodney asked Why can't we just...?

when the progressives/ dark girl-women/ rule
tell me...
...who's the oppressor now?

just because words vary in meaning/ say too much too little not quite what i
mean but did at one time/

really
that's just how i am

am

not

fence-sitting/ turned straight/ unable to caress that sound of socalypso-
reggae-hip hop-funkadelic/ not deaf to grrrl beats-hardcore-rock/ wearing
dreads-a fade-wigs-& nails...

feeling unashamed
about getting off
on Players / Pam Grier/

COCKsucking...

no longer subscribing

to herd mentality/
unable to be policed by the race-dyke-feminist elite

i am free.

inspired by those who lived honestly in difference
inspired by those who lived strongly in difference

chanting Audre, & Lorde knows: ...*I am constantly being encouraged to pluck out
some one aspect of myself and present this as the meaningful whole...* [1]

41

just because she's dark like me/ you think
"fucked up" like me   & why?/
when the struggle(s) means the freedom to
sex who be who we want?

NOTE
1 From *Sister Outsider* by Audre Lorde (The Crossing Press, 1984).

GLOSSARY
extra: as in being more than needed, bad attitude, calling attention to yourself
clicks: cliques
hittin': fucking
jimmy: condom
woody: hard-on
Crown: brand of condom
Pam Grier: Blaxploitation actress (films include *Foxy Brown, Sheba Baby...*)
Ebony Ayes: African American porn star
Mary J.: as in Blige
Rodney: as in King
Players: Black porn magazine

Shlomit Segal

The Rules of the Game

when I was nineteen
the rules of the game were explained to me:
you're one of us or you're one of them.

now I look around
I see us   them   us   them   us   them
some definitions have changed
others stay stubbornly the same.

we they us come together
in a somewhat different combination
as we discover we are also they
and they may not be who they seem to be.

Janice Williamson

Strained Mixed Fruit (after Gerber™):
an autobifictograph

> *I am not good at traditional narrative.*
> *Reality brings out the worst in me.*
> *I have tried and failed to lead a conventional life.*
> *When I try to be like other people, I fall out of bed.*

> — *Marian Engel*

MIX (15c) :

to bring into close association

What a phantasmagoria the mind is and meeting-place of dissemblables.

— *Virginia Woolf*

Strung out on *Orlando*, SHE rounds Gibraltar with the grace of a trapped whale. Almost everyone is sea sick but her. The third-and fourth-class dining room holds 175 one night. The next morning, seven show up to a breakfast of fresh figs. SHE is the only woman reading *Orlando*. SHE would have been kidnapped in Casablanca were it not for *Orlando*. Running like a maniac, SHE outsmarts her abductor, leaps from his speeding car and returns to the Pacquet ocean liner to finish her book. Just in time — SHE couldn't stand missing the final chapters...

> *In short, they acted the parts of man and woman for ten minutes with great vigour and then fell into natural discourse...Had they both worn the same clothes, it is possible that their outlook might have been the same too...Different though the sexes are, they intermix. In every human being a vacillation from one sex to the other takes place, and often it is only the clothes that keep the male or female likeness, while underneath the sex is the very opposite of what it is above. Of the complications and confusions which thus result every one has had experience; but here we leave the general question and note only the odd effect it had in the particular case of Orlando herself....*
>
> *Orlando kissed the spaniel with her lips. In short, there was the truest sympathy between them that can be between a dog and its mistress, and yet, it cannot be denied that the dumbness of animals is a great impediment to the refinements of discourse.*

FRUIT n. (12c)

fructuss pp.
of fruit to
enjoy, have the use of
-more at
BROOK

to enjoy

to stand for

<she would brook no
interference
with her plans>

Will the REAL bisexual please stand up!

[dozens of women rush to the front of the room]

MEMEMEMEMEMEMEMEMEMEMEMEMEMEMEMEMEMEMEMEME
MEMEMEMEMEMEMEMEMEMEMEMEMEMEMEMEMEMEMEMEME
MEMEME*

*TRANSLATION:
BISEXUAL HET;
HETEROSEXUAL BI;
LESBIAN BISEXUAL;
BISEXUAL LESBIAN;
BI -BI
IDENTITY
ETC.

STRAIN n :

lineage :
Broadly
a specified
infraspecific group
(as a stock,
line or
ecotype)

A bisexual woman, thirty-six, visits her heterosexual mother for lunch. Ham and lettuce sandwiches, a thirty-year tradition with an innovative salad for vitamins.

The two women love each other, giggle through familial gossip. The daughter is the much cherished *crazy* one whose escapades escape the *sanity* of her mother's measured life.

Conversation slows to halting.

So...what's been happening?, the mother begins, accustomed to being the interested party.
Not much. And you?, replies the daughter, concerned she is not a good listener.
I went out to the cottage with Gillian for the weekend.
Oh...(the bisexual daughter drifts, anticipating a familiar story about her mother's best friend)...Did you have a nice time?
No. Not really. Saturday we had dinner and Gillian drank far too much. I would have gone home by myself but we had come in her car. I couldn't bring myself to abandon her in the middle of nowhere. But she made me so angry...I went right to bed right after dinner, and then...
[Here, her mother pauses.]
Daydream interrupted by this silence, the bisexual daughter listens closely, echoes her last words...And then?
...then Gillian made love to me.

[SILENCE]

At this moment, the bisexual daughter, who for twenty years has kept her erotic life a secret, chokes on her lettuce. Mumbles. Searches for the right response — something supportive but neutral. Finally she settles on the following reply — inadequate, revealing too much of her own rigidities, but spontaneous.

(Let's back up to hear the sequence of call and response.)

...and then Gillian made love to me...

STRAIN :

inherited or inherent
character, quality,
or disposition

<a strain of madness in the family>

[Silence. The daughter's slow inhalation of breath.] Well...did you give
your consent?
I didn't say no...
How was it?
...terrible...terrible...She was drunk you know. Reminded me of your
father — DRUNK.
Perhaps if you tried it again, you might like it.
No. I won't.

Coward. Coward, the bisexual daughter feels she has let her mother down.
Won't speak up when the going is tough. Astonished at her own weakness.
The bisexual daughter has to admit her mother has caught her off guard.
Another missed opportunity.

Several weeks later, the bisexual daughter visits her mother again for lunch.
Screws up the courage to tell.

Mom. Since I was seventeen, I've been meaning to tell you...I'm...
bisexual.
Oh. That's too bad, Mother replies, you'll have an unhappy life.
The daughter says nothing.
I always thought your grandmother was a lesbian, says her mother.
When she made my clothes, she stood me on a chair to fit them to me.
Then she stuck pins in me. Touched my nipples. Made me cry.

Q: What is there to say?
Q: Grandma, an incestuous lesbian?
Q: Mother's child body, a fetish?
(No blame.)

STRAIN :

trace
streak

<a strain of fanaticism>

(the purée thickens)

The scientifically-minded
might like to see the GERBER™ connection.
The mother-daughter genealogical line
vacillates between several of the ingredients
listed on the label for the 128 ml of *STRAINED MIXED FRUIT*:

CITRIC ACID
&
SUGAR

STRAIN :

a stream or outburst
of forceful or
impassioned speech

MAY 1983:   It is difficult to write about fruited bodies after my bisexual practice changes so abruptly. Two of my former lovers inform me they are HIV positive. Fearful for their lives, I become fearful for mine. I visit the AIDS doctor who asks how I feel. With emphasis, I inform him that since I plan to give up sex for the rest of my life, I am *fine*. The AIDS doctor tells me my risk is somewhere between *a gay man cruising the baths and a monogamous heterosexual couple in Scarborough*...Is this an accurate description of the bisexual between?

Over the next ten years, my self-concern diminishes as I continually test HIV negative. But my anxiety about my friends turns to the pain of watching one of them ravaged by the disintegrating effects of AIDS.

JUNE 1992:   On my last visit, Alex is in decline. His wild and sensual gardens shift into full bloom. We sit side by side facing the sun, talk a little. I stroke Alex's back as he moves through words, no longer afloat in language. His mouth bobs above the surface to connect with my question, then retires just below the watery edge of conversation. As I turn to look at him, I catch sight of his roof garden. Above his head, a slant of sky-bound succulents and cacti colour the back shed in blue-greens and shining emerald. I gasp in pleasure as he explains with delight how he was inspired by a picture of just such a German garden.

Here in Toronto, we hold hands. Alex says he is *confused but alright*.
I cry unashamedly.

STRAIN n :

deformation of
a material body
under the pitch
of applied forces

<strained relations>

I like to think of my sexuality as a utopian space, uncontaminated by another's regard. But hatred interrupts this programme.

1982: At Yonge and Wellesley Streets, a peaceful demonstration protests another raid of homosexual baths by the police. No one asks to see my erotic identification as I march down the street to the tune of a disco-beat and the bitter denunciations of young neo-Nazi thugs. After our speeches and chants in front of the police station, these same boys beat us over the head with a white picket fence. Police take their own sweet time to arrive with:

Helmets.

Plexiglas shields.

Billy clubs.

(and *screams...*

...as the young homophobic thugs escape,
the police pause to beat us again...)

STRAIN vb :

L *stringere*
to bind or draw
tight, press together;
to injure by
overuse, misuse, or
excessive pressure

<*strained her heart*>

The privilege of
heterohex
looped glitter
a golden handshake
the diamond ring

(*You're doubly dangerous, she says. If you steal my male lover, you may steal his mistress too.*)

Seven women sit around the table talking about sex.
 It has been a while, says one woman. I miss talking like this.
 Openly. Without a censoring mechanism entering the
 conversation or my psyche.
She says, *My body changes shape in my nuptial bed. I become*
 stranger to my husband. He to me. We find ourselves moving
 toward each other anticipating nothing but what we do not
 yet know or understand.

MIX :

to be capable of mixing

Contradictions...are the moving force of history, writes Mariana.

One day in 1983, two women sit in a restaurant and talk about sex. My anxiety about exploitation and misrecognition is rooted in the potential to exploit lesbian women or to pass as het. Enmeshed in these contradictions, I feel an urge to tie myself up with single-minded solutions, short-lived resolutions:

> *Give up women.*
> *Renounce men.*
> *Abandon desire.*

Reread Foucault, advises Mariana. *Why insist on a stable identity when the flow of your sexuality offers surprising pleasures and desires.*

MIX vi :

to enter into relations

SHE follows this directive most seriously.

At the conference in Chicago, SHE meets S who only took up with strangers from faraway locations. The next morning, SHE reflects on how certain parts of her belly turn scarlet in the shape of the Maritimes. At breakfast, SHE orders tomatoes, while fishing out of her pocket, the ring S left beside her bed. The others stare, curious and surprised.

Quel surprise! There were other surprises. To their mutual discomfort as they embrace to say good-bye, they discover they live in the same city, a dozen blocks apart.

So they theorize on their backs. Strapped into contorted marvels with thongs and clanking O's, quoting *"pessimism of the intellect, optimism of the will."* SHE is always masked, swearing that closed eyes imagine the exotic more exotically. In the midst of the ongoingness of a most intense moment, collapsed in *ecstase*, they pause to marvel at the other's impressive pecs. (S pumps iron, while SHE articulates in headstands.)

Everything was hot and flushed until something failed. For a while, they continue to meet, somewhat wary and uncertain. One or the other complains of a sick headache or pressing engagement. Dutiful meetings dwindle.

THE PROBLEM IS IN THE CONVERSATION.

syn MIX :

coalesce

an affinity
in
merging
elements
usually
a
resulting
organic
unity

I live alone through most of my twenties and thirties. At forty-two, I find myself in a loving heterosexual domestic relationship. This is not an epiphany. I do not *find myself*, resolve lifelong dilemmas about desire, or divine perpetual spiritual release in this event. I try unsuccessfully to take vitamins. In spite of this, I find comfort and care and love, and sometimes...pain.

My amorous path to this point has taken me through moves to a predominantly right-wing province, through graduate school to a new adult life as professor, through first books, through anti-feminist harassment, denunciation and death threats. And into and through memories of child sexual abuse.

All of these experiences influence my choices. My lover is kind and caring, insightful and sexy, tender and awake to life, but my history is as relevant to my choice of partners as any intrinsic qualities in him, or any abstract desire of mine.

Is it this simple? To be a lesbian in this hostile workplace and social environment would have been difficult for me. The heterosexual community by and large is homophobic, and some women in the lesbian community perceive bisexuals as duplicitous traitors to their vanguard cause. *It is not this simple.*

J.W.: I can't say I have any regrets in that I don't feel there is necessarily
a lesbian one-and-only lingering in the wings....
But I know that the playing field is not equal.
One can make a choice and sometimes take the path of least resistance.

syn MIX :

amalgamate

a close union
without
complete
loss of
individual
identities

Q: What's in a name?
Is bisexuality the Janus-face of female sexuality?
Is the hybridity of our identity an infective dis-ease?
What is the Janice face of bisexuality?

Why not speak *of the margins from this position of relative centrality.* The troubling bilingual concern over authenticity and deception, loyalty and duplicity, faithfulness and betrayal lurk about the corridors of the academic feminist *and* the bisexual. Outside the academy, questions rise about whether the academic feminist is more academic than feminist? Inside, is she more feminist than academic? Outside the academy, she is a vulgar careerist. Inside, a dilettante and dabbler. Outside the academy, she is a double agent, her hat tipped toward the patriarchs. Inside, is she a double agent, her hat slouching toward revolution?

Q: Is the bisexual theorist or activist?
Authentic or deceptive?
Opportunist or dabbler?
Reprobate or revolutionary?

MIX vi :

to become mixed

My thinking about my libido shifts over the years. In my twenties and thirties, I explore my desire especially when it has little to do with "relationship"; any automatic connection between sex, love, romance seems corrupt and limiting. In my late thirties, sexual patterns change as I become more interested in *relationship* — though, unlike the rumours in the discourse of *relationship*, my libido doesn't die.

As I begin to work on child sexual abuse narratives and my own suspected incest experiences, I feel some pressure to renounce my sexual past. The story goes...*sex in the excess* (defined by various criteria) *is a compensation for childhood trauma. The child knows how to act sexual, translates all her need for love and affection into a sexualized vocabulary, and acts out a sexual melodrama at many moments throughout her adult life.*

Q: Doesn't this story of compensation amount to a repudiation of the woman's own desiring body? and of desire itself?

Q: Is this story making no more than a sexual theory of false consciousness where I am dupe to my traumatized history?

MIX :

mingle, commingle, blend, merge

commingle
a closer
or more
thorough
mingling

possibly I dream over and over of losing shoes so she will come
slide tongue along the long route back know it is a matter of time
before fingers clicking lips the teeth *am i hurting?* drive up my sting
the sounds hollow at neck urgent furred animals rifling female eyes
the crushed peach/lips/cheeks/teeth bared as in pain she is wet she
is smelling wet shaking wet brow rain on her hair couched
between my legs lose sight throat thin walls taste this aversion this
body we bathe to forget white light instructs the room rearranges
the furniture returns me to father framed in the doorway know that
I am twelve know that he has taken his shorts his cock cradled in
hand now offers this look the cool August evenings at sea full
blown steamed edges gape dehiscent strain forms like sublimating
slake out burst taut skin the lick the sing the lap of equilibrium

syn MIX :

mix may

or

may not

imply loss

of each

element's identity

At sixteen, SHE is an insomniac, inconsolable about her short history and the future SHE imagines awaits. SHE dreams of running away from home. SHE runs away from home. Just far enough to know SHE is missing.

Her high school English teacher takes her to his Rosedale apartment even though he has just married her high school French teacher, a *petite mademoiselle*. Post-honeymoon domestic life does not celebrate this consoling pedagogic threesome. All night long, SHE stays up talking talking with her English teacher. She is beside herself with despair. He introduces her to existentialism, a philosophy SHE uses to define the terms of her *anomie*.

Time passes. Days or weeks? SHE loves the English teacher for knowing and listening to how close SHE sits on the razor's edge. Her reading shifts from Camus to Simone de Beauvoir who speaks of jealousy, rage and the passion of women lovers. After *L'invitée*, SHE imagines gas jets in her electrically heated bedroom. Sometimes the jets turn on.

One afternoon as they walk in the park discussing how "theatre of the absurd" is not, the English teacher tries to kiss her. SHE begins to understand why her French teacher glares over the macaroni and shrimp salad *provençal* she serves for dinner.

SHE wants to run away again.

Instead, she calls her father who picks her up in his white car, top down. On the way back to the country, they talk, but don't. In the house, he slaps her hard enough. SHE knows he is angry and means business. SHE learns to understand a good family story does not include this one.

FRUIT :

a succulent part
used
chiefly
in a dessert or
sweet course

1973: At twenty-two, I leave my boyfriend in England. Again. Tears and some regret. On the train from Le Havre to Paris, I change into my vintage black lace dress ($2.00 in London's Soho market). Reemerging from the washroom, my rhinestone-studded hair combs and belt (15 cents, Soho market) sparkle. These black suede boots (gift from a Texan admirer) sound ready to dance. Several manicured women along the aisle look down well-powdered Parisian noses at my metamorphosis.

In France, I meet "Simone de Beauvoir," pet name for my desire, unspoken, but not unexplored. Simone takes me unambiguously in her arms before I meet her friends. One, boy, now girl, now bird, a transexual street mime, costumed in peacock plumage, whistles gender anarchy. This philosophical clown thumbs bi-Eros at the *petit bourgeois* passersby.

Life is less of a strain here because I have come from away. The doctor's wife, the woman in the shop with gilded cages, the pianist at the jazz bar. The architect's sister. The street vendor's mother. (The French way is not to tell...)

Glazed in flans or perfectly whole
orange petals swallowed one by one.
This fruited utopia remains,
not yet a figment of memory's imagination.

MIX :

mingle, commingle, blend, merge

mingle usu.
elements are somewhat
distinguishable
or
separately
active

Soon SHE will go to university to study English, especially poetry, and more theatre of the absurd and French *nouveau vague* cinema with dramatic enactments of tormented but pleasant *ménages à trois.* SHE studies Michael Snow's *Wavelength* in delightfully tortured detail. The romance of the pink room, the space SHE has encountered before. And another film which fascinates: <————————> (the camera pans back and forth, back and forth, hypnotizing her with the apparent randomness of events). SHE appreciates the world only when it refuses to make sense. SHE enters the dreamy phantasms of Maya Deren whose veiled female body dances phenomenal presence *and* absence. Watching, her very own lace-covered body fluctuates off/on. An apparition?

At the community hall, SHE attends a lecture by a feminist, a metal sculptor from Toronto. It is the first time SHE has heard much about this *Women's Liberation Movement.* SHE stays up all night writing a long letter to this newfound "feminist." The feminist writes back. This epistolary conversation makes sense of the senseless.

SHE goes on an abortion march to Parliament Hill and thinks about how SHE wants to get pregnant later in life.

SHE will not.

FRUIT b (1) :

the usual
edible
reproductive body

1970: In the middle of the night, I cannot sleep. At the pastry counter of The Party Palace, a local deli, I reach up to grab a sticky bun. At this precise moment, a tall elegant young woman reaches for a sticky bun. Our hands meet, grasp.... Laughter on both sides of the counter, and talk talk — sometimes over coffee and sticky buns. Later over *espresso* and *croissants*. We will travel the world together in a room. We will dress up in Paris and fill ourselves with dust and music in Djenne or Tombouctou. We fall off cliffs and wander through Dogon deserts. Teasing, we play the skin of canoe. Roller skate through circuses of pleasure.

Years later I ask about her lesbian lovers.
Oh you were the only one, she answers without hesitation.
I gasp, incredulous, *You mean, I was the seducer?*
Well you weren't the only one.

FRUIT *b* (1) :

especially : one
having a sweet
pulp

Elemental lungs breathe through eros
the florid dart,
the *movement toward*
alien stars tuned up
for this embrace.

[locate the *aim* not the *object*]

This room,
emptied of furniture before we begin.
This wrist drawing
desire's taut string

[release the whir]

Folds of sari or obi,
or fuchsia *blouse* (on first glance)
draped over the arm of this chair,
or fussy *shirt* (on second thought —
with this obscure pearl button
between my fingers

Before the bath grows cold,
my lover tells water stories without endings.

[watch her wave hands in the air like fish]

FRUIT :

the flavor or
aroma of fresh
fruit
in mature
wine

<*the fruits of our labour*>

Dear Alex,

I'm writing on bisexuality
and thinking about you and
how you lived.
Gay, and sometimes...
What's in a name?
And me?
Straight, then gay,
then bi, then gay,
then bi,...

How the times we made love,
certain of our sexuality?
Identity had nothing to do with it.
More like *fluxus*...
or *interwoven*...
or the crisis of this
alternating current
running between us
even as I write
months after your death.

PLURAL DESIRES

i cannot so casually attend to your voice in my ear
or touch mutual seductions
long fingers ripple the napes of our neck
the breasts you grew while we drifted apart have disappeared
and now your throat is soundless
northern birds dip wings in flight
while you find your own way home

FRUIT :

a dish,

quantity,

or diet of fruits

<please pass the fruits>

Her libido looks like a map of Canada.

In Toronto (PINK), bisexuality blossoms in gardens of irises, spartans and miniature roses. Plots are complicated enough that it appears everyone attends to the late-night conversations of multiple displacements, generous gifts.

In Edmonotone (BLUE), heterosexuality triumphs and lesbians clash. Locals attribute this to "alienation effect," claiming the North Saskatchewan drains along a rich river bed *in the feminine* when the break up of winter thunders along its shores. Some say tensions erupt in the shallows, ripple through territories of competition, hierarchies of scarcity and contempt.

Is it no more than clichéd rumour that on the wavy West Coast (VIOLET) lesbians from kayak to ballroom? Here desire shifts ground from fig trees to longing...

...For the woman who writes on gothic and plumbs her island cabin.
For the woman who finds her way through philosophical undergrounds
with the surety of a spelunker.
For the woman who writes about airports and breakfasts all night beside her camera.
For the woman who winds up her life and listens to it ticking.
For the woman who writes poems with kiwi lips this wide.
For the woman who camps out along Commercial.
For the woman whose tattooed shoulder bears the marks of a bear.
For the woman who peers into a sister's heart through the tart clatter of
Commercial cappuccino.
For the woman who plies this long night, heeled without apology or explanation.
For the woman who flies blind with the grace of a bolero's clicking heels.

For the woman who...

fruited (i):

dear m

I'm writing to you on Sunday after driving across mountains, made more glorious as I remember. Folding rock and green-glass rivers, landscape melt of peak and mist. Stuff of romance. I don't often write love letters. Regretful now I couldn't move myself to come close more quickly, but perhaps it is just as well since now I don't know what will happen. What you are wanting now? I write to you without knowledge of how you will read my words. How receptive will you be now that I'm so far away?

Here in the prairie parkland (larch, pine, magpie and ralph), thinking about you makes me lighten. Your incendiary devices (lips, fingers, inner walls and waves) make me a burnt-out star. Ignited. Fallen consumed and empty, failed and filled with regret — a black hole of longing for you. This charcoal waste of loss, this body I find myself inside, this aching cherry bloom of wanting you. Arched open and waiting, I imagine you sparkling, full of love and splendid anticipation of excessive limits, the tart and round watery spaces of frictive sense. I hear you in my inner ear, yearning toward the pacific skin of us: taut lessons against caution, restraint or suspicion.

Lunar phases know less about magnetic desire than I.

On our last night, unpursued by anyone but you, I pursue you, smoking with shared wicked delight. In the park, we dream of animals in the forest, glimpse masks, golden night eyes. A glint of how you look out at me, blind eye keening. Trees in this new city skitter with paws and furry wet. We hesitate until this movement toward each other; fingers, flesh, the bliss in us. The way my body shifts ground, finds your fragrance caught up in sand-covered shores, thighs at low low tide hug my hand into you, gush delight.

...*your lap gushes! Laps, lips, legs, slip into the frog-bound croak of throated love sounds in any underground garage. Concrete walls, unwelcome visitors, no match for your subterranean touch. Asymmetric crush of your breasts...all twelve of them...or twenty take shape in my palms. Soft slope of mouth nippled tight. Hard knot of breast tip between teeth, teases delight out of me into your mouth, tongue of you here on mine writes these words, close to breath. Left breast breathes full in my hands, right, languid pushing, pushing. My tongue latches onto you this prairie evening, cloudless, arcing clear blue across the taiga. Underground springs surface as waterfalls, come to light, bear fruit, root in the sodden moss of bodies (ours), caresses (ours) words (ours) love...*

fruited (ii):

for j

Kisses in and out of illicit crinolines: yours in longing; mine in jest.

Forbidden zones: your body pressed to my belly. Tenderness, scrotum hung up beneath us. The prick of you draws blood. Snow of white-out cries wrung out. Flurries of us write this home — sometimes rooms on ice and aching limbs. Or carpets of nails — sting of spikes pried out of our soles like prizes.

Your figure 8 skates across my back, skirts a syllable or two. This feels like...*is*...words, never wounds, running. A blade hollows out ribs, spine, the whole book of me opens into...red below us, blots our coming. Our bodies, displace volumes, kick out the history of romance.

A lull in your voice says temporary despair or long familiarity or mechanical fatigue. Stalled midway up a hill. Or renewed again. How can I forget this lilt in arms picked up with your laughter?

Just this. Our tongues: your hardness and mine. Up against you. Pushing. Pushing until tender collapse of lung in

abbbbbbbbbbb   all the way here.

Home, even in these intervals of blue. Up and down with the lack of it, or whatever loss we can muster this day. I cloud up with pain, no more than a purr in your ear. Or you gloom beside me. Tomorrow will your lips lick mine out of rain?

(In February, strawberries turn up between our ribs. Our domestic bed nippled with fret or fruit.)

The pink of us cares for this place and only.

fruited

FRUIT :

fruited?

(s/he wants to ask a complicated question)

was it the calla lilies or the candy
soother shaped like a ruby
ring to suck on raspberry or the thin line we
cross our hearts sweat rubber

Indigo Chih-Lien Som

Cinderella

when I was
a little girl
my favourite
record was
Cinderella.

I learned how
to play it
over & over
on grandma's turntable
while I danced
around her lvg room
& wore out my voice
singing along
w/ the words
every day
all day
never got tired
of it

Now
the scratched record
long gone/ I play
Cinderella
over & over again
in my sleep
in my bed

young handsome
Chicano Princes
read me revolutionary poems

Jewish hippie
East Coast princes
w/ breadbaking hands

even some
not-so-young
Chinatown Princes
talkin that sweet
familiar hometalk

hapa knights in
tarnished chrome
armour/ ride up
to my door on their
Harleys

to rescue me
from my
sleeping-beauty
ivory tower

from the safety
of my father's
American Dream

from the sound
of myself/ alone
talking to my
private thoughts
& knowing myself

Men sweep
me away/ let me
forget myself
so I can play
Cinderella
in my head
over & over

If i cd only go
back in time
to feel the edges
of that record
cutting my palms
once again
I wd smash it
to black vinyl ash
on my grandmother's
lvg room floor.

Zélie Pollon

Naming Her Destiny:
June Jordan Speaks on Bisexuality

June Jordan is one of the very few writers today who has dealt with bisexuality as a political issue. In "The New Politics of Sexuality," an essay in her most recent book, *Technical Difficulties* (Pantheon, 1992), Jordan speaks eloquently about bisexuality as an analogy to a "multicultural, multiethnic, multiracial world view."

June Jordan was born in Harlem and raised in Brooklyn, New York. She is the author of sixteen books of poetry and essays, including *Naming Our Destiny* and *Civil Wars: Selected Essays 1963-1980*, and teaches African-American studies at University of California at Berkeley.

ZP: How long have you identified as a bisexual woman and what does that mean to you?

JJ: For a very long time I have been trying to come up with ways of being in the world which do not depend upon choosing something out, but rather adding something on. In my own romantic life, I find myself attracted to men as well as women. I don't understand why becoming involved with a woman would mean that I no longer found men, or a particular man, attractive or romantically exciting. It seems the assumption is that once you become involved with women, it becomes an irrevocable statement of allegiance and commitment. I'm not sure that what I call an honest human body and an open heart can make an irrevocable commitment, to anybody — let alone a commitment along generic lines. That's like going through the world with half of it shut down to you, isn't it?

[At] UC-Berkeley, the students called a boycott of classes [to protest the lack of diversity in faculty]. Some of the key players in the leadership were bisexual. They explained to me that the first word [in their group title] was "bisexual," not "gay, lesbian and bisexual," but "bisexual, lesbian and gay." They felt it was very important that they achieve this kind of visibility in the context of a broad political event of their own creation; that it be clear that to be bisexual is not an afterthought.

I felt the bisexual contingent was very courageous in trying to affirm themselves in the context of freedom. They were in a situation where they would be attacked both by straight people and by people who identify exclusively as gay or lesbian. There was something wonderfully tentative about it and fierce at the same time. My feeling was that I was in touch with something that was really new in the world.

Many students at UC-Berkeley come from mixed parents, different cultures. I insist that they try to honour all the components of their identity and not make an either/or kind of choice: my father, my mother, white or black. That's not healthy and it's not honest. It's very difficult to try to embrace the complexity of origins as well as the origins of sexual response that any one of us may embody. But "easy" isn't usually worth a whole lot, and it's not too often connected to anything deeply real.

Melissa Benn, a feminist theorist in London, wrote about her bisexuality in *Sparerib*, which used to be the leading feminist publication in London. The response to her discussion — it was not a confession, she was not defensive — a *discussion* of her bisexuality was, 'This is bullshit! What this means is that when Melissa Benn wants safety and approval, she throws on a dress and calls up Bill or Johnny, and the rest of us do not have that option." In other words, she was playing where women were concerned and whenever anything would get tricky or dangerous, she would stop playing and take refuge in heterosexual relationships.

That was the nicest kind of negative response, what you would call "closely reasoned." There was *rage* because she was fairly well known in the women's community. There was a sense of betrayal, copping out. The overwhelming response was to read her out of the lesbian community; to identify her as an enemy, a Judas and a clown in the context of people whose lives are beleaguered in the battle with homophobic reality. I understood the anguish and the anger to some extent, but I think it was then that I came to a moral conclusion that this was wrong. To tell someone what to feel, that's the last tyranny. It's bad enough to tell people what to do, but to tell people what to *feel*, that's outrageous!

ZP: Can you explain your understanding of the sense of betrayal?

JJ: I think I understand it. I think the analogy [is a person of colour] who could pass for white whenever it was convenient or expedient; or somebody who would hang out with black people or have a black lover when that was convenient or expedient and when it was not, opt out of it. Meanwhile, for those of us who are black, we are *always* black and to have someone playing with something that is immutable in [our] lives [is wrong]. These women felt that [sexuality] to lesbians is immutable, and for that immutable characteristic, they have been persecuted or worse.

I was recently at a women's festival and there were a lot of older women there who had been [out] lesbians for a *long* time; they had paid a lot of dues. I wanted to read my essay on bisexuality, but I was scared and I didn't want to be disrespectful. I managed to say, "You know, people really *do* change. It's not like there are little people growing up to be just like you. That's not what's happening. We have *new* people growing up to be *new* people. The fact is that people who call themselves bisexual are out here fighting with you and for you. They are fighting for sexual freedom. The same people who would burn somebody because she's lesbian would burn somebody who's bisexual. Any time a woman is with another woman, you are undertaking huge risks just coming out the door."

I feel hopeful that people who have been in the struggle for sexual freedom for a long time will be willing to think about it in new ways. I have been in the struggle for African-American freedom all my life and, progressively, I realize that what I'm talking about is the right of *all people* to exist and to have equal civil rights and equal opportunities. It's not specific [to] African-Americans. The principle is bigger and deeper than that. The principle is the right of every single person out there to be whoever they are and to determine how they will spend their days on the earth.

What I'm trying to do vis-à-vis the avowed lesbian and gay community is to suggest that there is a principle by which the community abides, and the principle is that of sexual freedom. And if you acknowledge that, you will not participate in the persecution of anybody because he or she says, "I'm defining myself as bisexual." The inclination to regulate anybody's *anything* is wrong and carries with it, I think, the possibility of death.

ZP: Do you consider yourself a spokesperson for bisexuals?

JJ: To the extent that anybody asks me to speak for them, I'm a spokesperson. I don't think there's a lot written on the subject. I'm proud to be someone who has tried to write about bisexuality and has claimed that identity as her own, but I don't know that I think of myself as a spokesperson. I am aware that I have a kind of leadership function in the context of being a writer.

The realm of sexuality, including gender politics, is more difficult to disturb than any other, or to create anything new in. I think it's more difficult to disturb than the realm of [race politics].

ZP: Why do you think that?

JJ: I just wrote in an essay: "I have no problem talking about the police beating Rodney King, but apparently, I have a problem talking about whether or not Rodney King beat his wife." Our conditioning about gender [and] sexuality is deeper and more ferociously instilled and preserved by force than our conditioning on matters of race. [With the question,] "Does Rodney King beat his wife or not?" I lose momentum, I start second-guessing myself. Whereas with the issue of race, I don't. One obvious reason is that I feel completely supported. It's like being against apartheid — you'd have to be a psychopathic jackass to be pro-apartheid! There's no risk in that position — it's correct, and it *is* correct.

I don't think that freedom and equality for women, freedom and equality for different sexualities, enjoy anything even remotely similar. It just doesn't have the kind of righteous resonance to it that anti-racist *anything* has. I would like to see and to help build that kind of righteousness with issues having to do with what it means to be a woman in the world, and what it means to try to seek sexual freedom in the world.

ZP: Do you think there is a certain myth about a given community, an illusion of seamless unity that is promoted in order to appear stronger as a group?

JJ: I think that evidence of maturity as a people, however you want to define yourself, is that you're willing to criticize yourselves. Just because you have this sexuality or this skin doesn't confer some kind of innate virtue. There is a tendency to think that the way to achieve effective solidarity is to ignore self-destructive behaviour inside your own community. The whole point about being a beleaguered group is that you *do* have an enemy; why you want to become one, also, I don't understand.

Some people think that lesbians are disgusting and should be burned to death, beaten, harassed on the street; then you get involved with a woman and treat her as something despicable and contemptible — what is this all about? You should just go join the skinheads and be up front about it.

Take your self-hatred and join the neo-Nazis, if they will have you, and they
won't — they will *not* have you. If I really love myself as a black person then I
have to treat all other black people, to the extent that I am humanly able,
with respect and love. Ditto for women or for anybody I'm involved with;
otherwise I'm my own enemy and I'm not acting in any way different from
the people who, on a programmatic basis, really hate the fact that I exist!

ZP: You spoke in Pratibha Parmar's film *A Place of Rage* about the
disintegration of the Civil Rights movement. Do you see a way to have a
movement that does not splinter?

JJ: We don't generally tend to find out about other people's
histories, so we don't often benefit as we could from what other people did,
if it worked or didn't. Making yourself knowledgeable about other people's
political trajectories toward freedom would help a lot.

Also, it is necessary to seek a principle that underlies your sense of
justice. I'm not talking about tactics here but moral grounds for being alive
in the world. Too many of us avoid the moral formulation of an issue. If we
do not move to save life just because it's life — not great life, not bad life,
just life — then none of us is safe. None of us can assume [that someone]
who doesn't even know you, has never seen you or met you, doesn't know
your birthday, will care if you're being exterminated, burned, raped,
harassed or discriminated against.

I'm trying to promulgate a kind of moral framework for political
action in the world. I feel it's an uphill battle. The only people even willing
to talk about "right" and "wrong," or "evil," are on the right. People on the
left say, "I don't want to get into that kind of language." Why not? I think
there's a way to do it that doesn't make you into a baby fascist, or a big one.
I don't know what it is yet, but I'm working on it and I hope other people
will be interested to work on it as well. I think that's what's really missing
here on the side of progressive politics.

I support gay rights because the principle is that you have the same
right that I have: equality. That's a democratic principle that can be argued
in the courts and in the forums of newspapers, on TV, anywhere! And
people who are opposed to gay rights will have a hell of a time holding
their own! You put them on the defensive: you say, "Are we talking about a
democratic state, or not?" You don't do it just for tactical reasons, you do it
because you believe it. You're taking the time to say "what is this really

about?" in a way that can bring a lot of different people together and get you what you want, because it's right. But you have to be willing to say, "because it's right." It's so important to say that. "If this doesn't happen, it's wrong." You have to be willing to say that.

TRACY CHARETTE FEHR   Interwoven Faces © 1992
Ink on paper

HOW WE
ARE SEEN
& SEEING
OURSELVES

Indigo Chih-Lien Som

The Queer Kitchen

context is everything. here is mine: i was born in san francisco, a
cancer in the year of the horse. my spirituality is deeply rooted in
this place, the bay area, which is my home in every possible sense
of the word, from santa cruz in the south to point reyes and the
beginning of the wine country in the north. my parents are both
architects, originally from hong kong and canton. i grew up in
marin county (one scarlet bridge north of san francisco), which is
notorious for being rich — cocaine — rich, and just as white —
and attended an exclusive, oppressive private prep school there. i
left to go to college in rhode island, where i figured out that i was
not a white male, my upper middle-class background notwith-
standing. having made this discovery, i returned to the bay area
for art school and eventually graduated from uc berkeley in ethnic
studies. i am a writer, an artist ("in recovery from art school"),
radical and bisexual. i also happen to be vegetarian (although i
sometimes eat seafood if it's fed to me), a deadhead (in moderation)
and a hippie in general. i am happiest in mixed groups of queer
women of colour, especially if they are creatively oriented. i have
no disabilities that i know of (yet). i dream a lot, always in
colour. i am in my mid-twenties, living in the east bay for five
years now and plan to stay here for a very long time, probably
forever.

L ESBIANS LIKE TO ASK ME IF I AM A LESBIAN-IDENTIFIED bisexual, but I refuse to identify as anything other than what/who I really am, so I call myself a bisexual-identified woman of colour. (Not that different from being a woman-of-colour-identified woman of colour, right, sisters?) This assertion usually causes serious conceptual problems, until people can get beyond the rigid duality that hangs us up in our society: hetero/homo, male/female, good/evil, white/black. Being neither white nor black, & often invisible because of it, I learned early that this simplistic kind of categorizing system just does not work. Let's face it, folks, the world is a little more complex than that. Complex & wonderful. Of course it hasn't always been wonderful for me. For a long time I was in a sort of coming-out stagnation. Being bi was not something to be happy about; it was a problem. I only felt the oppression. I thought it would be so much easier if I were either straight or lesbian. If I were not attracted to men, if only I didn't have such great sex with them, then I could go running into the open cosy arms of the lesbian community and live happily ever after. I never really thought that if only I didn't find women so attractive, I wouldn't have a problem either; trying to be a straight female (womanist, actually) caused me no end of internal conflict, only some of which can be attributed to my coming-out process.

So there I was, twenty, twenty-one, then twenty-two years old and knowing the whole time that there were some incredibly fine women around who I would love to at least kiss or hug or maybe — just maybe — undress. (I was afraid to think about what I might do once I got past the clothes. Years of living in a homophobic world can cramp your style considerably.) However, as a supposedly straight womanist, I had been in enough contact with the lesbian community to know that I would get infinitely more shit from many lesbians for being bi than I was getting from my mostly straight, feminist radical circle of friends. Actually, I got a lot of support and encouragement from my straight friends, so for a long time I couldn't see why I should bother to try getting involved in the dyke community at all. I was very into being single and was content to have occasional flings or one-night stands with men. Just a couple of little things seemed out of place.

For one thing, and this should be obvious, I was isolated as a queer. No commonalities or validation or role models or any of that stuff that it takes to figure out what it really means to be queer. Supportive straight friends can't do all that for you. The other thing was that I was in love with a woman. Very minor detail. Both of us were in absolute, complete denial about it. I think her being *baole*[1] put me even more in denial about my feelings for her. We were incredibly close friends and always overjoyed to see each other. We sometimes flirted. I even had sexual dreams about her, but I wrote them off as being random coming-out dreams, having nothing really to do with her. A few times we even tried making out, laughing uproariously the whole time from sheer nervousness. Once I kissed her and she fled shrieking and giggling into the kitchen, where my lesbian housemate took one look at us and said, "Why don't you guys just go do it." We almost died laughing. This "friendship" of ours survived numerous long-distance separations while we each jumped from school to school trying to finish our undergrad degrees. I still have piles of her letters, and the phone bills are better forgotten. Eventually we both graduated. She came back to the East Bay and moved into the apartment I shared with "my other best friend," a very heterosexual Filipina American woman who was away in the Philippines at the time. Everything fell to pieces. Put into my coloured context, living in my coloured home, this would-be girlfriend suddenly seemed uncomfortably white to me. She was seeing a *baole* guy who also seemed awkwardly out of place among my friends of colour. Somehow they had a stiffness, a rigidity, something missing in their humour; they had those qualities that I always associated with other *baoles*, not my friends.

I was experiencing a time-earthquake. (This "earthquake consciousness theory" of mine comes from growing up in earthquake country. Things — plates of the earth, or your own personal growth — are moving past each other all the time, but you aren't aware of the movement, the change, until the edges of the plates snap past each other to produce an earthquake, and the landscape readjusts to its new reality.) While my friend was still in Rhode Island, I was in the Bay Area getting heavily into Ethnic Studies and the community of people of colour around it. I had grown to expect a highly developed consciousness around issues of race and ethnicity. *Haoles* who didn't have that kind of understanding and commitment couldn't be my friends. This woman, my best friend, who I used to think was "the coolest white person" I knew, suddenly seemed not to understand the first thing about living in a multicultural community, didn't know anything about people of colour beyond theory. I asked her to move out. She did. We tried to talk, but didn't get anywhere.

In the fall, my housemate returned from the Philippines, impossibly more man-crazy than she had been before. Or else I was just more aware of it. She resumed her dysfunctional relationship with her arrogant boyfriend, and they began to have awful fights. Meanwhile her self-righteously "radical," sexist older brother was homeless and crashing out in our living room with his girlfriend. They fought constantly as well. It all kept deteriorating until I moved out several months later in total disgust.

In the middle of all this pain and chaos (which included a real earthquake in October), I realized that something just wasn't working. Out of sheer instinct, I think, I made a new year's resolution to go to a support group of queer Asian women, most of whom were lesbian but turned out to be at least bi-friendly enough for me to feel accepted, if not completely understood.

While I was getting used to being in that community, organizers were planning the first national bisexual conference for June. I joined the people of colour caucus and for the first time felt that there was something really wonderful about being bisexual. Finally there were people like me! People who understood me exactly as myself, instead of trying to relate to only a fragmented part of me. At last I was allowed to indulge in my bisexual point of view, instead of feeling like I had to squeeze into the lesbian community's margins. The actual conference itself (although a little too white for my taste) strengthened my pride even more.

Not long afterward, I fell in love for the first time in years. My lover is a wonderful woman, a Japanese American musician who is the most bi-friendly lesbian I have ever met. She likes to tell people that it doesn't matter if she's sleeping with a lesbian or a bisexual woman, as long as it's a woman! She is attracted to a gender, not an orientation. It makes so much sense to me. I, on the other hand, am attracted to qualities other than gender, although I am not gender-blind by any means. Far from it. I appreciate different things about women and men, whether I sleep with them or not, just as I appreciate different things about different cultures: Chinese chow mein, Afro-Cuban drums, Navajo weaving...I only demand integrity, a creative spirit, radical understanding and an openminded willingness to struggle.

Bi is beautiful! I no longer accept falsely imposed limitations from either the straight mainstream or from lesbians and gay men. I can't be monosexual any more than I can be monocultural. The lesbian and gay community needs to see that we are not a threat, we are not confused, that we should be included as a visible part of the movement and that such inclusion can only strengthen us all. *We have always been here in the community. Bisexuals are queer too,* and like all other queers, we must fight heterosexism every day of our lives. "You can't have your cake & eat it too," they tell me. Well, sure I can, if I learn to bake myself. Then I can not only eat cake forever, but I can have all different kinds. I can even have bread. Bisexual inclusion can only make the queer community more rich and nourishing — more powerful. My beloved sisters of colour, welcome to the queer kitchen!

NOTE

1 *baole:* Hawaiian term for European/white people, literally meaning "outsider" or "without land." This word gradually seems to be creeping into common usage among mainland Asian Americans.

Cyndy Head

Untitled

To be bi   means   living on the fringe
means having my   of the straight
motives questioned   and lesbian communities.
Being considered
     untrustable
     complicated
     confused.

To be half black   means   living on the fringe
means having my   of black and white
motives questioned   societies.
Being considered
     too white
     too black
     confused.

It is not a choice I've made.
It is who I love,
who I am.

Bisexual   The fringe
always searching for balance   always different
Can I have harmony   wanting to belong
without sacrificing   but not enough
part of myself?   to hide who I am.

Susan Kane

Bisexual Slogans:
Snappy Comebacks for Daily Living

• 100% BISEXUAL, 100% QUEER • HOW LONG CAN I STAY IN THIS PHASE ? • DOUBLE YOUR PLEASURE, DOUBLE YOUR FUN • EVERYONE THINKS I'M GAY • TWO ROADS DIVERGED IN A YELLOW WOOD AND I TOOK BOTH • BISEXUAL BY LUCK, QUEER BY CHOICE • I LIKE GIRLS • COMPLEXITY IS THE SPICE OF LIFE • KINSEY HAD A LIMITED IMAGINATION • IT'S MY REVOLUTION AND I INTEND TO ENJOY MYSELF • WELL, I DON'T THINK YOU EXIST EITHER • KY-KY • HAVE YOUR CAKE AND EAT IT TOO • I JUST DO THIS TO SEDUCE GAY MEN • GET CURIOUS • PC SEX IS AN OXYMORON • I'M BISEXUAL AND I'M NOT ATTRACTED TO YOU • HATE PATRIARCHY, LOVE MEN • NO, YOU CAN'T WATCH • IF YOU THINK MY ROOM'S A MESS, YOU SHOULD SEE MY SEX LIFE • AC/DC • LOVE KNOWS NO BOUNDARIES • I AM OUT, THANK YOU • GENDER IS A SEX TOY • ASSUME NOTHING • FOLLOW YOUR NATURE • IT'S NOT MY FAULT THAT YOU CAN ONLY THINK IN ONE DIRECTION • FREEDOM IS SACRED • YOU CAN HAVE IT ALL • I LIKE BOYS, TOO • HE'S THE FEMME • DECIDEDLY BI • YOU DIDN'T OFFEND ME, YOU PISSED ME OFF • I'M LIVING A "BOTH/AND" LIFE IN AN "EITHER/OR" WORLD • EQUAL OPPORTUNITY LOVER • CROSS BORDERS • NO ONE BELIEVES I'M BISEXUAL • AND WHAT'S WRONG WITH A LITTLE PROMISCUITY? • EMBRACE YOUR LIFE • I LOVE PEOPLE • BEWARE: NON-MONOGAMOUS BISEXUAL APPROACHING! • POLITICAL LESBIANISM: NOT MY IDEA OF A GOOD TIME ON A SATURDAY NIGHT • GO THE WAY YOUR BLOOD BEATS • NO FATS, FEMMES, BUTCHES OR BI'S: I WANT HER THIN AND BORING • SWITCH-HITTER • HASBIAN, SHMASBIAN • WE'RE NOT FENCE-SITTERS, WE'RE BRIDGE-BUILDERS • YOU MAY BE CONFUSED, BUT I'M NOT • I MADE UP MY MIND A LONG TIME AGO • BE CAREFUL, YOU COULD BE NEXT! • DON'T TELL ME YOU'VE NEVER THOUGHT ABOUT IT • THIS IS NOT PLAYBOY, TRY AGAIN • WE'RE HERE, WE'RE QUEER, WE'RE FABULOUS: GET USED TO IT! •

GLOSSARY

Kinsey: Alfred Kinsey published the first major studies of human sexuality in the United States in the late 1940s and early '50s. He developed the "Kinsey scale," which describes sexuality as a continuum from exclusively heterosexual (0) to exclusively homosexual (6). His findings are the source for the popular idea that ten percent of the population is gay.

"Two Roads...": a twist on the poem by Robert Frost, U.S. poet (1874-1963).

Ky-Ky: in 1950s' lesbian bar culture, someone who was ky-ky (kiki) changed sides. This could mean bisexuals; more often it referred to women who switched back and forth between butch and femme.

PC: Politically Correct. Before its appropriation and distortion by the mass media, PC was an in-joke among progressive activists.

Patriarchy: a social and economic structure that upholds men's superiority and dominance. Sometimes confused with individual men.

AC/DC, Fence-Sitter, Switch-Hitter: derogatory terms for bisexual people, implying inability to make a decision about their sexuality. AC/DC refers to the two types of electric current. Switch-Hitter refers to someone who can bat both left- and right-handed in baseball.

"Freedom is Sacred": Religious Coalition for Abortion Rights slogan.

"Both/And Life...": Tom Robinson, *Bisexuality: A Reader and Sourcebook* (Ojai: Times Change Press, 1990).

Political Lesbianism: in the 1970s, the belief that women should choose lesbian identity as a form of political resistance to sexism. Still popular today among some lesbian feminists, who label bisexual women "male-identified."

"Go the way your blood beats": James Baldwin, U.S. novelist, essayist and playwright (1924-1987).

Hasbian: derogatory term for a woman who used to identify as lesbian.

Shmasbian: the prefix "shm" is a Yiddish way of making fun.

Leanna McLennan

Living a Bisexual Life: An Interview with Susan Arenburg

Susan Arenburg has travelled many roads on her personal journey. Her identity has been informed by lesbian politics in rural Nova Scotia, by her involvement as a musician in the women's music scene in Halifax and by day-to-day life in a small town with frequent visits to Toronto and Montreal.

At home in the farmhouse, where she lives with her lover and her eight-year-old daughter, we sit comfortably on the couch, with the ocean in the distance and a small tape recorder on the wooden table in front of us, and begin our conversation.

Identity: Questioning and Defining

S: I have always been bisexual. Even when I didn't know the word, that's what I felt. That's who I was. Before I could even identify with the name I was behaving bisexually.

L: When you found a name was it important to you?

S: I heard "bisexual" after I heard "homosexual." The term bisexual wasn't as commonplace as homosexual or heterosexual. So "bisexual" was a relief for me because I didn't have to choose to be straight or gay, I could just be who I was.

L: Before you heard the word bisexual, did you ever think, "maybe I'm straight or maybe I'm gay?"

S: Oh definitely yes. I was constantly thinking I must be one or the other. I must be straight... Oh, I'm straight today. Oh, now I'm gay. (*laughter*) Most of my relationships have been with women. My most recent relationship before the one I'm in now was with a woman who considered herself a lesbian so we used to argue about my bisexuality because it didn't fit in with what she considered me to be.

L: She considered you to be...

S: ...lesbian, which, of course, I was: I was an acting and practising lesbian. Another thing that is quite interesting is that when I am in a relationship with a woman, I exaggerate to my parents to clarify my position: to them I'm a lesbian. I don't want to talk to them about bisexuality because I don't think that they would get it. I present myself to them as a lesbian otherwise there might be false hope. There's this idea that if you're bisexual someday you could fall back over and become straight again. So if I told my parents that I was bisexual, they might not take the lesbian relationship I was in seriously.

L: But what if they know you're going out with a man? How do you explain that?

S: (laughter) Well then, to them, I'd be straight.

L: You said that when you were going out with a woman you were a practising lesbian. Did you still feel bisexual at that time?

S: The categories don't work when I'm in a relationship. But over my lifetime, I think of myself as a bisexual. I feel far more identified with being a lesbian in recent years than I did in the first twelve or thirteen years of being sexually active, when I was actively bisexual. In the last ten years, I've not been actively bisexual, I've chosen lesbian relationships.

L: But you still identify as bisexual...

S: It's a relief for me to call myself bisexual. It describes how my desires and how my relationships have been throughout my life.

For me to look back and say, well, I am straight and I've had quite a few gay relationships or, well, I am gay and I've had quite a few straight relationships, doesn't make sense. My life is bisexual; I've lived a bisexual life. If I don't continue to do that practically, it doesn't matter. That's still who I am. I think a lot of my identity as a bisexual is buried because I've been in lesbian culture for so long. As well, I think previous relationships may have influenced me. Particularly the last relationship I was in because there was absolutely no doubt in her mind about who she was: she was lesbian. And there was no doubt in my mind that I was bisexual. There was also no doubt that we were very much in love with each other and that we were in a lesbian relationship — obviously. It became such an argumentative point that I started to call myself a lesbian.

L: When you called yourself a lesbian did you feel that you were denying a part of your identity?

S: I suppose at first I did but then it didn't matter. I was in a relationship that I thought was going to be forever so it no longer was extraordinarily important that I identified as bisexual. It was more important to be in that relationship without having a repetitive intellectual argument about how I identified.

L: When you were calling yourself a lesbian were you still attracted to men?

S: Yes, I have always had attractions to both men and women. But my emotional and spiritual commitment seems to be only with women. I don't think I could be in a long-term relationship with a man. I don't believe that any more.

L: But you did before.

S: Yes. It's funny, but my relationships in my late teens and all through my twenties until I was twenty-nine, when I gave birth to my daughter, up to and including that year, my relationships went through a pattern of long-term couple relationships: two or three years with a woman, two or three years with a man, two or three years with a woman, two or three years with a man...I don't recall thinking, "Gee, it must be because men are so difficult, I'm going to be in a relationship with a woman now or, gee, it must be because women are so difficult, I should be in a relationship with a man."

L: You just were attracted to the person.

S: I believe so. I'm not conscious about being persnickety about one sex or the other or blaming my relationship failure on that sex. Then, I became involved in the lesbian culture, with feminism and all that wonderful woman stuff, and from that my commitment to women in general and my own identity were very much strengthened. So, it would be really difficult for me to be in a relationship with a man now. I would have to reshape how I incorporate a lot of my ideologies into my life. And, right now, I'm in a relationship with a woman that is beautiful and permanent, I hope. So I don't consider a man to be an option for me. I really don't think so, but who knows.

Motherhood and Bisexuality

L: Now you have an eight-year-old daughter...

S: How did that happen? (*laughter*)

L: You co-parent with her father, who lives nearby, and live with a woman. How do you discuss your relationships with your daughter?

S: We talk a lot about discrimination of all kinds and oppression of all kinds: that there are Black people, and there are fat people, and there are gay people. There are people of many colours, people of many sizes, people of many talents and people of many choices. She recognizes all of that and is very sensitive to all of the differences in the world and the differences between people, including the choices that people make about their sexuality. She knows about sexuality in relation to love and choosing life partners. A writer who I find very powerful in this way is Urvashi Vaid. She speaks in interviews about the gay movement and how we're often so single-minded in terms of what we're going after and reminds us that oppression of people in general is what's wrong with this world.

L: Making those connections.

S: Yes. And, because I have a daughter, those connections are very important for me to pass on to her.

L: Do you speak specifically about bisexuality to her?

S: It would be interesting to ask her about bisexuality because I think that she does know that term. But she is probably more familiar with "gay" and "straight." Remember I spoke about my parents and about how important it is for me to tell my parents that I am a lesbian? Well, that's also true with my daughter, because of simplicity. She really has a desire for her father and I to be back together again and hopes that someday we will reunite. So, for her, I have not elaborated a great deal on bisexuality because it could bring up false hopes that her father and I might someday fall back into marriage.

L: Do people in the community in which you live know that you are involved in a relationship with a woman?

S: Everybody knows. I believe that it's extremely accepted in this community. I also believe that sometimes it is accepted to the point of being revered, that it's titillating to some people. The position of gay men in the community is quite different. It is not, generally, accepted in the same way.

L: You think it's easier then...

S: ...to be a lesbian in a rural community than a gay man. Oh, for sure. I've been in the local tavern when people have made rude remarks to a gay man about his sexuality. Nobody would dare do that to me. Not only would they not dare to do it in front of me, but I don't think they would do it at all. Being a lesbian is sometimes seen as more funny or cute or something, which makes me very angry.

L: Because it's not really accepting.

S: No, it's entertaining. I'm entertaining and a gay man is not okay. That's how it is sometimes. It's not like that with most people. There is also a very deep, authentic, sincere acceptance here amongst many people.

L: Despite some of the difficulties of being in a lesbian relationship in a rural community, you mentioned earlier that, in some ways, you find it easier to have your sexual identity accepted in this rural community than in an urban community because people know you and accept it as part of you rather than seeing you first as a lesbian or bisexual, then as Susan.

S: Yes, it's true, because in a small community you are actively involved in everything that goes on in the community, you're always doing something: you're somebody who buys groceries, you're with a child at a baseball game or you're doing something that everybody else is doing. So, you're known for much more than your sexuality. It's part of your identity but people see so many more aspects of who you are.

Sarah Cortez

Reunion

There is a new family at our reunion.
Descended from a girl who died bloody
giving birth. Her parents lying,
saying no baby survived,
throwing my grandfather off the land.

This new family is from The Valley.
Parched land, endless highways
greying into brown dust. The dream of water
shimmering silver below noon-high sun.
My new relatives. Three sons, one daughter
from that baby left by my grandfather, hurrying
out of Mexico into the States at sixteen.

Carlos. Javier. Jose. Martha. Three sons,
one daughter. Jose, the unmarried one
with pointed, snakeskin cowboy boots, black
felt hat parked low on back of head.
A bandit moustache, silken and full,
hiding white teeth glistening strong
into easy smiles.

Jose. In a family
of men and women who love to dance
you dance every dance. Whirling
older aunts or teen nieces with grace.
Even your brother's toddler, dancing
with upraised, bent, baby arms
to hold your hands. Circling
your palm legs and black boots.
Small-baby, blunt white leather shoes
dancing in step.

I speak to you at the picnic on Saturday,
looking into wide pools
of tinted sunglass covering half your face.
Your grin broadens, full blooms. I see
a black star high in the soft pink gum
of your mouth. None of the children
are yours. You work on cars.

Mi primo, I come to you full
of the city's rush and starts,
where I sit encased in glass
behind a metal desk. I seek
the earth's warm, brown curve
in your hug. Between your blackened fingernails
stubbing out Camels, I search. Beyond
the rusty barbed wire prongs
curling through mounds of sand, along
the thin ridge of backbone curving into mattress,
I search.
Smelling the dusty soil in your sweat,
embraced by the Naval tattoos
spliced across your muscles.

I want to enjoy you. Slowly.
In The Valley's afternoon.
In a darkened bedroom, water cooler angled
in the doorway. Pink bedspread crumpled
on the floor. Before a rainstorm's heavy,
dust-laden drops hurl into parched earth.

Unfamiliar terrain. Where
passion becomes mother. Nourishment
from a man. You are
naked to the waist. Darkened chest,
scarred ribs, gaunt belly, hairless,
hairless. Black, laughing eyes.
Flat, sticker nipples.

Warm tortillas
fresh to eat
in a linoleum kitchen.

Stripped to belt buckle,
barefoot by the stove,
attending white dough rounds
of masa cooking, you laugh.
I wouldn't fit in
here.

Where dark-haired, handsome men
come home for lunch every day,
babies crawling underfoot and precious.
Where womens' shoulders are rounded,
soft and brown, for a man's fingers.

Mi primo, I look into my mirror,
I see you.

Shai Dhali

"Gender is a big issue in my life. Sexually, I am wearing two different buttons on my lapels. One says, 'I like girls.' The other reads, 'I like boys.' So the owl that I kiss by the bathtub remains masked. I don't want to see gender-specific features in this fantasy."

Leela Acharya, Amina, Amita, Farzana Doctor & Nupur Gogia

"Purifying" the (Identi)Ghee:
South Asian Feminists Gup-shup[1]

We came together not really knowing what it was that we wanted to talk about, only knowing that as feminist bisexual women we needed to articulate some of the commonalities in our experience. Part of the problem in developing a politics based on bisexuality stems from the fact that bisexuality encompasses such a broad range of experiences, from those who find themselves within the privileged institution of heterosexual marriage to those who have only dated women. Finding a commonality amongst this range has meant accepting the diversity of desire while simultaneously attempting to unravel the points at which this desire also inhabits a place of privilege. In the discussion that follows, we struggle with the issue of privilege as it presents itself within the South Asian context, and find that talking about privilege takes on a different dimension when it is placed in our particular cultural location. We also discuss, more generally, the issues of sex and sexuality within the South Asian context and how, as women, our practices and choices are labelled as sexually deviant if we do not conform to the norms of our community or the mainstream community. So much of the resistance in our daily lives is aimed at the institution of compulsory heterosexual marriage and the ways in which different communities regulate our lives as women. The awareness of these controls over our lives became apparent in our discussion around whether to use our real names or not, always conscious of the price that has to be paid for being viewed as sexually "deviant." While we realize that this is a choice that each woman has to make for herself, we have all decided to use our own names. This disclosure does not come without hesitation, however, as we realize that the backlash from our own communities, often a place of refuge from a racist society, makes us more vulnerable to self-doubt, shame and ostracism. The existence of the larger lesbian and gay community as well as the support we have gotten from each other has provided us the strength to do so, to come out and claim our existence as bisexual women. In the year and a half that we've spent on this piece we have come to view it as a work in progress, realizing that there are still many contradictions that we have not yet resolved. We invite you to our "conversation in progress" hoping that at least it will open up some questions around the issue of sexuality in the South Asian context.

I. Beti, (Baytee)² from which village do you come?

NUPUR: I was born in Montreal. My parents came to Canada in the late 1960s. I spent sixteen years in Montreal and then we were in Ottawa and now I've been in Toronto for a year. We're Hindu Punjabis. I'm twenty-seven years old.

AMINA: I was born in Pakistan. I came here when I was seven in the mid-70s. When I came here I was thrown off, because I was so immersed in my own culture and language. It was difficult to adjust, but I did. I went to school here in Toronto, grew up here and this is all I really know. I'm twenty-five. My father is a fairly conservative Muslim. My mother is more into Muslim culture as opposed to doing everything by the book. Me, I have my own feminist interpretation of Islam. But of course Islam has a big influence on my sexuality and the way I live my life. It's a determining force.

FARZANA: I'm twenty-four. I was born in Zambia, my parents came from Bombay and we lived in Zambia for five years and then came to Canada when I was six months old. My family life has been pretty areligious. Culturally we are more Muslim, but I didn't grow up knowing or practising Islam. We had Indian get-togethers and we celebrated different religious holidays, but there was always this sort of idea that "now we're in Canada and we're Canadians."

AMITA: My parents left India in the early 1960s. I've basically grown up here but have gone back and forth to and from India quite often. My parents were quite rooted in Indian culture. I wouldn't describe them as religious but they are very much into Indian culture and keeping it alive at home. I'm thirty and not religious myself. I am of Hindu and Punjabi background.

LEELA: I came to Canada with my parents in 1969 when I was six years old. We are originally from southern India, the area of Tamilnadu and Karnataka. I grew up in Edmonton, Alberta. Culturally, I'm from a Hindu background, and I'm thirty-two.

II. Looking for "Desi³ Deviants"

LEELA: Did anyone have any early awareness of bisexuality or homo-sexuality in a South Asian context? I had absolutely none. Everyone around me when I was growing up was very straight. It was only later, after I had some consciousness of my own sexuality that I began wondering about others, especially family members. I thought about the few South Asian women I know that never married men and how the middle class perceives them to be selfless, self-sacrificing women, committed to the economic security of the extended family, or some apolitical cause. They are also seen as a spiritual ideal, a social value and a conscience of the race. I think some of these perceptions of women are rooted in India's nationalist movement and how women are always assumed to be asexual beings.

NUPUR: Yeah, I remember always seeing these women in the Hindi movies. They always died in the end. Probably because they weren't seen as having a male counterpart, which is of course valued, and so it was thought there was no reason for them to exist without a man in their life.

AMINA: I have a recollection of my maasi, who was an older, single, female servant who looked after my mother and us children. A maasi teaches a woman how to be a wife and is her special companion. These women always had a special relationship that was not defined as sexual but only spoken of in functional and emotional terms. I think that it is possible that they fulfilled a purpose of meeting a woman's emotional and sexual needs, but this is never named or acknowledged.

LEELA: There was a woman politician in Tamilnadu, India, who had a married man as her lover — Jayalalitha, do you know her? In the popular culture of Tamilnadu, her affair with MGR was publically known. When MGR died, people said Jayalalitha became close to a woman, who later left her husband. In the Tamil media, this woman is referred to as Jayalalitha's special friend or companion, but maybe she was always involved with this woman and was actually bisexual. But their relationship was seen as emotional and functional, and the possibility of the sexual is absent. I know we can't just assume women like this were homosexual or bisexual. We can't conclude this based on the present historical moment.

FARZANA: I had never heard of any bisexual, lesbian or gay relationships among South Asians. Perhaps it is that these terms were not used, or that other words were used to cover the possibility of any sexual aspect of the relationship. I have more recently wondered if there are or were any lesbians in my family and have started to question different people about any possible "eccentrics" or "single women" in the family. I have yet to find out about any. I do remember seeing *Hijras*[4] on the trains in India and that my aunties were really afraid of them.

NUPUR: I remember seeing *Hijras* at weddings. They looked like men in women's clothing and I didn't understand because they acted very "womanish" but looked quite masculine, especially some of their physical features.

AMINA: Actually, I first heard about *Hijras* from my mother, before I had any understanding of sex or sexuality. We were in the market and she pointed to them and she said, "they're neither man nor woman, they're eunuchs." She said they're funny people, they live on their own and she described them basically as outcasts and now I know why. They were perceived to be sexually deviant.

AMITA: It's interesting that in sexually segregated societies, like in South Asia, close emotional bonds are formed between women or between men, because that is the context in which they interact and live their lives and have their experiences, and these unions are disrupted when women and men get married, because it's assumed to be "natural," but it's just the compulsory institution of heterosexual marriage.

AMINA: In my own experience, one of the beautiful things about being in a relationship with a woman is that I was allowed to express physical affection and emotional intimacy. Since we come from a sexually segregated culture, women can do everything together and men can do everything together. Unless sanctioned by marriage, men and women do not associate very much. When I see my mom and her friends and my dad and his friends, they walk arm in arm, and I don't know if this is something Muslim, but I know it is South Asian. Female intimacy among females and male intimacy among males that is assumed to be based on friendship and not at all sexual is wonderful because it allows you to experience so much with your family.

At home, we've been programmed to respond in a particular way. So even if we're all sitting together as a family and watching a show on television and suddenly sexuality is there, or sex is there, we change the channel! We do it for my parents, so they don't have to censor it for us! (*laughter*) Even when talking to my sisters, I have to force myself to talk about sex and sexuality. It doesn't feel comfortable, but I want to do it because I want to start breaking these barriers.

AMITA: It's very similar for me. I have always had to hide a male lover. In fact I could talk to women on the phone, but I couldn't talk to men on the phone! There are all kinds of policing practices by parents, family and community members around South Asian women's relationships with men.

AMINA: Also, anything related to a woman, including her body and sexuality, is taboo. And I know that we in our individual lives and in our families try to break down these taboos. But, at the same time, the expectation of "coming out" as the ultimate goal for lesbian and bisexual women to achieve is problematic since we live in a racist/sexist/homophobic society. To expect women of colour living in this society to simply "come out" without taking into account the dynamics we experience in our culture and in relation to the mainstream is a problem for me.

NUPUR: I'm still waiting for that big talk about the birds and the bees. I got the menstruation talk, but I never got the rest. I had to say, it's okay Mom, we got the rest at school!

AMITA: About two years ago, my mother said, "can you believe that in this society, by the age of twelve or thirteen, girls are starting to have sex with boys?" And she said, "I just can't believe it! And by your age they've all had sex!" Then she looks at me and says, "you haven't had sex, have you Amita?" She of course wanted to hear that I hadn't had sex yet. It seems she'd always make the lie up for me. And I'd just have to nod my head.

NUPUR: I remember, in one of our rare and close moments, my mother and I were having this hypothetical talk. I was asking her, "how would you feel if I had premarital sex?" She said, "no way, that's bad, I could never handle that," and I said, "well, what if I'm engaged?" and she said, "no, I *vodunt*[5] like it." (*laughter*) And I realized this is not the time to tell my mom

I've already had sex. However, she would want to know if I was pregnant and unmarried. But how am I supposed to tell her I'm pregnant when I can't even talk to her about pre-marital sex? It was such a bundle of contradictions.

LEELA: Yes, I know exactly what you mean. When I first became sexually active in my late teens, I was using contraceptives and my mother found them!

NUPUR: That's a nightmare for me.

LEELA: She could not understand me, and thought I was a "slut." I've come to understand why she saw me in this way at that time. When she was seventeen, she didn't even know about her body, never mind any aspect of her sexuality. I think she was trying to understand my teenage behaviour in relation to herself, but she couldn't, and she was so angry with me because here I was making my own decision to be sexually active and to control my fertility. She did not know how to deal with me. She tried to control me by not letting me go out, and she just didn't trust me.

AMITA: My mom feels the lowest thing a single woman can do is have pre-marital sex with a man. She would be a "prostitute" in her eyes. It's really hard, because when you grow up knowing this is what the judgement is, there's always the internalized shame to work through on your own, because you can't work through it with parents and family.

NUPUR: There's so much lying and deceiving to family and relatives that you are never fully yourself at any given time. But then you just get so used to relating in this kind of half way with family...

AMITA: It's funny 'cause I do think my mother has become suspicious of me. It's so hard to know if this is my own paranoia or what, I don't know how it gets trickled down, it's the networking that goes on, and somehow you think so many of us are so separate from the mainstream South Asian community, but somehow my mom will come back to me with something about someone in our community, and that element is somehow always controlling our lives in some way too.

FARZANA: My own experience of becoming sexual is quite different because I didn't have to hide my sexual relationships with men as much. When I was eighteen I moved in with my boyfriend and then called my dad to let him know my new living situation. He said that he felt "living out of wedlock" was "sinful" but told me that I had to make my own decisions. It was always clear to me that he would never try to stop me or try to change my mind. However, heterosexuality isn't discussed generally in my family and homosexuality is only brought up in the form of homophobic jokes and comments. When I speak to my relatives on the telephone, they never ask me if I am dating. They constantly suggest it is time for me to get married.

III. Sexing Saheli[6]

AMINA: I first found myself being attracted to a woman when I was about seventeen or eighteen and that time I did not define myself as a feminist, so when I found myself being attracted to her, I didn't have any analysis around sexuality. My only understanding of lesbianism was through the homo-phobic culture in high school. When I was with her I thought, okay, I'm a lesbian now, I better face up and accept it. I was fine with myself in spite of the knowledge that this was something condemned by my religion. It was just dealing with my own religious convictions and trying to sort all of that out for myself.

LEELA: From there, when and how did you come to bisexuality?

AMINA: After this relationship, I found myself being attracted to men, but I thought I didn't ever want to actually be with them again 'cause I was a lesbian now. (*laughter*) But then I thought, hey, hang on a second here, because I found myself attracted to a man and then in a relationship with him, I thought I'm back to being straight again. (*laughter*) At this point I realized that it's not so clear cut, and by then I was a lot more politicized and obviously had a greater understanding of sexuality and challenged myself on everything. So the great thing about it is that I was leaving all these options open and giving myself a real choice and I was practising this choice regardless of people saying you have to be straight or lesbian. And I said, no, I'm bisexual.

LEELA: When I came to Toronto, and fell in love with our women of colour community, I also felt there was nothing about me that mattered to anyone, except my sexuality. So the first question was "what are you?" I said I was bisexual, because that is my experience, and women were very...(*laughter*)

NUPUR: It's funny 'cause when I first got involved here that was the first question I was always asked and I thought, well that's such a stupid question, it's none of your business.

AMITA: It's true, you'd think people are so idle. Honestly, when I think of the world's problems...

FARZANA: I was asked the same question when I first came to T.O. too! I just want to comment about sexuality or sexual identity being based solely on who you're having sex with. Until recently, I hadn't come out sexually, which means that I hadn't had a sexual relationship with a woman. I had crushes on women for a long time and had always believed that I would eventually have a sexual relationship with a woman. Not having had sex with a woman before and coming out as bisexual was difficult for me. I often felt I had to "prove" myself to others, give them an inventory of all of the crushes and near sexual encounters that I've had with women or girls since childhood. People think the only way to "come out" is sexually. I believe it is a multifaceted process that includes, at least for me, the spiritual, emotional, intellectual and sexual aspects of myself.

Right now, I seem to be more interested in and attracted to women. I don't know if that will change in the future. I see desire and sexuality as being very fluid and sometimes I wonder where I'll be on the "bisexual spectrum" in a few years...

AMITA: So what does that mean to you when you say "I'm bisexual?"

AMINA: Well, I hate that term, I think a lot of people don't like it because it's so clinical...

For myself, as a bisexual woman, it means that I have a real commitment to women in my life, to loving women and being with them sexually, emotionally, politically fighting for our rights, but it also means that I like having relationships with men. (laughter) I have become really selective about the men in my life. And they have to be darn good! (laughter)

AMITA: Well that's the thing, I think once you become feminist, it's really hard to put up with anything. I was in a very long-term relationship with a guy at a young age. I had sexual experiences with women periodically, but at that time I had no kind of political understanding of it, and it was just kind of an interesting experience. I became involved in the women's centre when I was about twenty-four and then, for the first time in my life — being exposed to the politics of feminism, meeting all these women many of whom I felt attracted to — I really sort of had a crisis about what does this mean in my life? I felt sexually and emotionally attracted to women and very connected emotionally, which I wasn't feeling with men, and I really started questioning myself. And the experiences with women continued but the thing is I was also always in this long-term relationship with a man, so the whole issue of whether I could call myself bisexual or not was kind of...well, I felt I had no right to. So that's where the whole issue of how we define our sexuality, which is usually based on who you are living with or seeing, came up for me. I thought, I'm having all these desires for women so shouldn't I be identifying on the level of desire?

LEELA: Yeah I know what you're saying...I sometimes feel I am put in a position where I am questioned about my purity. And I think it's there for others too, whether it's in terms of your race, your class background, or your sexuality, you have to really prove whatever you claim. It's not enough to just live it and struggle against it everyday! I think this question of authenticity acts to silence women and I see this in women dating men and women or just women. It is hard for a woman in this situation to acknowledge and accept her sexuality and her desires unless she has a lot of confidence and believes in herself. Isn't that what you said, Amita, that you felt you had no right to call yourself bisexual?

AMITA: Yes, and then I started realizing that you have to really define at the level of desire. Because when you're walking around, who you're feeling desire for and how your sexuality is made up for you in your head has so much to do with desire, but as bisexual women we haven't found a way to politicize desire as lesbianism has.

LEELA: Yes, that's true, and in our culture there's so much repression in relation to sex and to the concept of desire. We are supposed to forego all our desires at some level!

When I first became sexual it was with men. The main messages while growing up were extremely heterosexist. And it was a certain type of conservative heterosexism. When I look back, I think I have always desired women, but it was much later, when I had my first sexual relationship with a woman, that it all came home for me. I went through a period of self-denial, unlearning the internalized homophobia, and I also struggled with choosing between men and women. I didn't feel I could determine which gender I would fall in love with. Then I heard about bisexuality and thought this must be who I am, in terms of my sexuality. I don't particularly like the term. But sexually, I do feel I embody a fluidity. I can't deny the possibility of desiring a male and I'm not being true to myself if I do. On the other hand, because of my own struggles as a woman of colour feminist, my politics are quite fixed, but I strive to keep learning and to eliminate any rigidity.

AMITA: There is an assumption that, for example, when I go to a straight bar, all of a sudden I've left my gay part at home and I'm not at all affected by the environment. But I'm feeling just as uncomfortable about not being able to express that part of myself. It's almost like splitting...as if you have this straight part and this gay part. It doesn't work like that. It's always in my head, it's everywhere, with whomever I meet. It's always an issue for me.

I'm not really happy with the term bisexual. I feel like it implies an equal kind of relationship to women and men. Like you could be with either in the same way, but you can't. There are very different political, social and intimate implications that apply to each. I started using "bisexual" last year because I was seeing both a man and a woman. I felt as if I was reinforcing the bisexual stereotype, you know what I mean, the "concurrent relation-ships," the "promiscuity," which can be a part of anyone's life regardless of their sexual orientation. When I told some people about my circumstance of seeing two people, they said, "Oh you bisexuals!" And I thought, why didn't they say, "Oh, you people who are in open relationships!" To me it's more an issue of whether you are having a monogamous relationship...or a non-monogamous one...

LEELA: I think the act of sleeping with a woman without a man in your life categorizes you as lesbian, and the act of sleeping with a woman with a man in your life categorizes you as straight. What if you sleep with a man and you have a woman in your life? It's so simplistic. My life is shaped by lesbianism, politically and emotionally, and I am definitely my own woman. If you ask me about my sexual desires, they are for both sexes. This does not mean I will act upon my every desire. Especially those related to men. But the desire is bisexual. It is this aspect which makes me feel I am bisexual, and bisexual is the most available term to explain it.

AMITA: But do you feel that you're attracted to men in a physical way? This becomes really interesting too, because there are a lot of lesbians who define themselves as lesbians and sleep with men.

LEELA: Yes, some men I am attracted to in a physical way. I cannot say it never happens. Why should I deny it or hide it?

AMITA: I can understand lesbians who sleep with men because if someone has decided that most of their life and lifestyle connect with women and that the person that they are going to live their life with is a woman, but they might sleep with a male occasionally, it doesn't have to entirely change who they are. It's like a straight woman sleeping with a woman, a one- or two-time encounter, but they still feel they are straight.

AMINA: But isn't that due to a lot of homophobia?

NUPUR: I think that's biphobia, I think it's because there is so much backlash against bisexuals.

AMITA: But there are differences among lesbians too. There are lesbians that will do that but keep it hidden, and then there are lesbians that will do that openly, and there are lesbians who would never do that.

NUPUR: But do you think that can really be, can a lesbian who fucks men be a lesbian? I find that such a contradiction...

LEELA: "Lesbian" and "gay" mean different things to different people, just like "bisexuality" does. I think it is important for us to explore what it is that makes us think we are who we are. I think some of it lies with one's sense of self and how you want to identify, in this case, your sexual self, your sexual desires, or explain your sexuality. So if a woman says she's lesbian and she sleeps with men, and continues to be lesbian, I feel that is her decision. I do not see it as a contradiction. To me the point is who is defining, and each one of us has the power and the right to define for ourselves.

AMITA: Because otherwise we are sexually defined by society on the basis of who we are sleeping with.

NUPUR: I think most of us would fall categorically into what we would call "lesbian lifestyle," just by the virtue of how we define ourselves in the culture of Toronto, where we go, who we hang out with, who our social lives are with, what we do politically, you know...

FARZANA: No, I say I'm bisexual, because it's more easily understood than a term like queer which is less specific. At the same time, though, I have difficulty with the term bisexual because it seems simpler just to say "I'm with a woman now" instead of having to explain my current relationship or preference and any possibilities for the future, or getting into long discussions about the theoretical definitions of bisexuality.

LEELA: Do you find these terms Eurocentric at all?

FARZANA: Maybe we need our own terms.

AMITA: It's very white, I like what it stands for, but I don't like the term.

NUPUR: Well, look who it was developed by, it was developed by white, gay men and white lesbians. It's not something that we've come up with, so I think it's understandable, the Eurocentrism, it's somebody else's term.

AMINA: I've actually never used "queer."

IV. Sharam,[7] Shame — Now I Know Your Girlfriend's Name

FARZANA: I am out to my sister, and that was a very gradual and easy process. When I was first starting to question my sexuality, I went to the Michigan Womyn's Music Festival with my sister. Over time, I've been talking to her more easily and I'm very close to her. I'm only out to an aunt and a cousin, and not out to anybody else. I think part of it has to do with the fact that I feel all of this is fairly new to me and it's still something I'm getting comfortable with.

AMINA: I'm out to my sisters. But even that was difficult in a family that does not talk about sexuality. I am sure and convinced that my parents think I am totally asexual, and have no sexual desires, or hormones whatsoever in my body...

AMITA: The way it "should" be.

NUPUR: Until you get married to a man and suddenly have this sexual explosion! (*laughter*)

AMINA: The only sign of sexuality will probably be my pregnancy.

Even that is seen as the "natural" thing to happen and only if married of course! I first came out to my sister and, although I would always talk about lesbians and there would be books and posters about lesbians all over my room, no one ever asked me, "so you hang out with lesbians, does that mean you are one too?" My sister just asked me and I said I'm bisexual. Then she said, "yeah I knew!" (*laughter*) I really underestimated my sister and so I told her about my first relationship with a woman. She said, "I knew you were lovers," and she thought it was a good thing that I've left my options open. I was really surprised, and thought that my sister may be coming from a homophobic perspective. Coming out to my parents is not even a consideration at this point in my life.

NUPUR: I'm out to my sister too. I came out to her seven years ago when I first started seeing a woman. She was cool about it and very accepting. About coming out to my parents, I was in a dilemma about how I would explain being bisexual to them and have them take it seriously. I felt they would only want to see half of it — that there would be some chance I'd be with a man or get married to one. I know that's how they would interpret it and they would ignore the part of it that involves women and would see it as "well at least she's not lesbian." I was always open about my feminism, so I don't think my parents had a lot of expectations of me. I really don't know how I'm going to tell my mother or even if I am. I had thought about it before when I was in an intimate and important relationship. It was so hard to hide and, because the woman I was with "looked like such a dyke," I couldn't see how my parents wouldn't have guessed. But you know ignorance is bliss and denial is a great way to stay ignorant. I've done a lot of things in my life and my parents have never questioned me. I used to live with a man in the same city as my parents and they never knew! In some ways my parents are really good at denying so I wonder why I should even bother telling them because there is so little they know about my life. What would be the point?

AMITA: I'm out to my sister too, but very gradually. I don't really share much about my life with my mother so it seems I would not share this aspect either. My mother doesn't really know what I do. The whole issue of sexuality and sex is just not talked about. There have been a lot of heated discussions about homosexuality with my mom and my aunt and I've argued my opposition to them and among some of my cousins. I guess I'm out to some of them, the others think I'm so far gone or weird anyways. They are very conservative in a lot of ways, politically, and other aspects. Even if sexuality came up they would be, "yeah, so what else is new" kind of thing. I had quite a heated discussion with my father about sexuality once. He gave me every argument against homosexuality and at the end of it, he said, "Amita, why is this so important to you anyways? Why are you getting so worked up about this?" and I said, "it is very important to me." After we had that discussion we never talked about it until quite a few years later when he for the first time said lesbian and gay rights is a civil rights issue. That was a big step for him, but still, if it came to his daughter...

NUPUR: We haven't even come out as heterosexual!

LEELA: I don't have sisters or brothers to come out to. But I am "out" to my parents. That does not mean sex is an easy topic to discuss with them. Like most South Asians of their generation, they are, like, anti-sexual and decently ashamed of their own sexuality! It has been equally important for me to get my parents to understand more about imperialism, racism, sexism and classism, especially in the historical context of our lives here as immigrants for the past twenty-five years. They have always known of my political involvements. In fact, my father thinks I hate men! The rest of my family — aunts, uncles and cousins in India, and more recently, more and more cousins in the U.S. — I think they see me as some kind of an eccentric, and I do feel like an outlaw in relation to all of them, their lifestyles and values. Anyway, each time I'm with my parents I try to get them to understand more about the different aspects of my life including my sexuality. The positive thing is I have not had to hide from them in any way and they have always supported the decisions I make in my life.

V. Purifying or Clarifying the (Identi)Ghee

AMITA: You know, we haven't really sorted out that heterosexual privilege thing.

AMINA: Well, that seems like a real monumental thing, because that's what is supposedly the greatest barrier to solidarity with lesbians, right?

LEELA: I think we're talking about the main criticism we get as bisexual women. One is heterosexual privilege, and then politically we are doubted, our solidarity and loyalty is questioned on the basis of definitionally keeping the possibility of men in our lives.

AMITA: Part of the privilege stems from the fact that bisexuality is probably more accepted by mainstream society than being lesbian or gay, because for some reason people think there's still that part of you that is straight and can be saved.

LEELA: It depends. People think in binary terms and they do privilege straight. But there are also people who cannot accept a woman being sexual with both women and men.

AMINA: But even that privilege is not shared and the way in which we experience that privilege isn't equal; I think we have to recognize that. First off, we need to define heterosexual privilege.

LEELA: Well, one form of it refers to societal and institutional privilege and legitimacy. A woman's relationship with a man is legitimized, the lifestyle is legitimized, you have access to the institutional benefits, like immigration and so on. It's those kinds of privileges that are the basis of criticism. Plus the question of sensibility, as in "lesbian sensibility" and loyalty.

NUPUR: But if that's the criticism that bisexual women get, once I've acknowledged it, now what do I do?

AMITA: It was like what you were saying, Amina, it's more complicated than this word privilege. When you look at it within a South Asian context, for example, I can't tell my mom if I'm going out with a guy, so the whole thing about being sexual in general is silenced. Then I guess it's the privilege of family thinking that one day you'll get married which, as a feminist, you might reject as an institution.

AMINA: But I know there are lesbians in my community who also face the pressure of getting married. The pressure to marry is societal. You can't necessarily control it according to your identity. In terms of physical intimacy in public, I fear I can't walk down the street and hold even my boyfriend's hand, because this is a city where all my relatives are, and I always bump into people I know who would see this as "immodest behaviour." I could be treated as a social outcast by my family and community. So I think it's really relative in terms of what culture you're talking about when you say "heterosexual privilege." Although I acknowledge when I walk down the street with a woman, as opposed to a man, and I 'm intimate with her, there's the possibility of me getting gay-bashed.

AMITA: But is privilege all about what you can and can't do? When you're with a man, supposedly you can hold his hand on the street, which we've already said is not necessarily true in the South Asian context. If you're with a woman you can or can't depending on where you are.

FARZANA: The time you would have heterosexual privilege is when you marry a man in the way that your family wants you to. That would be the one time. In terms of your own community.

AMITA: But, on the other hand, I think it's a bit more than that when I see my relatives or family friends, I don't go up to them and say "I'm a bisexual." Now if I were not to be exercising my heterosexual privilege, does that mean I have to out myself in every situation? Is this what I should be saying: "Oh, by the way, I sleep with women, I'm not getting married, I like potatoes and I'm bisexual." Is that how we relinquish this heterosexual privilege? This seems somehow tied into the whole issue of passing. Like, you can be a lesbian and still have this heterosexual privilege, so it's not just tied into who you are sleeping with. A lesbian can have heterosexual privilege if she doesn't fit the white dyke image and come out to every single person.

NUPUR: Is it a question of relinquishing it?

FARZANA: But do we give it up?

NUPUR: Well, can we even give up privilege?

LEELA: How do white people give up race privilege? How do we give up middle-class privilege or any other kind of privilege? We can learn to take responsibility for privilege. And I think you have to be honest to yourself at some level in order to take that responsibility, especially if you have a critical consciousness.

NUPUR: I used to have an argument with my ex-lover all the time. I was in this intimate relationship with her and she told me that previously she would never go out with bisexual women. She would say, "own up to your heterosexual privilege," and I'd say, "when I'm with you and we're walking down the street, where the fuck is my privilege?" Part of her problem with bisexuals is heterosexual privilege and the other thing is that bisexual women are male identified.

AMITA: You're attached to this man, and it's assumed that your whole sense of yourself is defined by this man and in relation to this guy, like you can never stand on your own. Also I find it's really interesting that there's this assumption, that a heterosexual woman has no agency. We really need to look at that too, because we don't give room for women to be straight and really autonomous and free-thinking, and if you see her attached to a man in any way, we automatically think, she's bought into that, she follows him, she whatever, whatever...without even knowing the woman.

NUPUR: The biggest thing that I hear from lesbians is "Well, if I go out with you, you'll leave me for a man." But lesbians and bisexual women could leave a woman for another woman!

FARZANA: For some reason it seems like it's worse, to leave a woman for a man than to leave a woman for a woman...

AMITA: There are a lot of lesbians that go around fucking a lot of women and aren't intimate with them. But then again, it's almost as if your relationship with a man is more important and that's how I found the situation that I'm in. If my relationship with a woman ended, it would definitely be seen as "she decided to go with the man." It's only seen in terms of a "male-female" thing, as opposed to what's your history or quality of relationship. The thing is, you can't really ever determine who you are going to fall in love with, under what circumstances, or you can't pre-determine what's going on for you in your life at that moment that makes you attracted to that person in a situation, you know what I mean...

AMINA: Then there's the other thing about being a bisexual woman and all this heterosexual privilege, so that when the KKK comes to get you or the Heritage Front, they are not going to say, well, we'll only cut off half of you. (laughter)

AMITA: I think there is a lot of mistrust between the lesbian and bisexual women's community... A lot of it is premised on — and this is the premise which I think we should break — that obviously bisexual women do not want to give up their heterosexual privilege, because if they really did they'd call themselves lesbian and when it's convenient for them they are lesbian, if not, they are bisexual.

I guess a lot of the struggle is about what the authentic identity is. Whether it's lesbian, straight or bisexual. There are so many different ways people have defined these and we're all constantly up against this criteria and whether we have a right to define ourselves.

LEELA: Yes, and in the meantime, what about forging alliances and building solidarity to achieve shared political goals? People say we are segmenting by further categorizing ourselves and making more divisions.

AMITA: Ultimately everything gets so ghettoized because your political identity is only based on what identity you inhabit. For example, if I'm straight I don't have to work for lesbian and gay rights, or if I'm white racism is your issue.

FARZANA: I agree with having coalitions but at the same time, how often do we let men into our movement or others who share our political goals? There are real reasons why we want to be with the people who are similar to us. For example, there are issues of safety, shared experience and power and privilege that force us to take exclusionist stands. So, on the one hand, there are real reasons for bisexual exclusion from lesbian space, that is, heterosexual privilege, and, on the other hand, even we as South Asian bisexual women are exclusionary in our own definition of community.

NUPUR: The more I think about it, I think identity politics is our greatest downfall because if you look at the movement of the right and of the left, I see that the right is getting so strong because they build alliances with anyone who believes in what they do. For example, we have all these people of colour who belong to the Reform party because they share the same ideology. I think there's a lot of strength in working collectively. Yet, in the women's movement we seem to be getting weaker because we're caught up in identity politics. We have these lofty political goals that sometimes appear unrealistic because we never seem to get beyond identity politics to have any kind of collective strength. I look at Toronto and I think it's insanity, because here you have such narrow divisions. I could never envision this happening in Ottawa and other smaller places in Ontario where it is a luxury to even have a South Asian community.

AMINA: The instances when we do work in the lesbian/gay community, our bisexual identities often go unacknowledged...

AMITA: The argument is that if it's the lesbian part of you that's oppressed, i.e., the homosexual part of you, then you should be struggling under a lesbian identity.

LEELA: I think bisexual women's visibility is slowly breaking that down because there are a lot of us who are defining our own politics, speaking out around issues of homophobia and the heterosexism that pervades our lives, and we are doing other kinds of political work as well, but we are still seen by many lesbians as traitors. And I don't know if or when that will ever change.

NOTES

1 *Gup-shup* means chit-chat.
2 *Beti (Baytee)* is a term of endearment meaning daughter.
3 *Desi* is a slang term referring to someone or something from "back home."
4 *Hijra* refers to a community of men in India who have become women.
   They do not necessarily have a sex change, but they physically appear as women.
5 *vodunt* means would not.
6 *Saheli* means woman-friend.
7 *Sharam* means shame.

Margaret Christakos

Marks

TWO DISTINCT IMPULSES WHICH BEND AND PULL. Thirst and a granule of dirt in the eye. Every story has its own lining which requires careful measure. On a very very hot day it feels worse to take a shower only to reemerge to the sweat. I'm dripping. I'm signing each letter with a different name. You who. If I tell will you listen? If I speak about you will I disappear?

•

Day by day I watch my body change.

•

Even though the first time was twelve years ago, or ten, but twelve sounds more dramatic — what is the past anyway except a riddle messed up in memory? — when I woke in your house yesterday I was reeling with dizziness. Was this the body or an intruder throwing off the body's balances?

Leaning into wind we grazed against a stormfront balanced bodies against the wall of possibility of one night touching. It was lunatic how we moved into the sideboard of a hurricane casual with the pretense of wanting to see Bertolucci's *Luna*. The layers of connection between moon, luna, lunatic, hysteric, his turn, terminate, nada. Where we went together.

Now you have the multiplicity of two daughters on your body, plunging and sucking, breathing as they sleep, your breasts generously dripping after their small lips relax and tumble beside your ribcage.

•

Recently I read again portions of Ondaatje's *Coming Through Slaughter* and felt the erotic brew of triangles. The names Bolden and Jaelin pulling equal tastiness for her, Robin. How I had loved to produce these in my own life for years and eschewed all jealousies then. Now I rage at small looks, my own distracted dreaming, any new thing.

•

A few weeks ago I realized I had not learned to write fiction because I had never intended to tell the story.

•

It's hard to believe how many solitary women go by with their lips pursed. And who this is for, or who it beckons. Beckons themselves into existence. From store windows, glib assessments of motorists passing, people hanging out of streetcars. Some concrete memory of the mother's eyes the way she smiled brimming with yearning to be young again and see you. Who sees who first is a riddle. All afternoon I watch joyful pairs of women come and park bikes in front of Grayno's bakery lock them side by side against an available meter duck out of the looming rain for coffee and I am watching for their reciprocal grin as they open the door together, for evidence. With them my triangular imagination is cells of hot pink. Floats ahead of the storm on the horizon's strict measure.

●

It appears I will live within a triangular tenet. My life fixed now, in two real senses, stationary and repaired, I am repaired by his listening and loving me. I am soothed working here on our technology, fingering codes into the room, pausing to touch my upper lip, look up at the orange wall that fixes me here. The room becoming like a mirror or mother's face. How I still look for her everywhere, for myself in the seams. Since the bus ride back with its lull of letting you go again all the women appear to me as confections I would put in my perfect bite. At the far-off vertice is the hankering. My neck rotates side to side. I draw triangles with my memory.

●

Maybe since I have stopped drinking red wine. The part it played in every seduction. How it made everything go pink, go rosey. Blushing and the why-nots like dominoes down the torso, tumbling. Temporary as a pregnancy, suffused with twice as much blood circulating emotion longing to be carried outward. An excess. Access. How we get into each others' pants. Panting. Ting ting. Tingles.

●

First of all the pulsing directly behind the bridge of my nose is worth worrying about, and second, so is my vision, which has gone bleary. At four in the morning it's hard to balance out the odds of peril. Hard to hear a mama's tune. But when I go, sit in the waiting room, rehearse my narrative, the doctors each in their turn swallow and nod as their soliloquy on condoms and foam is interrupted. When I say, well, I'm bisexual, so. How should I divide trust into a package marked "accept advice on mortal issues," from "dismiss subtle or overt homophobia?" Here I would be accused of a sociological voice intruding on aesthetics. A good edit is like a visit to a good doctor or a good lay where I can moan about wanting to, for instance, have a penis and push into his ass imagining he wants this. The last g.p. arranged to have my eyes checked.

•

What belongs in your living room. What belongs in your child's inner ear. What would be better conducted in private. What a good writer has gotten out of her system. What won't make it across the border. What is unfit for human consumption at dinnertime. What should be let go already. What they know and don't need harped upon. What will make it.

•

The marks left on my body by women and by men.

•

The marks left on my breasts after they are suckled by you. Certain cells that have never before travelled from the interior rise to visit this world, arriving so naive to the sun's apocalypse they flash pink instantly. My hot pink imagination rises to the surface just so, cell by cell, whether your lips are male or female. Whether you apply wetness or paper-thin words along with the suction there at each nipple. Marking me.

When I was fourteen I walked the overpass route to high school. The vista's strict measure was Lily Creek. From a momentary angle I could glimpse Nanny's stucco house and recalled other more childish times when this walk would have scared me. I am charging downhill late for homeroom again and dishevelled by the too-soon morning. Time's more than up. My stomach argues. On its return voyage my attention hooks on the tip of each breast and I slip inside each nipple, suddenly cruel, grimacing as needles pierce through the soft tissue. Two thin spikes the length of matchsticks flash into the story and then stick there, through its flesh. Who knows how the images become sewn into the hollow between brains. For a moment I am fourteen wearing black leather for a peep show. The cliff that drops down to Lily Creek's swamp is held separate by a civic installation of posts and link-chain. Law and order. Pain forgets itself at the same velocity as a body falling unconscious.

•

There was the absurdity and obvious boundary confusion of lying in bed between both of you while we read *By Grand Central Station* aloud. I remember I sat down and wept when you cooked the kidneys in my kitchen and I wanted you to leave finally, it was all too messy. I had never smelled such organ meat stewing in its juices. What had I done to deserve this!

•

I remember a mother's voice singing a throaty nighttime song as she sank down the stairwell and second, that I don't have any photos of her holding me.

I remember a father's operatic cowboy whistle waking us up Saturday mornings as he toasted the bread for exquisite western sandwiches. I have quite a few pictures of us playing.

The mother must have been holding the camera. My memory must hold her again and again, out in front of the father and me, gingerly, until I believe in this third dimension.

•

I have told far too many lovers they remind me of one parent or the other. Lovers do not, as a rule, like to hear this. Say instead, Kirk Douglas, or a political hero like Rosa Luxembourg. Keep relative memory to yourself.

•

Day by day my body ages like everyone else's. I carry tattoos of injuries and, more frequently, unpopular facial expressions. There was the wine-drenched boy who told me in the long run I'd choose women, he forecast it from my deep looking. This was just before we were about to have sex for the first time. Was he imagining his own father naked? He, discreetly, spoke of his family only in brief footnotes, like the crepe text unfolded from fortune cookies. Stories that last an hour and turn back into pumpkins, trundle down alleyways and sleep like dead acrobats. The contrast is its own excess. In a world like that triangles can't prop themselves upright. Horizons lead to dreams of conquest and booty for the queen, and cause me this vision problem.

•

It was a pussy love, but I guess you'll never know. The way a poor heart really feels, and why I loved her so. That year I chewed every mouthful thirty times, brushed my teeth with Pepsodent and secretly mailed the only heart-shaped locket my mother had ever given me to my grammar teacher

Mrs. Lindsey, whose birthday was on Valentine's Day. During the three weeks she was away in hospital for an unnamed operation I clutched tight to memories of her southern drawl. Maybe I thought, morbidly, she would never return. With one finger-snap she would banish the room lights and invent the humming of an overhead projector, floating prepositional clauses in haloes of greenish light just below the ceiling seam. We lifted our open gleaming jaws in unison to receive her confections, or so I choreographed. On every assignment I wanted her to mark me, and aah, she marked me well.

•

The place that is lunatic in me is imaginary. Where I have stored all of your images. Photographs are poor substitutes for the liquid desire experience motions as memory. After being touched indelibly by pleasure a cell dives from the body's surface to arc into the truth of the brain. One by one the grey cells turn hot pink. Telltale coda. The relationship is a triangular web suggested by the angle of the bakery door, swinging wide.

Re: Marks

Bisexual text.
Texture. Sure/unsure.
Sex. Bi-actual.

•

Currently, the most marketable sex either is bisexual or trades on popular notions of alternative sexualities, a 90s twist on 60s hedonism, along with grunge rock and body piercing. So to speak of bisexual identity as less than visible or privileged raises immediate problems. But in the same breath I do feel that the experiential texture of many bisexual lives is woefully eclipsed in both the straight and gay/lesbian viewfinders, leaving us outside operative imaginaries, dance clubs and community news-rags. Our culture is private, admitted over latenight telephone calls and under 100%-percale sheets only after we've known each other for a safe while. By-the-way-*sshhh*-sexual: I am.

•

Bisexual for me can mean being present. Letting go of all the I wases and I used to bes. Just is becomes admissible. Today and today and today: I ambi-sexual. Giving of myself with both hands and coming, clean.

•

The lexicon of contemporary identity politics forces closure, short and simple. "Bisexual" belongs to this look-book and its limits distress the bi-actual body and psyche. But our lips ache for naming, like any fact. Choose your poison, or poison your choice: by mime, be sexual. (Granted, this lip-syncing measure is ordinary practice for all identities.)

•

I live with a man and our infant son. Has it been easier to surround myself with "the male"? I prefer to ask what, in the context of the long term, is easy?

•

There is little to compare with a usually mainstream theatre filled with the gyrating pleasured bodies of women only en masse. We have feminist rallies, dances, a bar scene, at least in the major urban centres. A variety of bisexualities wrests space within this woman-on-woman social/political subculture, but usually garbed in dense emotional and material camouflage. Many straight women strive for that dyke hype now, so who's to tell? What's to know? Amid such manicured terrain, the bisexual "look" has few nets to fully want it, to catch it: neither the het net nor the homo net offers a similar balance of mesh and air, of clinch and space, of presence and absence. Both are (perhaps) less able to hold what is waiting in the wings.

•

In the touch is both memory and speculation. I want to harvest aspects of both in each encounter. No more boycotts. That's it. No more!

•

Not only is it simple and short, but naming self against an identity political creed promotes competition among claims. Since North American culture is vociferously individualistic, the more slots there are to fill, the more claimants climb out of the woodwork (what used to be called the "closet"). And clamouring to keep up, the more skeptics, a peculiar breed of vulture, inauthenticate the whole project. Ain't it just perfect that the new complaint is that it's becoming too crowded out here in the open!

•

It's incontestable that, in the private real realm, bisexual love and sex have a deep and hot history. What can this anthology offer? More than a space, a slice of the private intercut into the public: I hope for a spectrum. A fanning open of the notions "public" and "private," and of "fantasy" and "reality," where gender and sexual identification are framed, acted upon and fortified. Nowadays I'm pleased if and when "bisexual" happens even in the bluest of blue movies; when video rental stats affirm that Sharon Stone's real-life cemented heterosexuality continues to be far less interesting to a mass public than even the bi-murderous Catherine; when women plainly lust to know who that girl is as much as male viewers do. This is why, too, I read *Details* magazine. The popular imagination is escorting bisexuality into its commodifiably erotic hearth. Instead of seeing this as a dilution or appropriation of gay and lesbian facticity, I see it as an advocate wave gathering force against homophobia, and a useful tracer of a bi-actual presence. (In the way that black velvet paintings are useful tracers: tacky but true. True blue.)

•

Q: If bi-sexual is seen to be a-political, how would a bi-political fuck look?
A: Outward and inward, as far as the I can see.

TRACY CHARETTE FEHR Two Women © 1992
Pencil, pastel on paper

JOURNEYS OF
TRANSFORMATION

Tracy Charette Fehr

Accepting My Inherent Duality

I AM A THIRTY-FIVE-YEAR-OLD BISEXUAL WOMAN of Métis and Mennonite ancestry. Both my parents come from rural Manitoba. My mother's family is descended from the French Cree who lived in the Red River Settlement and fought in the Riel Rebellion. My father's family came to the prairies during the 1870s from Eastern Europe. My Métis ancestry runs on his side too, as his grandfather married a French Cree woman.

My parents grew up in communities close in proximity but far removed from one another in culture, language and religion. My mother's first language was French Métis and my father's first language was a low German dialect. They met and married in the 1950s. Because my mother was Catholic and my father Mennonite, they did not marry in either church and so each parent was excluded from their respective religious communities.

For most of my life, but especially after my mother's death when I was six, I have found myself straddling two identities; two cultures, two languages and two religions. Sometimes I feel as though I have been caught in an identity crisis since birth. Am I Métis or Mennonite, French or German, Protestant or Catholic, heterosexual or homosexual?

Recently I have come to appreciate, accept and understand more fully this conflict between my two selves. The biblical story of Rebecca reflects back to me the spiritual/emotional conflict within, as well as the resolution of new birth. The matriarch Rebecca is at first barren. After many years of marriage she finally conceives, but it is only after the extreme pain of a long labour and questions of faith that she gives birth to twins, "...two nations within herself." Rebecca emerges from a process that calls for profound faith and strength in the midst of despair and unknowing, what has been called the dark night of the soul, having given birth to two: a dreamer and a warrior.

This story speaks to me of my own journey: as bisexual, as Métis, as a recovering alcoholic, as an adult child of an alcoholic and as a survivor of childhood abuse. This path has not always been easy and it has often taken me, too, into the darkness. To be "in the darkness" is to be in a powerful place of transformation, somewhat akin to the womb or birth canal.[1] It is a place of power and potential. However, we sometimes fail to recognize positive power inherent in this experience of darkness and gestation until we have emerged into conscious awareness of the transformation that has occurred. What this difficult path has given me is enormous strength and much insight. Several years of healing and personal inventory have given me perspective and a renewed spirit. Out of this has grown an acceptance of my inherent duality: my bisexual, bicultural, bispiritual nature.

NOTE

1 Ann Decter elaborates on this important point in "Into the Darkness of Creation: An Editor's Journey" in By, For and About: Feminist Cultural Politics, ed. Wendy Waring (Toronto: Women's Press, 1994), 115-125.

Louise Bak

Soul-drought

Skewered
at eight
by a paper-mate rapier.
Retreated to dissociative antics
tessellating between
sticky-saccharine-white-picket-fenced-gardens
and
sunny-aqua-sparkling-Evian-queendoms.

Choking lessons
at twelve
from a wolf called neighbour.
Raged and ranted inwardly
in a labyrinthine inferno
while spit-o-ramming
and
washing the thick white fluid from my face.

Volatile
at sixteen
with past fuckery frigidized.
Pain coagulates with anger to
construct an arsenal of
don't-touch-me you S.O.B.s
and
mental icepicks perpetually poised.

The lifelings beckoned me
at nineteen
away from my emotional Gobi.
Up psyche scintillating peaks —
I bask in the luminosity of
revivifying love
and
unquenchable joy bursts over soul-drought.

Steph Rendino

Open Letter to a Teenaged Woman

THIS IS FOR YOU. I DON'T KNOW YOU PERSONALLY, but I'm writing this to tell you that you're not nuts or a slut if you find yourself wanting to kiss your boyfriend and your best female friend at the end of a great day together. Chances are you're bisexual, and that's just fine. You're not indiscriminate and you're not a lesbian who's just confused. This is how I figured it out.

I spent my teens in the mid-1980s. I had a boyfriend and some very good female friends. I loved them all in those days when the best bars in Washington, D.C., were gay and we didn't know about AIDS yet.

My then-boyfriend said he was gay-positive, but I think he had a problem coping with the idea of lesbians. I remember riding along in the car, eighteen and still trying to sort out this whole sex thing, and telling him I was attracted to women. He suggested I hit a bar and go home with a lesbian. I told him I couldn't do that; I'd have to love the woman first!

I remember my first encounter with a real, live lesbian and my reaction to her. She was in a one-shot, public access science fiction show and was chosen to play a general. So she was wearing a cool uniform that went wonderfully with her butch-short hair. She was talking to another woman about what it meant to her to be lesbian and later was the only one on the set who would stand up to the ditherings of the director. I thought she was great, but I was too shy to introduce myself.

When I broke up with my first boyfriend, several years of confusion followed. An experiment with anti-patriarchal dating (having two boyfriends simultaneously) blew up in my face. I guess the world wasn't ready and neither was I. I fell agonizingly in love with girlfriends and was terrified of letting them know, and, sister, was I jealous when they got engaged to guys! I theorized that my heterosexual attractions were just a passing phase and that I would find my lesbian footing eventually.

I finally discovered the word bisexual and applied it to myself. I came out to a friend of mine who had become a born-again Christian, more to be "in her face" than anything else. She of course asked the inevitable question, "Are you attracted to ME?" I wasn't and said so. She acted surprised, and a little offended. (And, teenager, they always do! I take this as a sign that more hets are really "one of us" than they will ever want to admit.)

I decided to become a nun because it was a life without men. I was delighted to see nuns who obviously had what are referred to as "particular friendships" sitting close with their arms around each others' waists with the other sisters either condoning or blessing their relationship. I wasn't so naive to think that there weren't long-time couples in the convent. I wondered if I would fall in love.

Well, I did, but with a guy, a very persistent guy from university. After a year of friendship we became lovers and I figured that I must be straight, even though hints of woman-love kept surfacing and surfacing in my emotions. Eventually, it became clear that it wasn't going to work out between us. I'm a seeker, always have been and always will be.

I got a cat, Badira. My then-lover was a rock-solid conservative American. This was at the time of the Iran-Contra scandal and he couldn't understand why I was so appalled. He didn't like my cat and Badira didn't like him. As I emerged from would-be nunhood I passed through a phase of non-threatening liberalism, and then started coming out as the woman-on-a-journey I have seen myself as for three years now.

Any rock-hard American pro-Reagan conservative with sense would have run away screaming. This one didn't, even though he knew I was in love with the woman I was living with. He and I were both miserable. He regarded me as being his, lock, stock and barrel, and I, rootless as I was, had to admit that I liked the stability and predictability if not the relationship. But he began standing in my way and at that point he had to go. It was easier than I thought. After three rocky years, I asked him to go and he went. Then my girlfriend and I settled down to happy domesticity.

Now I live with a feminist partner and two cats. I am a feminist writer and activist, definitely "out" about my bisexuality. I do protests, write articles and fiction and read Tarot. I work toward and look forward to a time when legal unions will not be sanctioned only on the basis of "one of each" but according to compatibility and the heart. I believe the concept of One Man Plus One Woman — based on marriage for reproduction and the passing on of property — is outdated and at this time sick.

So that, my dear nameless teenager, is my story. I know it's a little rambly, but I had a lot to say. Ultimately, my point is that, even though life can be confusing when you're young and bi, if you first off love yourself and devote yourself to finding out what's right for you, love for and from others will follow.

Pamela Lipshutz

The Creation of Myself

COMING OUT TO MYSELF TOOK ABOUT TWENTY-FOUR years. My process has included my sexuality as part of the totality of who I am as a person. How I came to view and feel about myself certainly affected why it took so long for me to come out as bisexual. I was physically and emotionally disabled as a child. The fashion in which I received my medical and psychiatric care taught me that I was at fault for the problems I had. I experienced a soul death: burying my sense of self, a happy, creative, free-spirited child facing frightening adult events. I was forced to deal with situations over which I had neither control nor adult knowledge and experience for coping. The emotions of terror and rage that I tried to express in response were invalidated, denied and ignored. My perception of how reality felt was made invisible by my caretakers who did not fulfill the responsibility of positively reflecting my sense of self and providing effective protective care. Now as an adult it is safer for me to be present in my body and in touch with my feelings. I have always associated my "intense" feelings toward females as wrong, sick and unacceptable. This is consistent with the way I have viewed myself in general. By connecting to and acknowledging my desire for both women and men, I have been able to discover who I am inside. My feelings of inner power, wholeness and self-love, and the ability to create my reality by changing my perceptions to form an existence that is healthy for me, have all contributed to feeling as though I am giving birth to myself in a spiritual sense.

Between the ages of seven and eighteen, I was under treatment for scoliosis. My spine was severely rotated and curved. Medical treatment meant numerous back braces and body casts extending from my head to my hips. I was frequently hospitalized through this eleven-year period. Between bleeding hips from the leather-bound brace, hot plaster applications from the casts, constant traction, losing total control of my body movement due to mobility restrictions and having very little contact with my family while hospitalized due to policies of enforcing isolation, I spent most of my childhood in a state of terror. I was also diagnosed with obsessive-compulsive neurosis — not too surprising since I was forced to endure these invasive medical procedures. I was also placed in special education from fourth to ninth grade where I was labelled mentally and emotionally disturbed. In fact the only "disturbance" I had was caused by all the medical and emotional abuse I endured. Years later I was to discover that I am also an incest survivor. Essentially I grew to view myself as sick, ugly and defective. I was labelled a "problem child." In painful contrast, my sister was labelled a "model" child. Shame was the foundation of my sense of self. Looking back over my relationships from childhood up to the present, I see how carrying and eventually healing from shame had been a key to how my sexuality and sense of self are integrated.

I had a series of significant relationships in my childhood that I now realize were early crushes or infatuations. We had a thirteen-year-old sitter named Janet. I was only nine and thought she was so sophisticated though somewhat stuck up. I also admired how mature and strong she seemed. I know now that I had a hidden crush on her. Our other sitter, Sharon, was wonderful, but I didn't feel drawn to her in quite the same way. I adored my third-grade teacher. I loved the way she read to our class *Pippi Longstocking*, a story about a very independent, mischievous little girl. How I longed to be like Pippi! I was so fond of my teacher that I gave her a gift for Valentine's Day. While in her class I noticed children disappearing from the school and wondered where they were going. Then I too was transferred out. I discovered that these classmates were shipped to a special school for disabled children.

While at the special school I met a boy named Jay who was wheelchair bound. We became good friends, despite my being frightened of his very shortened arms. During rehearsals for a class play, I hid behind his wheelchair because I didn't want anyone to see my brace. At this time I was experiencing compulsive behaviours in which I felt I had to periodically touch the ground. In addition to taking drugs to control these behaviours, I also needed to hold Jay's wheelchair as a way to control this embarrassing behaviour during rehearsals. I felt ashamed of these compulsions for many years. As our friendship grew, he gave me a silver necklace engraved with "To Pam, Love Jay." I was so flattered that someone liked me! I still have his gift. The same day I received his gift I was taken away without my prior knowledge to be committed to a hospital. I never saw Jay again.

I spent my tenth birthday in an adult psychiatric hospital unit. A few months after I was released, my family moved to Boston, Massachusetts. I continued with special education in a program that was located in a college setting for children considered to have psychological problems. By now I was convinced I was a piece of stupid, worthless junk. I also experienced frequent anxiety attacks which had begun before we moved up from Florida. To add to my esteem issues, a boy named Jackie used to call me "Joey Neck" because I wore the back brace. He treated me like the class freak. He never hesitated to bestow his attention on me by spitting, kicking and generally treating me like an ugly animal. I was terrified of him. Thank heavens he was transferred out after the first year. Also during this time, I became friends with a thirteen-year-old redheaded girl named Robin. She seemed sweet and tried to take me under her wing. Though she was only nine months older than me, I really looked up to her. We sat together on the school bus, and the smell of her cologne sent electric sparks shooting through me. I could not look at her without melting. Unfortunately, after the first year she was transferred out. The next year I developed a crush on a very handsome boy named Robert. That summer I attended an all-girls' camp. The other girls seemed to be so much more mature than me. I felt socially retarded and so ashamed of my body. I felt attracted to one of the girls who was athletic and husky in build. I was embarrassed about my feelings. I felt the need to keep them well hidden, and this caused me much pressure.

I was transferred to a special education class at a regular school which gave me the opportunity to attend some classes with "normal" kids. Believing I was stupid, I felt terrified of being in any regular classes in this school. I declined the opportunity because I felt out of place. On the other hand, I was thrilled because Barbara, a teacher from my other school, had also been transferred here. She was beautiful and sweet. As the year progressed, I became obsessed with thoughts of Barbara, constantly writing about her in my diary and incessantly talking about her to my family. I would spend hours in front of the mirror trying to make my appearance resemble Barbara's. I thought she had the sexiest lips. I used to peek at her thighs when she crossed her legs in her miniskirt.

I was finally transferred to the high school, where I was placed in Mr. L.'s special education homeroom. Again, I felt total terror at suddenly being placed into regular classes. Unlike the other students, I had not gone through the previous grades. I anticipated I would be found to be either mentally retarded or at least so lacking in any academic learning abilities that I would drown instantly. I felt socially embarrassed at being a sixteen-year-old freshman when other sixteen-year-old students were juniors in high school. Mr. L. was my first-year crush with his big dancing dark eyes and thick curly dark hair. I was in total lust with him. I felt so relieved to be attracted to a male too! After my obsession with Barbara at age fifteen, I had been certain I was emotionally abnormal, physically ugly and I had essentially wanted to die.

In tenth grade, I was transferred to a regular homeroom along with attending basic level classes (as opposed to honour level which my sister was in). After about seven years of missing regular school, I was officially out of special education at age seventeen. My self-esteem was shot and I had no concept of what self-confidence meant, let alone felt like. I assumed a student's knowledge built up through each grade level. Kathy was in my tenth-grade homeroom class. I was introduced to her by my sister the year before. She appeared very bright, independent and self-assured, and she liked me! By the end of the year I idolized her. I spoke of her constantly; I even wrote a poem about her. My feelings toward her grew very strong by eleventh grade. I became very uncomfortable and paranoid that others would know. I also had another crush in eleventh grade on Billy, a sweet, shy, handsome boy. Feeling ugly inside from the brace, I was certain no boy would want me.

I had corrective spinal surgery around age seventeen and a half, wearing three different body casts in a nine-month period. I would lie in the hospital bed, unable to move due to the surgical manipulation of my spine, and think of Kathy. I would have conversations with her in my head (which would continue in years to come), telling her how comforting it felt for me to think of her when I felt alone and scared. This was a powerful connection I was forming. I, who felt literally that my power was non-existent as a patient and a person, projected Kathy as an image of strength and love that I wanted, needed and could not acquire within.

After the braces and casts were finally off, I felt as if a part of me had died. I had become the brace. My entire life had revolved around the brace, and it was suddenly gone.

In twelfth grade, I wanted to spend as much time as possible around Kathy. I felt intoxicated by her. My physical feelings for her were so strong that I felt tense around her. I did not want her to know what I was feeling, yet I felt driven to be around her because it also felt wonderful. Now at age nineteen, preparing to graduate from high school, I was praying these intense feelings toward females would go away.

I entered Mitchell College and met Steve. Though he was sweet, I was not attracted to him. He ended up marrying a dorm friend of mine, Lynn, to whom I myself felt strongly drawn. I was almost twenty-one years old. My dad said one becomes an adult at age twenty-one — how wrong he was! Because of this "coming of age" concept, I thought these strong feelings of attraction for females were therefore supposed to disappear. Sharon was another woman in the dorm, who was large and very boyish. The other "jock-type" girls were spreading a rumour about her possibly being gay because her dorm-mate "thought she watched her as she dressed." I ended up being dorm-mates with Sharon and found her warmth and protective nature wonderful. Years later I heard she married and had children (which does not necessarily indicate one's sexual preference). I secretly hoped she might be bisexual.

I felt like a social isolate at college. I continued to identify myself as someone who had worn a brace and had been in special education. Kathy and I visited during school breaks. Once I took her out to a French restaurant. As she drove me home she began to cry, saying she loved me. In total shock, I was convinced she was trying to say she was "in love" with me. I had secretly hoped she was having feelings toward me, but that it was difficult for her to express them. I held her hand and embraced her. I was in heaven and could have easily considered this moment as one of the happiest in my life thinking my high-school love was also in love with me. At this point Kathy knew my affection was different from hers.

After graduating from Mitchell College, I met Billy back in my hometown. I told him how I had had a crush on him in high school. Apparently he had noticed me too! After dating for one year we broke up. I was influenced by my sister who felt I "could do better with someone having more of a future." This of course was a prejudicial and classist attitude, but I had always turned to my sister for guidance. Looking back now I realize my self-esteem was so low that I knew anything or anyone that I liked couldn't really be good enough since I wasn't good enough. I empowered my sister to judge the value of what was really worthy. After all, I was nothing, and she was God to me. I realize now that I strongly identified with Billy because he too had low self-esteem.

At age twenty-four I met Howard. We lived together for five years. He was fun-loving, romantic and inspiring. At last I thought I had met the perfect person. His confidence helped me feel secure. This relationship could be serious and prove I was really attracted to men. He thought we should have "stability in our lives prior to marriage, thus establish our careers." I realize now this turned into a form of control by him, since I felt pressured into finding a life career or he wouldn't "have me."

When I was twenty-five, just before I decided on my nursing career, my dad suddenly died at age fifty-seven. Initially I felt devastated and deeply depressed, and experienced panic attacks. As time passed I felt an emotional weight begin to lift. Along with my sorrow (as I had deeply loved him), I unexpectedly experienced a new sense of freedom. My dad was no longer able to make me feel stupid, sexually objectified or unloved. After my dad's death, I gradually felt safer to allow my true self to emerge, including my bisexuality.

During this time of mourning my dad's death, Howard became more controlling and self-righteous about his ways and demanded that I comply with what he thought was best for me. This occurred over a couple of years, cloaked in "love and concern" for me. Years later I took a course that included the topic of "Women in Abusive Relationships" and realized that I had experienced emotional battery, which is insidious. Because I had low self-esteem, I began believing that all of Howard's corrections and criticisms about me were right. I began to fashion how I ate, dressed, my frequency of sex, likes and dislikes to what he defined as ideal. He became withdrawn, silent and critical if I suggested something I wanted or liked. When I left Howard I struggled to replicate everything I had had with him. No longer under his direct control, I internalized the abuse by attempting to think and function the way he might have. This included how I performed daily activities. I tried to replace household items with identical or similar types of objects that we had shared. I left what is termed a "strangulating utopia." In other words, I was suffocating but he kept claiming our relationship was perfect.

The year before I left Howard I began obsessing about Kathy

again. My sister even suggested I call her to say I was in love with her and wanted to live with her. Now twenty-eight years old and attending Northeastern University as a nursing major, I began noticing women at school and wondering if they were lesbian. Suddenly I was overwhelmed with these "gay" feelings...(again). It felt hellish because as an adult I was supposed to have "outgrown" this gay business.

Kathy and I visited several months after I left Howard. I finally decided I had to tell her the nature of my feelings toward her. I was terrified she would walk out in disgust. As I explained to her that I had strong feelings for her and that thoughts of her were comforting to me when I felt afraid, she interrupted by saying, "You mean you find me attractive?" "Yes!" I exclaimed. Her posture suddenly changed, becoming softened. She said she had had a suspicion since our dinner at the French restaurant and had been waiting for me to say something. I still was not self-acknowledging lesbian feelings. I was certain that Kathy was absolutely the only woman toward whom I would ever have these emotions. At this point, I began dating "nice Jewish boys," aggressively hoping to marry and replace Howard.

I met Toni, a classmate, at Northeastern the following year. Later she introduced me to David, an ex-boyfriend of hers. David and I began to date and after I graduated he moved in with me. The relationship ended after eighteen months. Meanwhile, Toni and I got closer as friends. Having known her for several years I grew in admiration of her free-spirited and fun-loving manner. One evening we had dinner at my house. We sat on the couch and I asked if I could hug her. She said "Sure!" and jumped up to hug me. We cuddled for what felt like an eternal bliss. As it got later, she suggested she sleep over. I was puzzled as to where she would sleep. She suggested a pajama party in my bedroom. With a quizzical look, I agreed. She was going to sleep with me!? That night changed my life. I experienced passion and tenderness differently from anything I had ever felt from a heterosexual exchange. I was also terrified, having never been with a woman in an intimate, physical, sexual way before. For years I had been curious but terrified to try it. I was amazed how naturally the interaction came to me. The next day at work I felt confused and guilty. What had I done?

Several days passed and I began to make connections for myself. A series of thoughts became clear: the emotions I began feeling for Toni (adoration, passion and deep caring) were similar to the emotions I had experienced with Kathy. This combined with the enjoyment of sex with Toni told me I was a fledgling lesbian. I felt terrified. All the prejudices and myths I had learned about how abnormal homosexuality was came screaming out at me. I also knew what my personal experience was — wonderful! I could not wait to enjoy the treasures and pleasures of another woman again.

I began seeking connections with the gay community. The Cambridge Women's Center had a newsletter listing support groups. The title "bisexual women's support meeting" popped out at me. Having been alienated from my own feelings for so long, I felt as though a light had gone on. Seeing the term "bisexual," I started to realize that it meant having the potential for deep feelings toward both genders. I already knew what a straight attraction was because of all the examples I saw around me over the years. Having witnessed no role models for positive gay experience and being soul-dead at such a young age, it had taken all these years for me to connect with myself as bisexual and to connect with the world as a bisexual being. That was it, I thought, I am bisexual! Toni also introduced me to Wicca or Witchcraft, a feminine divine religion. New worlds began opening for me.

I began attending political rallies, and going to all the groups in the bi-network. I felt as if another dimension of myself was being revealed. I attended a rally protesting a public policy against gays and lesbians being adoptive parents. Television cameras were everywhere. I felt strong, yet scared I'd be seen on T.V. That June, at age thirty-three, I attended my first Gay Pride celebration. I had remembered back in the early 1980s driving through Boston, seeing lots of festive activity and noticing two men kissing. I was so surprised and happy that they could actually do that. Now I was in the midst of it. I attended the bi-brunch, bought a "Bisexual Pride" T-shirt and began walking outside. I felt overwhelming anxiety to be on the streets of Boston with a label across my chest, but I had to do it. I even carried the bi-banner in the Gay Pride parade.

I continued to seek all the resources that existed in the les-bi-gay community. By 1989 I had joined the lesbian-gay help line at a local community health centre (as part of my career search). While taking a class on the history of gay and lesbian lifestyles I was confronted with biphobia. During a discussion, students began expressing how people couldn't have feelings toward both genders. They claimed that anyone who called themselves "bisexual" was really afraid of their homosexual feelings and couldn't commit to really being gay. I was so angry and astonished that I spoke up and explained that in fact bisexuality is a very valid identity. Sometimes it is a phase, but it is also a way of life whose expression is as varied as a gay or straight lifestyle. The instructor later told me he was very impressed by my impromptu presentation and recommended I consider joining the les-bi-gay Speakers' Bureau. As a member of the Speakers' Bureau, I have visited several colleges and organizations giving presentations about bisexuality. I have discovered many pervasive myths including: "bisexuals are never happy with one partner," "bisexuals are always missing the opposite of whatever gender they are with at a given moment," "bisexuals are fence-sitters because they won't commit to either a straight or gay lifestyle," "bisexuals will rush off to be with the opposite gender once the homophobia gets too rough," "bisexuals always have to be engaging in sex." I tell the audience that bisexuals are as varied as the rest of the population. People can identify as bisexual, lesbian, gay or straight and may be celibate.

I have read many books on feminist politics and religion, Witchcraft and lesbian separatist ideology. Through this literature I learned that I have the power inside myself to define myself. Wiccan literature speaks of spiritual self-empowerment — being responsible for shaping one's own reality. I began to learn I have my own reality and that I can shape it. I have finally found a community with a large, ancient culture and history to which I can connect. Since my sexuality began to surface, my entire being has come out of the damn closet!

With the assistance of an excellent therapist, I have learned I am a survivor of lots of trauma and abuse. I have learned I am not to blame for my medical and emotional problems. My lesbian and feminist feelings are okay and I can feel proud to be me; this is a new feeling. I had learned to see myself as bad, evil and shameful. I now know that I was shamed by others. My feelings had never been validated. As part of my coming out process, I have evolved to refer to myself as bisexual/lesbian. I realize the vast spectrum of sexual feelings I have experienced. Prior to acknowledging my lesbian feelings I was behaviorally heterosexual and homophobic. Now I am celebrating my lesbian feelings as a bisexual being. Thus I use the phrase bisexual/lesbian to denote that I have the potential for attraction and romantic love for either gender, but currently have a stronger affinity toward women. By claiming my own descriptive terms, I claim who I am. Additionally, my feminist spirituality and philosophy have recently (1993) given me the strength to cope with the removal of both my breasts due to breast cancer. I have indeed given birth to myself. I am more than a back-brace and cancer patient. I am in fact a bright, creative, strong and attractive person.

Elehna de Sousa

In the Spirit of Aloha:
to love is to share the happiness of life here & now

T HE ISSUE OF MY SEXUALITY HAS BEEN SOMEWHAT
confusing to me of late. In fact, these days, there are times I wonder
if I am still a sexual being at all. Although I'd like to think that I've
finally evolved beyond the desires of my base chakra, in actual fact, I may be
simply suffering from serious burnout. Then again, perhaps I'm getting in
touch with some deep-seated developmental trauma, or past-life influence
(with its resulting impact on my present life). It is possible that I'm a 100-
percent pure lesbian, maybe a late bloomer, but I honestly haven't been with
enough women to know. Just recently, however, my doctor did send me for
hormone tests, convinced that my testosterone levels were abnormally
elevated. I wondered how she could tell. I thought that my external persona
was fairly feminine. Maybe she needs the money to maintain her lifestyle.

I think the truth of the matter is the fact that I'm just plain terrified
of intimacy after two full years of self-enforced celibacy. There was one
other time I made a conscious decision to eliminate sex in my life: it was in
the summer of 1984. I needed to figure out some things — exactly *what* I
wasn't sure, but it had something to do with the fact that my sex life with
men left me feeling shut down and unfulfilled. During this hiatus, I discovered that it caused me far less grief to channel my physical desires into career goals, and that is exactly where they went full time for a year and a half.

Then, to my fascination, I discovered that I had something called
sexual chemistry with women. This exciting turn of events unleashed a
passion within me unlike anything I had ever known before. Until four years
and three dysfunctional relationships later, when I made another conscious
decision in the direction of celibacy.

This time I knew I had to do some serious figuring out. I was
determined to get some concrete answers to my growing dilemma of sexual
confusion. As my only daughter grew up and moved away, I knew that it was
time. The moment was ripe for me to discover my own dream and to dance
it awake.

To ease the transition into my new life, my *ku* presented me with a mysterious illness for which modern medicine had no name. I lay in the safety of my bed for many weeks, drifting in and out of past dreams, learning to let go and full of fear, wondering if I was to live or die.

With breath held tight and heartbeat erratic, I knew the choice was ultimately mine.

In time, my power animal came to rest beside me, easing my pain and guiding me through the void of my life, across the seas to a place of magic. I was taken to the ancient and sacred island of Kuai, and left with a message that said, simply: THIS IS YOUR REALITY NOW.

I find myself in Anahola Bay, at the meeting place of the river and the sea, a border zone, where dreams become real. I thank my *amakua* for the protection and guidance I have received on this journey, and ask for clear direction on the path ahead. As my prayer moves beyond my lips to travel over the sand, sea, clouds and up into the sunlight, I know a shift has already occurred.

MY REALITY BEGINS FROM THIS MOMENT ON.

As directed by the map in my hand, I follow the red hearts to Angeline's place, an oasis of relaxation, love and ancient Hawaiian healing.

I was told to allow four hours for the treatment. Not bad for seventy-five dollars, I thought.

First, the cards are read. I turn mine over to discover that I have picked the Two of Cups...the card of balance, unity and perfect polarity between male and female. The next card I draw says simply: Synthesis. I breathe a sigh of relief at these good omens, which bode well for the resolution to my dilemma.

The next phase of the treatment takes me to the steamroom, the temple of purification through fire and water. I remove the floral pareo, draped modestly around my body, letting it fall into Angeline's arms.

Lying on the grass mat, naked and sweating, my brown body quickly melts into the heat and the rhythm of her firm hands.

"Auntie Angeline, tell me what you know about bisexuality in ancient times," my eager mind queries impatiently, as soon as it finds a space in which to speak. "The two-spirited ones were special, honey," she murmurs, rubbing a mixture of coarse salt and red clay into my skin. "They were often the great shamans and healers in our society. They knew how to be truly expansive with their love, sharing *aloha* with no limits...yes, they were very special indeed."

KALA: THERE ARE NO LIMITS. My mind drifts back to one of the basic shamanic truths I had read about. It seemed to fit.

"Breathe deep, honey, just let your body and soul open to the love...take it in, it's here for you now..." She croons softly, continuing to stroke my body with loving attention.

The thick steam encompasses us in a cocoon of wet fire.

"Love this body, it is yours...so beautiful, and serving you so well...without this beautiful body you would not be on earth."

New energy begins to awaken within me, tingling, prickling, moving through my arms and legs.

"Keep breathing, honey," she reminds me, kneading my buttocks and rotating my pelvis. "We'll get the *mana* flowing free..."

Even as my body lets go, melting into the heat of Angeline's hands, my mind, ever active, continues to struggle.

I, a grown woman of forty, once married, now single, with a teenaged daughter, and still unclear about my gender identity: How can I ask the universe for my perfect mate when I don't even know whether I want a man or a woman? It's true, I haven't been all that attracted to the male species in recent years, but then once in a while there's that certain spark of chemistry that can't be ignored. Maybe I am a late lesbian bloomer after all. I guess I'll have to get involved again to find out. At my age, and with the growing AIDS crisis, just how much experimentation can one person do?

Perhaps I'm polysexual. Is there such a word? I remember the time when I sat in the tropical sun beside a coconut tree, receptive and open. Slowly, on invitation, I moved closer, wrapping my body around its slender trunk, my hands caressing its bark with tenderness. In that divine moment of sensuality and magnetism, the tree and I merged, joined together in ecstasy like familiar lovers.

A stream of cold mountain water washes abruptly over my body, taking me by surprise, as red salt, clay and sweat fall to the ground, preparing me for the next stage of *lomi-lomi*.

"Stay open, darling, expand your beautiful self...take in the love...it's all here for you right now."

My consciousness continues to drift lazily over a bridge of

memories. Past loves, bodies soft and curvaceous, muscular and taut. I remember a picture I drew so long ago in an androgyny workshop, a being complete with breasts and penis. The perfect balance. Male and female. Yin and Yang.

Eyes closed, I hear the wooden door creak open to let someone else into this temple of love.

I become aware of both Angeline and Michael bending over me now, caressing, kneading, moving out the tension with warm oil. The fragrances of eucalyptus and coconut fill my nostrils with pleasure.

"Let go now, just trust...trust your beautiful body," I hear soft voices whisper into each ear. "You deserve to be loved...it is time for you to be truly happy." I tremble with delight as gentle lips lightly brush against my forehead, cheeks and heart centre. Electric energy travels from the soles of my feet to the crown of my head, coursing through my physical frame like a river unleashed and about to flood.

My tired mind finally gives in, abandoning its struggle in favour of a blissful truce with my waiting body. Together they dance, flowing into the steam and beyond.

I begin to soar, flying as free as the tropical birds I have seen over the Hawaiian surf. Tears of release and relaxation stream down my cheeks, blending with the rivulets of sweat and oil on my neck.

My *amakua* joins with me in this moment of ecstasy, sending the message of *Huna* even deeper into my soul.

IKE. KALA. MANAWA. MANA. I hear the words clearly and directly. I repeat these ancient truths, letting them flow forth from my spirit as effortlessly as birds are carried in currents of wind. Over and over I chant until the words crescendo into a symphony of silent sound, exploding into the emptiness of my universe.

In this moment of enlightenment I understand the truth of my quest.

This world is but a dream to which we give life. I do not need to know whether my perfect partner will be a man or a woman. I only need to remember how to step into the dream of my desire in order to make it real. I know that with focus, clear intent and harmony of spirit, my partner's dream and my own dream will find each other, manifesting into one reality of love and completion.

I send off a silent prayer of thanks for the wisdom teachings I have learned, for the knowledge that life and love are unlimited and for the spirit of *aloha* that surrounds me on this sacred island.

AMAMA, UA NOA, LELE WALEA KUA LA.

So be it; It is completed; fly off and manifest.

MAHALO.

GLOSSARY

ku: the subconscious.

amakua: power animal, spirit guide. Also means Higher Self, superconscious.

aloha: love, joy; to love is to share the happiness of life here and now.

mana: life force, animating energy that runs the body.

lomi-lomi: a unique form of Hawaiian bodywork.

Huna: esoteric teachings of Hawaiian shamanism.

IKE: The world is what you think it is.

KALA: There are no limits.

MANAWA: Now is the moment of power.

MANA: All power lies within.

AMAMA, UA NOA, LELE WALEA KUA LA: closing phrase used at the end of a blessing.

MAHALO: I give thanks.

Cyndy Head

Changing Beliefs

WHAT IS IT LIKE TO BE BI? WHAT IS IT LIKE to be straight? No, that's not a fair question. You can't really describe what it's like to be bi or female or tall to someone who isn't. I identified as straight for many years. I was one of those straight women who had perfectly normal, healthy fantasies about other women. They were useful when sex with a man wasn't being very interesting. How did I come to identify as bi? Let me tell you a story....

I grew up in a white middle-class neighbourhood. I was the only black child in my public school. My mother was, as far as I knew, the only woman in the neighbourhood who was divorced, had a full-time job and a university education. I grew up feeling different. By the time I reached high school, I had a pretty healthy scorn for those who ran with the crowd and an equally healthy cynicism. In my twenties, I began trying on labels — model, mistress, student, self-supporting (and low income), preppie, Queen St. cool, etc. I was struggling with my identity. When the journey that led to my acceptance of bisexuality began, I had just dumped the label of "B's together girlfriend" and I felt used and abused. My life was full of contradictions — working in and believing in collective action while living with a military man, fantasizing about women while being with a man. I had lost my sense of self — my self-confidence, my interests, my sense of humour and a few friends. Because B preferred more buxom women, I had come to dislike my body and everything about myself. My sexuality had become B's. I behaved in ways that he found arousing, expressed my desire in ways that he found acceptable. I had told B about my fantasies. He thought that fantasies were imaginary and normal but that attractions were real feelings and that same-sex attractions were abnormal. I kept my attractions and fantasies hidden like secret treasures that could only be looked at when I was alone. I had never heard the word bisexual. I wasn't even aware of the concept.

So, on a hot day in July, B headed east to a new city and I prepared to go west. I was going to drive a car to Victoria, sort out my problems and start a new life. I had shipped most of my belongings ahead of me and had only what would fit in the car. I also had four weeks to wait until my departure date. Like any good middle-class woman who wants to be loved forever but doesn't know how to change herself so that it can happen, I headed for the self-help section of my favourite book store. I soon found myself in the Women's Spirituality section where Starhawk, Zsuzanne Budapest and others were crying to be read. When I finally boarded a bus to Victoria (the car deal having fallen through), I was reading about one woman's journey into herself.

There I sat, engrossed in a book (*Map to Ecstasy* by Gabrielle Roth) that promised to show me how to free my body, express my heart, awaken my soul and embody my spirit. It didn't involve starving myself, getting up at indecent hours or a rigid routine — perfect for a Taurus. Ecstasy was defined as "a state of total aliveness and unity — unity of body, heart, mind, soul, and spirit." It was an expression of God(dess) and I wanted it. I wanted to feel whole again. I wanted to be me and not an extension of B. Gabrielle made feelings and expressing them seem honourable; she didn't hide the body and sexuality. That was chapter one. If she didn't have to hide her sexuality, neither did I. It didn't occur to me at the time that straight women have less to hide.

In between naps and rest stops, I re-thought a lot of my beliefs. Where had they come from? Did they truly reflect my thoughts and feelings? Did they serve me well? I discovered that many of them were adopted from parents, siblings and friends. If I did hold a belief that was different from someone important to me, I kept it to myself in an attempt to fit in. When I thought about my sexual beliefs I realized that they didn't correspond to how I felt. I defined my sexuality through limitations — what I didn't do, who I didn't sleep with. When I asked myself why I didn't sleep with women, the answers were "because my family and friends would flip out" and "because I've always been with men." I had so little in common with most of the men that I knew that it didn't really make sense to spend time with them at all.

They say that receiving a shock can change your perspective on things. Sleep deprivation works as well. Add to it a healthy dose of anger and the inspiration provided by Gabrielle's story, and you get a state of mind fertile for new ideas. A loving Goddess made more sense than a punishing

Christian God. Material possessions paled under the importance of my emotional and spiritual life. A vision of a more harmonious life began to grow. The phrase "a whole person" began to mean someone who had healed the wounds inflicted on them rather than someone who had studied both sciences and humanities. Somewhere in the middle of the prairies, my fantasies changed from a "normal straight" thing to desire for women.

By the time I reached Victoria, my new ideas had sunk into my heart and a sense of peace had developed. I felt stronger. I felt reassured by my new map for healing. I was looking at "people" as sources of positive or negative energy rather than at "men" as a source of bad relationships, and "women" as a source of good friendships. I wanted to meet some happy, loving, spiritual people. My trust was with the Goddess. I wasn't able to hail a cab but I was totally calm about it.

I spent the next few months visiting art galleries and museums as well as beaches and mountains. I cycled, swam, ice skated and meditated. I continued to read all kinds of spiritual literature from books on Catholicism to books channelled by spiritual entities. I wanted to understand it all. I was so full of confidence and peacefulness. I felt like the Earth Mother herself with roots reaching all the way to the earth's core. Every aspect of myself was perfect, everything about me was right for me. During those few months, I allowed my new ideas and self-acceptance to take root.

A few months later, I returned to Toronto and got caught up in the pursuit of outside love and approval again. One day I saw a book on a co-worker's desk called *Bi Any Other Name* and I thought, "Hey, that's me!" I grabbed it from her desk and left a note saying I'd borrowed it. I had a new label — that meant outside recognition of who I had become. It meant belonging to a group without having to conform, because the book made it clear that bisexuality isn't about right and wrong or about how one speaks or dresses.

Acknowledging my sexuality wasn't necessarily the most important or difficult part of my journey but it was the first big step. This journey has led me to other countries and to many interesting people. It has resulted in changes in lifestyle and a lot of learning. Part of loving myself is acknowledging, accepting and respecting every aspect of myself — my body, my beliefs, my feelings, my sexuality, my spirituality, my tie to the earth that nourishes and supports me. Recently, belonging to a group has ceased to be important to me again. My sense of belonging goes deeper than black or white, bi or straight. Deeper than labels. Perhaps it comes from a sense of something larger than myself or a deeper peace within myself. Perhaps it comes from a more open loving way of being with people. What is important to me is *that* I love and *who* I love, not the gender of individuals. Along with this sense of peace has come a feeling of great strength. The trick now is learning to maintain these feelings in a crazy, busy world.

My sexuality is part of the union of body, mind, heart and spirit. As one evolves, so do the others and the journey toward self, spirit and happiness continues.

Camie Kim

People Say I'm Crazy

THERE WERE THINGS MARY WAS GOING TO DO in her life, eventually, when she was older and a little wiser, and had finished with the things she was doing right now. She thought that her thirties would be a good time — to be exotic and bohemian, to go to Paris and smoke Gitanes and make love to many men and many women. Of course it would all just be temporary and speculative. She didn't want to expend too much energy on experimentation. It was enough to do it, and then to be able to say that she had done it. Mary admitted, somewhat proudly, that she was really just a collector at heart.

She was going to be an artist. She sketched, painted, took photographs and created installations. Her work had even appeared in several shows like *outside/inside* and *Brave New Art*. True, they had all been organized by friends or friends of friends, and there were always other names alongside her own on the slapdash posters.... But one day soon, just not yet, critics would hail her work as disturbing, challenging, politically astute and subtly compelling. There would be reaction, respect, and, at long last, remuneration. Until then, there were reviews to write for the school paper, rejections to justify from various art journals, openings to attend and plenty of cheap white wine to drink.

Mary was in art school. She admitted this sheepishly to the man who was cutting her hair. (There were many things in her life for which Mary felt slightly apologetic.) She had to repeat it twice because of the music blaring from the speakers in each corner of the room. The walls and ceiling were covered in what looked like tin foil and were vibrating in time with the music. Mary attempted a joke about feeling like microwave popcorn. Francis looked up into the mirror at her and squinted. He seemed rather surprised by the sound of her voice. As if her hair had suddenly started talking. Francis himself had black hair hanging down to his chin and over one eye. Mary thought he looked like a pirate. The ends of his sweater sleeves had been unravelled and the dangling fringes brushed against Mary's face. By the time Mary lifted a hand in order to brush the fringes away, they were already gone.

Mary stared at the the postcards taped onto the mirror: 'The Job That Ate My Brain"; "Silence = Death"; Rosy the Riveter. Francis nodded energetically whenever Mary said something and danced and sang and cut her hair. Snip, snip would go the scissors. Snap, snap his fingers. "Isn't 'art school' an oxymoron?" Francis asked slyly, and Mary closed her eyes and thought: If he cuts me I'll sue. Snip, snip, snap, snap. Francis asked her if she wanted it shorter. Mary opened her eyes. Maybe.

There were drawing classes on Tuesday evenings. This month they were sketching nudes. Amy was one of the models. Her body was strong and lithe and whenever she was the model Mary had to tell herself to concentrate on drawing and not on Amy. "Totallyfuckinghopeless," she would mutter and the student next to her would glance over curiously. Mary found Amy attractive and it pleased her that she could feel this way. It felt — liberating. But she could never draw Amy properly, or in any way at all, could not capture that long, oval face and those eyes that looked back at you levelly as she slowly disrobed. Pencils, charcoal, pastels, nothing worked. There was something about Amy, something either fleeting or inexpressible, that Mary wanted to see on paper but never saw. So she worked on, muttering, frustrated — elated.

The sheen of perspiration on her forehead. The taut line of her throat. A birthmark on the shoulder. Full breasts with dark areolae. The length of her fingers. A ring with a blue stone. Skin the colour of milky tea. The faintest of scars — appendix? The curve of her hips. A bruise on the back of a thigh. The muscles of her calves. A thin silver chain around an ankle. Pink polish on her nails.

Mary knows if she can fall in love with someone the first time she looks into the eyes. It's how they look at her and how they make her look back. Amy's eyes were the most beautiful she had seen in quite a while. When she saw them and they saw her, Mary knew just how long it had been. The third time Amy modelled she came up to Mary after the class and asked her if she wanted to go for a drink. She was still naked and her face was flushed with the warmth of the overheated room. The dark curls of her hair had been tied up and off of her face but a few tendrils had escaped and stuck damply to her skin. Mary thought of reaching out to smooth the hair back into place. She thought: If this was a student film, that's what I would do.

Mary was working on a series of "self-portraits." She liked to think of herself as the Cindy Sherman of paint. In the past she had used mostly acry-lics and sometimes pieces of wood or metal and the carefully cut-and-pasted pages of magazines. Now she was experimenting with watercolours and think-ing of doing frescoes. She painted herself as Joan of Arc, as Emma Bovary, as Ophelia. She painted herself into crucifixion scenes, or into still lifes. In each one she affixed a black-and-white photograph of her face onto the head. In the still lifes the face appeared on the curve of a piece of fruit, nestled amongst other fruit or atop the neck of a dead pheasant. It seemed to always be the same photo, grainy, slightly out of focus, the expression on the face one of mild surprise, as if Ophelia was thinking: How did I end up here?

Mary drove and they headed downtown over the bridge. The moun-tains rose above the city, blacker against the black sky. The lights of the office towers hung suspended in the fog and the street lamps shimmered in the rain, glowing. Mary thought of that painting, the one with all the stars, and imagined herself floating beatifically amidst them...They went to a wo-men's bar. It was the first time Mary had ever been in such a place, although she had vaguely known of their existence. It looked like any other sleazy eastside bar. There were even some men, Mary thought, but then she rea-lized that they were women. She was glad that she hadn't pointed them out.

There were dart boards on a wall and a pool table in a room off to the side. Gradually, Mary got used to the dark and the noise. A slow Ferron song drifted its way toward her through the smoke and women were dancing in couples, closely, leaning against each other. At one end of the floor a tall woman in a very short dress had her arms around another woman in jeans and boots. They were frantically kissing. Mary didn't know what to make of this. She wanted to ask someone what to think. She found it both repulsive and arousing. It made her feel conventional. It made her feel — insipid. She didn't want to be caught staring.

Amy came back with their beers and they sat in a booth across from each other and talked. There was a surprising amount to say and they both found the time in which to say it all too short. Mary didn't circle warily or hide behind wisecracks. Instead she asked too many questions, but Amy answered them anyway. She felt that Amy understood everything she said and when Amy talked about the woman who had been her last lover, Mary wished she could have done the same. She almost lied, a whole history of torrid affairs with women on the tip of her tongue. But then Amy leaned forward and kissed her and Mary was silenced by the softness of the skin, the softness of the lips.

Mary likes to think that when she drinks enough she can make love to anyone. She has always considered this to be a positive attribute. So she gets up to buy another round from the bar. Despite the dim lights and the smoke, everything is suddenly clear and distinct. It is always shape and colour that impress Mary first and on every face she now notices the lips, how strikingly different each pair is. The woman behind the bar takes her order and as Mary gives it she is aware of her own mouth and its slight saltiness. She stands there waiting and moves her tongue against her teeth, transfixed.... Someone places a heavy arm around her shoulders and whispers in her ear: I eat baby dykes for breakfast. Mary grabs the beer and ducks out from under the arm. She goes back to the booth, her face warm.

Mary is nervous. It's not the mechanics of things that worry her, although she does wonder what they will do, but her fear that she will be more repelled than aroused. And she is afraid Amy will be disappointed — what attracts her anyway? It seemed to her so much simpler with men, so much more obvious. And Mary is afraid that she will hurt Amy because, after all, she is only experimenting. Amy responds, "Oh, you straight women with your fence-sitting." And then she smiles and says, "Experiment away."

So Mary does and, with growing exuberence, she discovers she knows exactly what to do — and Amy knows even more. Mary says, marvelling, "It's almost like touching myself." And Amy drawls, "This ain't masturbation." Mary blushes and lowers her head to kiss Amy's breasts once again, the moist warmth of her sex. In the dark, her fingers slowly explore this new body, every curve and indentation, and she imagines painting what she feels. Her breathing quickens. There are those stars again, and there is Mary floating far above the earth, wondering which is more exciting, similarity or difference?

There are things to think about that Mary has never thought about before. She walks down a street and looks into the faces of women, wondering. And she watches men and women together with envy. Sometimes Mary and Amy will hold hands and nobody stares for too long because they are both young, both women and not men. But Mary wants to lie on the grass in a park with Amy and kiss and touch like any other couple. Amy shrugs: Why not? But Mary can't. She worries about who will see her, and what people will think. And she still isn't sure what she thinks. A woman walks by and smiles and Mary smiles back automatically. There is so much to be unsure about. Mary knows what Amy would say: But that's what's exciting.

Amy works at a community radio station when she isn't modelling. She is the station manager and is also one of the hosts of a show called *Women Do This Every Day*. Amy would like Mary to become a volunteer but Mary hesitates. She now sees Amy three or four times a week and they are wearing each other's clothes and using each other's shampoo. Mary thinks that if Amy had been a man, she wouldn't have allowed things to happen so quickly. She would have been more cautious. She thinks: I'm much too young for this. I should see other people. But it is Amy she wants to talk to at the end of the day and Amy who listens with that smile playing upon her lips. Amy who knows where to touch her and how. Mary sometimes tunes into the show and when she hears Amy's voice she says to herself: That's my lover. She rolls the words though her mouth slowly, as if tasting them, and deciding whether or not to swallow.

Once in a while Mary picks Amy up at the station. She has met most of the women who work on the show by now and they sometimes all go out for a drink. But there is one woman who seems to dislike her. There are scornful references to "lipstick lesbians" and women who are "AC/DC." Mary knows that they are all directed at her. It's upsetting. She is not used to being disliked and it all seems so — messy, so out of her own hands. After every encounter with this woman, Mary paints furiously, thinking about what Amy has told her: She thinks you're slumming, dabbling — you know, collecting sensations. She thinks you reek of straight privilege — and she probably finds you too middle class as well. Mary swallows hard and feels guilty. Isn't it all true? Amy shrugs: Ignore her — she's got a bad case of Dogma. But Mary is lousy at ignoring people. She gets swept up in the undercurrents of conversations and loses track of the words. She absorbs the emotions of others promiscuously, like a sponge, and Amy often finds her in bed staring at the ceiling, overwhelmed.

Sometimes instead of watching T.V., Mary rehearses coming out to her parents. She still isn't sure whether she has anything to come out about but she feels obliged to practise just in case, like reading up on what to do if there's an earthquake:

1. Be determined: Mom, Dad, I'm a lesbian.
2. No. Ease into it: I love women.
(Her mother would say: *We all love women, dear.*)
3. Don't be coy: Amy and I sleep in the same bed.
(*Oh, it's nice having a friend over.*)
4. Be patient: Amy and I fuck each other.
(Her father would say: *And just what kind of language is that?*)
5. Reveal no doubt: Well, actually, maybe I'm bisexual.
(*You young people want it all nowadays.*)
6. And don't whine: You've never liked my boyfriends, anyway.
(*We've always known that you could do better.*)

Mary decides that she really wants to be a lesbian. Really. They are soaking together in the bathtub as she announces this. Amy snorts: I think you've got a head start already. And she sinks lower into the water. But Mary doesn't believe her. I don't even look like a lesbian, she complains. Amy sighs: What do you think a dyke looks like? Mary doesn't know but she doesn't think she looks like one. She wishes she looked more powerful, stronger, more — What? Amy jokes: You couldn't look butch if your life depended on it. But they both know that's not what Mary means. Oh, she moans, what do I mean? Amy trails a sympathetic toe along her leg. Again, Mary doesn't really know but she's willing to try anything. There is a lot to try. And she even feels sometimes that things are finally connecting: outside/inside. What people think/what she thinks. But there are also days she feels like a child dressing up in her father's clothes — and they are way too big. She says tragically, staring at the ceiling: Hell is others. Amy sighs and adds more bubble bath.

Francis has dyed his hair violet except for the tips which he has left black. He has it pulled back into a chignon of sorts. An old Klaus Nomi song screams from the speakers: *Listen to me baby! You've got to understand! You're old enough to learn the makings of a man!* Today Francis wears a T-shirt with two men kissing on the front and the words "read my lips." He has taken to calling her "Mary, Mary, quite contrary" and with a wink he tosses a magazine onto her lap: This should spice up your vanilla existence, darling. Mary flips through it resolutely. It's a lesbian sex mag called *Quim*. *Listen to me baby! It's time to settle down! Am I asking too much for you to stick around?!* When Francis is ready for her she shows him a page: I want my hair to look like this. Francis whistles, impressed. Snip, snip, snap, snap. *Every boy needs a girl he can trust to the very end! Maybe that's you!*

Shorter, Mary says, even before he asks.

This term Mary is taking a class in filmmaking. She's decided it's time to branch out, to experiment with new forms. The medium excites her for what she can do with it. There are so many possibilities and she doesn't yet know enough about it all to be realistic. She thinks of making a music video, a documentary about the radio station or maybe even a feature-length production based loosely on her own life.... Mary imagines how the story would go: a difficult prolonged struggle and then eventual triumph. Maybe she'd make it an opera. She'd play with speed and colour and camera angles, and use her own paintings in the background. It would all be cutting-edge stuff, of course. And she'd hire Francis to do the hair. Mary can already picture the last scene: Her lover awaits her arrival impatiently, pacing back and forth. She finally sweeps into the room. They embrace. The music builds to a crescendo. They fall onto the bed....

It would all be wonderfully, seriously hokey.

She is making love with a man and the woman is watching them. Her lipstick is smeared onto her face. Her dress is pushed up above her waist. The woman watches, smiling enigmatically, and then walks away. She turns back to the man with relief, eager to continue, but now it's a woman in her arms and she kisses her hungrily. She strokes her stomach, her breasts, her throat. Then she hears something. She looks up and suddenly realizes that they are surrounded by people staring in silence. The crowd shuffles toward them, edging closer and closer. Their eyes seem to be growing larger. Mary closes her own eyes and tells herself to scream. She knows that if she screams she'll wake up.

Amy's birthday is coming up. They are going to treat themselves and spend a weekend at a bed-and-breakfast. Mary is supposed to arrange everything, but first of all she wants to finish Amy's present. It's a drawing of the two of them that she's done with Magic Markers onto a poster of John and Yoko in bed. It's just possible to make out the famous pair of lovers beneath. She's added a cartoon balloon above their heads and the words "People Say I'm Crazy" as if all four were speaking in unison. It's just about done and she's already cut a matt for it and made a bizarre frame out of some old ones that she found in an alley. Mary has no idea how she's going to get it to the bed-and-breakfast without Amy noticing but she is quite pleased. She thinks she has done a reasonable job on Amy, all in all. She adds a few finishing strokes. Well, she mutters, not quite.

The bed-and-breakfast is far south of the city along the coast. It's a breathtaking drive, high up on the cliffs above the ocean, and the weather is gorgeous, the sheer blue of the sky startling. They roll their windows all the way down and breathe in the salty air. Amy pushes some Brahms into the stereo and blasts it. Mary looks at Amy driving and she reaches over to help her keep her hair out of her eyes. She imagines Amy with another lover and is pleased by the sharp stab of jealousy. Every now and then she even deliberately invokes it. It's like fiddling with a loose tooth.

They have been given the Gertrude Stein suite. Mary asked for it especially. There are roses on the sheets and pillowcases, roses everywhere, ceramic cows on the windowsill and Picasso prints on the walls, the one of Stein looming over it all. When Mary sees the room she collapses onto the bed, giggling. Amy joins her. Oh no, this is too much. No, it's perfect. Mary suddenly bolts upright: Amy, can you act? And the urgency in her voice sets them off again. A few minutes later they have finally stopped laughing and they lie there quietly.

After a while Mary gets up for some tea. She also wants to go to the car and dig out the poster. With one hand carefully balancing the tray and the other carrying the present, Mary walks up the stairs slowly. She pauses at the top and looks out the window. The ocean is drifting in. Far away, people walk along the sand like little toy figures. A few gulls swoop down out of the sky and toward the sun. Mary can almost see the credits rolling and murmurs to herself: Wouldn't this make a great ending? She turns to walk down the hallway and pushes the door open with her foot. Amy is asleep. She places the poster on the sink against the mirror so that it will be the first thing that Amy sees. Carefully, Mary lowers herself down onto the bed. The cows have cast funny shadows onto the walls. She stares at the ceiling and then closes her eyes. She can hear Amy breathing, her body warm and close. There are things that will have to be decided, eventually, when Mary is older and a little wiser — she opens her eyes and reaches for the tea — but not now.

Victoria Freeman

Mama Nature

FROM THE REAR DOOR OF THE LAST CAR OF THE TRAIN, I watch the track spin out behind me: I am being pulled from my old landscape, dragged across a continent, and I'm glad.

I've walked the length of the train twice, politely evaded several men who tried to buy me drinks, listened to the tales of two recent widows. But when I talk about myself it feels like lying.

"I'm going to Vancouver to live with a man," I say, and it's true, but it sounds so simple.

Last night I dreamt of her as a warrior in breastplate and birdmask. She commanded me to swear allegiance, to ever be loyal. I pledged my heart to her. I have set off on an expedition into the land of men, but she will be my taliswoman, my kin, my faith.

In this inbetween country of muskeg and pine, this last desolate stretch of Ontario before the prairie opens out, the silvery rails disappear into swamp and impenetrable forest, veer swiftly behind boulders into memory. But her voice, the deep, rough bruise of her voice, can no longer reach me. Soon I'll cross the border and be gone.

This guy says he likes to make love after saunas but we are both dirty from two days on the train and I am bleeding. He says that with a woman like me he'll work harder and be steadier. He says he doesn't have to get off in Winnipeg, he could keep going, but I say, gently, no.

His name is Serge Brisseau. Or is it Brousseau? Broisseau? A bleary-eyed man in the bar car, but there's something about him, a sadness, a loneliness. A small man with a beard and ponytail, bags and wrinkles around his eyes. He seems almost familiar.

"I've got tequila in my roomette," he says.

"I don't usually go to the roomettes of strange men."

"You know, you have to watch out for three types of men: rapists, child molesters and rats, and I'm not one of those."

"That's jailtalk," I say.

"Yeah," he sighs, then offers me a joint from his pocket. "You're a lesbian, aren't you?"

I don't know how to answer questions like that anymore: I love who I love. But I'm more lesbian than not lesbian or at least that used to be true. So I nod.

In his roomette we speak French. He pulls down the blind and claims to know everything about me. He says we're both fire signs and there's heat between us, that I am soft, so soft, and he wants to make a real woman out of me. I laugh and listen to the clicking of the train as he moves closer. His body is warm and I like him. I don't want to say no, to draw lines for conventional reasons, but still I hedge, evade, tell him about the man I'm going to meet.

"Let Mama Nature decide," he keeps saying. "Let Mama Nature decide." As if she can be trusted.

Then we are two tangled crabs scuttling across the bed. But there is still the man in Vancouver, his long, lean, lovely body beckoning, his thin slip of a penis, a root, a branch — and I can't go on.

Serge pulls the sheet around him, becomes once again a separate being in his bag of skin, unreachable, unknowable, and I'm somehow ashamed.

Then he shows me a picture of his girlfriend who left him, a thin woman with two children, squinting into the sunlight.

"After she left," he says, "I tried to have the vasectomy reversed."

The whistle of the train, a shriek, a moan; now Winnipeg's behind me. I'm closed in again, solitary, as the hydro poles flash by outside my window, such relentless demarcations of time passed, of ground covered. The prairie seems empty, undemanding of commitment or attention, simply there to be passed through, a cocoon of snow and cloud.

My blood is thick and clotted and the colour of wine. No child this month: the egg is discarded, left behind.

Dim light seeps through my sleep, then rhythmic clicking and swaying, then the tiny closet, the blind pulled down, my bed over the toilet. A jolt.

Where am I? away away away I want go back, touch ground, touch Erin. Tears for her aching animal scent, for her keening cries. She touched the core of my being; she changed me.

When I met her she took me away, deep into the bush, to her sanctuary. We went off the map, into uncharted territory, out of time, into the wilds, left no tracks. I drank from her lakes and slept in her caverns; she sang strange songs of power and I healed. But she wouldn't allow men in her sanctuary and I missed them. I wanted to love them, to reinvent them.

But why with women do I dream of men? And with men of women? I'm like this country, encompassing too much geography, too many regions which threaten to break apart, which seem mutually exclusive.

I can't sleep. I pull up the shade and stare out the window: at dark houses, dark fields, slipping by. Where are you now, and now, and now? It's done, it's behind me.

Morning. But the train has hardly moved. Still the fields of stubble poking through the snow, the sky a grey wash of cloud. My body is heavy with blood — it's the third day of this inwardness. Male and female: I don't understand the words anymore. The Tao Te Ching says: "The further one goes, the less one knows." I repeat the phrase over and over.

Then it is noon in the dining car and the sun streams through the window. I sit alone, behind a white tablecloth, reading a menu. There's a single red rose in a vase on the table. A nervous dark-haired man passes my table, then returns and sits down. In the vague light of the afternoon we begin talking. There's something about him I find very attractive, some kind of affinity, perhaps because he is not heterosexual. It's as if we recognize each other as brother and sister.

He shows me a picture of himself with another man, a man with flowing blond hair, their arms around each other and radiant smiles. "Who is he?" I ask and he answers, "I loved him."

And I dream of the man in Vancouver. I take his hand, touch it, caress it. But I can't love a man again; it's too painful. He's the wrong size, the wrong shape; there's this funny thing between his legs and he's afraid of what's between mine. We are like children playing doctor, exploring each other's cracks and crevices and strange protuberances. But he is different from other men: I can see the woman in him.

He takes me in his arms. I feel her penis growing, swelling, his penis warm and soft against me, gentle, gentle. I am entering him. I am entering his softness. She is entering me. His face: female, male, female, male; the soft lines of his face, the strong lines of her face. He is waiting for me. Her lips are soft; his eyes, blue and wild. I gasp, weep, cry out in the presence of this spirit. We are starting over: the human race is starting over.

In my roomette I felt hemmed in by mountainsides. Here, in the observation car, I can see the peaks: high, remote, clear-edged against the sky. People are crowding into the lounge, filling up all the tables. We are approaching the great divide.

"You can sit here if you want," I say to an old man and his son, the father in a brown polyester jacket with a gold pin on the lapel that says Jesus Christ, the son in a green shirt with photos of wilderness scenes on it. "I'm only drinking ginger ale."

They accept my offer and sit down. They are ranchers, outdoorsmen, returning from a funeral in Edmonton. The father eyes me warily, tight-lipped. His neck is deeply creased; the whites of his eyes look yellow.

"Never get old," he mutters. "Only me and my sister left of six children."

"I don't know how not to," I say, but it's a terrible answer.

"I can't walk much now because I get dizzy," he begins, "and I can't fly an airplane anymore because I don't know what to do with all this new-fangled radio communication and how can I land the damn thing in bifocals?"

But I only half hear him; it is silence I am listening to, the stillness of his son, whose big hands lie curled on the table, whose hair is shaved at the back. He resembles his father but he is gentler somehow.

"Dad used to know every lake and landmark in the Yukon," he says, suddenly speaking, his voice with a faint twang like a cowboy's.

Then he tells me about the time they ran out of gas and landed on the sandbar of a lake, and the time they just missed a power line by flying under it and the time they tried to land in a valley near Kamloops and the windsocks were flying in different directions at each end of the valley; the whole valley was a giant whirlwind but somehow they were lucky.

The old man listens and sighs, then interrupts with his own anecdotes. I watch his gnarled body as it gradually relaxes, muscle and bone.

One night my love worked the hard knots hiding in my back; he said they were memories and I cried and cried.

"All people are fragile," he whispered, "incredibly fragile," and it fell away then, that pose of toughness, that protective barrier I had learned from my father. I turned toward him and and it came to me then, that it is the soft men I love, the fairies and the pansies and the sissies, the men who know they are as delicate as women.

And love loosened my body, reclaimed me. He came to me with the most wonderful tenderness. He was afraid and I was afraid, but there it was, that openness: he was as delicate and fragile and beautiful as a flower, the blossom trembling in full bloom, tears running down my face at the voluptuous softness of him, and why had I thought that men were so hard?

I sit in the observation car until it gets dark. My body is changing again; the flow is over. We are in British Columbia, passing through shadowy mill towns lost in the mountains.

I want to stay up all night. I want to stare out into darkness and breathe in the forest.

In the morning he will be there on the platform, waiting for me. I will write her and tell her that I have arrived.

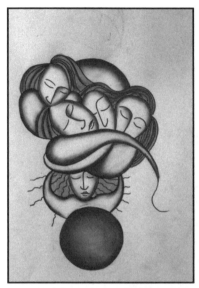

TRACY CHARETTE FEHR　Woman Circle #2 © 1992
Charcoal, pastel, pencil on paper

AGENCY,
CHOICES,
POSSIBILITIES

(*... does it bother you if i sit down ?)

(0 not at all !)

(1. ... you're really cute!) (2. ... you're not bad looking yourself!)

(1.... i've never slept with a woman!...)(2... because you're a fuckin' faggot?!)
(3....ya!... i'm 38 yrs. old and i've never wanted to sleep with a woman.)
(4... and now, like that, you want to fuck me?!)(5... oh, yeah!!)(6.... think what

(1. Oh yeah... i'd really like to...)(2... but i can't...)(3... my boyfriend's waiting for me at our place...)(4... we've been together 10 years and i've never cheated on him...)(5. But it was really nice! ... You're SUPER SEXY... especially for a woman!!)

Victoria Freeman

Love's Lessons

> *"...the either/or ways of thinking that are the philosophical underpinnings of systems of domination."*
> — bell hooks

> *"If you sit on the fence, all you end up with is a sore crotch."*
> — an acquaintance

I HAVE BEEN BI FOR A VERY LONG TIME. AS A CHILD I remember pleasurable sexual games with boys and girls. Later in high school, I had a regular girl friend — heterosexual — and boyfriends who I got all obsessed with, and then there was Virginia — small like me, a mime artist. I was too shy to do anything but I was very attracted to her.

I did not perceive bisexuality as a problem (perhaps because I didn't act on it) until I was older and in university, when I had some really bad experiences in relationships with men and when homophobia caught up to me. At a certain point I found myself much more attracted to women and agonized over whether I was "really" a lesbian. Eventually I overcame my fears and acted on these desires.

For a number of years I worked in feminist circles and met a lot of lesbians; it became clear to me that I was not "really" a lesbian either. My outlook was different from that of most of the lesbians I knew, especially separatists. While I had had lesbian experiences and I loved women emotionally, physically and spiritually, I came to identify as bisexual, for I loved men too — there is more room in that definition for me. I was always being told, usually indirectly, that I should belong to one camp or the other, but neither reflected the totality of who I was. For a long time I was very confused, because I kept thinking I had to be one or the other.

I met a bisexual man. At first we sought each other out because we were the only gay people at the writing workshop we were attending. He had been in a gay relationship for eight years but had decided he wanted to be involved with a woman. He understood gay sensibilities and respected (and liked) the lesbian side of me. It was even conceivable that I could have relationships with women in the context of our relationship, though I knew it would be difficult. Later we discovered we were both sexual abuse survivors and could help heal each other.

I learned the deepest lessons about love from seeing his struggle to love and affirm his ex-lover in spite of his love for me. This former lover is now like Mark's brother and a favourite uncle of our child. He and his lover have been our guests at many ceremonial times of year — I think of them as part of Mark's family. When Mark and I got married, his former lover was our best man and photographer; the first woman I loved provided the music.

I have been in the same long-term relationship with this man for twelve years (I am now thirty-six). Over this time I have had several secondary relationships — with men and women. Some of these have been rather rocky interludes, and Mark and I have had to really struggle to understand what was happening and why. But over time we seem to have worked out an understanding of what each of us wants and needs. Being with a woman sexually, even if only occasionally, or at the very least acknowledging and expressing my erotic feelings about women, is still important to me.

I don't know what it's like for other bisexual women, but for me it's not just that I have sex with women and men, but I love them in much the same way, to the same depth, with all of myself, including the physical. I'm not schizoid — I am the same person with men or women; it is the world that tries to split me into straight and gay, that is always trying to make me deny one half of my reality, my sensibility. It is individuals with whom I fall in love or to whom I am attracted, a particular fusion of body, mind and spirit. I don't fetishize body parts of either sex, or at least not of one sex more than the other, nor have I found either sex to be more loving or nicer (although more men are sexist). Different people bring out different qualities in me, not just males or females.

And yet to be bisexual is in some sense to be bicultural, to function in and value two different cultures and their respective ways of thinking and perceiving. I feel lucky to have this double vision. To me, it's like visiting one's father's relations and then one's mother's relations; in each case, you are aware of your family resemblances and you can love and enjoy both sides of your heritage. On the other hand, sometimes it's like the time I worked on an archeological excavation in England, where I was the only Canadian and everyone else was either British or American. The Brits told me I was so American and the Americans said I was so British. Similarly, it's easy to feel rejected — a lot of the time I'm too straight for gays, too queer for straights. I don't feel comfortable in a world composed solely of straight couples; I also need gay people to feel whole. I should mention that my daughter, who is four, knows straight, gay and bisexual people, including radical faeries and leather dykes, and knows that there are same-sex couples as well as male/female ones. It's no big deal to her.

Heterosexism and homophobia upset the balance that I feel in my attractions to men and women — my relations with men are socially approved of and rewarded whereas my love of women is not. I've experienced, at least to some small degree, the homophobia that lesbians live with every day. As a white, middle-class and generally privileged woman, loving women has been radicalizing — it has allowed me to look at society from a non-dominant perspective and deepened my commitment to working with others who have been marginalized, despised, rejected or excluded for who they are. While it doesn't give me much insight into the particularities of racial oppression or economic exploitation, bisexuality is a constant reminder that realities other than those glorified in the dominant mythology exist, and that so much of many people's essential experience — both their pain and their joy — is not visible to the dominant society. I think in that respect it has helped me to listen.

Everybody's bisexual deep down, I've heard many people say — usually straight people. It may be true — I really don't know — but I'm not out to convert anybody. Bisexuality is too difficult a lifestyle to recommend to others unless they are really drawn to it as their own particular path.

Who can understand these things about me? Who will accept them, when they are often confusing, even to myself? Who will see the special gifts that this sensibility brings? Spiritually, bisexuality is a very rich way of being.

There is also some part of me that just resists being labelled at all, that insists on my freedom to be whatever I want and to change as I feel like. Bisexuality has taught me that no one else can tell me what is right for me or who I am; it has made me aware of the endless permutations people are capable of and that are right for them, that conventional wisdom is not always the best, that I need to trust myself and find what feels right...to venture into the unknown. I have learned to live with ambiguity, and a deep sense of the complexity of things. Finding the courage to live as a bisexual woman has given me courage to move into other areas that are scary to me. I have learned to listen to the truth of my body, to the subtle energies that flow between me and other people, to respect the healing that touch can bring.

Nancy Chater

heat / wave

apparently the large purpley mark on that savoury
neck of yours was made by the mouth of *moi* yours truly
who's tickled pink knowing i had no idea i was sucking
like that this afternoon as you lay stretched out
on my bed in your white t-shirt for some remaining mystery
in front of my sixteen-inch oscillating
fan moving the thirty-degree-plus bath water we called
air today the length of your long drink of water self
and i found my fingers did the walking
or was it the talking

they travelled so freely cause i was standing up
and moving around the bed like a woman with a mission
to make you moan and tremble and hopefully tremble *and* moan

and then when you said *yeah squeeze my fingers with your cunt,*
i love it when you do that i squeezed all the more and
loved it and wanted to say *yeah baby tell me what you want*
me to do as in tell me how you *demand* that i let myself
pleasure myself every which way i can but i couldn't
say that because i'm too shy though i did manage to say
not for the very first time *tell me what you're gonna*
do and feel and at the sound of my spoken desire
i came on your lips face and fingers and you
loved it too i do believe

for john

christina starr

Making a Sexual Choice

for Liza, Margaret & Nancy & others along the way

I DID, AND THEN DID NOT, WANT TO WRITE ABOUT MYSELF as bisexual, as having a bisexual identity. Until a couple of years ago, I was involved in a long-term heterosexual relationship and had not had any other sexual experience. By the end of the year in which my relationship dissolved, I had made love with a woman. I had known for some time this would happen. I did not find, when it did, that a distinction had been irrevocably made. Though I discovered wonderfully new and passionate things about my sexuality, they did not include the revelation that I would never again want to sleep with a man.

If I say that I am bisexual, and write about that identity, what does that mean if in the future, maybe even by the time this anthology is published, I decide I want only to be with women? In the present moment of writing, I identify more clearly as lesbian but am still in the pupae stage of getting used to sexual labels and identities for myself rather than assuming the straight given. I feel like an anxious newcomer worrying about how to present a public self. Should I choose this label or that? Which one fits or feels comfortable? What suits me? And what is the cost?

Not that, every day, I worry much about labels, unless someone asks in which case I respond by explaining who I am. I am a woman who used to live with a man, who grew up believing (as I was taught) that living with a man and having sex with a man was the only natural choice, who figured out along the way that it wasn't, and who now is very interested, in fact, only interested, in meeting women to kiss. Does that make me bisexual or lesbian? Or should we, really, wait for the final count: at the end of my days say *No, she did not sleep with men after that and so in fact she was lesbian,* or *Well, who would have thought he would come along and so she was bisexual after all.* But the point in using a label as an aspect of identity is not a scientific one of data collection and analysis. Although the word bisexual was presented to me in my earliest encounter as a biological but unnatural and perverted phenomenon, I have come to understand it, to gain courage and inspiration from it, as a political, even intentional, choice. Sitting cross-legged on the thick woven rug in the living room of my family's house, I don't recall exactly what I was doing, killing time between high school and supper. My father sat close in his armchair, reading the news. He cleared his throat suddenly and shook the sag out of the paper. "Christina," he announced. "Do you realize that Elton John has said in an interview that he is bisexual?" The word had a definite emphasis, not so much out of astonishment as out of distaste, like the smelly bag of garbage you want to toss out the back door and forget. I was a huge Elton John fan. What I had just learned had implications to the very core of my fanhood. Was it okay to admire someone like that? Was his music still good? Or should I burn all my records and never hum *Your Song* again?

I knew the answers to some of these questions but was confused about what to do. My father had communicated clearly enough that it was not really okay to still be a fan of someone like that. So where did I turn all my reverence? All this teenage idolization of the funny looking guy with no hair and wild glasses whose voice was a gift and whose music I knew all by heart? In that first jolt of disclosure, bisexuality nearly outweighed all the talent.

Little did I realize how far ahead of his time Elton John was. Not as bisexual, of course, but for forcing the issue of sexual expression and sexual diversity into the public's eye. In some cases it shot into the heart of a fan and made her falter over the songs she sang in her head. But in other ways his statement helped to open up the debate. Being bisexual was big enough news that a small paper in northern Alberta picked it up from New York or London to print in the daily edition.

Would it, I've since wondered, have been such a big deal if Elton John had said he was gay? He has since identified as gay and it doesn't seem to have been world news. Would my father have mentioned it with such import in 1976? Perhaps. The concept of bisexuality, however, presents a specific and definite challenge to heterosexuals because of its proximity to their own identity. Bisexuality reflects heterosexual existence but also encompasses homosexuality, implying that love of one's own sex is a potential reality for all those who believe they are straight. Gays and lesbians are feared and hated by many but they are also, in the heterosexual mind, "like that," almost another species. Bisexuality makes visible the otherwise invisible and seemingly impossible choice. Bisexuals could, one might think, remain in a "normal" relationship, behave as they are expected, but, like a child oblivious to authority, maddeningly keep wandering off.

I believe that choice is a central issue the sexual mainstream, not to mention many in gay and lesbian circles, does not want to address. It blurs the lines between straight and not straight; it messes up the distinction of who and what can be oppressed, who and what enjoys privilege. Even those "liberals" who are tolerant of homosexuality would rather accept it on the basis that it cannot be helped. It's okay if you are born like that. If it's in your genes then, all right, we'll make room to accept you as someone who should not be persecuted, like we don't persecute those with red hair. As my own mother articulated in struggling to make sense of homosexuality, "I can understand if people say they are *born* like that, but why would anyone choose it?"

The fixed-in-your-genes stance is one that many institutions are taking in their debate over whether to allow full rights and privileges to those who admit they are gay. In 1991 Jim Ferry, a priest in the Anglican Church, came out to his Bishop, who immediately stripped him of all his priestly authority. In the ensuing trial in Bishop's Court (the church's self-regulating judiciary), which became a debate over the legitimacy of homosexual existence, the Anglican Church announced that they were waiting for "science" to show them the way. Even American Bishop John Spong, an outspoken and courageous advocate for gay and lesbian rights, cited, in his appearance as a defence witness for Ferry, scientific material to which he was privy ("though it is still being debated in scientific circles") to back up his belief that "homosexual people are born with their orientation. It is not abnormal."[1] If it can be *proven* that your orientation is biologically determined, then, okay, your rights will be grudgingly granted, we will try to accept you as normal. But if you choose? Then of your own accord you are relinquishing your rights and privileges, separating yourself from the crowd.

Bisexuality, I think, presents to the mainstream the challenge of accepting gayness as "normal." It also implicitly questions the legitimacy of dividing orientations into categories. It circumvents the fixed-in-your-genes argument since obviously bisexual people also have it in their genes to be straight. And it answers the question of why anyone would choose differently — because there is evidently something to gain (an answer that those in the sexual mainstream might rather not acknowledge).

Undressing a woman with passion did not become a tangible possibility to me until I considered it from the perspective of bisexuality. No longer was being sexually attracted to a woman something I couldn't experience because I wasn't "like that"; it became a choice I could make if I could break through my own homophobia, unlearn the compulsion of heterosexuality.[2] Getting to know women who identified as bisexual, who, like me, had relations with men and who also had relations with women made being sexually attracted to one of my own not only conceivable but also something I clearly could realize.

It sounds like bisexuality is something I challenged myself to, and I did. It sounds like being attracted to one's own sex is a difficult task not for the faint of heart. I mean that only in one specific way: overcoming homophobia in a heterosexist and heterocentric culture. The idea of kissing, touching, being touched by a woman was hard for me to imagine. I wanted to shatter that barrier, determine if whether, for me, heterosexuality was indeed just the disposable container that sealed in my sexual response.

In the tide of my rising consciousness, I have identified and pulled out with the undertow many other barriers behind which I had been carefully instructed to keep my life. Some of these have given way more easily than others. Heterosexuality took longer to emerge as artificial, as something I had been conditioned not to question in order not to dislodge my dependence on men. It just seemed so *natural*. To fall in love, to enjoy sex, to feel comfortable in the company of similar couples, to take for granted and as normal the blinkered heterosexual privilege. When I did, gradually, reach out and put my fingers on this one barrier I was not supposed to cross, it became something I wanted to get rid of if only for the continued loosening up of my life, the continued resistance to rules that were binding me in.

Yet while I write of and describe a deliberate choice, my approach to loving women did not come solely as a result of getting to know others who identified as bisexual. As I see from journals kept over the years, I have been considering the idea for some time. In 1987 I wrote a short story entitled "How I Became a Vegetarian" in which a woman chooses to become lesbian.[3] "No wonder," I concluded in 1988 after encountering some particularly disheartening misogynist crap, "so many feminists choose the all-women world of lesbianism." That same year I met a woman with whom I privately fell in love: I was terrified to call her, dressed carefully when going to meet her, imagined the excitement of kissing her but only vaguely the sex. I fictionalized the experience in my journal: "I would like to recreate in a story the mood of the late-night conversations. It's women's intimacy and it's beautiful. But I'll have to invent what they say to each other, how they reveal their lives, exchange gifts, undress themselves a little. What of a story of two women becoming friends and sharing their sexual stories which becomes, for one of them, a kind of substitute for real physical love between them?"[4] All this steaming desire, however, took place in a very safe context. The woman was straight and comfortable being so and I was certainly not going to push the boundaries for both of us.

Had she been a lesbian or more openly bisexual I'm not sure what would have happened. Probably I wouldn't have fallen in love, too terrified of the real possibility. Because one thing I still felt quite certain of, despite these experiences and my cerebral considerations of lesbian existence: I was not lesbian. How could I be? I had fallen deeply in love with a man (although that was seriously falling apart). I enjoyed heterosexual sex (although that was increasingly disturbed by the implicit and difficult imbalance of power). I had not, except in one very safe and riskless adventure, felt anything like love or lust for a woman. And as far as I was consciously aware — my memory of the afternoon with my father tucked invisibly away with other moments of life and revelation — there was only the gay or the straight.

How can we know if we really are gay or lesbian, bisexual or straight? "Heterosexuality may be the norm in our society but there is no way to know if it is actually normal," writes Kay Leigh Hagan; "We cannot know what our choice of sexual activity would be if left to our natural desires in an unbiased culture."[5] If left to our natural desires in an unbiased culture (if we can even believe that is possible), I suspect that there would be a lot more bisexual activity and that the statistical ten percent of the population that is gay might blossom to twenty or thirty. I believe we are born sexual, with a sexual capacity for love of other people, and that those who are genetically determined to love only one sex or the other are perhaps, in reality, the minority. Considering what great determination it took to allow myself to feel sexually attracted to a woman, however, I can imagine how unthinkable it is for the majority of people to question their orientation, to consider making a choice that contradicts the heterosexual norm.

But why do some question and some not? What is it that makes some push the boundaries of what is prescribed to come out the other side as lesbian, gay or bisexual? In my own case, despite my conventional upbringing, I do have a father who relishes exposing injustice and resisting authority. Perhaps I adopted his subversion. While I questioned my sexual conditioning, however, I could not move through the barrier of fear and ignorance surrounding my own sexuality until I could understand sexual expression as a choice. And I did not consider this aspect of choice until I witnessed the reality of those whose lives are bisexual. And whatever flux my identity takes, from lesbian to bisexual but never again clearly straight, I will always consider the gift of my sexuality and the potential for love as a choice. Which will be, for many, a threatening position indeed.

So she and I have made love. It is amazing to me that I write that down. That it happened so quickly and that I can say it at all. It was not entirely smooth. But we're new to touching each other and I am new to touching women. I'm sure it will only get better.[6]

NOTES

1 Bishop John Spong, quoted in *In the Courts of the Lord: A Gay Minister's Story*, Jim Ferry's account of his coming out to the Anglican church and his subsequent dismissal and trial (Toronto: Key Porter Books, 1993).

2 Interestingly, in availing myself of computer technology to get the most accurate meaning, I find that my built-in thesaurus gives "choice" as the antonym to "compulsion."

3 Definitely a story I must pick up and re-work.

4 Journal entry, May 1989.

5 Kay Leigh Hagan, "Orchids in the Arctic: The Predicament of Women who Love Men," *Ms. Magazine* (November/December 1991): 31.

6 Journal entry, November 1992.

Irene J. Nexica

antiphon

what was lying between us

we keep the nation's peace
with silence
lips presst tight together
with a thumb
seep red through the cracks
I have borne the weight of being
authentic
for too long

what was lying between us. what I pretended. what we could not say.
what has no name.

even if one layer of
brown skin peels off the new
pink is so young and tender it only burns darker scars.

what was lying, between us? we all have secrets to keep.

theeeeeeeeese

days are long

theeeeeeeeeeeeeeeeey
will not come back

she was never there those days
when i could not figure out what to do.
i'd look at my big toe slanting inward
and wonder if women's boots, big as
they were, were reshaping my feet.
we came to each other in bed
like small children
excited and afraid
wondering
what
ne
xt

wondering what the other would wish if we could ask

this love is messy
it glistens on what it touches
it will not colour within the lines

enveloping with clear egg
white a hungry amoeba

like a thorn in my side she's always with me
i have tried to see for my self and missed
what is there is no name

Indigo Chih-Lien Som

the fucker & the milkbottle

I hate running into you
in the Berkeley Bowl.
I was trying to decide
between a quart of nonfat
milk & a half gallon of
lowfat/ & there you were
threading your
slimy way through
shopping carts & rows
of sweet potatoes. My
girlfriend said later that
I looked embarrassed
when I saw you. Well,
I guess I was, because
I always manage to
get all flirty w/ you
in spite of my best
efforts. I want to press
the cold quart of
nonfat to my cheeks,
or maybe dive into the
nearest pile of red onions
to hide from what I
become when you're
around. My body rages
like a runaway vacation,
only vaguely homesick
for the wise guidance of
mind and emotion. My pelvis
seems magnetic. My mouth
smiles irresponsibly. I
let you hug me hello.

I can barely introduce
you to my girlfriend,
who immediately
disappears toward
the calm green
zucchini & peppers, it seems
helpless miles away.
I let the bottle slide cool
to the floor of my cart as I
escape to where she is.

Andrea Freeman

Nympho Next Door

I MANAGED TO LIVE IN MY NEW PLACE FOR THREE WEEKS without realizing that my window looks straight out into another window, the window of the bedroom of a man who lives in an apartment in the place next to mine. After three weeks already passed, three weeks of dressing and undressing, three weeks of jerking off and fucking, one day I just happened to look over and realize he's been there for the same three weeks, doing basically the same bedroom things, well it just seems ridiculous to all of a sudden think about curtains or blinds or turning out the light. So I don't. And neither does he.

For a while I acted exactly as I had before, as if I had no idea there was someone watching me, which I didn't, before. Then ever so often it would occur to me, usually kneeling on all fours over my girlfriend's face, or fucking her ass with the dildo, that we might not be the only ones getting a kick out of it. And that made me smile.

Then I started wondering what he might be up to, and I figured he didn't mind me finding out, or he would have done the curtains or blinds or lights thing, right? So I started checking in on him. And he turned out to be the kind of guy you figure most guys would kill themselves to be, or figured they really were on some level. I mean the kind of guy that never sleeps alone. I guess he's got some kind of problem, like incurable loneliness or insecurity, but he's doing a damn good job of helping himself forget about it, I'll give him that much.

So somehow this guy, who seems pretty good looking, as far as men go, is luring different women to his place every night, and not just any women, but really beautiful women, I mean hot women, and this guy's got them in his bedroom, naked and working up a sweat every night, and I wasted three good weeks not noticing.

Watching became more than a habit — pretty soon it was a bonafide obsession. My girlfriend works nights, so I was always alone anyway, and I couldn't ask for a better way to get over the frustration of not having her with me.

It wasn't long until this guy caught on to the fact that I wasn't just a casual observer. But he didn't get mad. All he did was position himself so that he could get a good look. At me. Looking at him. And he concentrated. He figured out what I liked and he did it more. Like he'd set the woman he was with up against the window and fuck her from behind so I could watch her face. Or he'd get her to lie on the bed with her legs spread toward me. Him kneeling on the floor eating her out so that I almost felt like it was me doing it. I'd see her from the angle I love best, all curves and bumps, and on warm nights with both windows open I could hear her coming.

I started to wonder what I could do for my friend. The thought of turning him on made me feel a little queasy, but I knew I owed him something for all the pleasure he was giving me. So I started paying closer attention. I was surprised to see he still had energy and sperm left over in the afternoons but he did. He always grabbed his dick when he saw me jerking off. So I asked my girlfriend, nicely, to jerk off beside me, although I failed to mention why, and pretty soon it was a regular thing, the three of us rocking happily together and me turning my thoughts to innovative fucking techniques, the kind that wouldn't just feel good but would also look great.

I spent a little money. Bought both of us some sexy lingerie and devoted some time to leafing through men's porn, searching for the ultimate male fantasy. I opened the window, turned up the music and enjoyed her stripping for us. I tied her up in full view of the window, teased and tortured her, dressed her up in stupid clothes, made her beg and crawl. She didn't know where it all came from, but she loved it.

And he worked harder to please me. He brought two women home and we all got off on them doing each other. He asked them to strip slowly, so slowly I almost couldn't take it, performing expressly for me, thrusting their hard nipples and dripping cunts almost into my drooling mouth. I thought I could smell them, so strong I believed I could taste them. I ached for them and came dozens of times watching them but felt no guilt, committed no sin of the flesh against my love, fucked her harder and more often thanks to these anonymous women and my friend.

I also tried to oblige him in other ways. Although he didn't get my juices flowing, I knew I turned him on, so I took extra care dressing and undressing. I did it like I meant it. Slowly and deliberately covering and uncovering my body, getting off on each part, stroking skin, remembering how damn good I look. And I did other things, like change my style. I got tighter things. Special bras, a garter and stockings. Half the time I wouldn't wear underwear — only we would know. And kinkier things. Like those little balls you stick in your cunt and walk around with all day. And improvised nipple clamps, like paper clips — secret reminders we both got off on.

My masturbation techniques became more outrageous. Taught myself to ejaculate and flooded my room. Coaxed all kinds of household items up there in all sorts of positions. Taught my cat to put her rough little tongue to good use, licking me in just the right spot, and put up lots of sexy pictures. Even drew a few of my own.

Things just got more and more intense. Neither of us got much sleep and it was impossible to concentrate on anything else. For the first time I let my cunt rule my life and kind of wondered why I'd let my head run things for so long. I knew I couldn't keep it up forever, but at the same time, I didn't see what could stop it. I guess if I really thought about it, I could have come up with a thousand different scenarios. Like anyone besides the two of us finding out. Like actually meeting him, even running into him on the street or finding out we have a mutual friend or acquaintance. Or one of us getting arrested for indecent exposure.

In the end it was simpler than any of those things, and more obvious. He moved. He never said good-bye, which makes sense, since he never said anything. Just one day a curtain was up and I knew it couldn't be his. Then sure enough it happened to open and the room was totally different, and I don't even know or care who lives there now. Things are pretty much back to normal and I hope I never come across him anywhere again because I don't want to ruin one of the greatest times of my life.

Sarah Cortez

Dream

If I was a dark and beautiful man
this is what I would do.
Wear sharp, red shorts
gathered at the waist. Run
around the park twice, every day,
and see my legs grow strong and thick.

I would shave every morning, the clean
stainless sweeping the contours of face, chin,
around moustache. I would rub
aftershave, cool
stringent juice over jaws, chest,
armpits, stomach, crotch.

Loving women, I would choose
carefully. Prolonging the desire,
waiting, making myself wait. Coming
home to jerk off before bed.
Not choosing back seats, back
alleys, motels, parks, parking
lots. Waiting to be in her house,
where *la chica* lives. Watching
her sleeping breath before I leave,
knowing when she wakes she'll find
my scent in the morning's rumpled sheets
and remember.

I would be a good dancer. All the men
in my family are. Even *los viejos*,
bald, with rock-hard melon bellies.
I would clasp my beautiful cousins
close against the hardness of stomach and cock
at family reunion dances. And whisper,
"Prima," before I placed soft, quick kisses
onto lipsticked smiles. Low sparking
desire careful in our eyes.

Finally, I would marry
a girl from my school. Beautiful,
with smooth brown skin,
long dark hair. She will go to Church
every Sunday. Give me children.
Raise them well. Fuss
when my newly polished shoes mark
the kitchen floor.

I will die an old man
in my favourite chair,
dreaming the high shallow V of geese
in the clear night sky.
Moustache whitened with age,
bristly staccato against dark
dark skin.

Sarah Cortez

Avenue de l'Opera

I N THE EVENINGS I USUALLY WALKED FROM THE OFFICE
to my hotel. The apparent simplicity of life during my Paris stints always
beguiled me. My evening strolls were a celebration of that ease. No
dinner to be cooked and eaten. No discussions with or about our sixteen
year old, Mark, who was approaching either manhood or complete
annihilation with a careless impetuosity I found alarming. His fast driving.
Two wrecks: one in Jim's car, one in mine. His total nonchalance. Listening
to records by groups with names like "Foetus" and "Fudge Tunnel." Alone
with his door closed. For hours. His hands had been lengthening from
some time now. His legs too. As his fingers grew into an unfamiliar thick-
ness, I sometimes felt my throat catch glimpsing them. I wished that his
body's new dimensions indicated a new sense of responsibility. But no, he
remained loyal to his old habits of skipping deodorant and doing acrobatics
in the stairwell.

After the first round of dinners for the members of our project team
had subsided, I could politely dine in my room. No more discussions over
rich food about the Spring collection. Endless questions preceding difficult
decisions. Would the buyers like this fabric? Which colours? My digestion
improved. The power struggle with the coordinator of the French team had
abated. Maybe it had all been in my imagination. It was too complicated to
try to figure out if the arrogance was her intuitive response to me alone, or
to all Americans. I ignored her icy stares and made sure that my boss back
home knew every time the French team missed a deadline. Once or twice I
awoke myself from sleep, not realizing until the following day brought
aching jaws that I must have gritted my teeth all night under the hotel's
high ceilings.

The final deadline had been set at least two weeks too early. Only
one week remained. I knew I could force the project to completion in the
allotted days. Jim called every third or fourth night to offer encouragement
with his precise words. We both knew that these long assignments away
from home gave me the experience of a simple, uncomplicated life. I knew

he could manage regular meals even in my absence. I missed him. I had already bought the bottle of champagne for my return. We'd go upstairs early and close the door. I found a turn-of-the-century set of "naughty" postcards and sent him one each day. Seeing those broad Edwardian buttocks encased in endless rows of starched ruffles would no doubt convince him that I had gone mad. But I also knew he would laugh and prop them up on his dresser where he could see them even without his glasses.

I couldn't find anything to send to Mark. I saw nothing French that wouldn't look out of place in his abrupt life. I wanted to find something for him. Something he wouldn't dismiss with a "Gimme a break, Mom." I was scared to pick something out. The tension between us was still too fresh. Too heavy to be lightened by a pair of soccer shorts or a logo'd T-shirt. I finally decided on some sunglasses. The expensive ones for skiing. I could see their red, squarish frames with the opaque silver reflecting across the bridge of his scarred, sunburnt nose. One blonde hair glimmering on his cheek, the only one that needed to be shaved.

I didn't know how to get through to him. I wavered and worried. And got angry and yelled, "You're ruining your life. You'll regret it." He fought back by slouching around and taking several times too long to complete every assigned chore. When he used my bathroom, he no longer flushed the toilet, the yellow, acrid fumes gripping me when I got home from work. I wished I didn't know. I wish I hadn't seen the prophylactic. He was flipping through his wallet. He didn't know I recognized the shape and size. Didn't even know I'd seen it. I said nothing. Later, when I told Jim about it, he dismissed it. "Every high school kid has to carry one. Don't worry. It doesn't mean he and Carla are sleeping together." Mark's fascination with her had replaced concepts like scholastic achievement and "the right college." I kept digging to see if he still cared. But all that resulted was a deadened silence when I tried to talk with him. His grades dropped.

Cleaning his room, I found copies of *Hustler* rolled up in his sleeping bag. I flipped through the pages. Young girls posed, legs spread, with spotlights accenting their openness. My mind went blank at the thought of trying to talk to him, laying open the pages on the kitchen table, demanding an explanation. So, I put them back. Not able to find the words to talk to Jim. Knowing I'd be dismissed again. Hating them both for being male.

Mark's light steps through the carport as he ran across the cement to his dates with Carla were the only times I heard him come to life. He gunned the engine of Jim's car around the curves of our street. Even muffled the sound came back hasty and excited. I didn't know what to write, so I relayed messages through Jim, feeling out of touch with my son and his precipitous existence. Angry that he had changed. Scared that I had somehow lost him already. Unable to do anything but worry while I was away in Paris.

I had seen the girl every day for three weeks. One evening as I had walked home from work her figure appeared in the window of one of those fashionable dress salons along the Avenue de l'Opera. Her face floated against the darkness as clear as a flowering water lily against dank leaves. That image held constant before my eyes all the way to the hotel in the swirling autumn mists.

Each evening as I passed the shop, I could feel my body tighten. My pace slowed. My face grew hot as I felt my breath quicken. I prayed no one on the street could feel the energy in my body for hers. It started with a certain heaviness in the middle of my chest. As I approached the place from where a glimpse of her was possible, the constriction would dissolve into a melting warmth that flowed out into all my limbs making me lightheaded and acutely conscious of the distance between us. If I did catch a glimmer of her pale skin, the blood flowed from my head to my legs making my footsteps ring sharp and taut all the way to my room. Once there, I would imagine swirling in dance steps around the polished floor cradling her in my arms as our skirts billowed out from stockinged calves above pale satin pumps.

One evening, her blouse was heavy green silk, the collar low enough for small slivers of creamy flesh to shine through. A simple design flowed in jet beads around her breasts onto one sleeve. Another day she wore lavender, simply cut, tight through the bodice with pearls and a white skirt.

Lingering one day at the window, I watched her hand remove a trifle for a customer. When she leaned forward to return it, the yellow silk she wore fell away revealing lace against paleness. I looked directly into her face drinking in the full mouth, its redness drawn with precision, unable to walk away.

That night in my dreams I slept against her slim paleness. My hands holding her beneath me. I kissed her face now devoid of make-up. Her breath touched the fine hairs at the back of my neck.

"Good evening, madame, may I help you?"

I stopped breathing, enjoying her closeness. Her waist was cinched with a bright scarf. A heavy, black dress clung to her hips and breasts. Those fingers which had clung and scratched me the night before tapped an impatient litany on the countertop.

"I need to purchase a silk blouse. In mauve."

Sliding off the stool, she inclined her head and licked her upper lip, the lipstick remaining intact. A mechanical smile and a direct glance at my torso.

"What is madame's size?"

"Small."

Looking at her, close for the first time, I could only think of undergarments: lace bras, delicate slips, tiny web-like garter belts, silk stockings peeled away from waiting thighs and moist lips.

She walked to a rack at the back of the store, black leather placed on the lush carpet in measured steps.

"Does madame prefer buttons in the front or in the back?"

Awakened by her voice, I returned from my fantasy. I focused on her eyes. I didn't even know their colour.

She looked closer into my face, no doubt puzzled by my lengthy meditation on the question of buttons. She hadn't lost patience with me yet but I saw the inquisitiveness begin to harden. I groped for an answer.

"Front."

"Would madame wish to try on this blouse today?"

Then I realized my mistake.

The dimness of the salon made her skin luminous just as the thick autumn mists had done the first evening I had glimpsed her. The street lamps outside were not yet lit. I saw her lips open beneath mine; the cool eyes flame with desire; her black leather shoes askew at my bed; her toes curl as her back arched in ecstasy. Could I go into the dressing room and have her stand at my side while I unfastened each button of the blouse I was now wearing, slipping each covered button through its tailored enclosure each time to reveal more flesh? Could I stand exposed to her, my breasts ready for her mouth, nipples hard beneath the translucent camisole I wore? Could I restrain the impulse to seize her at the back of her neck and bend her face up to mine as I leaned into a first kiss? Could I resist the fevered need to reach over to her breasts shaped by the black, clinging material and trace the outline of her nipple daring to believe she would do the same with mine? Would I dare to stand half naked angle upon angle of my body reflected and refracted by dressing room lights as she stood there uninterested and composed?

"I am sorry, mademoiselle. Some other day, perhaps." Turning on my heel, I left her.

I walked into the evening's reassuring stillness. I didn't dare look up. I wondered who on the street knew. Surely my desire had made me transparent. I didn't notice the dampness until I reached the hotel. I pushed the mist off the fur of my coat feeling the soft nap of a young girl's unshaven thighs.

Alone in my room I flung my coat across the bed. I didn't want to eat dinner there alone. What if Jim called? I doubted that the roar of long distance would be enough to disguise the chaos in my voice. Without thinking I slipped into my robe, then into the shower. Drying myself I reached over and wiped the steam away from the mirror over the marble sink. Jim had recently started joking that I'd make a sexy grandmother. I turned around not wanting to look. As I unzipped my dress I imagined the metal teeth folding back sinuously to expose porcelain flesh down the curve of her backbone, not mine. I must go to dinner.

I had worn the black dress. The one I wore to feel beautiful. The heavy starch of the white tablecloth reminded me of childhood. The nuns always rustled as they walked, white habits billowing, smelling of soap and other holy things. If they were angry the rosary beads roped at their waists would click; an angry walk faster than a godly walk. What parts of me had survived those years of bent knees, holy water and statues of virgins' eyes straining upward, wounds gaping as plaster-of-Paris blood dripped downward?

When I glanced at the waiter to place my order, I took in my surroundings for the first time. At the next table a couple ordered their wine. The man inclining his head as the woman whispered a few words into his ear while running one fingertip along her refined jawbone. Her large earrings flashed in the candlelight. Her companion must have been pleased because he cupped her small hands in his and kissed her lacquered fingernails one by one.

I unfolded the crisp napkin against my thighs. The roughness against my fingers, the warmth of my legs through the silk of my dress, that first caress. When had it been? Long before boys were real. In the hazy, uncharted time when my whole world revolved around God, the nuns and my best friend, Mary Beth Russo. We had chosen each other in the first grade. Spent the eight years of grade school calling each other every night. Attended the same all-girls, Catholic high school.

There was nothing we didn't do together: sewing lessons, tennis, homework, guitar lessons, slumber parties. The furry pink flannel of my nightgown. Her blue striped pajamas. Everyone else asleep on the den floor with us sharing the bathroom's small gas heater against the cold. I, fumbling with blouse buttons, scared to be naked in front of anyone. But, finally, pulling it off, careful of the blue licks of flame in the heater. Seeing her hand placed. Seeing her hand lift my bra. My breast emerging. Watching the nipple unfold in the uncertain light. Feeling my hard intake of breath. Mary Beth whispering, "What if a boy did this? What would it feel like?" Not knowing if this was a setup for one of her jokes. Feeling her tongue back and forth. My body's response. I brushed back her hair and turned slightly, offering my other nipple, lifting the bra higher, knowing the door would spring open and Martha's mother would find us and call our mothers and tell the whole school. So, I closed my eyes and waited. Paralyzed by the improbability, or, perhaps, the probability. Not touching her again.

When we flopped on the den floor to sleep with the crowd, I couldn't go to sleep. Again and again I relived the soft insistence of her touch and the inexplicable sensations. There were never any apologies. No confessions or admittance. Only memories of that incompetent gentleness and hurried insistence. The tight ache between my legs. The hand placed.

The couple at the next table rose to leave. As the man pulled back the chair, the woman removed one earring, and massaged her earlobe. Slowly and deliberately her thumb and forefinger worked the tiny nub of flesh. Coat on. Purse found. Glance to maitre d'.

Back in my room I waited for sleep. Instead, the phone rang.

Jim's voice sounded tired. It must have been the middle of the afternoon there. He had probably been at work since six-thirty that morning.

"How are you doing?" he asked.

"Fine. Really...fine. How are you? Have you eaten lunch yet?"

"Naw. No time. Budget meeting in fifteen minutes."

"I wish you would take better care of yourself," I found myself saying. Knowing it was useless, but needing to say it, needing to supply my half of the formula from an ocean away.

"I'm okay. I'm okay."

"How's Mark?"

"Still blowing and going."

"What's he up to?"

"Soccer. Weights. T.V. Everything but homework."

A blurred vision of the woman and me waltzing through the night swirled through my head. The little jerk. Why did he have to ruin his future by refusing to study? What had happened to the obedient child who had so proudly brought home report cards for display and reward?

"He's going with Carla and her parents to the cabin next weekend."

That did it. I felt my teeth clench as the headache started. I focused on the wallpaper to stop the harsh words.

"Jim, you know I don't want him doing that. How could you?"

"Oh, sweetheart, c'mon...you'll make me late for my meeting."

"No, I mean it. Her parents don't care if they sleep together. We do care. I don't want him sleeping with Carla. It's not fair to him and it's not fair to her. Besides, it's not what two sixteen-year-old kids should be doing."

"Carla is a good kid. They belong to our church."

"Jim, I can feel it. Something's different. When they're around us. It's there. In the air. Please, can't you do something?"

"Sweetheart, what can I do? He's too old to be spanked. Besides, I hardly ever see him anymore anyway, except at breakfast. How am I supposed to impart the benefits of my collective male sexual wisdom to him at six a.m. when we're both still half asleep? It'll be okay. You like Carla, remember? She likes you. Probably more than she likes her own mom. Relax. Being away is making you uptight. Listen, I've got to go. My meeting starts in a few minutes."

"I'm worried. What if she's pregnant? What will happen then? They'll both be trapped. They're too young for that."

"What about us? Remember sitting out in front of your parents' house? We went pretty far then. In the front seat of a goddamn Mercury. Remember? I lived for those moments. You were the sexiest girl alive for me. You still are. C'mon, honey. Come home. We'll hold each other and make love, and it'll be okay. God, I miss you. You don't know. I'm going crazy. These budget projections aren't helping either."

I thought about the bottle of champagne and hoped Mark would be out late the night I returned and that Jim wouldn't have to work until all hours.

"What are you thinking?"

"Oh, I don't know." I didn't expect to get away with that one, but he let it pass. I felt so helpless. Sixteen short years, then sex. The next generation would be ten or twelve.

"Honey, any chance you could get an earlier flight back? I can't wait to have you here."

I knew he meant it, but I also knew he'd be working twelve and fourteen hour days until the budget was approved. I could see him at his desk. The unwatered plants bending toward the grayish half-light between the buildings. The curve of his chin darker because of the faint stubble that couldn't stay away any longer. I felt a sudden need to fall asleep against his body. To feel the unexpected jab of bony knees when he dreamed.

I knew the exactness of the days. Five more postcards for Jim. Five more days to see her. "No, we won't be finished." I said. "I'll be home on the ninth. I can't wait either. I love you."

"Are you okay?"

His voice sounded faint and worried but also rushed and exasperated. He would be pulling off his glasses now. He had explained years ago that everything was easier when the world was blurred.

"Yes, I love you. Don't worry about me. I'll be all right. We'll talk more about it the next call. Have a good meeting."

After I hung up, I felt lost. I went to the mirror. Would the woman have been surprised? Would she have been glad for a chance to experiment? I fingered my nipple. Did her boyfriend put his mouth against her with gentle competence? Did my son do the same with Carla?

I got into bed. I reached to turn out the lamp. Darkness descended. I closed my eyes. I saw Mark and Carla in the car. Half reclining. His lips seek out her breasts. She holds his head. His hand goes from her waistband to the centre of her stomach, reaching past the sweater, lifting her bra slowly. One breast emerging. Nipple unfolding. Head bent. Tongue extended.

TRACY CHARETTE FEHR   Woman Circle #1 © 1992
Conte, pastel, ink on paper

COMMUNITY,
POLITICS,
ORGANIZING

The Bisexual Anthology Collective

(Leela Acharya, Nancy Chater, Dionne Falconer,
Sharon Lewis, Leanna McLennan & Susan Nosov)

Toward a Feminist Bisexual Politic: A Discussion
Edited by Ravida Din & Nancy Chater

NANCY: I would define a bisexual politics firstly within an anti-racist feminist framework which considers ways that sexuality, especially women's sexuality, is political because of how it intersects with power. All kinds of power — state power through institutions, capitalism, which commodifies and exploits sexuality, and social relations of power. From that perspective, women's sexuality, in effect all sexuality, has now been *politicized*. Another important element is that, within this feminist framework, a bisexual politic is about women's sexual agency, rather than women's sexual victimization. Whether heterosexual, lesbian, bisexual or otherwise, it's about women as sexual subjects, not objects. So it's part of a politics of empowerment.

DIONNE: I lost part of what you were saying, Nancy, because the language is really theoretical.

NANCY: Yeah, I know my language was theoretical, but this is one of the ways I think about it. I'll try to clarify. I'm setting the politics of bisexuality in a framework that is coming out of feminism and out of gay and lesbian activism. Those are the main arenas in which sexuality has been struggled over and organized around, and talked about in a more public and political context. Instead of seeing sexuality as something "natural," something given, these movements have said, no, it's socially constructed. It's controlled by the state. There are all kinds of institutions and ideologies involved that attempt to define our sexualities for us.

SHARON: So are you saying that as bisexual feminists we are trying to locate a definition that isn't socially constructed? Because that to me is impossible. Something that I'm trying to keep in mind as an end goal in defining a bisexual politic is that what we are really doing is *reshaping* the social construction of sexuality.

NANCY: And bringing it out in the open, making it conscious. The ideologies of sexuality as natural and "God given" and so on obscure the way that particular agendas are at stake.

SHARON: I wonder how we do that and remain self-reflexive about it. As we push forward with our socially constructed vision of feminism, anti-racism and sexuality, how do we remain self-reflexive?

SUSAN: I wouldn't conceptualize a reshaping of the social construction of sexuality as the premise for, or end goal of, defining a bisexual politics. I do believe, though, that movement occurs through our visibility, through our naming ourselves and through our reflections on how we identify within a social and perhaps even biological context. This movement plays a part in how changes are being made in current definitions and social/biological constructions of sexuality. This reshaping occurs along with a recognition of bisexuality as a legitimate sexuality and is largely hinged on bisexual visibility and community. This for me is closer to an "end goal" regarding a bisexual politic.

DIONNE: I think part of what bisexuality is is a challenging of the existing social construction which is an "either/or" concept; either you are heterosexual or you're homosexual — gay or lesbian. Bisexuality shows that sexuality is not so clear cut as either/or and that, in fact, there's either, or, both, neither and all kinds of permutations and connotations.

NANCY: The politics of bisexuality also challenge the institution of heterosexuality, which is defined as the norm. From the queer side, from the non-heterosexual side, we have to look at heterosexuality and its institutions, how they work and therefore how to fight them.

LEELA: I think part of the politics is to take power, to self-identify and to challenge the norms you've all mentioned. But there is still more. We have yet to politicize the desire aspect of bisexuality in the way that gay male desire or lesbian desire has been politicized.

LEANNA: The important thing is to integrate a politicized interpretation of bisexuality with other empowerment struggles, to create space. There has to be a context. If you are breaking down the way that sexuality is constructed, it's not just bisexuals who are going to benefit from it.

DIONNE: I hear what you're saying. Like even the notion of a "bisexual politic" I don't see as something that exists in and of itself. I look at it within lesbian and gay struggles. You know, if there's anything I see bisexual politics outside of, it's heterosexuality. I don't know if opposition is the right word, but I see it in opposition to heterosexuality and challenging the notions presented by heterosexuality.

SUSAN: I too see the exposure of a bisexual politic, existence, identity or what have you as a challenge and opposition to heterosexism. Bisexuals present an opposition by virtue of our existence. Naming this existence within a sexual politic is a confrontation of heterosexism on another level. The unfortunate piece in all of this is that, to fight hetero-sexism, we end up creating new labels. Even though I believe that labels are often created by and for the dominant, who never have to label themselves, I use this label "bisexual" as a way of resisting heterosexism because by saying that I'm bisexual, I'm also saying that I'm non-heterosexual. And I'd rather say that I'm a something than a non-something, you know?

LEANNA: I'm not suggesting there should be no politics around bisexual identity but that it doesn't have to be defined as a singular "bisexual politic." Identifying as bisexual can also be a provisional means of calling into question the ways sexual identities are constructed.

LEELA: On the question of the social construction of sexuality, women's sexuality has been historically constructed at many points in time to meet the needs of a capitalist-patriarchal society. But there is a lot of variation in exactly how women's sexuality has been constructed according to factors like class, age, religion and history. But that construction has always been heterosexual, and has served to suppress and control women's sexuality and fertility.

NANCY: Yes, sexuality is very much mediated by or affected by notions of race, class and gender. For instance, in the history of slavery in North America, specific racist sexist ideas were promoted about African women's sexuality. Various types of sexualities are ascribed to particular women at different times in history.

DIONNE: The thing is, race is sexualized and sexuality is racialized. I said before that I don't know if opposition is the correct word in terms of bisexuality but when I think about struggle and organizing with lesbians, gays and other bisexuals, it is about opposing heterosexuality. Within that organizing context, different issues emerge for bisexuals, lesbians and gays. But I do locate the alliances and coalitions and the struggle together within that.

SHARON: For me it's not so much an opposition to heterosexuality as it is an opposition to heterosexism.

NANCY: That's an important distinction. Otherwise we could be suggesting that it is wrong to be heterosexual, which isn't the point. It's more (*in unison with Sharon*) the domination.

LEANNA: I'm trying to get away from definitions that put homosexual and heterosexual as opposites, which leaves bisexual somewhere in the middle, moving between the two. So I think that's a really good point, that you can oppose the domination of heterosexuality and not heterosexual relationships in general.

DIONNE: That is a good point because I think even heterosexuals need to challenge heterosexism.

SUSAN: Absolutely! If an individual lives her/his own life as a heterosexual without owning privilege and challenging the system of heterosexism, which discriminates against all those who are not living that heterosexual life, then that individual needs to be accountable just as much as the system, because systems cannot function without individuals. I consciously use the term "heterosexual individual" because non-heterosexuals challenge the system by virtue of our existence. Granted, we do this to varying degrees, but the concept of accountability is important to create a certain level of allegiance.

DIONNE: So do you think it is possible to define a bisexual politic?

NANCY: Not completely. I think it's something that is very much in process, especially in Canada. But it's a good question to go back to and look at.

LEANNA: I don't even think that the goal is to define a "bisexual politic" because there's no way that all bisexuals will ever agree. Feminism has become feminisms as women have acknowledged and insisted on different ways of seeing things.

Where is Our Struggle?

SHARON: For me the question to be asking is, in what shape or form do we want power, since the basic struggle and end result is that we're asking for power. What we need to strategize about more is what do we want this power to look like?

NANCY: I wouldn't say "asking" for power. I would say taking power, or exercising power.

LEELA: I would also say taking power. The fact is, though, we are used to viewing power negatively, because that is our experience historically, as women of colour, as workers, etc., power has been exerted over us. Power is relational, and at a broader level, in an advanced capitalist society, we don't have direct control over the larger, external forces; but in relation to strategizing and maintaining the self-reflexivity that Sharon mentioned earlier, we do need to question the ways women *do* have power, in the smaller arenas. For example, through our own grassroots organizing and community building. In this case, the question for me is, why do we, regardless of our sexuality and politics, re-create the very same relations of power we criticize in the first place? There is too much hypocrisy around the issue of women and power...

SHARON: Yeah, not necessarily exercising power over.

LEANNA: ...As in the term empowerment.

DIONNE: I guess for me it's all still located within capitalist society and therefore even when we talk about power — and there's nuances, you know, race impacts on class and that impacts on gender — it's still power within capitalism. And I don't think that under capitalism you can have that kind of power. Within that framework, it's problematic.

SUSAN: It's true. If I am truly wanting to set up or define a bisexual politic and understand it within a system of oppression, I would have to locate it within oppressions, plural.

LEANNA: Oppressions that can't be separated out from one another.

SHARON: Does that mean in order to be bisexual activists we have to be anti-capitalist? In order to strategize? What I'm hearing is that to be activists we have to question our active role...

SUSAN: Within capitalism or any other hierarchical institution.

NANCY: I would say we do that as feminists. We attempt to look at the way that all these forms of power mediate and affect each other.

SHARON: I don't think that's true for all feminists.

DIONNE: I think it should be...

SHARON: Not all bisexual activists are anti-capitalists but what I find appealing is that we're saying we are.

NANCY: That's why I say "as a bisexual feminist." By feminism I mean an analysis of all systems of domination and relations of power. That to me is feminism, therefore I'm a bisexual feminist.

SHARON: Does our struggle imply that it's sexuality we are looking for — I go back to that same question: is the end result to create an anti-oppressive structure? Do we have one we're working toward?

NANCY: I think our struggle is part of a larger, multifaceted one. We work as bisexual feminists both on bisexual politics and also on issues which may include bisexuality less directly.

SHARON: But if those struggles are not just reactive but proactive, what are we making all the links for?

DIONNE: I look at whether that end place has been defined yet, because I think it's a process. The creation of a vision takes time and it takes different people's input. Organizing around gay and lesbian and bisexual rights is a creating of that vision — and incorporating feminism within that, feminism that looks at racism, anti-Semitism, imperialism, colonialism — all of these things are creating that vision; and I don't think the vision is complete yet. We kind of know what we're working toward but to say in a clear-cut way "this is what it is," I don't think that's happened yet. As Susan says, it's complex and because it's complex, I don't think we need to try to simplify it either. Is that all tying in?

Community: What Does It Mean to Us?

LEANNA: For me community is somewhere people can integrate different aspects of their identities.

DIONNE: I know that I don't belong to "a" community. I belong to communities, because there are different communities that incorporate different parts of my identity and my being and there are some that incorporate more of those parts than others. Where I work is community and that's very different although there are people and politics that carry over from other communities, say within the AIDS movement. There are pieces and strands of community for me within the gay, lesbian and bisexual movement, feminist movement, anti-racist movement. But there are other pieces missing, just as there are within the feminist movement or within Black communities.

SUSAN: Community is very important to me. When I look at who makes up my community there is a role for my bisexual friends and allies, but my community is made up of many of the parts I have within me and many that I don't, as well. My community is not focused entirely on my sexuality. But in terms of my sexuality, I would say that I need bisexuals in my life and, in fact, as long as I can remember, my community has been almost entirely women, most of whom are lesbian.

SHARON: Here, we're a group of bisexual women. But we're not just bisexual women, we're all feminists. We all have some sort of understanding of anti-capitalist strategies, you know, so there are things that have brought us together, besides our bisexuality.

LEELA: Speaking of the multiple identities and communities we inhabit, it means there are many parts to our whole being. And these parts are not necessarily fragmented. They can be whole. We can work, socialize, move and mix with different people but still remain whole. So in terms of community, I agree that it's not that simple. To me, a community based on a shared identity is not always enough. I also need more.

NANCY: I think some kind of bisexual community is useful. Especially at this point historically, in terms of bisexual presence and visibility and activism. When I was first coming out, the fact that I saw a notice somewhere that said "bisexual feminist support group meeting at the 519"[1] was very important to me. I went to that group for a brief time. Even though I didn't relate that much to the group, it was important to see that name. To have that group was part of a process, it was one step in a process. So I think one good use for bisexual groups is that they create a presence, a space where bisexual women can find each other and forge community. Not that we only need to be in bisexual groups, but there does need to be a community bisexual presence. Access for bisexual women to all kinds of community spaces, in the sense of public cultural spaces and groups. Where does community take place? Partly in public spaces. How does it grow? Partly through having access to a public voice. Such as having magazines...

SUSAN: The only real experience I have had working within a "community" of bisexual women is this anthology collective and it's been a unique and meaningful experience in the work we've done, but also in the ease around discussing issues related to sexuality and oppression. I'm sure that our coming from shared standpoints around sexuality is a major factor.

DIONNE: Yeah, and probably part of the reason is that bisexuality is still being defined. Whereas people have more set or rigid ideas about what it means to be a lesbian, to be a gay man. With bisexuality people are still asking what does it mean; you talk to me and I go on one definition, I talk to you and you go on another one.

NANCY: Uh huh. And it might be a strength of bisexuality. It seems to me that we often have to be flexible, creative and constantly negotiating with different meanings, different contexts and all sorts of power relations in our day-to-day lives. For instance, if we're with a man and dealing with heterosexism, how do we negotiate our own relative empowerment within that situation? If we're in a relationship with a lesbian, how do we negotiate that? Or as a bisexual woman with a bisexual man...We shift around so much that we have to be creative and flexible. And I think that can be a strength that we bring to our political work and thinking.

SUSAN: We shift on various levels. Who we are loving, who we are desiring. Not just who we're with physically but also in our everyday way of being in the world.

Building Visibility Through Organizing

LEANNA: It seems quite easy to put "bisexual" in the name of an organization without educating yourselves about bisexuality and issues that affect bisexuals. Changing the name of a lesbian and/or gay group or organization doesn't necessarily address what really needs to be addressed.

SHARON: You don't even have to have bisexuals in your organization, you can just put it in the title.

LEANNA: I think that people who add the name bisexual usually do it for positive reasons — they're recognizing links and making those links — but to talk about changing a name as if that's the solution is really limiting. A group could have a really integrated analysis of bisexuality and not have changed their name. I think it's more important to see that people are recognizing the importance of working together in coalition than it is to look at whether they change their name or not.

NANCY: I don't think it's an either/or thing. Ideally they both change and their name and recognize those things. What I mean is that if they do change their name, it's for sound reasons and actually reflected in the way they work. The circumstances in which I would want to see a name change include when there are bisexuals working in the organization, so it's a way of recognizing their work, or if the organization seeks the work and contributions of bisexuals, it's a way of recognizing that; or when an organization sees a coalition between bisexual, lesbians and gays as useful.

DIONNE: So you're saying, Nancy, that they should?

NANCY: Yeah, that these are the circumstances in which I would like to see "bisexual" in a name. Another one would be if an organization is aiming or claiming to represent or speak for "gay communities" broadly defined, which I take to include bisexuals. We are still so invisible. We are building visibility through organizing and through doing work in the community, or communities.

SUSAN: I don't want bisexuality to be an add-on either. I also think that while we are challenging broader definitions of "non-heterosexuality" we need to be working for the inclusion of other groups presently omitted.

NANCY: Are you saying that you wouldn't want the name bisexual added to a gay and lesbian group?

SUSAN: For me the question focuses more on why there is resistance to including the name bisexual alongside lesbian and gay. I believe there are many reasons for this, but when the reasons are biphobic they are not acceptable, and this is where we must push for change.

LEANNA: As much as I have a problem with an add-on approach and see the limitations of just adding a name, something you said, that Sharon also mentioned, inspires me to think that including the term bisexual can create space and let bisexuals know they are welcome. Including "bisexual" in the name of an organization could also be useful to people who feel they have to decide to be either lesbian/gay or heterosexual. If they see "bisexual" it may open up the possibility of not having to decide between dichotomous alternatives.

LEELA: For me, one form of visibility through organizing has come through in the "South Asian feminist *Gup-shup*" that appears in this book. It took a lot of time and commitment, but five of us got together and articulated ourselves for the first time around the issue of bisexuality and what it means to us.

Being BI, Being OUT

DIONNE: I guess the operative question is, what is a bisexual identity? Is it enough if I'm in a relationship with a man or with a woman to just say that I'm bisexual and that is affirming my bisexual identity? Does that mean my bisexual identity has to be played out in some kind of physical way by fucking men and women at the same time or...

LEANNA: I think there is a kind of myth attached to bisexual identity, Black identity or any kind of identity. No one version of an identity will work for everyone. For some people who identify as bisexual, bisexuality is about an openness to the desire that they feel for people of both sexes, which does not necessarily have to be expressed physically. What's so interesting about bisexuality, or any sexuality, is that one does not have to act out one's desire to identify a certain way.

SUSAN: Another aspect of sexuality is the question of visibility and invisibility. As bisexual, how I am seen in the world may not reflect who I am. For instance, when I am seen with an intimate partner, there is the assumption that I am monogamous, which may or may not be the case. My sexuality is generally defined by others in relation to that one person, be they male or female. As a bisexual woman, this process always omits a piece of my identity, and so my bisexuality is rendered invisible.

LEANNA: Maintaining that openness doesn't allow you to make assumptions about other people based on who they are with, which is another thing that's interesting...

DIONNE: For me, the main way my bisexuality is made visible across different kinds of relationships is by me affirming that's who I am. Most often my relationships have been with women, so the assumption is I'm lesbian. So anywhere I go, I am bisexual. I don't change how I identify based upon the space I'm in. People can make assumptions about my identity. However, when it comes from these lips, it's always the same thing and has been for a number of years, and that's how I have been able to maintain my bisexual identity. It isn't necessarily through what you see. You just create things and make assumptions from what you see.

LEANNA: Things are more complex than they seem. You can't just slot people into categories.

NANCY: For me being out is one of the ways I strive to incorporate my bisexuality into my day-to-day life. That may not mean announcing to someone "I'm bisexual," though I do that quite often. Working on this anthology has been great that way! Talking about it creates the perfect opportunity to come out — and I don't feel alone because of this editorial collective and the nature of the project. When it's not a matter of making that statement and more when I'm talking about my life and something comes up that involves bisexuality, I strive to "speak from my bisexual centre," in other words, to just say it and be myself. I don't take on how the listener may respond or judge me or whatever, I just want to be myself in that moment. Which isn't always possible because of homophobia and stuff — sometimes their judgements matter or I feel too exposed and vulnerable. But the more out I am, generally the better I feel.

SUSAN: Being out, I think, means being visibly non-heterosexual, read: homosexual. It's trickier now that I am living with my male lover. Now it means changing my name to have B.I. as my middle initials. I feel like I need to label myself and speak "as a bisexual" more often than if I were involved with a woman, or if I were celibate. I'm struggling not to be "invisibilized," or assimilated, into the straight mainstream. This becomes painful because I don't want to have to live that way. Having to say it over and over again feels like a rip-off. That's the piece I find most difficult. It doesn't represent me fully. The love and desire I have for women and men is euphoric and not a struggle in itself.

LEANNA: In what ways do you think that experience is coming from the inside and in what ways from the outside?

SUSAN: It's hard to say whether it's coming from outside or inside. That's almost irrelevant. All I know is that it plays into feeling swooshed into assimilating. A lot like how I feel about being seen only as white and being Jewish gets erased by that process.

SHARON: It would maybe help to be involved with a bisexual man who's got his politics, but —

LEANNA: Then it doesn't necessarily integrate class or race and other things.

SHARON: Regardless of the man, it doesn't take away from the invisibility that Susan was talking about. It doesn't matter if he's straight or gay or bisexual or he's done his work or not, you still have to deal with that invisibility if you are a bisexual woman with a man.

With a man, I don't want to have to think, well I shouldn't kiss him in public because I'll be labelled, and that's ridiculous, right, but I've done that and I've thought, well I won't kiss you or I won't do that — so what the fuck's the point? It's a really painful thing and it's such an odd thing, cause you're constantly coming out then: "I'm bisexual, really, I really am." (*laughter*) Being with a man is a different coming-out process than if I'm with a woman and I'm labelled lesbian. In that case, fine. I don't need, or don't have the same urge to say, well, I'm not actually lesbian, I'm bisexual. I have that need with a woman in terms of negotiating in our relationship if I'm gonna sleep with a man and that becomes an issue. But I don't have the need to come out as bisexual in the same way.

This brings up two issues, strategizing and trying to educate.

LEANNA: But it's also personal.

SHARON: I guess, yeah, on a personal level, when I'm sitting with a group of women, they usually know I'm bisexual.

LEANNA: Often that's the case for me now, but it's taken time to create that in my life. It wasn't always that way.

SUSAN: It's not an all-or-nothing thing when we talk about visibility and invisibility. Being seen as a lesbian doesn't have a negative impact on my sense of my identity. Being thought of as heterosexual does deny a part of who I am, the part that is seen as "wrong" or "different." Because of that I correct wrong impressions of me in different ways, be it in lesbian or heterosexual worlds.

DIONNE: A key here, though, is where we want to be socially and politically. It's because we want to locate ourselves around lesbians, gays and bisexuals, around like-minded people — 'cause I mean who wants to hang out with a racist, homophobic, sexist dog (*laughter*) — so that's also what makes it so much more complicated.

Sometimes I think about when I was dating a couple of guys and some of my friends never knew, they just never knew. Only those who came to my house or whatever knew, but other people didn't know about it because I wanted to locate myself within a certain place, right? In a way it's like a — I was going to say sacrifice, but it's not sacrifice because it's also a clarity that this is a space that gives me a clearer affirmation of self than to be in that other space — a straight space, that is.

NANCY: That also has to do with the point that is often made about lesbianism, that it's not just a matter of who you're sleeping with, it's a world view or a way of life or whatever. I think that's true for bisexuality or bisexual feminists, anyway. It's not only who we're sleeping with but, again, it's a sense of community, a sense of shared values. And so to lose that and be cut off from that is very painful and a major loss.

LEANNA: It's important to make a distinction here, because I don't want to set up heterosexuality as this space where there's no room for bisexual, lesbian or gay identities. In certain groups of straight people, there is the space for those who don't conform to a conservative heterosexual norm.

LEELA: Those are important points you have raised...Sometimes I'm not sure what to do about the invisibility I experience, whatever form it takes, whether it's vis-à-vis a relationship with a lesbian or in the straight mainstream. For me, it depends on the situation and how important it is to me, and I think the only way to address this is to keep taking initiatives to prevent the erasure, but like you say, it's tiring to be constantly coming out, and explaining yourself to everyone...

Thinking About Privilege

DIONNE: One of the ways heterosexual privilege has played out in my relationships with men is they have been *private* relationships, whereas my relationships with women are much more public in terms of scrutiny, in terms of the criticism and in terms of the affirmation.

LEANNA: So, if you keep it private then it's privileging it because it's not being criticized?

DIONNE: No, it's more than just the criticism part of it. It's also that aspect of heterosexuality which says that relationships are private and what you do behind closed doors is your business and nobody else's and all of that stuff. So it's also the privileging of all of the things that are attached to that privacy. Not just the criticism, but that was another part of it.

LEELA: I find the issue of heterosexual privilege often turns into a judgement and a dismissal of women. It's very convenient for us to dismiss women in this way. Privilege is something that exists in many forms and it calls for taking responsibility. I have a hard time judging women, dismissing them and assuming they have no agency because they have men in their lives. I feel it's a lot more complicated than that.

SUSAN: As well, privilege, be it heterosexual privilege, bisexual privilege or what have you, is something that cannot be measured. Privilege and oppression exist on various levels. How we are accountable for that is often unmeasurable by onlookers.

SHARON: And it's complicated by race and gender. And it's about legitimacy. If you go to the bank for a loan, as a straight-looking couple you'll be more likely than a gay couple to get a loan regardless of how much you make, so legitimacy also translates into power on some level.

LEELA: Definitely. It's the layers of legitimacy a woman gains when she is attached to a man in any patriarchal society. But, that legitimacy is just not there for single women, who might be lesbian, bisexual or straight. So I see two things here. There is the legitimacy of having a male partner. And there's also the legitimacy associated with coupledom. In any case, privilege exists in many forms. I think taking responsibility is the key to addressing issues of privilege.

DIONNE: When I think about privilege, I don't think about it in an individual way. I think of it in structural ways, like going to the bank for a loan, like housing, different things...

SHARON, NANCY: Children, adoption...

DIONNE: ...Losing your kid if you're a lesbian. I mean those are the ways that privilege manifests itself. In terms of ourselves bringing it down to individual levels and how we struggle against it — even the thing, you know, Sharon, that you were talking about, like walking down the street with your male partner, I'm not gonna hold his hand. I'm not gonna do any of that because I know if I do that with my woman lover somebody can bash our heads in, right? The difference is if I'm with a man and I do this, it does accord me that kind of legitimacy. When I see heterosexual couples kissing on the subway it really annoys me because I know two women doing that, no way, people would freak. So I think about it in those kinds of ways because when you work out the nitty-gritty, like who is this man and it being compounded by race, language, religion, all kinds of things, right...

NANCY: Then it's a question of, so what do you do with that privilege or how do you use it? I'm in a relationship with a man and he's heterosexual. One political strategy I take is that I'm never going to get married. I'm thirty-five and I've never been married. I don't support the institution of marriage because, for one thing, it's heterosexist.

DIONNE: But would you do that with a woman in terms of having a commitment ceremony — I guess that's probably another story.

NANCY: Oh, a commitment ceremony is a possibility even with a man. But I do not want — I reject — state and church sanctions of my relationship. Now, I don't know if that's really dealing with heterosexual privilege but it does have an impact on family. I'm choosing not to get married. And then people ask me, "you know, you're in this long-term relationship. When are you getting married?" That gives me an opening to say that I don't support marriage and these are the reasons why, and say that I'm bisexual, and so challenge heterosexism. That's one thing I do in terms of privilege.

SHARON: I just want to go back to one thing Dionne was saying around whether or not we're kissy-kissy on the street. For me it's a complex issue and every time I engage in it I think about it, but I also think that I don't want to *not* do it. I want to think about a positive way to do it. A positive way to have that freedom to express myself. And when I'm with a wo-man, I want to be able to do it. At the same time, I recognize the dangers. Does it mean, then, and by what Dionne was saying, that if I hide my hetero-sexual relationship I'll be seen as being a "good bisexual girl?" So if I'm not all over him or we're not very public, does that mean that I can be "good"?

NANCY: But then people can accuse you of closeting your straight relationship as a way of gaining credibility in lesbian circles.

LEANNA: The bottom line is you have to be true to yourself because everyone's not going to love everything you do anyway. It's a matter of finding ways that you can work in your relationships around issues of privilege and oppression.

SHARON: Trying to negotiate feminism in a relationship with a man is for me also a paramount struggle.

NANCY: That's something I deal with a lot too. One thing I do is I have my priorities and my political commitments and I take that space within my relationship. I go to a lot of events. I go to demonstrations or I work on projects or whatever, most often without my male partner because it's a feminist setting and a women's setting. I take that space within my relationship and I set those priorities. That's one of the ways I negotiate being a feminist involved with a man.

SUSAN: So what is responsible bisexuality?

DIONNE: Yeah, I guess it's about self and self-analyzing and doing all of that, right. Talking about accountability and being "responsible" is again tied into what I said earlier about where we want to locate ourselves. I'm locating myself within a lesbian/gay community so you know I'm gonna have to speak to some of these issues within that community. But the challenging of heterosexism also exists for lesbians and gay men. Just because somebody is lesbian or gay does not make them immune to having certain kinds of thoughts or behaving in certain kinds of ways...

NANCY: ...Or being politically conservative.

LEANNA: Or being given heterosexual privilege in situations...

NANCY: ...Where they're in the closet.

DIONNE: Or even in terms of how people look and if they don't fit the stereotypes of "what a lesbian looks like," they are assumed to be heterosexual; so some of this is not just particular to us as bisexual women. Lesbians need to challenge themselves around some of these issues and sometimes that doesn't happen. In fact, the stuff around bisexual women having heterosexual privilege blah, blah, blah, I think sometimes is used to invalidate what we have to say and who we are.

And I think heterosexual feminists need to think about how they sometimes have relationships with men that nobody hears about...

LEANNA: And also putting the responsibility onto heterosexual men who are pro-feminist is important.

SUSAN: The other piece that's been mentioned, and where it comes home for me too around privilege and accountability, is that responsibility regarding privilege is a responsibility outward, but also toward myself.

NANCY: Integrity strikes me as a good word here because of its double meaning; integrity as in ethics, being ethical, and integrity as in wholeness.

NOTE

1 The 519 Community Centre, at 519 Church St. in Toronto.

Michele Spring-Moore

Queergirl

To be read aloud

What a state I'm in, Day One post civil–rights: Karl cuts his
      Hallowe'en costume Sister Domestica habit into strips for black
      armbands
my body is under siege, my stomach so cramped I can't go to school
      and teach the joys of iambic pentametre, my eyes leaking so I
      can't read in my room alone at night, can't catch my breath,
feel as if I've been kicked in the chest, run over by a Chrysler,
      torpedoed in the teeth, punched out by thousands all over the
      state yelling *Yes! Yes!*, X-ed in the ballot box
by a mob of robots chanting *the wording was confusing*.
Mike returns this week from the South Pole where he's been
      studying. His exact science I can't recall, only that he
      silkscreens Hitler's face
on T-shirts so we can show our friends the connections to
      contemporary fascism
I could say he's a meteorologist examining the political climate,
      but that would be too obvious. All of us are blatant these
      days,
in your face, up half the night screaming at the Democrats' balls,
      crying alone or in our lovers' arms,
planning the next rally, meeting, fundraiser, strategy
I'm tired. Tired of going door to door, leafletting windshields in
church parking lots, delivering
campaign brochures at 5 a.m., writing letters, making phone calls,
      protesting,
demonstrating that I'm a human being, that I care about my
      family, that I don't molest children, that I deserve a house
      a job   a car   a bus ride

a movie ticket and popcorn with artificial butter flavouring
that I have a right to exist
It's been just us for so long, picking up the pieces and moving on.
I'm tired of movement. I want to plant myself in moist dark
        earth, handfuls of clay stuck together in my fist, rich
        as night.
I've been outlawed, pushed outside the margins of the books.

What a state I'm in. But I haven't always been illegal. Last
        year
I camped out at the House of Edgewood
named after the cramped apartments in *Paris is Burning* where
        African-American New York drag queens sew tulle, invent
        costumes, create realness
real executive, real movie star, real prom queen, real homeboy
        homoboy hustler slut cheerleader model anything but
In the kitchen, under the blue neon art deco clock Jim saved from
        his grandfather's movie theatre in Buffalo, Wyoming
Karl bakes chocolate roll-outs with my cookie cutters: dark
        brown Santas in March, camels, bunnies, teddies, hearts,
        while my favourite fags discuss their next fundraiser's guest
        list:
Miss Thing!? In this *house!? No* way, *girlfriend!*
Well, how about him? Isn't she just?!
Crystal and Rob, white lefty men raised Christian turned
        Buddhist turned queer spiritualist turned radical
        disillusioned atheist and Jim, Jewish PhD student activist,
strut around their living room in Boulder, Colorado, sounding like
        a bunch of burning drag queens they've seen on the big screen
a pale imitation, a celebration
to be real...
celebration of themselves
        of us

I'm different here than I am with women friends
you guys give me permission to be raucous, politically incorrect,
       out of line, out of step, offensive to anyone who hates what's
       queer in us
I can put away goddess-worship, politeness, quiet, solitude, fear
       of cattiness, dirt, sex, pain, camp   fear of fear
can say *tit* and nobody will glare. No one cares to keep the boys
       and girls straight here
we vogue and limpwrist and runway up and down the halls all
       night, turn on the VCR and turn bad Hollywood movies into
       high camp,
become academic queens, debate the functions of drag or the
       symbolic meaning of a poem's cocksucking scene

then go dancing at the gaybar, watch gayboys and girldykes,
       bykes and bi-boys
dance while their civil rights are being stripped faster and
       slicker than the disco fags peel off their white T-shirts
       beneath the mirror balls,
everybody shakes their asses and bulging crotches and unbra'd
       breasts under one-size-too-small shirts and silk blouses
till the lights come up at 2 a.m. last call last pickup last chance
       last dance for love for

queers unafraid to move hips, thighs, rears, hands, arms, fingers,
       shoulders, heads, torsos, chests, feet, legs, knees
display themselves in mirrors, stare, play, vogue, posture, strut,
       gyrate, grind

       a few jerk their stiff limbs, shuffle awkwardly
       as if they haven't met their bodies yet

snap divas, the newly-out awakening from long hibernations,
>   fags soused in cologne, pool dykes at the table, cue sticks like
>   oversized dildoes in hand
disco queens/drag queens/leather queens/size queens/chicken
>   queens/marriage queens/new age queens/snap queens/ do-me
>   queens/drama queens/grass is always greener queens
>   men who collect brown-skinned boys, intellectual bisexuals, PC
>   lesbian feminist sometimes separatists, working-class diesel
>   dykes in sneakers and jeans, gay women in designer sweaters,
lesbian hippies dressed for a Dead show in limp cotton T-shirts
>   torn strategically to show off their shoulder and breast
>   tattoos of Ishtar and the Egyptian goddesses' asps
and I have lusted after all: Black dreadlocked dykes
compact brown-skinned working-class Sicilians who eye me across
>   the room
waspy blondes with miniscule ponytails who look like twelve-year-
>   old boys from the back
graceful femmes in black silk pants, dancing with arms akimbo
dark-eyed Chicanas with wind in their hair
the white pair in black leather, she in a dress, she in pants, one's
>   hands cuffed to the other's belt

light switches:
all stop dancing and drinking and drift out the door to little
>   sports cars and big pickup trucks,
head for La Diner or the Royal Queen Restaurant or home with
>   lovers to snuggle in bed
or with tricks for more acrobatics than they could manage in the
>   dance floor's dark corners

Hallowe'en, our national holiday, the show's even better for
      tourists out slumming,
boys dressed as Miss Furr and Miss Skeene, the Terminatrix,
      Sisters of Perpetual Indulgence: the Order of Vagina Dentata
butch or femme girls, bitches, witches, virgins and whores
silk stockings, black leather jackets and chaps, handcuffs, tit
      clamps, high heels, flats, flaming lipstick, jockstraps,
      G-strings

But we outdid this ritual once, in '79, and the second and third
times, when we took over the capitol — Hallowe'en
      and San Francisco Freedom Day Parade rolled into one and
      add half a million or so:
March on Washington 1987, 1993
queers, queers, everywhere
and not a drop to drink
Jack said *I just went to a bar and it was either the cruisiest*
      political scene or the most political cruise scene
I've ever seen. Dupont Circle wall-to-wall men till the wee
      hours,
and the women all went over the D.C.-Maryland line to see a
      lesbian comedian, packed into little red Toyotas named
      Rojita for the ride back to the city,
sat up all night talking in hotel rooms, bars, baths, bookstores,
Lambda Rising open twenty-four hours for out-of-town guests, so literary
      types would have somewhere to cruise
and you could stand on any northwest corner and converse with a
      dozen strangers from around the country

like one big queer party to end all parties, everyone out on the
      streets with no fear of baseball bats and spit

I called you, Brian, that weekend from the D.C. Greyhound
        station where I waited for my bus north
didn't think much about the incongruity of calling my male lover
        from that greasy phone at dusk, believing you'd understand
        why I cried
tried to tell you about meeting Michael Hardwick in nonviolent
        civil disobedience training and thinking, *he looks like a*
        straight California surfer boy with big hair,
about the march motto, *For love and for life, we're not going back,*
about the PWAs leading the pack down Pennsylvania Avenue,
about the dykes arrested on the Supreme Court steps, arms linked,
kissing as cops in bright yellow latex gloves pried them apart, as
        hundreds of us chanted
Your gloves don't match your shoes! Your gloves don't match your
        shoes!
Loud and Clear! Lesbians are here!
The whole world is watching! The whole world is watching!
Cameras were watching.
                I was watching.
You didn't understand my tears and any explanation I could have
        given would have flowed like the Potomac through our lives

I came out to Martin in D.C., while marching in circles, when he
        volunteered for the *Empty Closet*, that little queer paper
        paid for by the little queer organization run by little queer
        volunteers in that mid-sized city, that rag, the oldest queer
        newspaper in New York state
Martin: always layers, all those labels, multiple identities:
        bisexual-identified, Asian American, queer activist, Nisei, twin,
        colourblind, feminist, skilled writer, safe sex educator, gay,
        hearing-impaired, ASL interpreter, member of TOFU, Tough
        Oriental Faggots United, adopted son of Sansei Catholic
        missionaries in South America, "native" speaker of Spanish,
        fluent in six other languages, former Mormon, incest survivor,
        conversion "therapy" survivor, recovering alcoholic and
        addict, person with AIDS and Chronic Fatigue Syndrome

continually coming out as something that someone or other in that
community organization didn't understand   including me but
        once in a while I kept my mouth shut, stopped pretending to
        know everything, learned,

came out at a Lesbian Resource Centre meeting when I was eighteen, to
all thirty-five of you, the first dykes I'd ever seen out   side of photos in
        books
I thought you'd all been sex partners at one time or another,
had no idea this is what it looked and felt like to be a member of
a group that expressed friendship openly by touching casually,
        hugging, kissing, holding hands
So these are lesbians, I thought; *they look like normal people,*
        just like everyone else.

Cynthia: you read my coming-out story when I went public in
        print. We helped found the bisexual women's group, then
        spent the next two years wrangling
with the same man and talking about dyke sex and lesbian porn,
        sat around your kitchen, eating fudge, discussing latex squares
        and how to use them, embarrassing politically incorrect
        gossip
in your living room among your collages and assemblages and
hand-me-down chairs, Rapunzel plants, scraps scrounged
        from construction sites and the curb
        You were the only one who could see how I got stuck, always
said *we're too het for the queers and too queer for the hets*

I wanted Ron's arms around me, my head buried in his teddy bear
        stomach so I'd be left alone and I wouldn't have to face my
        difference, my indifference
but the rest of the time I wanted to woman the barricades, fight
        to be able to hold Kim's hand anywhere without stares or
        taunts

I was hired as *Empty Closet* editor, called my lesbian friend
        Anne long-distance to catch up
You're editor of the gay and lesbian paper and you've been seeing
Ron? she asked
Yes   it dawned on me her tone said *betrayal*
thought of defensive replies till I remembered

                                      static
on the line
she'd been in a relationship with a woman for three years but
        had fucked the two most sexist men in our work brigade in
        Nicaragua:
nights humid with the sea
palm leaves rustled like paper
dogs barked at people walking the dirt path to the cinderblock
        outhouse
roosters crowed every hour
norteamericanos snored under mosquito netting
Anne and Eric kissed on a sleeping bag in the cabin's corner
while I wrote in my journal *I don't know who I'm more jealous of —*
        her for having him, or him for having her
the next day in the fields my face said *betrayal*

I've come out to you namechanging sisters over and over in the last
        decade
your fear takes you not to aspirin bottles, but to the bong
you give me stern lectures on physical and spiritual cleansing and
        why I shouldn't eat grilled cheese sandwiches or Milky
        Ways
you womyn-loving wimmin not into material possessions who
        spend seventy-five bucks to have the Venus of Willendorf tattooed
        on your left cheeks   after you changed
        from Mary Jean Miller to Firewalk Stargazer
mysteries disappeared and you knew
Mary Daly invented the wheel, or the goddess did, or men did
        and therefore the world would be better off without it

I too got my knowledge of lesbian feminism from books, but I
    started with magazines:
came out to myself by reading porn snuck from Dad's room when
        everyone was at work, stories of women having sex with
        women, stories for straights and the stray bi like me
My first lesbian thoughts, like yours, were theoretical, but mine
        were based in lust as
I rocked myself to sleep, childhood teddy bear stuffed between
        my twitching legs
I didn't know penetration was patriarchal and women weren't
        supposed to want each other that way

whe I turned eighteen and discovered the bars, I responded like
        Pavlov's dogs to butch,
that hand in the jeans pocket, little boy's tight round ass, that
        casual air as if she could take you and take you then leave
        you however she wanted to,
that barely perceptible once-over, slight smile, leaning on one
        hip and squinting across the green felt,
        chalking the cue stick, strolling, legs spread
that makeupless face so much clearer than so many straight
        womens'
that body, compact or fat, taking up space like a man, looking
        everyone in the eye
never apologizing for existing
How this plus a pair of hightop sneakers made my cunt salivate,
    I can't say,
nor why I was a feminist at twelve, had my first crush on a gay boy
    the year before
but I know it wasn't planned and the feelings came from my gut,
    not my books
and when you fix me with that dead earnest stare and begin to
    drone about the evils of pornography

I wonder if your feminism has ever sent your fingers into a
              woman's soft wet vagina making loud slurping sucking sounds
again and again till she sighs then groans then rolls over
squeezing
like C-clamps
like a vise
till you know you'll never type with that hand again
talk all you want about loving womyn energy
theory's fine, but sometimes I'd rather suck nipples

Your face says betrayal. We keep fighting, both of us convinced
deep inside we're not legitimate queers
I'm just bi, not a real dyke   you came out only
last year, haven't had a girlfriend yet, a lover, a life
              partner, whatever word is in vogue this week

both of us ask *where's home?*
in a forest of crisp pubic hair, in a warm armpit, in a snake-
              tongued mouth, in my own body
sitting on a cock standing ship's mast above the belly
inside the sea coves of a woman, heading toward the womb
inside the latex bags we can't fuck without
inside the head   the gut   the cunt
wherever lust is manufactured, then the theory to support it, the
              will to resist the world's crushing refusal of it

Porn was closet fantasy, something to do instead of my high
              school homework. Senior year, I came out to Amy in the most
              roundabout ways
watched her at her locker greeting male and female friends:
did she kiss her?   hug him?   touch her lower
back?   again?   does that mean she's bi?
I dropped hints, listened to gossip, read her Christmas card over
              and over,
finally became her pal, got Dad to drive us to The Who and
              Beatles movies

went to punk rock concerts where she danced like a dervish with
      college boys who barely glanced at me
but I didn't care about them, wanted only to run my hands where
      they ran theirs, through Amy's carrot-red soft spiky hair, to
      feel her large breasts hugging my small ones
I tried for months to impress her by sketching John Lennon,
      murdered early that winter,
staging '60s-style happenings, sitting in a giant trash bag
      chanting *peace* like Yoko Ono
Amy loved it   She also began dating my kid
      brother's best friend
they played electric guitar in our basement while Amy screeched
      lead vocals, then sat in the living room chairs on each other's
      laps
acrobatic positions that made me wonder whether they'd
      had sex yet
after they kissed cutesily Amy said they were going to get
      married, have seventeen kids, call themselves the Rainbow Family
I thought she was losing her cool
when David's parents went camping one weekend, Amy slept
      with him and told her mother she was at my house
I told Mom, she told David's mom, all the kids were angry at me

but I didn't care by then because I wanted Craig more than I'd
      ever wanted Amy
Craig who didn't try to paw me or call me ugly as other guys had,
      who had a cute little ass in Jordache jeans
his brother, my good friend, said *Michele, Craig is gay*
but I thought he was jealous of the attention I gave his brother
we dated a few months, neither of us came out and I didn't care
      what his sexual preferences were or how he was oriented
in a year we'd graduated from the suburban malls and holding
      sweaty hands at roller rinks
to drag shows at the downtown bars

Craig and I came out to Maya, Liza and Marcella when they
        waited our tables and teased the boys for tips
or at their hair salons or cafés or whatever small business they
        owned so they didn't have to work for another boss who
        hated fags and feared they'd give the customers AIDS
they spent hundreds of dollars at Fabrics and Findings, hundreds
        of hours at the sewing machine
sequinned cloth, feather boas in thirteen colours, tight gold lamé
        minis slit up the sides, foam-rubber fake tits
elaborate sets at the bar's Sunday tea dance, their perfect lip
        sync, constrained dramatic torch singer hand gestures, arm
        flailing
to be real...
there is an art to this, no matter how many pro-feminist sensitive
        new age guys say it's a misogynist stereotyped portrayal of
        women and makes heteros believe all gay men wear dresses
Honey, if I looked that good in a short skirt, I'd wear one onstage
        too
and I think genderfuck is the most fun you can have with your
        clothes on

Let's do the Time Warp again: I went to college, came out at *The
Rocky Horror Picture Show*, watched a cast of teenagers act
out their own queer fantasy in front of the screen,
stared at the star, a girl playing a man dressed as a woman,
Sweet Transvestite
her painted-on tattoo said *Pure Sex*   I didn't
        know how girls did it, but I fantasized about kissing her,
        finding her
alone in the women's restroom, taking her
to the last stall and running my hands over her tall slim body,
        under her black garter belt, panties, camisole, platform
        shoes, smearing her exaggerated lipstick, eyeshadow
I was an eighteen-year-old virgin, had never even french kissed

but I sure could talk dirty. Six months later, a Rocky Regular,
     had a homemade photo ID so the
     suburban mallplex theatre managers would let me in free,
a new gang of friends, fledgling gays and bi's finishing high
     school, starting community college
coming out, getting kicked out of the house
Shari's father beat her mother till the last fight
                                 Shari punched
     a hole in the wall, broke her hand
and she and her mom left. Patrick was an Air Force brat whose
     father had retired, found a job with Kodak, bought a house in
     Chili, New York
Patrick missed England for years because he didn't have to worry
     about being masculine there, could wear whatever sorts of
     clothes he wanted.   His mother tried to kill
     herself
Perry and I were lucky   our parents were divorced
only once. Each of TJ's parents had married four times

Rocky became our family, three-hundred amply-stuffed red acrylic seats our
     home
TJ took over as transvestite, the girl I licked my lips at went on to
     community theatre, I discovered my own talent: downing
     Shari's Jack Daniels or blackberry brandy, hiding empty
bottles behind the stage curtains,
yelling lines to the crowd of teens as stoned and confused as I was
when the soundtrack sang *and when worlds collide*
said George Pal to his bride
I'm gonna give you some ter-ri-ble thrills
I hollered *like a fuck!*   Every Friday and Saturday
     at midnight for the next year and a half I screamed words my
     mother and great-aunt had taught me nice girls not only
     do not say, but pretend do not exist:
orgy, orgasm, vibrator, douche, slut, incest, asshole, hard-on, beat
     off, blow-job
bisexual

not only did God not drop the roof on me, but I got laughs, loud
       ones, lots of them, weekend after weekend
I was afraid to speak in my college classrooms, but in my celluloid
       haven I could not shut my mouth

until I came out the next year with Maria, my first lover, and I
       discovered the worst kind of silence: believing someone you
       care about knows what you're thinking
a few weeks after we began dating, we went to a Holly Near
       concert,
returned to my cell-block dorm room, kissed and caressed, clothes
       on,
my narrow bed against the wall   later as I drove her home,
       she said I'd teased her
bewilderment: I thought only men said these things to women

Maria, while you were at work and I was in class or the campus
       pub,
I began the push-me-pull-you of hetero men,
came out to them, those who didn't know what coming out was,
       those who asked ignorant questions
       because I was the first out dyke they'd met
those who thought *split down the middle* meant going on the
       road

A decade after you and I broke up and I realized I wasn't a
       lesbian, I came out to Guy on the road, riding in his lime-
       green '70s VW van as he drove through the pass,
through the whole Colorado Rocky Mountain High aging hippie
       trip
I saw the little lift of the eyebrow behind his wire-rimmed
       glasses and I could hear him think *bisexual women are exotic,*
       insatiable
but I was too desperate for hugs to get offended, though *OK, let's*
ride this one out and see where it takes me

next morning I said I could be a dyke if I didn't like sucking cock so
    much
he just groaned and moved, appreciating my snaildarter tongue
    but not this candour unusual for me
I can do it but I still can't talk about it, not even in the dark
but I did get out one more thing: *no, we're not having sex without
    a rubber*
I waited for the raincoat line, but he was too slick for that,
said he'd lose all sensation, quoted me Centers for Disease
    Control statistics on white heteros and AIDS, said the risks
    weren't as high as I thought
because I hung out in a community that was going through an
    epidemic
He and I didn't fuck that weekend.

I taught a creative writing class and you sat in the back left
    corner
which I've now dubbed the queer seat
because some non-het kid always sits there the entire semester.
My ol' reliable gaydar went off the first time I looked your way,
    Mike, but I never assume anything any more
not till I got your gray recyled-paper environmentally-correct
    journal loaded
with drunken rantings written alone in your bedroom in your
    parents' good Catholic house when you could get away from
    babysitting the six younger kids
you slept twelve hours a day and I could see the pills coming, the
    rope, the knives, the gun at your temple,
but I was wrong: it was razor blades at your wrists,
not a serious attempt and I was drunk that night, you said
I came out so you'd feel safe with me, tried to give you the card
for the campus counselling centre, tried to
    talk to you, tried not to feel like a failure because I couldn't
save another kid, but you thought I was trying to drag you from
    the closet so you held onto the doorframe and kicked

you couldn't tell your parents, it would devastate them, they
         were very religious, the family was already messed up
         enough, you had to set an example for your brothers and sisters
Yes, I said, you have to do what you feel comfortable with, just
         take the card in case you want it later, the counselling centre's
         free.   *Yes, you'll make a fine example for the other kids*
         if you off yourself at twenty-one.

I was drunk the night I tried it in a dorm room when I was three
         years younger than you,
nothing around to swallow but a bottle of aspirin
which doesn't mix well with vodka so I slept for hours, woke up,
         got sick, slept, got sick.
Probably didn't make any more fuss than the hundreds of
         bulimics and alcoholics on campus, so no one paid
         any attention.

The rhythm is missing from this work, the beat
in every good gay film of the past ten years
I don't mean porn, I mean *Tongues Untied*
the poetry that goes: *lemme fuck it lemme suck it lemme taste it*
         lemme...
It's hard to be rhythmic when I write about the government
         suppressing reports on youth because they reveal
most teen suicides are queers.
It's hard to be rhyming when I realize how easily my friends and
         I could have been drowned.
It's tough to be pretty when we can't walk in public without being
         called *faggot*
The right to walk   I'm pro-walking   Like most people
         of colour, we can't walk undisturbed
One spring night Kim and I in our leather jackets and five friends
         with short haircuts went out to the beach
caused a gang of teenagers to exclaim *God! Fuckin' dyke*
         mayhem!

Another bunch of boys walked to the end of the pier and screamed
LEZZIES! LEZZIES! top of the lungs. We made them the
butt of our jokes, decided to design T-shirts with FDM logos,
strutted around and said, Tha's right! But I remembered
a man named Charlie who lived in Maine, killed in '83 or'84
when a couple kids threw him off a bridge and he drowned

'cause he was a faggot. He was a good faggot, he minced and
pranced with wrists that had springs
where bones should be
but he was no loud and flaming faggot, no, he lived quietly, in an
apartment with two toy poodles, not to disturb the good
heterosexuals trying to lead their ordinary lives
He felt guilty, suicidal, apologized daily for living, called his
mother on Sundays, went to church and a psychiatrist,
prayed to God to make him straight, and when it became too
much to bear, he went off to the tearoom and found himself
someone to fuck, never got a name or phone number, lived his
whole life this way

She married at eighteen because that's what girls did, because she was
pregnant, because she feared she wasn't normal, because she
had to get out of her parents' house because her father raped
her
she had three kids after a few years, a decent marriage,
but something didn't fit, and she knew she'd have time to figure
it out when the kids were
out of diapers, in school, at Boy Scout and Girl Scout camp, high
school, college, out of the house
time to breathe, away from her strange and estranged husband.
Now that the kids are grown, at least he can't fight her for
custody.

she's a big butch bulldagger ballbusting manhating cuntlicker
tomboy lezzie bulldyke

he's a little queer sissy fairy pansy punk limpwrist fudgepacker
      cocksucker maricón faggot queen

and me: an AC/DC fence-sitting confused swinger heterosexually
      privileged flip-flopping can't make up my mind switch-
      hitting AIDS-carrying high-risk parasite on the movement

I came out at a Boulder Queer Collective meeting, Bisexual
      Women's Voice meeting, Gay Alliance meeting
wearing a pink triangle button in the office, boycotting stores,
      participating in queer poetry readings, speaking as the token
      bi on community panels or in Human Diversity courses,
      arguing for sliding-scale fees, on the PBS station's news and
      entertainment show
reading a bulletin board in the Castro, glancing at you on the El,
      chatting and browsing at Silkwood, Smedley's, Lammas,
      Wild Seeds, People Like Us, Book Garden, Lambda Rising,
      Category Six, Full Circle, Antigone, Old Wives' Tales
at the San Francisco Lesbian and Gay Freedom Day Parade, the
      Rochester Lesbian/Gay/Bisexual Pride Parade, Stride With
      Pride March on Albany, March on Washington, my third
      ACT UP demo, my fiftieth queer rights protest
eating at a potluck, a brunch, a party, a picnic, listening at a
      conference, a speech, a workshop
saying *so am I* when you sneer *she's bisexual*

                          embarrassed
                          you fumble with
                          apologies

but I don't have to come out at all because I can easily pass, can
      talk about my ex's in class and throw in a *he* so all my
      students say is *you've had some weird boyfriends*
                        you don't know the half of it
I don't have to come out. I can walk the streets and shop
      supermarket sections full of bright applauding tiers of corn
      flakes and fabric softeners

while holding hands with a male friend, kiss a guy in the
      condiments aisle while passersby, embarrassed or not
by PDAs, think *ah, love* or *mm, lust* instead of *fucking dykes*
I don't have to come out. I can shave my hairy legs, cram them
      into pantyhose, paint my plain cute face till I look like
      someone else
slip a dress over my head, stuff my feet into high-heeled pumps
      and listen to my professors' comments:
You look really good   *Michele, you have legs*
      You have a nice ass, Ms. Moore

I can pass, but every time I touch a man in public I'm aware I can
      be threatened, beaten, killed
for holding a woman's hand at the wrong time / *slash* / in the
      wrong place. I celebrate each time I see two women face that
      danger and live
I only feel at home in my short hair, boys' jeans
hightop sneakers I dyed purple, neon pink cap with the bill in
      back, *Queer Girl* button in front
style stolen from gay men
Read My Lips T-shirt with the photo of two women kissing
and the back I embellished because I was tired of all my white
      liberal friends saying *I hate labels*
I love 'em, they let me know who's who, I want as many as I can
      collect in one lifetime
bisexual/feminist/lesbian-identified/queer activist/snap
      diva/Kinsey 3 to 5/non-monogamous?/androgynous/
anarchist/fag hag/size queen/tomboy/pervert/kiki/butch
      girl/bitch/woman/lover

I can pass as queer more easily than as het   at bars, parties,
       meetings consider it a compliment when someone calls me
       lesbian
I slip back into my boys'-cut Levi's into my butch stance
       spread my legs, drape my arms over chair backs, take up as
       much room in theatre seats as men do, sometimes even play
       dueling knees with those next to me
slide my hands into my pockets without realizing till a student
       writes about it
and I become self-conscious: do I look dykey?
                           do they know?

It's safer to come out at demonstrations, where we wear pink
       triangles inverted, taken back from the Nazis and turned
       around
We picketed malls: *We're here, we're queer, we're not going*
       shopping!
We created chaos at FDA headquarters: *ACT UP! Fight back!*
       Fight AIDS!
28,000 people are dead! What do the candidates say about
       AIDS?! A year passes and the chants don't change   much:
32,000 people are dead! What does the president say about
AIDS?!
It seemed as if nothing changed but T-shirt slogans: *Power*
       Breakfast; Men Wear Condoms or Beat It; Kissing Doesn't
       Kill, Greed and Indifference Do; Silence = Death
demo after demo after demo, a string of rosary beads, barbs on a
       wire fence, if we only chant enough, chant the right chants,
       we'll get our rights, we'll get enough people angry, someone
       will notice, we'll get enough adrenaline moving that
       something will happen,
we'll save someone

Every day I live Colorado for Family Values, Citizens for a
      Decent Community
like deer ticks with Lyme's Disease in the folds behind my knees
      and elbows after I walk in the mountains
I try to ignore them but they burrow beneath my tenderest skin
      and suck my blood

the slow grinding sound of words like weight belts wrapped
      around wrists and waists and ankles when we run:
abomination in the eyes of God   people that don't reproduce
immoral   sick   perverted lifestyle
threat to the family

        those *people*

I have been an Other all my life, became proud of it at twelve when I
      realized there was no strength in fitting in
if nowhere is home, home can be everywhere
there is power in being among America's most-hated
      most-feared   most-hunted
they're right: we're dangerous
we want to burn up the white picket fence that impales us
we want to change the nuclear bomb family, stifling school,
      condemning church, neighbourhood silence cut
only by motorized sheep every Saturday morning at ten

but they don't kill most of us with baseball bats, fists, guns
most of us strangle slowly on our own
find our way to the bar, tell ourselves we're happy during five hundred
      months of nights stuck on the vinyl stool, that the dim
      coloured light shining through shelves of liquor bottles is
      pretty
trying to smile, talking to strangers, smoking another pack down
      to butts, skin getting dry, eyeing the younger and younger
      bodies that come through the door

of the bar, site of a thousand little depressions and deaths, the
        dark stinking rancid bar breath of exhaled liquor and
        cigarettes
where we're ignored, abandoned, cajoled, seduced, insulted,
        danced with, kissed
tossed out into the night, the curb, the neon gleaming streets of
        rain and cars
The cold bathrooms where we vomit rum and Cokes while the
        barkeeps stick their heads in to make sure we haven't passed
        out and klunked our heads on the floor

we join the priesthood, enter the convent, remain celibate, adopt
        stray cats and call them our babies, get married and have
        kids and try to wish it away, contract HIV from sex with
        nameless strangers in adult bookstores after work so our wives
        don't know,
get kicked out of the house at twelve, sell sex on the streets, get
        knifed, get beaten up, get our ribs broken, get into and out of
        the hospital, get into drugs

we know we're worthless and no one will ever love us
we take dozens of sleeping pills
tattoo our wrists with razor blades in cold white porcelain
        bathtubs
put handguns into our mouths because a clit or a prick was in there
        last week
jump off bridges onto cement beds
drive too fast around curves so our families can say we were an
        accident

death like water
death like release
blame it on a lover who slammed the door when she left
a lover who never was
a lover who wanted too much of us
a lover who never sent flowers or gave us Valentines

but we know it's because something there is that sure must love a
    dead fag
and the only good dyke is a dead dyke
and our deaths are brought to us courtesy Reagan, Helms and
    Bush
and those who say a holocaust can't happen now were wrong a
    decade ago
we remember our dead
our individual dead, our seventeen-friends-who-died-of-AIDS-
    last-year
the fifty-two of them who died in the last five
our memories like videotapes
patches on quilts so no one forgets the names
the quilt grown so big it takes an army of lovers to transport the
    damned thing and it can't be displayed in one place at one
    time
photos on walls, in books so no one forgets the faces
of the old and the young.

Why are you killing my people? Jim asks
I must admit that phrase has pretty good rhythm, like a brisk
    little stroll down the pier
When I get angriest I say OK, *fuckers, drown us, kill us, shoot us,*
    mash our organs to pulps with baseball
    bats in alleys
and who'll teach your kids and wipe their butts in daycare
    centres?
Who'll nurse your sick and care for your dying mothers in nursing
    homes?
Who'll take your photos, play your symphonies, make your
    touchdowns, shoot your movies, cook your burgers, serve your
    meals, perform your plays, drive your trucks, write your
    books,

make your change?

Melina

pete

defiant lesbian space so named and claimed was a gift to me. was a warmth a confirmation place of growth and self-definition.

how handy it was for explaining some of the gross inconveniences and outrages in my life. some of the abuses suffered teenage traumas that opened scars in my flesh which only the hands and mouths and words women kissed and healed with me.

a sensation of selfhood made on my own time is the gift i have received from women.

this self is allowed to roam encouraged to risk affirmed as steps are taken bringing me farther from home closer to me.

now, i took the power to shape myself and have done something which leads me farther from here closer to me. and i feel it is empowering, healing, good.

i pose a question to you — does this particular journey which makes my own life fuller make me more of a lesbian — a self-defined woman — or an alien?

after nine years — a plenty long time, think of all that's happened to you over the last nine years — i decided to have a thing with a man and i did it. it was great, full of sun and talk and comfort...

fifteen minutes from work, so i'd walk over in the middle of the day. we'd play on his magic futon. it just fit in a green-painted balcony enclosed with big paned windows. lying down all we could see was blue sky and leaves and branches of the tree hear people playing tennis and basketball the streets of downtown mid-day. what a great month of june i had two-and-a-half-hour lunches sandwiched in my nine-to-five day.

fear i had to overcome. fear hurt hate to touch this man let his touch touch me. touch him i did touch me did he. and i kept thinking in the first days, "okay, it's going to hit me and i'm going to panic and feel like shit."

the oddest thing is i didn't feel odd. the nicest thing is i felt nice.

i confessed my terror and mistrust shared with him some of my personal history, told him about the women i was in love with. he told me he had been terrified the night i "bagged" him and he shared with me his hurts and loves. we were we are friends at ease having travelled a little ways together on the journeys each to our own selves.

i've told friends about my discovery that this man is people too. one friend said "everybody's turning bisexual these days!" and we had a good laugh.

i guess one of the things i got from growing into dykehood is a need to connect events, people, places. nothing exists unattached. i put myself in many different environments and exist for that time in that group of people, that history of happenings, that viewpoint. if you asked me "where is home?" i could not name one city, one circle of people, one language, one time of day, one texture that would speak all of me.

marginality is a process, the location changing with the surroundings. inclusion is also fluid —

comfort, support, mutual and honest trust is what i wanted from my time with this man, and is what i found.

to break the mould is a way of life for a chinese dyke, it has gotten me hooked on asking why must it be this way? the answer usually is that it doesn't. trust is never to be taken for granted for it often comes tied to prescribed manners and values. am i a trustworthy sister? yes. what if i say, this man is helping me extract pains like slivers of glass grown over with skin.

i don't feel like i've abandoned my sisters. i am stepping into another environment to feel the texture of life unique against my skin.

and i am not willing to trade my desire for challenging the gates of the gilded cage for conditional solidarity. membership in any particular radicalism/outlook/society is deadweight around my neck if it doesn't let me dream and gather round me that which i need to find my voice and speak with honesty.

so is my sensibility to be suspect, or shall it be seen to be enriching our discussions around selfhood? am i a better dyke for striking out finding new footholds in the trip farther from here closer to me? or am i essentially now a non-lesbian?

i have no problems with how i live. i have no time for re-boxing me to fit the title or redoing the title to fit the history.

all i know is that the process has been honest and cathartic, and is a building upon experiences rather than a severing of beliefs. well, like the way life goes, it is as much a jolt and a shift as it is an evolution and a continuity.

the essence of what i've learned from my sisters is that boxes cut you up into convenient cubes so you are managed and functioning within a grand hierarchy. and these boxes have nothing to do with that fluid beautiful energy that emanates from those who refuse the box and let us recognize each other.

and so i share with you my concern,

don't make dykedom another box. don't view my choosing to have sex and trust with this man as switching boxes, because that's not how i experience it. understand it to be part of my way of respecting the fluidity of living, taking nourishment i need, helping me heal and grow, and breaking out of that killing reflex to amputate deviations from the norm. don't manipulate dykedom into a norm against which you judge deviants.

Huda Jadallah and Pearl Saad

A Conversation About the Arab
Lesbian and Bisexual Women's Network

PEARL: Hello. This is Huda and Pearl and we're talking about the Arab Lesbian Network and the Arab Lesbian and Bisexual Women's Network. We want to talk about how the groups formed so that other women know how we came together. Our group is very important to us and its formation is really significant. To the best of our knowledge, our group is the first such coming together in the U.S. of Arab lesbian and bisexual women.

HUDA: Well, let me start. The group first got together in May 1989. I started the group because I had wanted to meet other Arab lesbians and bisexual women for quite some time. It was so isolating not knowing any other lesbian or bisexual Arab women. I didn't like hearing some Palestinians say that I should stay in the closet if I wanted to remain a part of the Palestinian community. I could not accept that. And hanging out with white lesbians felt really alienating. They didn't understand who I was. I was an outsider to them, I felt as if I was in these two worlds that were separate from each other. That I was cut off. And I wanted to be whole, to experience all of who I am. When I was in Southern California, it became a joke with me and my friends, "in search of." I was in search of Arab lesbians. When I moved to the Bay Area, I actually took the steps needed to get the group going: I put ads in the papers, talked to people and gathered names and phone numbers. That's how the group got started.

PEARL: I'm so glad you did that work, took those steps. When you said "in search of," I related because I heard about the potluck through Paula. I met Paula in 1981 or 1982 and I came out to her as lesbian and Lebanese. Together we were looking for other Lebanese lesbians. She's part Lebanese, and together we were wondering where we could find other Lebanese lesbians. When she told me you were having a potluck I was very excited. Excited and scared.

HUDA: What was it like for you at the first meeting?

PEARL: It was intense, it was as if I was in a dream. I was afraid we weren't going to get a parking space, because I thought there would be cars and cars — that there would be hundreds of women there. But, when we got to your house, there were no cars parked on the block. None at all. So, I thought, okay, maybe they're all coming over from San Francisco on the BART. It was really powerful that first time. I was scared. I thought you were a *real* Palestinian.

HUDA: Well I am.

PEARL: Well, I thought you would be a real one, like...

HUDA: An immigrant?

PEARL: Definitely, definitely an immigrant. But also "real," meaning that you were connected to culture and family in a way which would have overshadowed everything else about you. I imagined you would have been cooking all day because we were coming. When I saw you had falafel in a bag I began laughing inside.

HUDA: So who I am made you more comfortable?

PEARL: Yeah, I could identify with you. And I thought you were so beautiful.

HUDA: You could identify with that?

PEARL: Well I thought that I must be beautiful, because I felt I could see myself in you and what I saw in you was a really beautiful woman. That is something that is important to me about the group — images. For me, not being raised within an Arab community, I don't have a lot of images of who I am. Seeing Arab women as the norm, as a standard of beauty, that is very powerful to me. How about you, what was it like when people started coming?

HUDA: Oh God, I was nervous, because for a while, no one showed up. I thought "Oh no! I spent all this energy, what if this is a bust?" But, the thing I remember most is the sitting around the table. At the first potluck, and at all the potlucks, just sitting around the table, and how we would each go around and talk about ourselves, who we are, why we are here. The telling of our stories. That's just been really powerful for me, getting to know each other in a deeper way. That's one of the things that sticks out the most for me over all the year — sitting around the table. We were probably outnumbered by the Lebanese at that first get-together. I finally found more Palestinians. It is interesting to see who the people are too. Remember how we joked about having an artists' caucus: a lot of people in the group were artists. That was really interesting to me. Just seeing who the people were.

PEARL: You're right. There were filmmakers, writers, weavers, a photographer, painter, sculptor. That's a lot of different types of artists.

The Group

PEARL: Do you want to talk about some other things that happened in the group?

HUDA: Well, at first we had women only at the meetings. I had put an ad in the San Francisco Bay Times (a lesbian, gay and bisexual newspaper) advertising an Arab Lesbian Network. This was one of the ways in which women found out about the group. Then, someone from the paper told me that lots of men were calling the paper to see if there was a group for men.

PEARL: The ad was for Arab women, right?

HUDA: Arab women only. And the men were calling because they were interested in the group as gay Arab men. When I heard that, I brought it to the group and said, "What do you think about having some men come to our meeting?" I had been thinking about it in the back of my mind, so when the men started calling, I thought this was a good time to bring it up to the group. We decided that we definitely wanted to retain our women only group, but that we also wanted to meet the men. We thought it would be fun. We decided to invite them and have a joint potluck. So we did. And it was great. At that first meeting, I think everyone had a great time. It was very exciting for all of us. The energy.

PEARL: Yeah, that first night was a real high for me too, us being together, women and men. That was a real high. It was very contagious and exciting. I felt alive and happy and delighted.

HUDA: It was a real celebration.

PEARL: Yeah. And there was so much food.

HUDA: That's because the men cooked. Don't you remember, the women went to the delis and bought their food and the men cooked up a storm.

PEARL: That's right, that's right!

HUDA: So of course we were very excited. "Let's invite them again! Let them bring the food." So that's how the men joined in and then that's how we started the Arab Lesbian, Gay and Bisexual Network. We still had the Arab Lesbian Network (which was to later become the Arab Lesbian and Bisexual Women's Network), and now we also had the Arab Lesbian, Gay and Bisexual Network. As we got together more and more, we began to form our identity as a group. We decided to write a formal statement of purpose.

PEARL: We worked together as a committee on a statement of purpose for the group, and then we brought it to the larger group where we had a lot of discussion about it.

HUDA: Let me read the statement of purpose for the Arab Lesbian, Gay and Bisexual Network:

> The purpose of the Arab Lesbian, Gay and Bisexual
> Network is to provide social, cultural, personal, political
> and spiritual support for Arab lesbians, gays and bisexuals
> of all ages. For us the term Arab encompasses people who
> racially, ethnically or culturally identify themselves with
> the Arab world. This includes individuals born outside of
> the Arab world who grew up being denied the right to
> call themselves Arabs, as well as people of mixed heritage.
> We are not a religious organization. Specifically our goals
> include the following:
>
> 1. Celebrating the richness and diversity of our Arab heritage;
> 2. Challenging myths and stereotypes about Arabs;
> 3. Working for Arab rights internationally.
> We are an anti-Zionist group;
> 4. Working to increase the visibility of Arab lesbians, gays
> and bisexuals within the Arab community and in the lesbian,
> gay and bisexual community;
> 5. Working to provide a safe community for Arab lesbians,
> gays and bisexuals.

PEARL: As things turned out, two of the biggest discussions we had were about Zionism and about bisexuality. Do you want to talk about why it was important for you that the group be anti-Zionist?

HUDA: As a Palestinian it was very important to me that the group be anti-Zionist. Whenever anyone called to find out about the group, or was interested in joining the group, I made it very clear to them what the group was. This issue is very present for me and I had to make sure that all people who came to the group were anti-Zionist. It was so important to me that the group be anti-Zionist because I wanted a place in this world that I considered a safe place for all of who I am.

PEARL: Yes, I know that is really important to you. I remember when you went to that protest at the Israeli consulate.

HUDA: Yes, some Palestinian had been shot by an Israeli and there was a large protest in front of the Israeli consulate. And I carried my big sign "Arab Lesbians for a Free Palestine." That was interesting. There were lots of people at the demonstration, mainly Palestinians. So it was interesting for me to carry that sign. In general, people didn't say anything. But one person, one young man did approach me and give me his dissent. He said I shouldn't carry this sign, that I was hurting the cause. My response to him was that twenty percent of San Francisco was going to read my sign before they read his. And that's the truth of it. I kept carrying the sign.

That was a powerful moment for me. Being in front of Palestinians with that sign. Saying I am a lesbian for Palestinian freedom. I am a lesbian and a Palestinian. I feel it is very important that when Palestine does become a country that the contributions of lesbians, gays and bisexuals be recognized. Because if we are not out there now, sharing in the struggle, then when the country becomes independent, we're going to be oppressed. Others will say, where were you, you weren't part of our independence struggle. It's important for me to say I participated, I fought for independence and I don't want to be oppressed.

PEARL: When you were talking your action struck me as really powerful and I imagine you must have felt really vulnerable being there and carrying your sign. I wish you had been there with fifty or hundred out Arab lesbians, gays and bisexuals. I know what you did was really important, too, that you were taking the steps to create visibility for Arab lesbians, gays and bisexuals. One of the things I notice about you is that you identify yourself as a Palestinian woman born in the U.S. That's different from saying Palestinian American. It's a very clear political statement, "I am born in exile from my country, I am born and raised in the United States, but I am Palestinian, I'm not Palestinian American." That's a critical political definition of self.

HUDA: It is. And it is who I am. So another issue that came up was bisexuality. Initially the group was called the Arab Lesbian network.

PEARL: Right, and then when we talked about inviting men to join us, there was that big fear of letting bisexual men join the group. The feeling was that, it would be okay for gay men to join the group, but not for bisexual men to join the group. Women within the group felt fear that bisexual men might come looking to find a wife.

HUDA: Even though bisexual women and men were a part of the group from the beginning it was hard for people to be out. Even though we agreed on the name change, not everyone in the group felt open to having bisexual people in the group.

PEARL: That was really hard because some people would say things that I would now identify as biphobic, but since I was not out to the group or myself about my bisexuality I was hardly in a place to challenge some of the things that were said. And I didn't know who else in the group was bisexual. But I did know that I belonged.

HUDA: But the joke about the whole thing is that in the midst of the discussion about how people didn't want bisexuals in the group, there were already bisexual people in the group who were closeted about being bisexual. The people who were afraid of bisexuals were sitting right next to bisexuals. And they were not afraid of them at all. And the bisexual men were not hitting on the women.

PEARL: I know for me a lot of issues came to a head around the Lesbian and Gay Freedom Day parade one year. Our banner said "Arab Lesbian and Bisexual Women's Network." There were two issues around that banner. One was that the words "bisexual women" took up more space than the word "lesbian." The other was that some individuals didn't want to stand behind a banner that said bisexual because they wanted it to be clear that they as individuals were lesbian. That caused contention within the group. At the parade itself people came up to me and said, "Oh I'm so glad that your banner says Arab lesbian and bisexual." I thought they were saying that I was bi. I was closeted, and I was uncomfortable with people having this positive response to the word bisexual. I didn't know it, but the same weekend the first national bisexual conference was happening in San Francisco. I have this feeling that what we did and what we went through was historic and absolutely a part of what was going on within the larger gay and lesbian community at that time.

HUDA: Right.

PEARL: Bisexual women came out within the group as bi people began coming out more within the larger lesbian and gay community. I felt the beginning of a bisexual identity. And political visibility. Bisexual people are in every group. Bisexuals are in every gay and lesbian group.

HUDA: But nobody knows it. Nobody knows it unless you are out as bisexual, or friendly with people who are out as bisexual. Then you know everybody. It's the underground of the lesbian/gay community.

PEARL: It's not an issue of whether or not "we" as gays and lesbians are going to accept "you" bisexuals. We're already here.

HUDA: One of the issues I recall when we were discussing bisexuality was that the men felt strongly that they didn't want bisexual men in the group. They felt that in the Arab world bisexual men had a lot of privilege over gay men. They talked about the "top-bottom thing." That the man on the bottom is gay, and the man on the top is bisexual. That the bisexual man just wants to get what he can get sexually, but that he wasn't really interested in the man. It was just a matter of getting sex. So, the issue of how gay men and bisexual men are seen in the Arab world was a real issue for the men in the group.

PEARL: That's a big difference.

HUDA: Yeah. And for the women, I think privilege was one of the big discussions we had around bisexuality.

PEARL: I don't really remember.

HUDA: Too bad.

PEARL: I guess so. I just didn't want anyone to know I was bi.

HUDA: Right. But there was also a lot of support from lesbians. I think things were helped by the women who were supportive of bisexuals and who encouraged us to examine our feelings toward bisexuality.

PEARL: Yeah, that's right. Within the group one of the most vocal supporters of the inclusion of bisexuals was a lesbian woman. She just kept saying, "We have to include bisexuals." She was totally bi-supportive. She would point out that there are different kinds of bisexual women — would we react the same toward lesbian-identified bisexuals as we would toward a bisexual in the group who was going out with a man, or a bisexual who was married? Would they still be welcomed?

HUDA: There are so many issues to discuss around bisexuality.

Same as with lesbian identity. And in addition to having lesbian and bisexual women, we had so many other types of identities in our group. It's what happens when you bring people together — we come from different backgrounds in terms of class, age, race, country of origin and sexual iden-tification. There are so many things that come up. That's what we found. That joy of coming together and seeing the whole spectrum of colours and experiences was really empowering.

PEARL: There were people from North Africa and the Middle East, including Yemen, Palestine, Lebanon, Egypt, Iran. There were Berber from Algeria, Assyrian from Iraq, Armenians. And we had mixed-heritage people too. There is the whole experience of being mixed-heritage Arab American, and the experience of people who are mixed-heritage in the Arab world as well.

HUDA: We really learned a lot about each others' cultures and that was really exciting. In some ways I think we didn't want to learn about each others' cultures because we wanted to minimize our differences. It was so important for us to be one. We were so glad we had found each other, we didn't want to have any differences come between us. I think there was an effort among us to ignore differences, since this was such a big deal for us to be together as Arabs.

PEARL: Right. I think that one of the main things we came to the group with was a hunger for community because that was something none of us had experienced before. That was our common bond, that desire to be with other Arab lesbian, gay and bisexual people. We were in a gay/lesbian/bisexual circle where we could have our Arab culture. We could share everything together. Like you said in the beginning, we each had a chance to be Arab lesbian, gay or bisexual, to be totally who we are as opposed to being different things in different places.

HUDA: I could be accepted for the whole person that I am. We really created a community. To this day we are a community and it's a really tight bond, a really close bond.

PEARL: Thanks for bringing us together.

Laurie A. Cooper, Michelle E. Hynes & Edith R. Westfall

The Kinsey Three

> *"I want to be able to express the truths of my life, and my sexuality, in a language that does not obscure. The word choices available now restrict me. I am not tolerant of these restrictions, of a world view that consigns dissidents to limbo. I want some place to belong, a name to be called."*
> — Carol A. Queen[1]

THE THREE OF US WHOSE VOICES APPEAR IN THIS writing wanted to explore what it means to us to be young, professional, bisexual women in Washington, D.C. Our home city, particularly the neighbourhoods we live in, provides easy access to bookstores, restaurants and other public spaces that are owned and frequented by lesbian, gay and bisexual people. The recent March on Washington filled our neighbourhood with "family" for days, and affirmed our pride in living in a place that could host such an event. However, in our day-to-day lives, we struggle to make clear for ourselves and others the significance of bisexual identity.

Michelle is twenty-five, Edith is twenty-seven and Laurie is also twenty-seven. Michelle and Edith are White; Laurie is Black. We have all lived in Washington, D.C., for six to eight years and have been "out" to ourselves and our friends for most of our post-college life — between three and four years. We met in the Adams-Morgan apartment two of us share, ordered Chinese food, decided what topics we wanted to cover and then just talked for about an hour. Then we transcribed and edited our conversation.

In particular, it was important to us to confront myths we encounter about our sexual orientation and to talk about how our bisexuality affects our relationships with partners, friends and families.

The Importance of "Bi-Identity"

EW: It's important for me to identify as bisexual because I think it's an accurate label for me. I don't want to be forced to hide in a closet by the gay movement any more than I want to hide in a closet because of what straight people perceive. I'm equally attracted to men and women. Although I've been in relationships with women for three years, I don't rule out seeing men in the future.

LC: I spent a lot of my life worrying about how to fit in and how to be "normal." I think I've finally figured out that it's whatever I want to be — what is sexually and emotionally normal for me is that I'm attracted to women, I'm attracted to men, I do not go through periods of not liking women or not liking men, and I believe that that's what bisexuality implies. I've been out for about three years. I'm sorta single in that I've just met somebody — a woman — and we've just started dating.

MH: I'm in a relationship with a man I've dated on and off for seven years, continuously for about four years. Calling myself "bisexual" gives me a way to name how I feel about my relationships with people, with women, with men...so the naming is important for me, and it's also indicative for me of an openness to being in different kinds of relationships with anyone I might meet. It's not important to me whether it's a man or a woman; there are things that I'm attracted to that go beyond someone's gender.

The "Double Closet" and the Coming Out Process

LC: For me, the easiest people to come out to are women, usually women I end up meeting in social situations, like bars. When I'm nervous about getting to know a woman I usually say, "well, I am bisexual..." to see if there's some kind of barrier, or final hurdle I need to get over.

MH: How do you do that? Do you just say out of the blue, "My name is Laurie, and I'm bisexual?" "By the way, I want you to know that I'm bi, in case this is an issue for you?"

LC: Yeah, exactly. With the woman I last dated, we met and we began to get along fairly well, so on our first official date, our second official meeting, I said, "I want you to know that I am bisexual, and if this is a problem for you I'll understand, but I think you should know where I'm coming from." And she took it fairly well...it kind of depended on what day it was. I've never met a woman, told her I was bisexual and had her say, "I cannot get involved with you because you're bisexual." With men, it's something that I've been wrestling with ever since I came out. It's much easier to tell men that I used to date that I am bisexual than it is to tell men that I am dating that I am bisexual. And that's something that I think complicates my current relationships with men. Since it's less difficult to tell a woman that I'm bisexual, it's easier for me to be in a relationship with a woman. I don't know if this means that I'm never going to be in a lasting relationship with a man again, but it is harder. If I meet a man in a bar, he's not going to assume that I'm anything but straight. The reason that you're in the gay bar meeting women is primarily because of your sexuality. The subject of sexuality does not come up in a conversation between a woman and a man in the way it does between two women.

EW: For me it's hardest to tell lesbians, because I have had...no one necessarily says anything to me, but they give me "the look" — "oh, you're one of them" — and that's very uncomfortable. It's easiest for me to tell gay men, because they have no stake in it. They're not going to date me whether I'm straight, bisexual or transgender. They're just not interested. Straight women, for the most part, are not worried, or wary. Part of my discomfort with lesbians is because of those lines in the personal ads in the *Blade* [the local gay newspaper] that say "no bi's, emotionally insecure women or psychos" — I really don't like being lumped with the psychos. That's why when I put my ad in I was very explicit about being a BI female, the implication being if you can't deal with it, don't call this number.

LC: Or "tortured." The "tortured bisexual" is a phrase I've heard used, most commonly by tortured lesbians.

EW: Or "you're confused." I'm not confused; I know exactly what I want. Sometimes what I want lives in a man's body, sometimes it lives in a woman's body. I don't want to be hemmed in by other people's labels. I feel like I get that a lot from the lesbian community.

MH: I guess that's been mostly my experience too. I've had a lot of acceptance from gay men, and so it's easier for me to come out to them. Because, like you say, they don't really care. They're doing their alternative thing, and you can do yours, and it's okay. I've come out to some straight men, but mostly in hostile situations, like coming out to my brother, who just thinks the idea of women together is *so* gross.

LC: Sometimes I feel like instead of saying to co-workers, "I don't like that comment and I have a personal stake in it." I'd rather say, "Excuse me, I don't think we need to have this kind of conversation at work." Which would be nice, if they would shut up. But there's also an issue of "I want you to notice that I'm here, and I can't sit across from you day after day knowing that you're thinking those thoughts."

MH: Why do you think we're talking as if we're all so comfortable with this naming and this space within ourselves, and it seems so scary to other people we know?

LC: Well, it was really scary for me for a long time because I didn't know any other bisexuals. I didn't know this kind of feeling existed. I think depending on how you grow up and what kind of exposure you have, it's fairly easy to assume that if you're not straight, then you are gay. Period. There isn't an in-between. Most of the first lesbians I met had never slept with a man, and didn't want to.

EW: The first time I came in contact with gay people was at Georgetown [University], and there you either were a gay man or you were a lesbian. I never heard anyone identify themselves as bisexual. When I started identifying that way, I felt like it was a long time before I heard anyone else say that about themselves. I guess it wasn't really that long, it was only four months, but it was a long four months for me.

MH: I guess when I came out, I had Edith as one model for that process. Also, Bi Any Other Name was published around the time that we came out, which was really important for me — not only because the voices in it really resonated for me but because I received a copy as a birthday present, as a gesture of acceptance from someone. I guess I never really felt alone in that process, and I can see how it would be scary if you did.

LC: Exactly.

EW: For a long time I had the feeling of "is anyone else out there?" But I'm comfortable with it because...why am I comfortable with it? My mother just raised me to be very independent, to make my own decisions. I'm used to having to define for myself what I want and how I'm going to get it.

LC: I talked to this new person that I've met about it, and on our first date I said, "Well, I'm bisexual and is this going to be a problem for you?" And to my surprise she said, "Well, I'm bisexual too. But you're the first person I've met who's publicly identified as bisexual. And it's certainly something I've thought about, but not something I would necessarily call myself." And I told her why — if I must label myself and others must label me — this is what I prefer, rather than "dyke." As it turned out, we had many of the same reasons for identifying this way. Going back to that earlier question — going through all these cartwheels with coming out to men that I am/would be/going to date — means that for me the coming out process is not complete. There are some other issues, like whether I really do think that queer is okay. Right now it sounds like a perfectly wonderful idea, and when a man once asked me — in the throes of passion — "so which do you prefer?" I said "NEITHER." I have moments like that. But I'm also wrestling with issues of whether to come out to people at work, by way of saying, "excuse me, I don't like that comment." And I'm still not comfortable talking to my mother about it.

EW: I wonder about...I think I'm the only one here who wants to go into corporate America. And I wonder what I'll do if I'm in a board room, forty years old, trying to build a company and someone starts a rumour that "Edith's a dyke." If perceptions about queer people haven't changed by then, what am I going to do? How open do I want to be; do I want everyone in the company to always know, so it's never an issue? Do I always keep it really close to myself? Part of it is my privacy issue, that I don't really like to talk about my personal life at work. But I may need to, and I'm not sure I'm really ready to do that.

The Lesbian Litmus Test

EW: I keep getting told, especially by lesbians, "you can pass," because I have long hair and long nails and no one's ever going to mistake me for anything but female — it's really offensive, because I can't pass. I can't turn off my feelings for women or let those comments go by. These things trivialize my sexuality.

MH: That whole issue of passing is one that's difficult for me, and one of the things that makes it very hard for me to come out when I'm with lesbians, or really with anyone. Because first of all, people never would think that I'm anything but straight because I've been dating this guy for so long. So for me to come out to someone I have to make an issue of it; it's not like it would come up in conversation because I was out (so to speak) last night with someone, or whatever. And if I'm in a women's bar people think I'm a lesbian, if I'm in Lambda [a gay and lesbian bookstore in D.C.] people think I'm a lesbian, if I'm in Lammas [a lesbian feminist bookstore in D.C.] people think I'm a lesbian. So I feel really locked in at both ends, and I feel like it's really hard for me to make space to say who I am and to be accepted for who I am rather than for who someone assumes I am. I have long hair and wear an engagement ring and go around with this six-foot guy, and sometimes I want to go around saying "HI, I'M QUEER!" just to get people to look beyond that.

EW: The same people who get mad at you because you can "pass" for straight are the ones who don't want you to make any waves in the lesbian community by saying "I'm different."

LC: Or they want you to "pass" for lesbian when you're not "passing" for straight.

EW: Or they say, "You're not really bisexual because you haven't seen a man recently." Well, does it count that I slept with one a year ago? I get mad that I have to prove I'm bisexual. And then if I've slept with men and women at the same time, they say, "well, you're just promiscuous." It also frustrates me that bisexuality isn't allowed to exist historically. Strong women, like Eleanor Roosevelt, who was married and loved FDR and also reportedly had affairs with both a woman and a man, is classified as a lesbian by the lesbian community.

Our Intimate Relationships

MH: I should start on this one with my coming-out process. My partner decided I was bi before I decided I was going to identify that way. And when I woke up one morning and said, "I think I need to call myself bisexual," he just said, "I was waiting for you to get to that."

EW: Why did he decide this for you?

MH: It wasn't ever that he did the naming for me, it's just that he was really there for me and talking to me throughout that process, and there was never an issue of whether he was going to accept it, or whether it would create some schism in our relationship, it was just, "okay, what does this mean to you?" I was still Michelle, his girlfriend, friend, fiancée, all the permutations our relationship has been through. At the same time, it's really important to me to have close female friendships, it's really important to me to have women in my life, and sometimes the boundaries that are established in a traditional monogamous relationship feel confining in terms of expressing how I feel about my women friends. Patrick and I have had many conversations about this; and, while we have an agreement that it's possible for us as a couple to be involved romantically with another woman, there aren't that many candidates for that third person. And occasionally I want to say, "Couldn't I just sleep over at so-and-so's house?" but he really pulls back from our relationship being any less structured than it is now. Which I can definitely understand...even for me, the lack of some boundaries I might feel as a straight, partnered woman can be kind of scary.

And also, it can be difficult to be a queer woman involved with a straight man...sometimes there are things I want to do with my partner that are queer-space, or woman-space, and so if I were dating a woman I would take her, but for him they're off limits. And that creates a sort of weird split in my thinking.

EW: In my first relationship with a woman, my bisexuality wasn't really an issue because D. and I didn't talk about most of this stuff. She was just, "yeah, whatever, fine." We had an agreement that it was okay to be non-monogamous, that we would start no new competing relationships, but that if we really felt the need to go sleep with someone that was okay. And you would just use your judgment about it.

In my current relationship, I was very up front before I started dating this person and told them I was bisexual. I met her through a per-sonals ad that I placed which said, "Me, Bisexual Female." So anyone who called that ad knew that I was bi. On our second or third date, she said, "so, okay, what do you mean by bisexuality, how does that affect your ideas of monogamy, etcetera?" So in terms of our relationship, my bisexuality hasn't really had an impact. She figures if I'm going to leave her it doesn't matter who or what I leave her for, she doesn't have any hidden anger toward men, she doesn't think I'm going to leave her for a man. As a matter of fact she'd probably be more hurt if I left her for another woman, because that would call into question her own worth. We have a much bigger problem discussing my need to explore the terms of the relationship, things like monogamy and distance and personal space.

LC: I'm fairly recently out of a relationship with someone who would state that my bisexuality was not a problem for her but in serious discussion situations, she would say, "I know this man was really important to you, you're going to leave me for a man." Every once in a while she would say something like, "well, you really prefer women, don't you?" And I would say, "I really like being with you, I enjoy you, this is wonderful." I think part of her inconsistent feelings of me as bi were that she had some feelings that she might be bisexual and didn't really want to deal with that. She wanted to be a lesbian, or she wanted to be straight. She did not want to fall into this nameless chasm of bisexuality, because going there was just anguish and suffering for the rest of one's days.

Family Issues

MH: I 'm still not out to any of my family, except to one of my brothers. And as I said before he's hardly supportive. I probably could come out to some other people in my family but I don't know how to make space for that to happen.

EW: It was about a year before I came out to any of my family. When I first started dating D. I said to myself that if it lasted X length of time then it was real, and I should tell my mother. I set all these hurdles I had to go over before I would tell her. And then it was very anticlimactic.

MH: Somehow I don't think that would be the case with my Catholic mother.

EW: It's different than any other "coming out to parents" story I've ever heard. My father doesn't know. He's seventy, and he already knows he's not getting any grandchildren from me. So I've decided that it would take so long to explain to him what I'm talking about that it's not worth it. If I were a lesbian, I think he'd understand, that would be clear. But this, no.

LC: I decided to tell my mother after I started dating the third woman I had been involved with. I thought very highly of her, and I figured, "This is not a fluke. I'm sensing a pattern here." My mother and I are very close. There's nothing she doesn't know about me, and I didn't feel right about eventually, or ever, having to lie to her on the phone. At some point she would ask me what my social life was like. And I'd have to say, "... Charles. I'm dating Charles." Or I'd have to, 'fess up. Basically, it was an ugly scene. It was something she chose to ignore, as I had chosen to ignore earlier. We've gotten close to each other again, I brought C. home to visit, which went as well as could be expected. My mother's also had to reconcile herself to the fact that I date white men a lot, so this was just the latest in the series of "things you wish your daughter would never do to you."

The thing she says every time something happens, like "I've met somebody new and he's white" or "I've met somebody new and SHE's...," is "well, darling, life is hard enough; why would you want to complicate it any further? Why would you want to expose yourself to the evil thoughts of others around you? There are people who will deliberately make your life miserable because you are...whatever." For her, it's easier to either conform to societal norms or erase yourself, as she's done. She's done a lot of unconventional things, but no one knows about them.

I gave my mother *Different Daughters*,[2] written by mothers of lesbians mainly, just so she could see she's not the only person out there whose daughter's not...whatever it was she's thinking. But six months after I bought her the book, I asked what she thought of it, and she said, "I haven't been able to read it yet." So that's where our relationship is as far as my sexuality is concerned.

MH: You've definitely had the roughest time of the three of us.

EW: I think that the idea of choosing an easier path is a theme with moms. A year after telling my mother, I found out this wasn't as easy for my mom as she made it sound that first night. I was trying to decide whether to tell my brother, and I asked my mom how she thought he'd deal with it. And she said, "Well, he'll probably be like me. It'll be a little bit hard at first but under it all you're still his sister and he's still going to love you no matter what you do." I kidded her about being so nonchalant at first, and she told me, "Well, you've had an awfully hard life up to now, why would you want to make it any harder? I would have chosen an easier path for you. I know you're doing this because you need to but I still would have picked a different path." Every once in a while she'll come out with one of these gems...kind of like when she cooks. (*giggles, laughter*) She doesn't do it often, but when she does, she does it well.

Inclusion/Exclusion and the 1993 March on Washington

MH: I was really happy that "bi" was included in the title of the March. And I thought the Action Statement for the March was really great. So I was really, really disappointed when I got there and *they weren't talking about me!*

EW: The contingent for bisexuals was buried in the marching order. So we didn't get to march, and didn't get to march, and didn't get to march...and part of that was logistics, part of that was the number of people that attended (which was more than what the Park Service said, I just want to record that for posterity). Although Laurie and I had planned to march with the bisexual contingent, the wait was so long we went ahead to meet our friends on the Mall. It was a really empowering experience, being at the March for Lesbian, Gay, Bisexual and Transgender Rights. I was happy 'cause I was in the title. Finally I wasn't this hidden sexual minority anymore.

LC: Would you have marched if it hadn't said "Bisexual?"

EW: I would have marched because I support gay and lesbian rights. I would have marched, I would have gone no matter what, but I was really...Like Michelle, I thought the March Statement was really good. But it raised my expectations. In a way, it would have been very different if I had gone to a march for gay and lesbian rights. I would have been a little disappointed that bisexuality wasn't recognized as part of the sexual rights march, but I would have been really happy to be supporting gays and lesbians, I would have enjoyed the whole process much more. As it was, I kept hearing "gay and lesbian." "Lesbian and gay." "Lesbian sisters." "Our gay supporters." "Our straight supporters." And I just never felt included; in four hours I heard the word bisexual mentioned twice. And I was waiting for Lani Kaahumanu [co-editor, *Bi Any Other Name: Bisexual People Speak Out*] to speak, and she was supposed to speak at a certain time and she didn't speak till an hour later. And I heard her speech, it was really great, but I'm sure a lot of other people didn't hear her because it was the end of the day, people had been out for a long time, they were tired.

The March was more than willing to take our help putting people up; three people stayed at our apartment. I felt empowered and excluded at the same time. It was really *great* to have so many people here for the March.

LC: I guess I'd say empowered and enveloped. It's probably characteristic of being bisexual and associating with the gay and lesbian community in any city. Being bisexual means that there's a certain amount of envelopment, of lumping in, of assumptions that you deal with in the gay community that you either put up with because — at least here, you can go out with women, you can dance with women, you can kiss women and no one will get upset with you — it's better than being in a straight environment, let's put it that way. But it's not great, and on some level, are you going to argue envelopment or go and have a drink with this cute woman over here? I wanted to march because I felt that, once again, it was our rights in danger, my rights as well as those of my lesbian girlfriend. It was for anyone who has been made to feel that their sexuality is wrong. So if loving another woman is wrong, if loving another man is wrong, if loving more than one woman is wrong, if loving women serially is wrong...

EW: It was really fun to go and just thumb my nose at the establishment.

LC: Yeah, waving at those CIA helicopters, which could have inspired fear in a previous generation. And it was great to be down there and not have any place to move, to not have any room to walk, on the Mall.

MH: The best part was going into Dupont Circle the day before.

EW: That was so wonderful.

LC: For two days before. And to be in the majority...maybe we weren't in the majority in Cleveland Park, but for darned sure we were from Connecticut Avenue all the way down to the Mall.

EW: All those wonderful dykes were here. I don't usually like graffiti, but they painted "Dykes are in D.C." in big letters. It's faded now, but it was nice.

MH: And just really feeling like we were all there having a good time, and celebrating, and recognizing each other, that felt really empowering.

EW: The Metro was overflowing with people who were obviously "family." And you know, probably, when they get back home they're going to be back in their three-piece suits looking straighter than ever. Because they're from a place where they can't be out of the closet, but here they could. And here, everyone was out, and you had everything from Dykes on Bikes to women with big hair to men with big hair.

MH: It made me really appreciate living here. It made me really proud that this is my home. That that could happen here. And it wasn't just the march, but it just spilled over into this raucous, *raucous* time.

LC: Yes, raucous is probably the best word.

Organize or Integrate?

EW: How did you feel about the Dyke March the night before the main march?

MH: I thought it was neat that it was done. But it brings up the issue about language including or not including us in the lesbian community. When the Lesbian Avengers, who organized that march, started organizing here, I felt, well, it's nice they're here, but does that mean I can join? And then a couple weeks ago they had a discussion about it and they put an explicit invitation in the *Blade* that bisexual women were welcome to come and join and participate. I felt really good about that, but at the same time, it would be nice if you didn't have to ask that question.

EW: I just feel that groups are more concerned with their acronyms than with inclusiveness — I don't care if I'm messing up the acronym. I don't think it's wrong to ask that "bisexual" be put in the title because then it includes you. If the name of the group only has lesbian in the title, how am I supposed to know that bisexuals are included? The word lesbian is not inclusive — lesbian means women loving women only. And I'm a woman who loves women and men. I think it's okay to have strictly lesbian space or a strictly lesbian group but if "bisexual" or "supporters of" or some other inclusive language is not used I assume that I am excluded.

MH: Right, and sometimes you can tell from people's literature, like GLOV (Gays and Lesbians Opposing Violence) has on its stickers to report violence as a result of your bisexuality. I guess that brings us to the whole question of how is it that you make change? And what kind of change is it that you want to make happen?

LC: Well, the issue of — going back to the acronym thing — including bisexuals in the title came up in BLSG (Black Lesbian Support Group) discussion on bisexuality. That was one of the last things that was talked about. And apparently it's been something that the group has discussed, whether they should be the BLBSG. I know that the Coalition of

Black Lesbians and Gay Men has, this year, I think, changed its name to Black Lesbians, Gay Men and Bisexuals, which I think is good. Elias (Farajaje-Jones) said it best when he said, "Well, you guys aren't going to do anything that you don't want to do. If you want to be a group that welcomes bisexuals, then the name change will not seem as something, you know, some kind of big hurdle for you to get over. You know, who cares what you call yourselves? However, if this is still an issue, then don't change the name." One of the bisexual women on the panel said, "Whether you change the name or not, it won't really make any difference in the amount of times that I show up here," because on alternate discussion days she feels comfortable at a BLSG meeting and uncomfortable at a BLSG meeting. It's a tough question. Whenever I think about creating space for anybody, there's an issue of separateness that I don't like, or potential for separatist thought, that I find ugly. You know, if one creates a group for bisexuals, are lesbians and gay men invited? Are they made to feel welcome? Is the name of the group the Bisexuals, Lesbians and Gay Men Whatever Whatever, or is it the Bisexual This-and-That?

MH: So you think then that what's important is for the groups that we have to be inclusive, rather than splintering?

LC: Yeah. I guess that I wish it was easier for any group to realize that there are larger issues to fight over than whether somebody's truly one of you because of their sexuality.

MH: I was thinking about this — it's like, who can be a feminist? What do you have to believe to be a feminist? And that there's all this splintering around colour issues and class issues, how and what you think about choice and other kinds of political issues. That we use all these litmus tests for whether you can be here and talk to us and will we hear what you say, versus these are the issues that we're working on and we need everyone to get this work done.

EW: Yes, it's a dispersion of energy and power. Things that you could get done if all these groups were cooperating — they're not getting done because everyone's putting their energy into separating. Look at the local bi community. We've got AMBi, we've got the BiCentrist Alliance, and one says that you have to be monogamous, and one says however you want to define your sexuality is fine, as long as you're bisexual or even bi-friendly you're welcome, however you express that is your private business. So what to do is very confusing. Do you just go to lesbian groups, do you go to splinter groups that aren't getting anything done?

LC: It's weird. I find that I enjoy knowing other bisexuals, I'm certainly not averse to meeting other bisexuals, but I've not made any attempt to seek out bisexual groups or to be part of bisexual discussions other than this one.

EW: The thing about going to gay and lesbian groups is that I always feel like I have to say, "I'm bisexual," and educate about what that means which is very tiring. You have to spend time proving that just because you're bisexual doesn't mean you don't have a place there. You get caught between two ends. Do you just go along, knowing that your energy will be better spent fundraising for something, or do you keep stopping and saying "this is what I am?"

MH: I like to meet other bisexual women and men. Because I think it's interesting. I think that people who have the choice to identify in a way that a lot of people see as ambiguous, or confused, or just different are interesting people. And I always enjoy talking to them. And I feel a sort of kinship around these issues. But I don't want to be in a group that's just organizing around that. I feel like the education that I do around bisexuality is in my daily life. In talking to people about who I am and what that means to me, and letting them see that it's just another person, not something to be afraid of. And that's why I do things like — what you're saying, Edith, about putting energy into fundraising and other things that need to get done. But I really shy away sometimes from dealing with what it means to be bisexual and work within the gay and lesbian community. It always seems so scary, so hard. And it's hard for me to put the energy into the work and to put the energy into putting myself on the line personally about whether I "deserve" to be there, whether I belong there.

LC: It's a tough one. I'm glad that we're talking about this question. I wouldn't want to join a group that just dealt with bisexuality. I did my work on the [Washington Area Clinic Defense] Task Force because of abortion rights. Not because it was a wonderful source of empowerment for women — though in many ways it was that. It would be nice to know that local bisexuals had items on their agendas such as health care, abortion rights or other feminist issues.

EW: From a purely social standpoint, it would be nice once a month or once every couple of months to get together with a diverse group of people who identify as bisexual for dinner. One of the bi groups sponsors a weekly dinner at a local restaurant — AMBi does. And I think that's a nice idea, because it's just social, and you get a feeling of belonging and get replenished, re-energized. The issues I work on are mainly abortion rights, women's rights, things that are close to me as a woman; not that I don't care about explicit rights for gays, lesbians, bisexuals, etc. — but I wouldn't join a group that works primarily on those issues.

MH: I think the coalition building is really important, and I guess I feel more comfortable doing that on an individual level than as a member of a group around my sexuality.

LC: I think we're all at a stage in our lives when being part of a group is sometimes more trouble than it's worth. (*giggling*)

MH: A theme that runs through all our comments, wanting to push those boundaries — and how we identify and how we relate to other people are part of how we push those boundaries — not just to "thumb our noses at the establishment," as was mentioned before, but for ourselves. Sort of finding out more about who we are and where those lines are for us.

EW: I think it would be easy for all of us to identify ourselves to ourselves, and then present a different self to the world — Michelle calling herself straight and sometimes sleeping with women, my identifying as a lesbian and sometimes sleeping with men but not talking about it, Laurie identifying as straight and sleeping with women on the side and not dealing with that. I think it would be really easy to take that path. So I like the idea that we've all chosen to label ourselves according to what we feel we are, which may not be what other people feel.

NOTES

1 Carol A. Queen, "The Queer in Me," in *Bi Any Other Name: Bisexual People Speak Out*, ed. Loraine Hutchins and Lani Kaahumanu (Boston: Alyson Publications, 1991), 17-21.

2 Louise Rafkin, *Different Daughters: A Book by Mothers of Lesbian* (San Francisco: Cleis Press, 1987).

Hannah Hoffman

Celibate Bisexuality:
An Identity or the Ultimate in Fence-Sitting?

THE HUMAN RIGHTS COUNCIL IN BRITISH Columbia recently field tested, with various gays and lesbians, a draft brochure on sexual orientation protection under the Human Rights Act. There was a spirited debate about whether bisexuals should be specifically mentioned as a "group" under the description of sexual orientation protection. Many feel that bisexuals are discriminated against when they are involved with people of their own sex, and therefore perceived as lesbian or gay, and that they do not experience discrimination when they are involved with people of the opposite sex because then they are perceived as hetero-sexuals. They could not perceive that bisexuals could be discriminated against because of their bisexuality. In the end, bisexuals were specifically included in the brochure's description of sexual orientation, but it was not without debate.

I find many aspects of this debate problematic. The piece I carry away with me (and into this article) is the attempt to legitimize "homo/-heterosexualities" according to who we are partnered with. This leaves those of us who are single/celibate bisexuals in either a non-category or a "heterosexual by default" category. For me, and hopefully for other celibate bisexuals, this is tragic. The need for recognition of who we are and the particular life challenges we face every day and every step of our lives is relevant and deserving of recognition and protection under human rights acts and everywhere else.

Although this exclusion of me and my reality is frustrating, it inspires me to wonder about how I have lived my life and about how and where I have built community. As I have been living with a progressing disease, the need for a truly supportive community has become ever more important.

Over the past few years, as my health has deteriorated, my concept of living has changed drastically: I've worried about being remembered; I've worried about being heard.

Emily Dickinson said that to live is so startling that it leaves little time for anything else. I have to agree with her. Since discovering that I have leukemia, I've been concerned with building and identifying my tribe — in a Jewish, historical, cultural, spiritual sense of community and place of belonging. Our tribe is a place for us to create our legends, where we tell who we are, in the way that our foremothers did.

Getting sick made me very angry for a long time. After spending most of my life being active in feminist lesbian movements, I felt that I was missing out on too much. I felt angry and resentful that life was going on without me there. I worried about my friends, about who would be my community, who would stay with me and who would be able to go through this process with me. I was tired and afraid, and very lonely. I felt that I was losing too much, too fast. Who would I be when I settled and could begin to examine my new self? Would I even be someone I would recognize and like?

I had gotten angry as my health began to fail. I couldn't walk without a cane. I felt humiliated that I needed help with the basics: laundry, shopping, bathing. My image of myself has taken a beating. Buying a cane for the first time forced me to come out about my disability. After reconciling myself to my need for a cane, I made it down the three steps at my front door and went shopping for a cane. I had friends who were quite happy to go cane browsing with me. In the end, it was fun. I found a very classy black cane, which I promptly decorated with magenta holographic sticky paper. My friends don't mind my pace, or driving me around when I can't drive. They laugh with me and I still feel included and enjoyed.

As I have begun to wonder who my tribe is and whether my community is bisexual, heterosexual or lesbian, I've discovered that my community is very much all of those things. I have friends who are gay and lesbian, some heterosexual and a few who identify as bisexual. Most of my community is women; a few are men. Also included in my tribe are my doctors, who have been like friends to me. I have also felt privileged to have a wonderful cousin, Susan, with whom I share so much of my process and life and with whom I laugh a lot. I love my friends and I could never have made it through these last years without their love and support.

Being ill has created a new chapter for me, not only in terms of friends and community but also in terms of lovers and sexual relationships. When I've been in a relationship with a woman, I've wondered if I was a lesbian; when I've been in a relationship with a man, I've wondered if I was heterosexual; now that I'm celibate, I wonder what I am.

Certain questions remain unclear: am I still sexual if I'm celibate? Am I still sexual if I don't have the energy to engage in sexual relationship or if I have so much pain in my body that even the sheets on my bed hurt when they touch me? Am I bisexual if I'm celibate? For me, these are basic questions about sexuality, yet I never hear them raised at human rights commissions, included in political theories or even discussed around the table with friends.

Last year, at dinner with a group of friends, we were discussing the fact that as lesbians we are invisible. All but two of us were in couples. As usual, I was the only bisexual. At least the only one who identifies as such. After a lively conversation, we decided that, perhaps, we should write Sapph at the end of our names to identify ourselves. I asked what I, a bisexual, would write after my name. One of the women suggested "half-Sapph." I thought it was quite hilarious at the time but when I thought about it, I realized that I don't feel myself half-Sapph, I feel whole Sapph, even though I'm bisexual.

I don't feel that I am sitting on the fence unable to make a decision or commitment to being lesbian or heterosexual. I truly and totally love when I love. I have always been willing to be committed to a relationship.

I believe that not having a clear bisexual identity is due to the fact that we have been trying to come up with a definition of bisexuality within a pre-defined framework of sexual politics. By doing this, we are, then, forced to look at our sexual relationships as the sole indicators of our sexual identity. Some of us are more woman-identified, some more male-identified, some Jewish-identified, different ability–identified and, certainly, different class-and colour-identified. And, of course, there are those of us who are celibate. If we work solely with a "sexual relationship" framework of sexual identity, will celibate bisexuals be the ultimate fence-sitters?

Sexual orientation is about more than who we make love with. Sexuality is about the attractions we feel internally, not only the acting out of these attractions. When we find ways that allow all of our ways of identifying to be heard, the community we form and take part in will be truly liberating. I look forward to living through this step of the journey.

Robyn Ochs

Excerpts from the Bisexual Resource Guide

I. The full directory can be ordered from:
International Directory of Bisexual Groups. Robin Ochs.
(U.S. $8.00) ECBN, P.O. Box 639, Cambridge, MA 02140.
Updated twice a year, lists bisexual and les/bi/gay groups in fifteen countries
and forty-two U.S. states.

II. Bi and Lesbigay Groups in Canada

LESBIAN, GAY AND BISEXUAL COLLECTIVE
Douglas College
PO Box 2503
New Westminster, BC
phone: 604-527-5111

OPTIONS
British Columbia, Canada
Social group. Phone answered live on Mondays 8-10 p.m.
604-681-8815

BI-FACE
PO Box 20524
723 Davie St.
Vancouver, BC V6Z 2N8
phone: 604-681-8815
Support group, meets first and third Tuesdays, 7-10 p.m.
Also "BiCycle," a bifriendly activity group that
cycles, hikes, rollerblades, etc.

BI-FOCUS
Box 34172, Post Office D
Vancouver, BC V6J 4N1
phone: 604-737-0513

LESBIAN, GAY AND BISEXUAL STUDENT ASSOCIATION
Vancouver Community College
Student Union Building, 100 West 49th Ave.
Vancouver, BC
phone: 604-324-3881

BGLAD
Dalhousie University
The Dalhousie Student Union Building
University Avenue
Halifax, Nova Scotia B3H 4H6
phone: 902-422-0116
e-mail: BGLAD@ac.dal.ca

LESBIAN, GAY & BISEXUAL YOUTH PROJECT
100-6156 Quinpool Road
Halifax, Nova Scotia B3L 1A3
phone: 902-492-7155
fax: 902-492-7155
Youth group meetings, social outings and
educational workshops on heterosexism and
outreach to isolated youth.

ONTARIO BISEXUAL NETWORK
519 Church St.
Toronto, Ontario M4Y 2C9
Phone: 416-925-XTRA ext. 2015
Fax: 416-649-1356

DIVERSITY
c/o Ontario Bisexual Network
Contact group for people of all orientations.

EMBRACE
c/o Ontario Bisexual Network
A political voice for bisexual people.

KINGSTON LESBIAN, GAY AND BISEXUAL ASSOCIATION
(LGBA)
51 Queen's Crescent
Kingston, Ontario K7L 3N6

AL ANON - LESBIAN, GAY AND BISEXUAL
St. Pierre Community Centre
252 Friel
Ottawa, Ontario
phone: 613-234-3781 or 613-237-XTRA, ext. 2031
Meets Thursdays, 8 p.m. Al Anon 12-steps self-help
group for lesbians, gays and bisexuals who are affected
by someone else's drinking. All welcome. For more
information, call the main office number above.

ALGO PAC
318 Lisgar, 2nd floor
Ottawa, Ontario
phone: 613-233-0152, or 613-237-XTRA, ext. 2049
Gay, Lesbian and Bisexual Committee.

ASSOCIATION OF LESBIANS AND GAYS OF OTTAWA (ALGO)
Gay, Lesbian and Bisexual. Home of many gay and
lesbian artistic and cultural events and the Saturday
Lavendar Laundrette women's bar. ALGO is home of the
GO Info Community Paper.
GO INFO
PO Box 2919, Station D
Ottawa, Ontario K1P 5W9
phone: 613-238-8990

CARLETON UNIVERSITY GAY, LESBIAN, BISEXUAL
CENTRE & LENDING LIBRARY
Carleton University – Unicentre
Ottawa, Ontario
phone: 613-788-2600 or 613-237-XTRA, ext. 2022

OTTAWA UNIVERSITY GAY, LESBIAN
& BISEXUAL UNICENTRE
Ottawa University
Ottawa, Ontario
Phone: 613-788-2600 or 613-237-XTRA, ext. 2022
Includes bisexual group, anti-homophobia workshops
and Sexuality Awareness Days information campaign.

SEX ADDICTS ANONYMOUS (SAA)
Ottawa, Ontario
phone: 613-339-0217 or 613-237-XTRA, ext. 2028
Sex addicts 12-step self-help group for lesbians, gays
and bisexuals who require support to stop compulsive
sex behaviour. All welcome.

BIVERSE
290 Rubidge Street
Peterborough, Ontario K9J 3P4
phone: 705-743-5414
e-mail: TLGC@TRENT.CA, attn. BiVERSE

BISEXUAL ESSEX COUNTY SUPPORT TEAM
Brenda – Tecumseh South Postal Outlet
PO Box 21004
Tecumseh, Ontario N8N 4S1
All bi people and their partners and friends welcome.
Meetings held monthly. Founded 1993.

CAMBRIDGE, KITCHENER, WATERLOO
BISEXUAL LIBERATION
PO Box 28002, Parkdale Postal Outlet
Waterloo, Ontario N2L 6J8
Founded 1992.

III. Electronic Mail Lists:

BI WOMEN'S DISCUSSION LIST
(Bifem-1@brownvm.brown.edu)
BI ACTIVISTS' DISCUSSION LIST
(Biact-1@brownvm.brown.edu)
BISEXUAL DISCUSSION LIST
(Bisexu-1@brownvm.brown.edu)

To subscribe to any of these three lists:
send e-mail message to listserve@brownvm.brown.edu.
In the message text, write (for example):
subscribe bifem-1 yourfirstname yourlastname.

IV. Non-Fiction

Women and Bisexuality
by Sue George. London: Scarlet Press, 1993. Findings of a
UK study of 150 bisexually identified women.

Lotus of Another Colour:
An Unfolding of the South Asian Lesbian and Gay Experience
ed. Rakesh Ratti. Boston: Alyson, 1993. Includes three
essays by bi-identified women.

*On Intimate Terms: The Psychology of Difference in Lesbian
Relationships*, by Beverly Burch. Urbana & Chicago:
University of Illinois Press, 1994. Psychotherapist Burch
draws an interesting distinction between "primary" and
"bisexual" lesbians, and posits that there may be a comple-
mentarity, or attraction, between the two. "Bisexual
lesbians" are defined as women who come to identify as
lesbian later than "primary lesbians" and who may have
had significant heterosexual relationships and/or continue
to recognize heterosexual relationships as a possibility.
This book is primarily about women who identify as
lesbian but deals extensively with bisexuality.

Odds Girls and Twilight Lovers
by Lillian Faderman. New York: Penguin, 1991.
A history of lesbian life in the twentieth-century U.S.
Includes numerous references to bisexuality,
especially in the 1920s and 1930s.

Witness Aloud:
Lesbian, Gay and Bisexual Asian/Pacific American Writing.
The APA Journal, Vol. 2, No. 1, Spring/Summer 1993.
Available for $10 (U.S.) from: The Asian American Writers
Workshop, 630 First Ave. Suite 4K, NY, NY 10016.
Includes writings by bi authors Indigo Chih-Lien Som
and Jee Yeun Lee.

Bi Any Other Name: Bisexuals Speak Out.
ed. Loraine Hutchins and Lani Kaahumanu. Boston:
Alyson Publications, 1991.
Seventy-five essays by bi-identified people, ranging from
the highly personal to the theoretical. Has been referred
to as the "bi bible."

Closer to Home: Bisexuality and Feminism.
ed. Elizabeth Reba Weise. Seattle: Seal Press, 1992.
Twenty-three essays by bisexual feminist women
discussing bisexuality, feminism and the intersection
of the two.

Bisexuality: A Reader and Sourcebook
ed. Thomas Geller. Ojai, CA: Times Change Press, 1990.
A compilation of interviews and articles on bisexuality.

Two Lives to Lead: Bisexuality in Men & Women
ed. Fritz Klein and Timothy J. Wolf. New York:
Harrington Park Press, 1985.
Formerly published as: *Bisexualities: Theory and Research.*
Compilation of articles on research on bisexuality.

The Other Side of the Closet:
The Coming Out Crisis for Straight Spouses
by Amity Pierce Buxton. Santa Monica, CA: IBS Press, 1991.
Primarily focused on female spouses of gay
and bisexual men.

Bisexuality in the Ancient World
by Eva Cantarella. New Haven & London: Yale University
Press, 1992.

Bisexuality and HIV/AIDS: A Global Perspective
ed. Rob A.P. Tielman, et al.
Buffalo, NY: Prometheus Books, 1991.
Collection of essays about bisexual behaviour in a number
of modern cultures. Most of the essays are recommended.
Interesting introduction and summary of several research
studies on bisexual behavior.

Bisexualities: Theory and Research
No. 11 of the Book Series, *Research on Homosexuality.*
ed. Fritz Klein MD. and Timothy J. Wolf.
New York: The Haworth Press, 1985.

The Bisexual Option
by Fritz Klein MD. 2nd edition.
New York: Larrington Press, 1993.

Dual Attraction: Understanding Bisexuality
by Martin Weinberg, Colin Williams, Douglas Pryor.
New York: Oxford University Press, 1994.

Gay, Straight and In Between:
The Sociology of Erotic Orientation
by John Money.

Sex and Bisexuality: Index of Modern Information
by Dr. Rosalie F. Zoltano.
Washington, D.C.: Abbe Publishers Association, 1990.

Half Straight: My Secret Bisexual Life
by Tom Smith. Buffalo: Prometheus Books, 1992.

V. Journal Articles and Chapters in Books

Ronald C. Fox, "Bisexual Identities," in
A.R. D'Augelli and C.J. Patterson, ed.
Lesbian, Gay and Bisexual Identities Across the Lifespan.
New York: Oxford University Press, 1995.
Dr. Fox discusses the results of his study
of 800+ bisexually identified men and women.

Carla Golden, "Diversity and Variability in Women's
Sexual Identities," and Rebecca Shuster, "Sexuality
as a Continuum: The Bisexual Identity," both in
Lesbian Psychologies: Explorations and Challenges,
ed. Boston Lesbian Psychologies Collective. Urbana, IL:
University of Indiana Press, 1987.

Deborah Gregory, "From Where I Stand: A Case for
Feminist Bisexuality" in S. Carledge and J. Ryan, ed.
Sex and Love: New Thoughts on Old Contradictions.
London: The Women's Press, 1983.

Robyn Ochs and Marcia Deihl, "Moving Beyond Binary
Thinking," in Warren J. Blumenfeld, ed.
Homophobia: How We All Pay the Price.
Boston: Beacon Press, 1992.

Jay Paul,
"Bisexuality: Reassessing our Paradigms of Sexuality,"
in *Journal of Homosexuality* 11(1/2), 1985: 21-34.

Michael W. Ross and Jay Paul.
"Beyond Gender: The Basis of Sexual Attraction
in Bisexual Men and Women," in
Psychological Reports 71, 1992: 1283-1290.

Paula Rust, "The Politics of Sexual Identity: Sexual
Attraction and Behaviour Among Lesbian and Bisexual
Women," in *Social Problems* 39 (4): 366-386.

Paula Rust, "'Coming Out' in the Age of Social
Constructionism: Sexual Identity Formation Among
Lesbian and Bisexual Women," in *Gender & Society*,
7 (1): 50-77.

"Bisexual and Homosexual Identities:
Critical and Theoretical Issues," in
Journal of Homosexuality, 9 (2/3).
John P. Decerro PhD, Michael G. Shively MA, eds.
New York: The Haworth Press, 1984.

VI. BIOGRAPHIES/AUTOBIOGRAPHIES

John Cheever, *The Journals of John Cheever.*
New York: Knopf, 1990.
Journal includes accounts of this writer's bisexuality.

Florence King, *Confessions of a Failed Southern Lady.*
New York: Bantam Books, 1985.
About growing up Southern, white, female and sexual.
"No matter which sex I went to bed with,
I never smoked on the street."

Kate Millet, *Flying*.
New York: Simon & Shuster, 1974.
and *Sita*. New York: Simon & Shuster, 1976.
Two autobiographical novels by a self-identified
bisexual woman who has been a leader of the modern
women's movement.

Nigel Nicholson, *Portrait of a Marriage*.
London: Weidenfeld & Nicholson, 1973.
Biography of Vita Sackville-West and Harold Nicolson
by their son. Vita, born in the late nineteenth-century,
was a self-identified bisexual woman of the British upper
class in love with Violet Trefusis.

VII. SELECTED FICTION
(Only books with a prominent bisexual theme.
This list represents only the tip of the iceberg.)

Lisa Alther, *Bedrock*.
New York: Ivy Books, 1990.
Two married women, best friends, trying to
come to terms with their love for each other.
Also *Other Women*. New York: Knopf (Random House),
1984. A woman with a bisexual history comes to terms,
through therapy, with herself and her love for women.

James Baldwin, *Another Country*.
New York: Dell, 1985.
First published in 1960, a book about race, sexuality
and friendship with male bisexual characters.

Ernest Hemingway, *The Garden of Eden*.
New York: Collier Books, 1986 (written 1961).
His last work, about a male/female couple
and a woman who enters their relationship.
Deals with transgender issues, jealousy, bisexuality.

Edith Konecky, *A Place at the Table.*
New York: Ballantine Books, 1989.
About middle-aged Rachel, "a perfectly ordinary woman
who sometimes falls in love with other women."

Hanif Kureishi, *The Buddha of Suburbia.*
New York & London: Penguin Books, 1990.
Set in suburban London, the story of the bisexual
son of an Indian father and English mother.

Marge Piercy, *Summer People.*
New York: Fawcett Crest, 1989.
The story of two women and a man in a ménage-à-trois.

Manuel Puig, *Kiss of the Spider Woman.*
Story of two men, a homosexual window
dresser and a heterosexual revolutionary, who are
imprisoned in the same cell in a Latin American prison.
Involves situational bisexuality.

Ruthann Robson, *Eye of the Hurricane.*
Ithaca, NY: Firebrand Books, 1989.
Short stories, some with bisexual characters.

Tom Spanbauer, *The Man Who Fell in Love With the Moon.*
New York: Atlantic Monthly Press, 1991. Several bi
characters in this novel set in nineteenth-century Idaho.

Carole Spearin McCauley, *The Honesty Tree.*
Palo Alto, CA: Frog in the Well Books, 1985.

Alice Walker, *The Color Purple.*
New York: Harcourt Brace Janovich, 1982.
Shug, a major character, is bisexual.

Jeanette Winterson, *The Passion*.
New York: Vintage International (Random House), 1987.
Set in France and Italy during Napoleon's reign,
one of the protagonists is a bisexual woman.

VIII. Additional Resources

There are a number of periodical and newsletters by
various bi groups around the world. *Bi Women*, published
bi-monthly by the Boston Bisexual Women's Network
(PO Box 639, Cambridge, MA 02140, USA) and *North Bi
Northwest*, published by the Seattle Bisexual Women's
Network (PO Box 30645, Greenwood Station, Seattle,
WA 98103-0645, USA) and a 'zine called *Bi Girl World*
(Karen F., 99 Newtonville Ave, Newton, MA 02158, USA).
A mixed-gender quarterly called *Anything That Moves:
Beyond the Myths of Bisexuality* is published by the Bay
Area Bisexual Network (2404 California St., Box 24, San
Francisco, CA 94115, USA) and *BiNet USA* publishes a
quarterly newsletter (PO Box 7327, Langley Park, MD
20787-7327 USA). There are several others, in New
Zealand, the Netherlands, the U.K. and the U.S.
The Bisexual Resource Guide (already listed) is the most
up-to-date resource on what's out there.

Contributors' Notes

LEELA ACHARYA is a South Asian activist who has been working in different areas of community development. She is trying to be who she is and not who she isn't...

AMINA is a social justice activist living in Toronto. Although her formal involvement with the women's movement began in 1988, she's always been a trouble-maker. She has been active in working with the feminist communities, anti-racist coalitions, progressive Muslim and South Asian organizations, and currently works in the area of housing rights.

AMITA is a student and hopes to get out one day to do work at a community level. Recently she has found a new love for music and can spin a tune or two. She has two short stories in *Fireweed's Awakening Thunder: Special Asian Women's Issue* (1990). She has tons of incomplete short stories she hopes to publish one day.

SUSAN ARENBURG, a musician who manages her own business, lives with her ten-year-old daughter and her German lover in rural Nova Scotia. She is currently engaged in a lengthy process to gain immigration status for her same-sex partner.

KAREN/MIRANDA AUGUSTINE is a Toronto-based writer and visual artist of Dominican and Carib Indian heritage. She is the founder and managing editor of *At the Crossroads: A Journal for Women Artists of African Descent*.

LOUISE BAK is a twenty-two-year-old Chinese expressionist who lives and works in Toronto. She likes trust(ing) her dvende — no longer a closet idealist.

NANCY CHATER is a Toronto writer and poet. *Bodies of Knowledge: fear*, a book of poetry, was published by Ragweed Press. Her work has also appeared in *Fireweed: A Feminist Quarterly of Writing, Politics, Art & Culture, Canadian Woman Studies, Fuse, Room of One's Own, Open Letter, Contemporary Verse 2* and in the anthology *By, For and About: Feminist Cultural Politics* (Women's Press, 1994).

MARGARET CHRISTAKOS has published two books of poetry. *Not Egypt* (Coach House, 1989) and *Other Words for Grace* (The Mercury Press, 1994), as well as two poetic chapbooks. Her poems have appeared in a range of Canadian literary journals and critical essays have been published in *Tessera, Room of One's Own* and *Open Letter*. She was an editorial collective member of *Fireweed: A Feminist Quarterly of Writing, Politics, Art & Culture* from 1991-1994 and works as an editor, teacher and parent. Based in Toronto, she attended the bisexual potluck parties out of which this anthology was spawned.

LAURIE A. COOPER is looking forward to being a wise old woman. Currently she works at a non-profit organization in Washington, D.C. Her professional interests include African and Latin American development and politics, local politics and women's issues. Her private interests are too complex to deal with here, and may scare people.

SARAH CORTEZ is a native Houstonian. An Aquarian. Her blood comes from Spain and Mexico. Also from the Sioux, Cherokee and French, who are the women that the men from Spain married.

ANN DECTER is currently working on *Honour*, a sequel to her novel *Paper, Scissors, Rock* (Press Gang Publishers, 1993). She is co-managing editor for fiction and poetry at Women's Press in Toronto and has recently co-edited two anthologies, *Out Rage* (Women's Press, 1994) and *Resist!* (Women's Press, 1995).

SHAI DHALI lives in Victoria, British Columbia, with a martial arts stick fighter and their pitbull dog, in a 1966 Ford bus. It excites her to girl watch.

FARZANA DOCTOR is a twenty-four-year-old South Asian woman born in Zambia and originally from India. By weekday, she is a social worker. By weekends, a member of *Saheli Theatre Troupe* — a South Asian women's theatre collective based in Toronto.

DIONNE A. FALCONER is a Black bisexual feminist working in the Black community around AIDS prevention and support. She lives with and loves Jennifer in Toronto.

TRACY CHARETTE FEHR lives and works in Winnipeg, Manitoba. She has a Bachelor of Arts in Labour Studies. She is a visual artist and a Tarot practitioner. Tracy spent her first twenty-four years in the heterosexual world and the next seven years in the lesbian community. She is currently involved with a male partner. Through this she has maintained her sense of humour and hopes that her cats Chocky and Delilah will live long and happy lives so that one day they can tell it all.

LILITH FINKLER is an activist commited to both personal growth and social change.

LEANNE FRANSON was born in 1963 in Regina, Saskatchewan. She is now a bilingual, bisexual, bicycling illustrator in Montreal. She has been self-publishing her comic zine *Liliane* since 1992 and has had her work appear in newspapers, books and magazines. A catalogue of her zines can be ordered from P.O. Box 274, Succ. Place du Parc, Montreal, Quebec H2W 2N8.

ANDREA FREEMAN is a poet, playwright, performer, counsellor, adventurer and filmmaker living in Toronto. Bisexual Jewish vegetarian movie fanatic traveller insomniac basketball fan. Dreamer.

VICTORIA FREEMAN is a Toronto writer.

NUPUR GOGIA is a woman who lives her life and struggles with friends, laughter and hopefully new adventures.

·

CYNDY HEAD lives in Toronto. She enjoys photography, travel, cycling and her friends. This is the first story she has written.

HANNAH HOFFMAN is living — in Victoria, British Columbia, in a wonderful old house by the sea, with her companion Cat Esther. She is a Reiki master, healer and astrological consultant. She is currently working with those living and dying of terminal illnesses and learning ways to put language to this profound experience.

MICHELLE E. HYNES lives with her partner of eight years in an urban apartment filled with sunlight, clutter and books. She works for a non-profit organization in downtown Washington, D.C., and volunteers in the lending library of a gay and lesbian health clinic. In her spare time, Michelle haunts various coffee bars with her friends and reads paperback mysteries by women. "The Kinsey Three" is her first published writing.

HUDA JADALLAH is a Palestinian lesbian. She was born and raised in the San Francisco Bay area. She is the founder of the Arab Lesbian, Gay and Bisexual Network, P.O. Box 460526, San Francisco, CA 94146. She is currently compiling an anthology of writing by and about Arab lesbian and bisexual women.

JUNE JORDAN — poet, essayist, political activist and scholar — is the author of twenty books including *Technical Difficulties, Naming Our Destiny, On Call,* and *Living Room.* Her commentary has appeared in the *New York Times, Essence, The Nation* and *Ms.;* and she is a regular political columnist for *The Progressive.* She is a professor of African-American Studies and Women's Studies at the University of California at Berkeley.

SUSAN KANE was born in New York City, and raised in the midwestern United States with fond memories of life in the old country. Her poetry has appeared in *Whiskey Island Review* and *The Femme Mystique* (forthcoming). These slogans were previously printed in *Anything That Moves,* and are also available as a T-shirt. She presently lives in Cleveland, Ohio, where she manages her family's coffeehouse and tries to find time for political activism, performance poetry and flirting.

CAMIE KIM lives in Waterloo, Ontario. She has been previously published in *Fireweed: A Feminist Quarterly of Writing, Politics, Art & Culture* and in an anthology called *Asian Voices* (North York School Board). In 1994 she won the Writers' Union of Canada's prose contest for emerging writers.

SHARON LEWIS is an actor-activist, generally a happy woman.

PAMELA JEAN LIPSHUTZ a.k.a. Phoenix (rising from the ashes) Benson is a perpetual student of philosophy, political science and spirituality of women's culture. She holds a Bachelor of Science in Nursing degree from Northeastern University in Boston, Massachusetts, where she resides. She wrote this story with the hope that others will find strength in their own struggles for survival and celebration of life. Special thanks to the publishers and editors of this anthology, to Neal Buchalter for his computer and hugs and to Tala Lipshutz (mother) for her excellent sense of humour that has gotten her and Pam through life.

LEANNA MCLENNAN is a Toronto-based poet and writer who dreams of returning to the Maritimes and living in a farmhouse with plates that don't match. Her poetry has appeared in *Contemporary Verse* 2 and *Fireweed: A Feminist Quarterly of Writing, Politics, Art & Culture*.

MELINA is in her own life now. Humour and love will bring you to trust and peace.

IRENE J. NEXICA is a Chicana born and grown 5' in Albuquerque, New Mexico, U.S.A. Her gramita Amada L. Soto crossed the border and picked cotton, had a daughter who had a daughter who kept her alive so she could make herself into the multi-culti generation equis postcolonial postmodern reader artist writer listener she seems forever struggling to realize. She feels she is lucky to come from these artisans who have kept her going with their own creations. For a job Irene goes to school and mostly studies what she loves around her wherever she is. She adores her bike, and was riding her when both the poem and this blurb's composition were begun.

SUSAN NOSOV is a Jewish feminist activist. She is presently writing, speaking and presenting in the areas of community development, Jewish identity, sexuality and violence against women and children. Her writings have been published in *Fireweed: A Feminist Quarterly of Writing, Politics, Art & Culture, Canadian Woman Studies* and *Bridges* as well as in several community-based periodicals and newsletters.

ROBYN OCHS is a bisexual feminist activist. She is the editor of the *Bisexual Resource Guide* and all eleven editions of the *International Directory of Bisexual Groups*. Her works have appeared in several anthologies. She has taught three university courses on bisexual identity, and travels around as widely as possible speaking and doing workshops on bisexuality, coalition building and other fun stuff. She lives in Cambridge, Massachusetts, with two cats, Emma and Luca. Oh, and she also works full time as an academic administrator.

ZÉLIE POLLON is a San Francisco–based writer and associate editor of *Deneuve*, an internationally distributed lesbian magazine. She has been an advocate of bisexual visibility and involved in AIDS activism and education for many years. Her most recent project was translating from the French teachings by the Dalai Lama.

STEPH RENDINO is originally from Brooklyn, New York, and spent much of her time outside Washington, D.C. She currently resides in Montreal, Quebec, where her writing can be found in the oddest places.

PEARL SAAD is a mixed-heritage Arab American woman. She is a writer and painter living in Oakland, California.

SHLOMIT SEGAL likes to express herself through the written word and visual images. She is also a student, a tradeswoman and a political activist. Her poetry has appeared in *Fireweed: A Feminist Quarterly of Writing, Politics, Art & Culture*, and *Outrage: Dykes and Bis Resist Homophobia* (Women's Press, 1994), and she is an editor for *Bridges: A Magazine for Jewish Feminists and Our Friends*.

INDIGO CHIH-LIEN SOM is a garlic-chopping, book-binding, shuttle-throwing cancer & fire horse. She is a bi-dyke abc (american-born chinese) born, raised & planning to die in the San Francisco bay area. Her publications include journals and anthologies such as *APA Journal, Piece of my Heart: A Lesbian of Colour Anthology* (Sister Vision Press, 1991) and *Beyond Definition: New Writing from Gay and Lesbian San Francisco.* Most recently she contributed the title poem and other pieces to *The Very Inside: An Anthology of Writing by Asian and Pacific Islander Lesbian and Bisexual Women* (Sister Vision Press, 1994). Under the name bitchy buddha press, she makes one-of-a-kind, altered, letterpress and xerox edition artist's books, as well as blank books to order.

ELEHNA DE SOUSA was born and raised in Hong Kong and is of Portugese–East Indian ancestry. She currently travels between the garden island of Kauai, Hawaii, and the urban jungle of Toronto, Canada, where she practices the sharing of *aloha* through teaching, counselling, writing and just plain living.

MICHELE SPRING-MOORE is a legal citizen of the evil empire known as the United States, a founder of the Rochester (New York) Bisexual Women's Network and a former editor of the *Empty Closet*, New York state's oldest lesbian and gay newspaper. She wrote "Queergirl" partly in response to biphobia in lesbian and gay movements and right-wing attempts to pass anti-gay/lesbian/bisexual legislation in Colorado in 1992. Spring-Moore recently completed an M.A. in creative writing at the University of Colorado, writing residencies at Cottages at Hedgebrook in Washington state and Ucross Foundation in Wyoming, and her first book of poetry, *The Order of Things.* Her work has been published in *Fireweed: A Feminist Quarterly of Writing, Politics, Art & Culture, Bay Windows, Hanging Loose* and *Standards: An International Journal of Multicultural Studies.*

CHRISTINA STARR is an editor, activist, mother, poet and writer (when she has time) currently living in Toronto. Her most recent accomplishments include: seeing Elton John live (for the first time) in 1992, and (more recently) explaining the concept of sexual choice to her family just in time for them to witness the staging of her first poetic monologue, *holding...*, which was produced at the Edmonton Fringe Festival (summer 1994) and explores the snags of a lesbian love triangle.

EDITH R. WESTFALL's current existence is best described by her recently placed personal ad, "Coffee overflows my freezer, books clutter my apartment, work fills my day — night owl trapped in morning person's schedule." While she also lives in Washington, D.C., unlike her co-authors, she works in a decidedly for-profit corporation.

JANICE WILLIAMSON's most recent books are *Tell Tale Signs: fictions* (Turnstone Press), *Sounding Differences: Conversations with Seventeen Canadian Women Writers* (University of Toronto Press) and, as co-editor with Claudine Potvin, *Women's Writing and the Literary Institution* (University of Alberta Press). She is an associate professor of English at the University of Alberta. Excerpts of "Strained Mixed Fruit" were performed in Catalyst Theatre's 1994 *Loud & Queer Cabaret*.